COMEBACK

Levity Brown

This novel is entirely a work of fiction.

The names, characters and incidents portrayed are the work of the author's imagination. Any resemblance to actual persons, living or dead, is purely coincidental.

Comeback

ISBN: 978-1-0682391-4-4

Copyright © Levity Brown 2012

Editorial support and publication assistance from Creative Words Ltd www.creativewords.cc

www.levitybrown.co.uk

CONTENTS

CHAPTER 1

September 2012

The oak door to the Chief Executive's office sounded to the knock of a woman, then his secretary entered and approached to speak in a whisper.

Godfrey Shilling nodded, and, while his secretary retreated to perform her duties, once more addressed the small gathering. 'We shall reconvene after lunch.'

In their gradual fade, Shilling kicked back his chair, picked his way across the spongy carpet and poured another cup of decaf. Beyond this conclave of financial executives were matters of doubt relating to a pay-out on a million pound life policy. Already an inch thick file prepared by the best intelligence available sat on his desk. Sadly, this never laid the ghost. What the Chief Executive of Fair Life Assurance needed was a witch to fly on her broomstick and perform her magic. At least that was the theatrical endorsement given by the best intelligence available.

But the comparison between the perceived notions of a witch with the elegant figure in grey walking into his office, emphasized by her silvery grey hair bound by a diamond comb, was striking indeed. It did not contradict the physical rarity but it did disguise her intuitive qualities.

'Miss Grey?'

'Yes,' and shook his hand.

'May I offer you a coffee?'

'Please; one sugar.' Grey unbuttoned her ankle-length raincoat, slightly flushed by the stuffiness of his office. 'Who gave you my number?'

'Ben de Wit, the best intelligence I could find.'

'Is he stumped or are you stubborn?'

'Let us say a bit of both.' Shilling, bespectacled and middle aged, gestured to a leather chair as he himself took to his own. 'But, yes, limiting liability is a huge priority for this company.'

'Does the smoke bother you?' she asked tapping a long-tipped pink cigarette from her pack.

He shook his head. 'They look different.'

'Homemade herbals. Would you like one?'

'No thank you…now, to business. How much do you know about our industry, Miss Grey?'

'It makes a lot of people glad when their home is flooded.'

'That may be so,' he said with a mellow almost professional baritone. 'But insurance is not viewed the same as assurance. For instance, insurance is linked to material things such as cars, contents, property and so forth. Assurance is linked to a person. You are assured that if this happens you will receive the contracted amount. Fair Life Assurance is a UK company dealing in life assurance, pensions, and investments. Due to the subjective nature of our business, the internet only serves twenty percent of the company's income. The rest is achieved through established agencies, such as solicitors, financial consultants, and estate agents. Are you with me so far, Miss Grey?'

'Mr. Shilling,' she said with her notepad open, her pen poised, the blank pages like listening ears. 'I am with you so far because I am your last resort,' and followed it up with a smile.

'Then let me begin with 53-year-old Peter Tudmoor who took out a life policy for one million pounds. It was to run a term of five years at an annual premium of £270 per month. This was based on a risk assessment after we wrote to his doctor for a PMA report…that's a-'

'Post-medical assessment.'

'Yes, precisely…when we received the all-clear, we sent him for a fairly stringent medical and again, the all-clear. His occupation was a watchmaker, had no hazardous hobbies or sporting activities. The policy was held in trust for his sister, twelve years his senior, that should he die before his planned retirement she would have the very best of care for the rest of her life. It all sounded plausible and was very uncomfortable when he died in his sleep.'

How inconvenient. 'Post mortem?'

'Heart failure.'

'Nevertheless, you have misgivings?'

'Indeed I do.' The Chief Executive removed his rimless spectacles, suspicion etched behind brooding eyes. 'This man paid his dues for a little over one year before he died yet in that year, he had sold his premises and cleared out his bank account.'

'Perhaps he had a premonition of his own death.'

'Is that possible, Miss Grey?'

'Anything is possible, Mr. Shilling. The brain is an unsolved mystery. Some say we are able to home in upon death, like elephants walking miles to their resting place.'

'I ask because there is another, probably. Lenard Green, died three years ago, did the same thing, went the same way. He was insured for three hundred thousand, the money held in trust for his dog. Are you now going to tell me he too had a premonition of his own death?'

This was interesting. She left her seat and went to the window lost in thought, perhaps listening to the distant sounds from the narrow streets of London below. At twenty-seven she had acquired sufficient political skills in the male-dominated investigative field to attempt such work where there were tangible as well as monetary rewards to be had. Coincidence or not, this was a case worth taking on. She turned back to the savvy executive limiting his liability. 'You have your Trojan Horse, Mr. Shilling.'

'Good. Have you eaten?'

'I could do with a cheese-and-pickle on brown, with a nice cup of tea.'

The Chief Executive spoke into the intercom. 'Get a pot of tea for two, a cheese-and-pickle on brown and my usual,' and then addressed his new-found arsenal. 'I held up the payment on reasonable doubt but Ruben Stone curtly reminded us of the terms of the contract, to either pay up or produce evidence. Since this company can ill-afford bad publicity, we settled on the full amount.'

'Ruben Stone?'

'Your target,' he replied, prodding a photograph across the desk. 'Along with his grandfather, they run a shop selling dollhouses and related items.'

She studied the picture of Ruben Stone in thick-soled boots and careworn jeans, brown hair flicked over his brow like the Victoria Falls, facing an older man with a pipe gripped firmly between his teeth like some mythical creature trailing clouds of smoke.

'Peter Tudmoor had two sisters,' Shilling continued, 'one of whom was married to Charles Stone. What we have here is the great-nephew arguing with the great-uncle on the day he died. A local informant was certain they crossed words in the gardens of the Green Dragon, with Ruben Stone walking out after saying something to the effect *this will be the end of you.*'

'Has he a record?'

'Clean as a whistle. Drives an old Sunbeam Alpine and seems to occasionally latch on to his old school chum Amy Pots. His closest friend is in the army, Sam Dingle. Other than that, he appears bereft of companionship.' The maniacal grin came next.

Grey lowered her cup, now comprehending how this ruthless captain of industry viewed her. 'I slip in with credibilty, Mr. Shilling, not between sheets.'

'You cannot disagree an attractive woman would lower his guard.'

'A man who has something to hide is not readily influenced by fluttering eyelids.'

'Sorry, what was I thinking?'

'Below the waistline, I should imagine.'

Like an irritating penitent politician, he was a master of silky contrition and was only saved by his secretary when she entered with a loaded tray, an indefatigable marcher who never got nearer than the edge of his desk. No one quite relished the powers this office held than Godfrey Shilling, a man who routinely summoned and dispatched his staff like domestic orderlies.

'Ruben Stone,' he continued. 'An enigma who rarely attended school, passed every exam thrust under his nose and chose carpentry over a place in Oxford.'

'His preferred subject?'

'Chemistry. Interesting?'

'More interesting, why should a man with so much talent choose to be a carpenter?'

'It could possibly have something to do with his upbringing. At three days old, the father died in a car crash; later the mother slashed her wrists leaving the grandfather to raise the child. Since then, they have lived above the shop in what appears to be a hand to mouth existence.'

In the lull of conversation, Grey painted a picture in her mind of the grandfather on that long journey; the expectation when his grandson was born, not knowing what their future held when so much was lost. 'Do you know if he or the grandfather benefitted from Tudmoor's estate?'

'Tudmoor left everything to his sister.'

'And his sister? How gullible is she?'

'Your guess is as good as mine.'

'So, you have this vision that perhaps Ruben Stone, being of competent mind to thwart the autopsy, killed his great-uncle for the money?'

'I do.'

'Then tell me why an intelligent man should leave himself open to such speculation?'

'Desperate times, Miss Grey. In my business I have seen all sorts of scams and shenanigans. Most certainly he was anxious for the money to be paid to his great-aunt.'

'Where do I go?'

'Here,' Shilling indicated to a map. 'Wymondham has become a dormitory town for Norwich. This and many other things you will learn for yourself. Your contact is Michael Fuller; runs his own company, Fuller Estate Agent. It was he who dealt with the policy.'

'Are you satisfied he played no untoward role?'

'On the contrary, I am dissatisfied in the way things have been handled. Three years ago, our Investment Department received a complaint from Stone who claimed Fuller used his position to capitalise on the ignorance of his grandfather. The grandfather being the sole proprietor of the shop, had entered into a leaseback arrangement with Fuller. Harris, our departmental head found no case to answer and suggested the matter be referred to the Financial Ombudsman. When this was put to Stone, Harris heard no more. Of course, this only came to my attention in light of Tudmoor.'

'Perhaps this was another reason why you felt it prudent to settle?'

'Hem…yes, precisely; though Fuller would be a very stupid man to bite off the hand that feeds him. We pay him a good rate of commission and not only that, he does his job well.' Shilling pulled out a drawer as though it was his secret origin. 'You will discover newcomers are accepted into the bosom of Norfolk only having done a stint of thirty years or more, which makes your task even harder. This disc contains the information to what I have here. Any points you need to raise, Ben will clarify.'

Plunging the notepad and disc into her shoulder bag, she had no doubt whatsoever this was going to be an interesting case. 'Twenty percent of the money recovered.'

'Agreed.'

'I shall leave messages with your secretary when to contact me.'

Mindful of a ticking clock, Shilling pushed back his chair and sprung to his feet. 'Just make sure you keep me informed.'

CHAPTER 2

Leaving Celia gave Ruben Stone as much pleasure as supping a pint of best ale at the Green Dragon. She was tall and strong and had intricate paintings on the secret parts of her body. But this was not enough to see her again. She also rode a classic Norton Dominator. But still it was not enough to see her again. As she sped away drowning all other sound out, he glanced at his chiming pocket watch under the glare of a moon and considered he was just in time to catch the nine o'clock news.

Upstairs, above the shop with a magical window display, an old man in a leather-bibbed apron had watched the long goodbye from the window as the kettle behind him sighed its way to the boil. Never let it be known this was the best place to bring home a date. The sills were choked with plants, the walls supported clocks and from room to room ornate plaster ran tired over the ceilings. Sadly, it did not offer complete shelter from the rain, the bitter cold of winter was only lessened by the fireplace and over the years several small tragedies had occurred to the furniture.

But this was their home, the cracked linoleum on the stairs, the stained walls from steamy cooking and when Ruben entered, he looked at Charlie whose bearded face fell back on him. With great disparity in their years as well as their outward appearance, they were, in every other respect alike as two men could be.

'Charlie,' Ruben said, kicking off his shoes, 'we should get a card transaction machine.'

'We hev no need fer one.'

'People don't carry cash anymore.'

'Thass the bank's fault.'

'Look, we need to diversify.'

'Why?'

'We make no profit.'

'Starbucks don't make any profit and they're still trading.'

The old man's lightness of tone, his little joke, did not cause Ruben's expression to alter, nor did he move, only studied the hole in his sock as though he saw right through the globe and into the immensity of space beyond. Age 33 and standing a touch over six foot two, he often dressed as if he had never found his way out of the seventies. He liked to shave with a wet blade, the only suit came with a waistcoat and he never went anywhere without his nineteenth century pocket watch. But for all of his peculiar qualities, he was far more than just a carpenter who liked to whittle wood into miniature figures and furniture.

After the news which only conveyed Britain was in a financial crisis just like their business, a shout echoed from the street below. Ruben moved to the window and craned to study the figure of Michael Fuller.

The old man went to stand but Ruben pushed him down. 'I shall handle it.' Ever since his grandfather fell into the trap created by a money-hungry estate agent, it had become his personal campaign to make the man's life a misery.

In the lee of the shop entrance, smoking a cigarette between thumb and forefinger was Fuller. Tailor-made suit, monogrammed shirt, and initialled gold cufflinks, his three inch heels gave further stature to his height. He sidled into view when Ruben came to the door. 'You took your time.'

'That's what monkeys do, wait their turn.'

'Just hand it over, Stone.'

'The roof needs fixing.'

'So, get a roofer.'

'It's your responsibility.'

'I told you; the roof gets fixed when you stop pissing about and make payments by direct debit.'

'And miss your illustrious company every month.'

'What is it with you? I never twisted the old boy's arm. I even offered to sell it back.'

'But not at the same price you gave him.'

Unruffled, Fuller flicked his dog-end into the gutter and returned his gaze. 'Listen to me, Stone. You had the chance to take your grievance to the Financial Ombudsman but you chose not to, so that puts me in the driving seat. Now give me my fucking money and get over it.'

Typical Fuller response, Ruben mused and surveyed him with a look of cold contempt. 'Since it appears you are not listening to me, I shall reinforce my point to educate your pea brain. The rent is withheld until you make good on this roof. Should you feel disinclined to do so, it will give me the greatest pleasure to write the epitaph on your grave. Now run along to mummy and give her the good news.'

With the door slammed shut in his face, the estate agent shook uncontrollably, his features mobile with the vision of anger and desperation. No one was present to notice.

CHAPTER 3

With no traffic to fight, Grey walked with laptop in one hand, the other a small suitcase, matching her outfit of course. She was leaving behind the railway station, taxis and brown-clad hoarding, moving on towards the centre of town awash by the tail end of a rainstorm. Expecting any moment to see Michael Fuller roll up in his black Mercedes, she reached the crossroad and sighed. He was probably plotting his next course.

The medium in which he elected to converse was nothing less than email, acting with an innate sense of theatre and coming dangerously close to upsetting her plan. In contrast, Ruben Stone worked very hard at not being seen. He had no web site, brochure, ads, listed phone number, or anything else that might attract further business. In some way and by some means necessary, his grandfather's shop had plodded into the twenty-first century even more fortuitous than the fossilized remains of a dinosaur.

As the last few drops fell on to an already steaming pavement under the returning heat of a September sun, women removed their plastic macs and their young jumped in puddles to annoy them. All seemed at peace with the world. So bright, so different to the noisy sounds of London, only those that had a certain look about them as if they were stuck in the past. She stayed her journey outside Peter Tudmoor's shop now sold to a part-time fireman who tinkled with gems and silver. Butcher, baker, but no more a watchmaker, the town was steadily losing its traders one by one. That many had grown in these surrounds, the shops had become their string of life to which they cleaved but just as they had been asking more of a compromise, so the Council's willingness to bear the weight of reality had lessened.

A black Mercedes halted alongside her, a perfect haircut poked out of the driver's side. 'Well, hellooo,' he said to the breasts. 'Let me guess, you must be Grey.'

'Let me guess, you must be late.'

'Mick, call me Mick. Hop in.'

The scenery changed swiftly. Shops and offices transformed into houses and then bigger houses with a backdrop of the Tiffey Valley. It was an outlook this estate agent enjoyed. His residence sat neat in mature grounds, the double garage doors electrically operated. White walls, blond-wood floors and leather sofas made a further statement of wealth. Fuller was not proof against this fortune but rather his mother framed in oils over the mantelpiece.

'She has a rather impressive home.'

'She lives in Norwich.' Fuller slid out of his jacket, hung it neatly over a chair, and then walked to the wide and elongated window to stare at the valley beyond. 'When she goes, I shall have it all.'

All being a wonderfully vague term that covered just about anything. 'Shall we get down to business?'

'You can be my secretary.' His eyebrows slid independently, the habit strangely suggestive, a trick that no doubt ascribed much of his success with women.

'I am a Financial Consultant.'

'You never said.'

'You miss the point. I am not here to service your clients. I am here to service my own, that being the Chief Executive of Fair Life Assurance which brings up the rather larger issue of your deceased client, Peter Tudmoor.'

'He came to me.'

'And what exactly did he say?'

'That he wanted a hefty life policy.'

'Was it he who suggested the amount?'

'No amount was suggested, no specific amount then we got talking after five hundred grand and I told him the monthly payment wouldn't be much dearer if he went for a million.'

'Which would double your commission?'

'Hoy! I never twisted his arm.' This greedy estate agent moved uneasy to the drinks cabinet and poured himself a dose of verbal mettle. 'He came to me, just like that, walked in my office and asked for a quote. I gave sound financial advice, spent more time on those bloody quotes than a cow spends in a field.

And do you know what that sod did next? After I signed him up on a good deal, he had the damn cheek to use another estate agent for the sale of his premises.'

'Did you think it rather odd at the time?'

'Yeah, I did. He said he intended to retire in five years then he was supposed to sell up and move in with his sister.'

'Umm…what about Lenard Green?'

'Ah, Lenard, he lived in Norwich.'

'Did he say who recommended you?'

'Nah, just walked in, asked for a three-hundred-grand life policy and wanted the money in trust for his dog.'

'He had a daughter, so why not leave it to her?'

'She married a rich bloke, no point.'

'I gather she is guardian of the dog.'

'Yeah, strange that. When he died, I went to see her, thought she could do with some financial advice but there was no dog…so I asked, where's the dog and she said it died out of bereavement.'

'Did you do any other business?'

'That's another strange bit. She said she gave the money to the dog's home.'

Retiring herself to a comfortable seat, Grey brought out her trusted notepad and crossed her legs, one click to the biro. 'Tell me about Ruben Stone?'

'Ah, I get it. This is his doing, yeah? I went out of my way to get Charlie a mortgage so they could diversify and what do you think that prat did? I'll tell you what he did, accused me of trying to cheat the old boy out of his property.'

'If I recall, it was no mortgage.'

'I couldn't get a mortgage, not for the amount he was asking.'

'Can you give me access to the agreement?'

'Why?'

'So, I can read the small print, Dick.'

'Mick,' he corrected.

'Mick or Dick, both are incompetent.'

'What's with you?' Fuller scowled. 'That deal has nothing to do with Lenard Green.'

'But everything to do with Peter Tudmoor. You claimed to have overheard an argument between them yet all I have is your word.'

'Who told you it was me?'

'It's written on your forehead.'

Fuller muttered something indecent under his breath and then found the good manners to ask, 'Do you want a drink?'

'I want the truth.'

'Amy Pots told me.'

'Why would she tell you?'

Fuller made light of her request, endeavouring to divert her attention. 'We went to the same school, been friends for a long while. I know lots of people from around here.'

'I am not interested in lots of people only Ruben Stone who, as I understand it, is a close friend of Amy Pots. So, I ask again, why would she tell you?'

'Pillow talk, okay? And don't let it go beyond these walls. I have enough on my plate without him giving me grief.'

'Am I to understand those two are an item?'

'The only relationship he has is with his car.' He laughed at his own joke and came to sit on the armrest of her chair. 'What about you?'

'What about me?'

'Where do you come from?'

'Where I come from and what I do is of no concern to you.'

'Are you a lesbian?'

Grey gave him a sharp look with a clear and unremitting message. 'Any attempt to poke your nose into my private affairs will see yourself with a police record. Have I made my position clear?'

Fuller took her rejection with a pinch of salt, looked at the notepad and breathed down her neck. 'Have you got a bad memory?'

'If you must know,' she said changing seats, 'I prefer using a notepad. May we now move on?'

'What do you want?'

'I wish you to inform your staff, Lulu, I believe her name that I am a Financial Consultant working from your offices. I also want it made clear that I am not restricted to office times, that I come and go as I please, that I make my own appointments and visit people in their homes. I also want an apartment in town, as promised, and I also want access to the deal you made with Charles Stone.'

'Yes to everything but no to the last.'

'If we are not on the same page, you give me no alternative but to pass the bible to God.'

Fuller slugged down his drink and said nothing because there was nothing to say.

'The acquisition of wealth is no longer the driving force. One should work to better themselves.'

'And what do you get out of it?'

'I get my mortgage paid. Where is your bathroom?'

'Through there and off to the left.'

The sad part about her occupation was the inevitability of making enemies that were often catapulted behind bars or given a slap on the wrist by a lenient judge. Thankfully the air smelt fresher in the bathroom albeit heavy with potpourri.

When she returned it was plain to see Fuller looking like a wet weekend, no doubt contemplating the number of people he turned over, self-sewn seeds that made him a very rich man. 'I suggest we meet up at your office, say 5 o'clock?'

'Where are you off to?'

'That need not concern you.'

CHAPTER 4

With a plan to acquaint herself most thoroughly of Wymondham, Grey considered her first port of call should be Betty Tudmoor who, on paper, had never worked a day in her life. But like most well laid plans, she strayed into the Lemon Tree Café, enjoyed a cup of Americano and stepped outside only to be drawn to the shop next door with a magical window display. Viewing a range of dollhouses and related items that seemed to be borrowed from fairy tales, she rather fell in love with a pink-washed terrace. How sweet. Then she pressed her nose to the window, cupping her hands either side of her face to view a greater world of magic inside.

'Yew might see better if yew come in.'

She turned to the gruff voice of Charlie Stone wearing his leather-bibbed apron with majestic pride. His white hair and white whiskered face against dark bushy brows made him look like an advert for fish-fingers. 'You have an extensive collection.'

'All hand made from good wood, no rusting parts, none to give grief to child or collector.'

'Collector?'

'Dollhouses are not recent toys. In fact, they were not fer children. As long ago as five hundred years, the gentry had their properties copied into miniature form to show off their wealth. Hev yew a young un in mind?'

'No, but that's not to say I refuse to play with one myself.'

'Best yew come in, my woman, let me wrap it up fer yew.'

'Do you take Visa?'

'I take anything I can handle.'

Smiling as they entered, Grey drew towards the pink-washed terrace, almost forgetting why she was there. 'Ohh, I love this,' she said. 'Is the furniture extra?'

'Fer such enthusiasm and thass a big word fer me, I shall throw in the top floor.'

'Then I shall buy the bottom floor.'

In the quiet interlude that followed, she regarded the collection, occasionally bending to peep through furnished rooms, picking up pieces that caught her eye. Next, she gravitated towards a wall where painted a large facsimile of a mushroom, the stem catered for a door much smaller than herself. It raised such curiosity that she took a peek inside and discovered nothing more than an empty paint can left on the floor in the middle of a windowless room.

'Where do yew come from, my woman? London mores like by the sound of it.'

'No, yes, correct. Actually, I have just secured a desk at Fuller Estate Agent.'

'Never knew they sold furniture.'

'No, what I mean to say, a desk working as a Financial Consultant.'

'Hev yew now.'

'Yes, a bit boring compared to your wonderful dollhouses. Do you make everything?'

'My grandson makes the related items, keeps him happy.'

'A rare gift to be sure.'

'Do yew make anything apart from money?'

'I dabble a bit on canvas.'

'Wat sort of dabble?'

'Contemporary, mostly contemporary, would that I wish to go further than my cat.'

'How about our Abbey?'

'Not sure I know her.'

The old man blinked in a moment of silence, thought twice what to say then grew a smile on his whiskered face. 'Best yew go to SpecSavers and get yerself a pair of glasses if yew intend to visit church on Sunday.'

Laughing, she popped her Visa card into the machine and told him to turn away so she could enter her pin.

'Any chance yew can finish it off?'

'Have you never operated one of these?'

'Ruby usually does them.'

'Ruby being your grandson?'

'He's older than he looks.'

Side-stepping behind the counter, she worked her fingers over the situation and completed the transaction.

'I would love yew to work here. I could train yew up on a sewing machine, make little outfits fer the little people.'

'Then you would need a little washing machine.'

'Wat makes yew think I heven't got one of those?'

'You probably have. Is there any chance of leaving this here?'

'I can get Ruby to drop it off.'

'Because he's older than he looks.'

'How roit yew are, my woman.'

The carpenter was charming and wonderful, just like his beautiful dollhouses. And as she bent to zip up her shoulder bag, Ruben strode by with a downward glance, paying more attention to his thick-soled shoes than to the woman who was about to turn his world upside down.

Betty Tudmoor lived in a terrace which stood in a dip by the river. There was little remarkable about it except that it was old and only visible when one got close. Vestiges of a stone pathway still engraved the grass as well as the memories of locals who recalled the ancient disaster of her watching the man she loved marry her sister before macular degeneration set in, and what followed thereafter, a touch of senile dementia.

Betty knew her callers like a person would know their own pet. The milkman's knock was twice and gentle, the postman's once and hard, Charlie had a key and the neighbour would shout through the letter box.

'Who's that?'

'Betty Tudmoor?'

'Don't be daft. I'm Betty Tudmoor.'

'Yes, of course. My name is Miss Grey. I am a Financial Consultant based at Fuller Estate Agent, Michael Fuller who helped your brother to give you security?'

The door creaked open three inches to a lone little creature wrapped up in a shawl with hair so fine, smelling like a cart load of lavender. Save for her pickled white eyes, Betty had sustained her beauty into maturing years based solely on ear and nostril.

'Were you very close to your brother?'

'As close as we are now.'

'Can you be more specific?'

'Look dear, at my time of life there are no specifics. He went sad and come back happy.'

Come back? 'So, who died?'

'Peter of course.'

'Did you see him? I mean, did you see him in his coffin?'

Betty sniffed to obliterate this insinuation and stared straight at her caller from who knows what eyes of comprehension. 'He grew taller, got older and ran a watchmaker's shop, so don't you be telling me that I'm blind when you can't read the sign on my door. No callers till after five. Have you got any more stupid questions?'

'Do you keep a lot of cash in the house?'

The door slammed shut. Perhaps she should have rephrased that question.

Deciding there was nothing further to be gained in talks with Betty Tudmoor for clearly, she was three bricks short of a house, Grey moved on. But in her mind was a kind of uneasiness in the way Betty had said, '*He went sad and come back happy.*'

First, she resolved to stroll up a street for half an hour, then up another for half hour more when she went straight to the florist, bought a huge bunch of roses and returned at Betty's door.

'Who's that?'

This time her answer was prepared. 'Red roses,' and again the door edged open. 'I must apologize most sincerely. You are perfectly correct. I ignored the sign.'

The lone little creature pushed her nose into sweet smelling buds then set them aside to explore the face like a moth to a light bulb. She nodded her head a great many times and frowned just as much. 'How old are you?'

'Twenty-seven. How old are you?'

'Young lady, I'm already midnight. You go in there while I'll put these in water,' and pointed somewhere southward.

Now that Grey had been accepted into Betty's world of make believe, she squeezed past junk where it took effort to move from the hall to a room that was spacious enough, as large as many modern rooms with a bay window emblazoned with stained glass. She made note of the miniature dolls stored in the glazed compartments above the fireplace and turned when Betty stepped into the room.

'I can't see true enough but I can see you meant well.' The vase was placed on a side table with precision before Betty took to her seat. 'Those around here will miss their watches being mended. I expect you have one with a battery.'

'No, actually, I wear my grandmother's watch.'

'Has she no need of it?'

'She definitely went sad and never came back.'

'Oh, my Peter was sad but I told him, don't be worrying about me. I can manage. Come back happy and do what you always wanted to do, buy a nice little place by the sea.'

'Where is a nice place?'

'He loved Cromer but there's no guarantee he would come back there. He might come back in Australia. He went there once, thought it was too hot. Have you been to Australia?'

'I rather like England, not altogether a green and pleasant land, most certainly it's been designed by nature at pleasure for the tourist.'

'You have a lovely voice.'

'Thank you, Betty.'

'You can call me auntie. Who are you?' This had come to be the established state of affairs, the rebellious act of disassociation.

'Grey, I work at Fuller Estate Agent. I never meant to be so blunt. I just wanted to know if I can help with your investments.'

'What investments?'

'When Peter went sad, the assurance company paid you a million pounds and-
'

'Oh, it's not mine dear, it belongs to Peter.'

'So, you gave him the money?'

'Don't be daft. He's not come back yet.' Her nose went high, sniffing the air. 'Oh, those roses smell lovely.' Next, she took up a pill box and tapped the lid, elegantly feeding her mouth with a tablet.

Then sentences broke and went floating away in her head and the chatter went on and on, round and round until Grey struggled to catch their sense. Sometimes she was lucid, and sometimes she dozed off. And it was in a stage of napping that Grey took the moment to study the things in the room, little dolls stored above the fireplace, balls of wool on chairs, a piano for dust, and china ornaments, some cracked and some with pieces missing. These were the blind woman's shapes, worn smooth by her constant nuzzling.

'Water everywhere,' Betty said, kicking Grey back into conversation. 'It come up to my step, it did. Have you ever heard anything more stupid than telling everyone we need more rain? Peter would have laughed.'

'Betty, may I be frank?'

'Make no mind to me.'

'Your brother left you a sizeable fortune but the moment it went into your bank it was taken out again. Who helped you to do that?'

'Why Charlie, of course. I loved him from the moment I clapped eyes on him, and he loved me too but he got my sister in the family way, done the decent thing and married her. I was young, like you when I saw him looking all dapper going down the aisle. Lord, did I cry. It meant no mind to her but it did to him. He never ate his wedding cake. I still got some. Would you like a piece?'

'Thank you but no. And then what happened?'

'Well, she had Teddy and did Charlie love him, loved him to bits. But she never hung around to see him get married. No, she was off with the coal merchant, a shifty little devil going behind Charlie's back.'

'But you never married him.'

'Why would I be marrying Teddy?'

'What I meant to say, you never married Charlie after his wife ran off with the coal merchant.'

'Oh, that's because Teddy got himself killed.' Betty felt her way along the mantelpiece and fondled the dolls one by one. 'This is Teddy. Charlie said if I can't see him, I can feel him. And this is my Peter, left knowing Charlie would look after me.'

'So, Charlie is looking after your money?'

'Lord no! He buried it so Peter could dig it up.'

This was getting worse by the minute and conjured up a frightful scenario which Grey lodged at the back of her mind as she followed Betty into the kitchen. 'How long have you lived here?'

'I was born in this house, right up there with the midwife coming in too late. How do you like your tea?'

'As it comes with a spoonful of sugar.'

'Helps the medicine go down…' Betty sang to the boil of the kettle then she alerted to a key being turned in the lock. 'That's Charlie,' she said and Grey froze.

'Who hev we got here then?'

'This is Frank,' Betty answered.

'Frank?'

'She said she wanted to be Frank.'

'Did she now.'

'Frank bought me roses.'

Another *did she now* and the old man guided Grey to the front door, delivering words in a far less understanding way. 'Next time yew hev a mind to call upon Betty Tudmoor, make it after five.'

'Because you will be here.'

'Yew catch on quick.'

Although an incident to quicken the pulses it was enough to bring doubt about the Stones. Undeniably, Betty had a screw loose but she also had coherency on things that mattered. And it mattered to her that Peter had gone sad and come back happy. So, was it possible that Ruben Stone with his chemical brain had found a way to cheat the post mortem? Assure the life, liquidate the assets, murder the gullible victim and collect one million pounds. Perfect. Dead people cannot talk. But live ones can. Most of it was supposition, but Grey knew even supposition had some basis in truth.

At the heavy glass door, Fuller stood awhile looking at his watch, fair-haired and expressionless before processing the mottled blue carpet to the portal of his office. 'You're late.'

'What time do you normally close?'

'Five-thirty,' and passed over a key. 'I got you a first floor apartment overlooking the Abbey. Your things are already there.'

'That is very thoughtful. Thank you.' She looked at him for a long moment, a pattern of bruising just below the eye. 'What happened to your face?'

'Stone tried to re-arrange it after dropping off your dollhouse...so what's new.'

'He certainly holds a grudge for a long time or was it about something else?'

'Let me tell you something about Stone.' Fuller sat down in his executive chair and placed his feet on the desk, his hands laced behind his head. 'As kids we used to muck about by the river, a whole bunch of us. Sam Dingle was closer to him than the rest of us. Then one day he decides to throw him off the bridge, stood there watching him drown. I went in after him and Stone went mad, tried to stop me. After that, none of us would have anything to do with him, not even

Ding who told me something I shall never forget. He said Stone pushed him off the bridge because he called him Jeffrey. Does that sound like a normal person to you?'

'Who is Jeffrey?'

'It was just a name he hated, like he hates me or anyone who makes good in life. So what? I seize an opportunity if it arises just like Tom Hutton, just like anyone who has a mind to do business. Some people around here get in a jam, too bloody lazy to sort themselves out before the bailiffs come knocking.

They know where to come. I don't twist their arm, I give them an alternative, take it or leave it, as simple as that. Charlie Stone came to me without him knowing, and that's what really got his goat, the same with Amy Pots, his girlfriend. She was in a financial fix so I offered a deal and got a black eye for my trouble.'

'Do you ever see Betty Tudmoor?'

Fuller smiled. 'Is that where you've been?'

'Yes, she is rather scatty. Sad really, very sad to watch the man she loved marry her sister, then the tragedy which befell the family. Is it any wonder why some people find it hard to adjust to the reality of life?'

'I went to see her after Peter died. Of course, Charlie had to be there. It wasn't something I relished, not with the payment being held up. So, what's she done with the money? Gave it to Stone?'

'Would that surprise you?'

'Hell, nothing surprises me about him. You think he killed Tudmoor?'

'Post mortem revealed a natural death.'

'Maybe he paid off the pathologist.'

'What I need is to get close without arousing his suspicions.'

'There's a charity do at the club on Friday. We have one every year for the Christmas lights. He never misses. We could go together and you take it from there.'

CHAPTER 5

In the Green Dragon, and occupying a bar stool, Ruben was supping a pint whilst reading the local rag, appearing somewhat intelligent in his chalk-striped suit. But the chance of an intellectual conversation seemed very remote given that Amy thought a spread sheet was a quilt. Collecting dirty glasses in fishnet tights, her fashion crime rendered only slightly less shocking by the fact she was a woman with no help from a bra.

'What you need is a grin and tonic,' she suggested and Ruben looked up. 'Who cut your hair?'

'Charlie.'

'Did he put a basin on your head?'

Ruben ignored that remark and went back to reading the news.

'If you could make someone dead with your mind, would it be Mick Fuller?'

'I don't have a problem with Fuller. It's you who has a problem with Fuller.'

'Have you got plenty of money?'

'I wear an expensive suit.'

Placing a hand on his arm, Amy leaned to whisper in his ear. 'I'm dying for a cig, Ruby. Can you watch the bar?'

'Sure.'

As she rattled off a guilty titter, her four-inch heels drove over the tiled floor, click-clack, click-clack through a 15th century timbered building that once belonged to the nearby Abbey. Legend had it that an ancient tunnel used to run between the two, the monks being frequent patrons.

Five minutes later an unquantifiable perfume switched his gaze to the floor where he spied a woman on her knees. 'Can I be of assistance?'

'I think I dropped my gloves…somewhere.'

To be accommodating, he rolled off his stool to lend a hand as she climbed to her feet like a secret breath of witchery. Charlie was right, she was so far removed from the likes of Amy that he kind of got the feeling his whole life had been a prelude to this moment.

'Actually,' she said snapping him out of his spellbound state, 'perhaps I made a mistake,' and darted off.

Odd, Ruben thought, for he saw in her expression that he troubled her, that perhaps a piece of toilet paper was stuck to his chin.

'Did you see Mick's new girlfriend walk in?'

Ruben turned to the publican. 'Do I smell?'

Tom Hutton, a mountainous man who walked with a stutter and spoke with a limp, came close and sniffed a few times. 'You gotta stop using Charlie's aftershave.'

'Old Spice happens to be my choice,' and went back to reading his paper.

'What do you make of Mick's claim?'

'What claim?'

'That Tudmoor was murdered.'

'A load of bollocks.'

'Did you kill him?' Hutton never so much asked questions as hurl them in like hand grenades.

Keeping his emotions in check, Ruben gulped down the last of his pint, left for the open space which was planked under foot and stole a cigarette from Amy's packet.

'I never knew you smoked.'

'I don't.'

'Okay, lover boy, what's going on?'

'Hutton just asked if I killed Peter.'

'Oh, so you haven't heard then?'

'Would you care to enlighten me?'

'Well, Lulu was at her desk when she heard Mick laughing in his office. Next, he comes out and says Peter Tudmoor was murdered. She says, what's so funny about that and he says, because Tudmoor was scammed into thinking he could come back from the dead. Then he shoots back into his office when Miss la-de-da walks in. I wish I could steal money and get away with it.'

'And then what? Buy a wardrobe full of dresses, spend time on the beach, lose your sense of self and become a lazy ingrate smoking pot.'

'Wow, you just described my ideal lifestyle.'

'What do you see in him?'

'Extended credit,' and fluttered her eyelashes making him smile. 'What did you see in that picture post card?'

'I have absolutely no idea to whom you refer.'

'Yes, you do. Celia, wears leathers and rides a bike, never seen anyone look so twerpy.'

'Every girl I meet is twerpy, including Fuller's.'

'She's not his girlfriend.'

'Oh?'

'She's a Financial Consultant working out of his office.'

'Name?'

'Miss Grey.' Then Amy took on an aristocratic accent. 'But please call me Grey.'

'I take it you're not keen.'

'Did you get a load of her talons. She saw me looking at them, told me they were real.' Amy gazed at her own nails, bitten down to the quick and began laughing. 'She said all I had to do was to soak them in salt for twenty minutes then suck them dry. You should have seen Mick's face. Then she gave me one of her herbal cigarettes, except it stunk of mint. I tried patches.'

'I tried a lot of things, still find sex better.'

Amy, being a woman some two months senior to Ruben, and having shared their pencils at school stubbed her cigarette out in the ashtray and nodded her head as if she had acquired the wisdom of age. 'You should marry the crash helmet and retire Charlie.'

With that, Hutton appeared. 'Amy, don't forget you are at the club tonight.' Then he gave Ruben a thoughtful once over. 'They had those suits in Marks and Spencer about ten years ago.'

'Gee, got anything else to make my day?'

'Who cut your hair?'

Ruben rolled his eyes to the sky and picked up his feet, tired of being caught in the tangle of human living. But most importantly, he had established the woman who seemed to be taking a keen interest in Betty Tudmoor, that her name was Grey, a Financial Consultant, and blindly considered that whatever challenges she held, he would surmount them without difficulty.

The market square had already been emptied of stalls, its meagre holders moved on and in their place a party of cleaners picking up rubbish. Round an obscure corner the clubhouse, a temperate building for many uses that would otherwise go unnoticed.

He sent a passing glimpse at the velvet interior stretching back to the stage where a local band was setting up their equipment. Elsewhere, pockets of shopkeepers ready to do their bit, poverty and obedience, each had pledged themselves to buy a raffle ticket. On the turn of his head, he caught sight of Fuller advancing with the one-shoulder dress. What he would give to fly on her broom.

'How's business, still bad?' Fuller asked as if he wanted to provoke something.

But Ruben only had eyes for the witch. 'You left your gloves on the bar.'

'Do you have them with you?'

'No. I left them with Tom Hutton.'

Fuller quickly covered the formalities. 'Stone this is Miss Grey, a Financial Consultant.'

'Are you leaving us, Fuller?'

'No.'

'Pity.'

'Ruben,' Grey interjected, 'what an interesting name, he led the foremost tribe to Israel.'

'It also took him a very long time.'

'I met your grandfather. He makes wonderful dollhouses, simply wonderful. You must have a great deal of patience to make those teeny weeny legs on teeny weeny foot stools.'

Again Fuller. 'Like his teeny weeny prick.'

Ruben squared his shoulders, was about to respond when Grey stepped between them. 'Will you join us for a drink, Ruben?'

The choice was quite easy when he turned to a light tap on his shoulder. It was Sam Dingle. Two friends embraced, briefly raking over each other, gaining fresh layers of change.

'When did you come home?'

'Yesterday.' Battle scarred and weary, the soldier gestured to his gammy leg. 'Shit happens, got hit on a poxy roadblock.'

As they gravitated towards the bar, the soldier spoke of his luck, how death near robbed his eyes of the sun while an Iraqi shepherd boy wandered aimlessly with his scrawny sheep.

'Two pints,' Ruben ordered and turned back to his friend. 'Insurgents you say, six?'

'The first shot blew out the front tyre. Shit, some of them are well organized and some are downright dangerous. Cheers.'

'Cheers.'

'I tell you, it was close, Ruby.'

'Are your dancing days over?'

'Just a flesh wound. Did you hear Pat got married?'

'I heard. One cannot help but hear when your mother gets news. So how long before you go back?'

'Until I get signed off, hopefully we can spend some time together. How are things? Mum said something about Charlie retiring.'

'Speaks about it, never does it. We got a new lathe and cutting tool, bought off a company that went bust. You have to come round and see for yourself, yes, business isn't that bad, keeps him busy and complaining as usual.'

'You still got your motor?'

'Jim keeps it well-oiled and dandy.'

'Didn't we have some good times in that?'

But the question floated over Ruben's head. He was holding his steady gaze upon Grey, almost forcing her to meet his look. And when she did, there they remained staring at each other.

'I think you fancy her.'

'I couldn't agree more.'

'I also think she fancies you.'

'Shall we find out?'

Tentatively, like skeletons emerging from a tomb, they picked their way across the floor and placed their drinks on the table. As Fuller stood to welcome the soldier home, Ruben used the moment to take his seat.

'So…you're a Financial Consultant.'

'We all have to start somewhere. Your shop was very impressive. It was hard to extricate myself without buying everything up. I'm curious as to why your grandfather was unfamiliar with card transactions.'

'Anything outside of wood, he's lost.'

'Ah, yes, of course, like so many blinkered souls who plod the ground wishing to still time.'

'What made you move to Norfolk?'

'For a quieter life, less crowded.'

'What's your Christian name?'

'Grey.'

'Everything you wear is grey.'

'Not so hard to forget my name then?'

To say Ruben had lost interest in small talk would have little meaning for it was clear that his mental and professional mind was, at this point in time, on taking her to the moon and back. So, he upped the level of conversation. 'Did you know the power of population is greater than the power of earth to produce food?'

'All the more reason for men to have vasectomies.'

'Well, err, yes, I suppose that's one way of curbing the population.' As the band struck up, atomizing the air with *Can't Live Without You* music, Ruben tried another tactic. 'Do you dance as bad as your ideas?'

'As long as you keep off my feet, I think I shall manage.'

Without further word he remained close behind her as she walked to the dance floor, his hand hovering above the small of her back. And there, holding her, he became someone else, someone more like himself.

'Do you like your job?'

'Absolutely love it.'

'Is that why you paid a visit to Betty Tudmoor?'

'And glad to hear your grandfather is looking after her welfare as well as her money.'

'Hard to trust people these days.'

'Oh, I so agree.'

He brought her closer, bathing in the smell of her hair, dancing as though language had surrendered to music.

'I looked for you in Yellow Pages,' she said.

'Why, when I'm here.'

'You may be here but you're not there.'

'Maybe that misfortune could herald a springboard for my future.'

'Do you like being a carpenter?'

'Too dumb to do anything else.'

'I would peg you as an intelligent man.'

'It's the suit.'

He lied. She lied. They both lied and denied everything out of self-preservation, poised among others in the corrupt sands of commerce, the earth spinning round their feet and still spinning when the band stopped playing.

At that juncture, the local gossip waved a book of raffle tickets under their noses. With the blank watchfulness of an insect and ears like a bat, Marge Dingle could see though keyholes and hear a pin drop on a carpet of grass. 'Buy five get one free,' she said.

'What's the first prize?' Ruben asked.

'A set of miniature furniture.'

Ruben shook his head and dug in deep trusting his grandfather never offered a teepee for the second prize.

'Did you hear about Kings Head Meadow? It's a green space not to be built on.'

'I thought that was already established.'

The gossip shone her false teeth in pyrotechnic brilliance then grabbed another unsuspecting soul, leaving no room for argument.

Ruben glanced at his watch then at Grey with a third tactic in mind. 'I need some advice.'

'What sort of advice?'

'Forgotten your trade already?' Carefully crafted for a yes or no, he saw the refined beauty of her face dissolve into confusion. 'There's a business plan at the shop, look it over, see any missed opportunities?'

'Advertising springs to mind.'

'Is that a no?'

'I shall get my coat.'

Breathing a little easier now Ruben walked on, a man with the weight of curiosity on his mind. To him, she just seemed too perfect and the meeting too coincidental. Before stepping into a swoop of fresh air he looked back and saw Fuller looking at him with a grin plastered on his face. Perhaps there was something far, far more to worry about than the snooping, beautiful Miss Grey.

'You know,' he opened up, 'there's a conspiracy to kill off this town. The joint core strategy to manage growth in what is called the Greater Norwich Area, nobody wants it, leastways nobody with any brains.'

'Are there not consultations?'

'Ha! Now there's a novel get-out-that clause.'

'Is this about Kings Head Meadow?'

'It reaches further than a green space. No, we cannot pretend to have all the answers, but we have a right to ask our elected councillors to stop representing themselves and start representing the people.'

'Oh, I so agree. When a man lies, he murders some part of the world, and most assuredly England has been murdered enough.'

In the pause of their conversation stillness followed in the empty streets, yet the echoing music appeared to haunt on, a reckless attempt to put Wymondham on the map.

'Once called Kinmundy House,' Ruben said outside a high street building, 'demolished in 1880, in its place a surgery until 1983. Next door used to be a chemist now it's a charity shop. All these buildings have history. In front of you was the Rose and Crown dating back to the 1500s, now occupied by one of the oldest family businesses in town. What do you see?'

'A sold sign.'

'And soon to become another charity shop, which only hinders genuine businesses who, unlike the charity organizations that pay just ten percent of their rate bill, struggle to survive, more so when the council adopted Park & Ride. The museum, you should go there, learn about our town's history, before it too closes.'

'Why when I walk beside a history lesson.'

'Do you wish me to continue?'

'Oh, please, it's fascinating stuff.'

'The Service Men's Club where we danced used to be a cinema. In the post war years, the Regal struggled to compete with Norwich and closed in 1962. Architecturally, economically and socially this town has an eclectic and vibrant history. It was once the centre of the woodturning craft, then it became synonymous with the weaving industry, and later brush making became the main source of employment and remained so for almost one hundred years.'

'Life goes on, Ruben, regardless of competing enemies. Shopkeepers probably feel they are alone and unprotected, faced by a struggle which require new techniques to pay off their burdensome rates.' Which brought up the rather larger issue who was going to be next? 'Are you struggling to make ends meet?'

Ruben had been struggling with his own disquieting ruminations about this, but now, with Grey's probing questions, he was feeling an added unease over the issue.

In the living room he slipped out of his jacket, flung it across the arm of a sofa and loosened his tie. 'From what I can ascertain,' he said, filling two glasses with warm Chardonnay, 'this business is able to compete if two objectives are met. First, establish card transactions and this I have done, though I am hard pressed to teach Charlie how to use it. Secondly, rather than cheapen the product with inferior materials, we came up with a new design for boys, saloons and tepees, cowboys and Indians.'

'Where is your business plan?'

'In front of you.'

Grey picked up a few scruffy notes off the coffee table and slowly sat down, narrowly missing a protruding spring. 'Did you compile this in your sleep?'

'It's not too difficult to work out what comes in and what comes out.'

'But you make no allowances for staff. And what is this, two thousand pounds for advertising?'

'Yes, I know it's a large sum but that's for the year.'

For the year! 'You must be living on the fiscal moon if you think two thousand pounds will market your new line.' She grabbed a pen and scribbled a few figures. 'You need at least two thousand to cover web design and a further three for marketing in the first year.'

'Why when we have word of mouth.'

'You asked for my advice and here it is. Either do this properly or wave goodbye to money badly invested.'

'So, we close the shop.'

'What, just like that, close the shop?'

'Charlie has a pension and I could work in the building trade as a carpenter.'

'Ruben, for goodness' sake, one of the great pleasures of shopping away from the city is the discovery of hidden treasures. There's always something to be said for knowing precisely where to go, especially when time is short. Whatever, happy accidents, discoveries and rarities tend not to be part of the chain-store offer which is where local shops come into their own, and you want to invest a poultry sum of-'

'What other alternative is there?'

'If you used the web-'

'If is a very big word.'

'I have a bigger one. When you use the-'

'Are you going to operate it?'

'I do wish you would stop interrupting me.'

'I do wish you would limit your words to one.'

There ensued a fidgety biro-chewing silence when rebellion raised its standard, to which Grey wrote *bollocks* on his white sleeve. It might have ended there, and having ended would have been forgotten. But no. Ruben took the pen out of her hand and wrote *double bollocks* on her bare arm. This immature behaviour continued for several more minutes, each scoring a few random points in senseless conceit.

'Ah! Ah!' Ruben exclaimed, exulting in one-upmanship when the ink ran dry. 'Nil point to you, one to me.'

Her eyes glinted. 'Is there a chemical to remove biro print from your shirt?'

'You have been doing your homework.'

'That is more than can be said for your scanty business plan. If I never knew better, I would be inclined to think you brought me here under false pretences.'

'If I never knew better, I would be inclined to think you came here under false pretences.'

'Ruben, you have a cog missing. I came because you asked me to…and look at me. How am I able to help when you are reluctant to listen to my advice?'

He sighed, reason and reasonableness in his voice. 'When my grandfather goes, and he will as do we all, this property will revert to Fuller or had that escaped your attention? I would be surprised if it had seeing as he enjoys playing the role of landlord.'

'You appear so close to your grandfather and yet he signs away your home?'

'With good intentions, believing the deal to be a temporary arrangement, a security on this property in return for a lump sum to tied us over. I was away at the time.'

'Then take it up with the Financial Ombudsman.'

He had his reasons not to, none of which may be so bold as to think there was a long term future in this shop. No profit, no loss. No gain, no shame.

'Your silence speaks of guilt.'

'My silence prevents me from making an ass of myself over a tight-knit contract which Fuller covertly shoved under my grandfather's nose along with a pen.'

Grey paused for a moment. 'Flatpacks.'

'Flatpacks?'

'I presume you are capable of making dollhouses in wood as flatpacks.'

'Selling is the problem, not making.'

'Just continue as you are and introduce flatpacks to another retailer. The margins will be less, admittedly but at least it will maintain the quality which is so rare these days and keep your business afloat.'

A long silent moment passed. Ruben thought hard. Who the hell was this woman? Financial Consultant she was not. He put down the pen, not knowing what to do about her, nor did he know what not to do.

She decided for him. 'I think you need to sleep on it,' and grabbed her coat and bag.

Politely they exchanged goodbyes, see you tomorrow or sometime soon, and then Ruben picked his way to an open yard, beyond where walls held secrets.

Plants and petals, not in gardens but in small receptacles like ancient teapots and redundant buckets softened the brick-built workshop that sat as a bedfellow to the main shop. With its iron-grills covering its green-painted windows, a cast iron stove kept the cold nights at bay. Its floor was uneven, its rafters blackened by the hand of time. The workbench ran along one wall, tools displayed for all to see, and far in the corner tucked by the breast of a chimney was an undisclosed gateway to a smaller chamber that held the truths of Ruben Stone.

He brought out a bottle of best malt from the underside of the bench, blew the sawdust off two mugs and sat on a stool opposite Charlie who was reading his paper by the cast iron stove.

'How'd it go?' the old man asked.

'She's not who she claims to be.'

The old man fell silent and took off his reading glasses, scrutinizing some invisible speck of dirt on the lens. 'I take it we hev a problem.'

'It depends how immutably fixed she is on solving her own per se in how to handle me. Fair Life is behind this, of that I am certain, illustrating their desperation and stupidity, sending something out of Vogue…not that she's stupid or skinny, no, she's nicely rounded, cuddly, smelt good too.'

'I see she made her mark on yew alroit.'

Ruben's shirt was covered in biro print, and looking into his malt, he said, 'Charlie, she came up with an idea that sort of caught me on the hop but the more I think about it, the more it makes sense. Flatpacks, what does that say to you?'

'A man should be able to buy a woman as a flatpack then he can put together the pieces he likes.'

CHAPTER 6

Mid-October 2012

Grey set her coffee cup on the bedside table and stood by the window peering at nine hundred years of history through rain. The Abbey Church still played a vital role in the community, like every street had a story and every building a memory.

It seemed forever had elapsed when last she spoke to Ruben Stone as if his interest had waned. The only breathing she encountered was Fuller's laboured efforts to palm her off with a one bed flat. She turned into the room, rolled her hair into a French pleat and smeared on some lipstick when the signature tune on her mobile echoed to the melody of *Ding-dong-bell, Pussy's in the Well*.

'Are you, my angel?' Shilling enquired.

'You are not yet God.'

'What's Fuller been up to?'

'His business was acquired by virtue of his mother, as you know a partner in a firm of solicitors. She divorced his father ten years ago, gained a sizeable pay out and took over the house. Since then and between them they have amassed a healthy property portfolio by targeting homeowners that are sufficiently old and sufficiently naïve to accept Fair Life is unable to provide additional income with no repayments. To make the deal even sweeter, the mother drops her legal fees. Fuller then values the property thirty percent lower than market valuation, claiming the differential is a risk contingency. The vendor is then given a tenancy agreement. Naturally the monthly rental goes in his favour as do the terms. Although morally reprehensible, they both stand on a secure legal footing. The next part is even more inventive. Now that the vendor has his or her assets reduced to cash, Fuller sells them an income bond linked to the stock market for maximum commission, and a life policy to cover funeral expenses.'

'Except in the case of Peter Tudmoor, what?'

'He never purchased Tudmoor's premises. In fact, Tudmoor used a different estate agent to sell his property. And I think I know why.'

'Enlighten me.'

'It begins,' she muffled in the process of lighting a cigarette, 'when Charlie married the wrong sister. Instead of Betty, he married Peter's other sister to whom he made pregnant. What followed thereafter, as you already know was the loss of Ruben's parents under tragic circumstance.'

'It reduces the notion Stone would do harm to his great uncle.'

'Not harm but favour. Macular degeneration set in after Betty witnessed her sister's marriage to Charlie, and thereafter she became less coherent. I think Peter was frightened of going the same way and asked Ruben if it was possible to cheat the pathologist. And there a plan was in the making. Teach Fair Life a lesson and provide Betty, Charlie and Ruben security for the rest of their lives. To get over his problem with Betty, Peter told her that a way had been found for his re-birth, that although he would go sad in leaving her, he would come back happy and collect upon his fortune.'

'How did he do it?'

'There is a little known drug which constricts the heart muscle making it look like a heart attack. The beauty of this drug is that it dissipates in 36 hours and becomes totally untraceable. Ergo, a clear post mortem. This drug is not widely known let alone widely available but of course Ruben Stone has the brains to produce it.'

'Do you have evidence?'

'The only way to obtain evidence is through Ruben Stone who is currently tip-toing around me like a keeper to an untrained bear.'

'You think he knows who you are?'

'I dropped enough hints.'

'May I ask why?'

'Mr. Shilling, it is far wiser to let him think he has the upper hand, a tactic well used in the past to bring results. Though I must admit he's taking his time.'

'And if waiting proves fruitless?'

'He will make contact, I assure you. Men are very predictable when threatened. The mere fact of my continued presence is enough to be a thorn in his side, which leads me to say, Amy Pots has requested a quiet word in my ear.'

Apparently Fuller broke his cardinal rule and acquired her property. If I can be of help to her she may be more forthcoming about him.'

'And no doubt soften him above the waistline.' The Chief Executive had earned some brownie points. In minutes he would be building bridges to protect his company from adverse wrong-doing created by his agent, Michael Fuller.

Now gazing out of the window, Grey could see nothing but rain clouding her view of the Abbey. She pushed her feet into grey boots, swept on her grey raincoat, and closed the lid to her laptop before leaving a modest apartment.

She walked hurriedly through a pelting shower and into the Lemon Tree Café where jolly faces gathered to eat home-made cakes. Beyond the main area where tables huddled and people heard other peoples' conversations, there was a small alcove for two and that was where she spied Amy with half a pound of make-up.

'Sorry I'm late.' Grey whooshed back her hood and parked herself in front of an Americano and scone. 'I was under the impression East Anglia had the least rain.'

Amy smiled as she chewed, then when she could speak she said, 'we're arse about tits with the weather. Is coffee okay? I can get Nick to make tea?'

'No, this is fine. How much do I owe you?'

'It's on me. So how do you like Norfolk? Boring most like, nothing compared to London, yeah?'

'Do you like living here?'

'Sometimes I feel like living in France, sun on my back, dishy men with dishy accents.'

'They are generally shorter there. Much better to look up to a man, don't you think.' Grey held the cup to her lips, aware that Amy looked the right side of slutty in her figure hugging sweater. 'Ruben is tall.'

'Is he just and good-looking but he's way above my head at times. We've been best mates dating back from the year dot.'

'But not good enough to share secrets?' She watched the face grow red from the neck upwards. 'Amy, no one knows how painful it is to be taken for a ride.'

'Can you speak to Mick, get my house back?'

'Did you bring your Agreement?'

They both delved into their handbags. As Amy passed over her documents so Grey brought her notepad and pen to the table.

'What's that for,' Amy asked.

'I assure you this is for my eyes only. Now tell me, what possessed you to sell your property to Michael Fuller?'

'Nan left me the house so Ruby gave me ten thousand to fix it up. I offered to pay him by instalments but he wouldn't have it, then I felt bad when I heard Charlie sold out to Mick.'

'So, your affair began three years ago?'

'Yeah, just after Nan died. It wasn't serious, just the odd randy moments. I told Mick about Ruby giving me money so he came up with the idea of buying my property and I could still live there by paying him rent. I never liked that idea and asked if he could sort me out a mortgage for around twenty thousand. Then things got stupid. Tom cut my hours down and Mick got involved with some girl from Cambridge. About eighteen months later we were back in bed and then it got serious. The lying shit was still getting his rocks off when he signed me up.'

'When was this?'

'Late last year.'

'Did you pay Ruben?'

'I tried to, bad mistake. I told him I got a mortgage but he said don't be stupid, put the cash in your bank. Then you came along and old memories got stirred, Mick opened his big mouth to Tom-'

'And Tom told Ruben who gave Michael something to think about, yes, I can see it now. That was the day I arrived. Have relations been severed between you and Michael?'

'I don't sleep with him anymore, if that's what you mean.'

'How much did he give for the property?'

'A hundred and twenty-two thousand but it was worth more than that.'

'Thirty-eight thousand more to be precise, based on a thirty percent risk reduction. Dare I ask if you have that money available?'

'I tried to give it back, another stupid mistake.'

'I puzzle why you came to me.'

'Because he has this thing for you, dah! If you're okay by him then you gotta be okay to sort out Mick.'

'Are you talking about Ruben?'

Amy pealed with laughter and plonked her glossy bag on the table. 'Everyone was talking about it,' she said in the midst of rummaging for her lipstick. 'You two smooching on the dance floor then him whisking you away like a cream bun. For the first time he paid attention to someone, got a retailer to take the flatpacks and boy are they up to their necks in work. I thought about getting streaks in my hair, something like the colour of yours. Did you have it done in London?'

'My hair is naturally grey.'

'You know Ruby calls you a witch.'

'Most people do, wish that I had the ability to cast spells my job would be a doddle. Did Ruben get on with his great uncle?'

'Peter? Mick told you, didn't he?' Amy shrank to the size of her bag. 'Oh, God, I feel terrible about that. I was pissed as a newt.'

'What was the argument about?'

'It wasn't an argument. It just got silly. One minute they were having a drink and joking about then Ruby got angry about something Peter did, told Peter it would be the end of him.'

'The end of Peter?'

'No, silly, the end of Ruby whatever that means. So, what do you think? Do I stand a chance?'

Grey sat back and looked at her watch with minutes to spare. 'Why did Ruben throw his best friend off the bridge?'

'See,' mumbled Amy, the talkative barmaid applying her lipstick, 'Ruby went through a bad patch, thought he could bounce off the planet and be someone else. Understandable really, seeing he lost his mum and dad, so he spent more time gazing out the window than paying attention to Miss Stinky. But when he signed his name Jeffrey Cane on an exam paper, she clipped him round the ear and made him stand in the corner, so we all knew about him making up a fake name. Ding was only messing about like kids do, teasing him for getting into trouble in class, then he lost his footing and fell in the river. Ruby went after him and Mick tried to drown him. He never tells the story right. He always says he saved Ding just to cover his arse.'

'He mentioned Sam Dingle never spoke to Ruben after that.'

'He didn't, not for ages because Charlie kept Ruby locked up in that shop. If you want my opinion, it was the wrong thing to do because he hated school after that, I mean really hated it.'

'Why did the teacher treat Ruben so badly?'

'Well, the bloke was his idol, like that man Epstein-'

'Einstein?'

'Yes, that's him, Bernie Einstein.'

'Albert.'

'Whatever, anyway Miss Stinky said the man was mentally deranged like that painter who cut off his ear. But I want you to know Ding and Ruby have always been the best of mates, even kept in contact when Ding went into the army.' She put her lipstick away and forced Grey to meet her gaze. 'Can you get back my house?'

'We can do it one of two ways, the legal route which, no doubt, you wish to avoid or the direct route. In doing the latter I may be creating conditions that might threaten your long term survival.'

'What's that mean when it's at home?'

'Michael could turn very nasty.'

'Ruby would sort him out if he laid a finger on me.'

'By then it may be too late. You must tell him, sooner rather than later. It will give me more leverage when I confront Michael.' Grey sensed the hesitation, the shame of cavorting with the enemy. 'Amy, true friends rarely part company because of silly indiscretions. Tell Ruben the truth and put this behind you.'

'I never have much luck with men.'

'Try a different lipstick.' They smiled. 'Are you off to work?'

'Yeah.'

'Have the cheque made out to Michael. I'll be in touch, okay?'

Leaving Amy's anxious nod behind, Grey returned to her apartment post haste, her boots sloshing on the pavement like a runaway train. If ever there was need to think outside the box, it was now.

Prior to this day, she had made the usual enquiries for a Jeffrey living in Norfolk which brought no real satisfaction. The only factor limiting her abilities to refine the search was the lack of information. Now she had something else to go on and immediately began a systematic investigation into a Jeffrey Cane. But research was utterly tiring. Google threw up so many opuses that by the end of the day she flopped on the bed thinking about Ruben Stone. He was such a contradiction; tall but short on arrogance, gentle but hard on himself. And those brown eyes which bore hatred in company of Michael Fuller had all the mournful characteristics of loss.

Ding-dong-bell, Pussy's in the Well.

'Hello?' she answered.

'Are you hungry?'

'Starving.'

'Green Dragon in five.'

Panic! Off came the sweater, on went a silky white blouse and opal ear-studs, quick splash of water to the face, two squirts of perfume, an argument with the hairbrush, a shuffle into grey jeans then a last look in the mirror. Perfect. She threw cash into her bag and scrambled out the door, then scrambled back to collect her raincoat with an overwhelming desire to change her shoes.

There was not one face among thirty that had the looks of Ruben Stone until she travelled into a smaller room. Here a table for two upon which sat a lighted candle and two glasses of red wine, the neat haircut bent into a menu and home spun cardigan over a white shirt and tie. Was this an attempt to weaken her resolve?

'Have you ordered?' she asked.

'Steak, I thought.'

'Good choice.' They chinked glasses and smiled to the spluttering wicks. 'A little birdie told me you obtained a major outlet for your flatpacks.'

'Yes, a fluke really bumping into an old friend. It transpired he had connections in the trade so when I showed him the flatpacks, well…next day I was sitting in front of a buyer. I also raised the price of our finished goods.'

'I thought at the time they were undervalued.'

'To you, Grey,' he said raising his glass. 'Did the idea just pop out of your head?'

'Things generally do.'

'And you, closer to your own goals?'

'I have a cat.'

'All witches have cats.'

Grey opened her mouth to speak then closed it upon the approaching meal, sizzling and brimming, steak with sauté potatoes, peppered sauce and two side helpings of mixed vegetables. And watched breathlessly at Ruben's swooping spoon stacking his plate with runner beans, leaving the rest for Ron.

'Ron,' she enquired.

'Later on, when I have more room.'

'We learn something new every day.'

'And what did you learn about me?'

'That you love runner beans.'

Their Ping-Pong conversation developed into an intellectual game conducted in wayward outbursts of laughter, while they drank wine by the gallon.

At cheesecake dessert topped with strawberries, Ruben finally chanced his luck and glared direct into her eyes. 'Do you think me that stupid to believe an intelligent woman rubs shoulders with a man like Fuller?'

'I was trying to be discrete.'

'A polar bear has more discretion than you.'

'Ruben, I can help Amy.'

'Is this why you're here, to help the poor sods who were sucked in by his scam?'

'I can only help those who help themselves, which leads me to ask why you failed to take up your complaint with the Ombudsman?'

'Let's talk about your job.'

'Yours is far more interesting.'

'I shall tell you what's interesting. How you intend to get back her house when his mother crosses the t's and dots the i's.'

'As a matter of fact, he broke the cardinal rule in Amy's case, forgetting to cross the t in motherly love. What do you think she would do if she learnt her son had dotted the i with another solicitor?'

'My, my, you are a clever girl…blackmail?'

'I prefer coercion, a word he understands all too well as do others who step over the line.'

Grey contemplated the man who now appeared lost in thought, perhaps listening to his own heart rapping hard against the walls of his rib cage or dwelling on the nearer sounds coming from the bar. Then, quite unexpectedly, he floated a cheque across the table made out to Michael Fuller for one hundred and twenty-two thousand pounds.

'Make sure he gives you a receipt.'

'You were very generous giving Amy a hand.'

'No big deal.'

'You plead poverty and it's no big deal.'

'It was spare.'

'Could you be more specific?'

'No, I do not wish to be more specific.' He leaned back and folded his arms as the customary notepad was placed on the table, one click to her biro. 'If you think I'm about to hand over my life story, you're very much mistaken.'

'I am giving you a receipt.' She smiled, points to her advantage building up nicely. 'Who is Jeffrey Cane?'

'An idiot who lost his way in the world.'

'Yet you admired him.'

'I admired his achievements as I admire any scientist who makes a valuable contribution to this world.'

'And what was his contribution?'

'Why not cut to the chase and be done with it.'

'I think you facilitated Peter Tudmoor's death and in so doing defrauded Fair Life Assurance out of one million pounds.'

'Huh! Is that what your crystal ball told you?'

'I do not need a crystal ball when the man who sits before me has the capacity to manufacture a drug that constricts the heart muscle leaving no trace in the body after 36 hours, and that he makes a point of hiding in the shadows for fear of being discovered.'

Ruben pushed his dessert plate aside and leaned forward, keeping his voice trim. 'Let us say that if such a man existed, he would always be one step ahead. If not, would the subject of such a man ever come to light in a court of law without proof?'

Grey had faced worse, was no less frank. 'Let us say it would make an interesting story for the nationals.'

'I do not intend to be your victim.'

'Does Betty intend to be yours?'

Ruben scraped back his chair, his face mottled in animosity. 'Fly back on your broomstick and be grateful of coming this far.'

Grey watched the fuming mystery swing out of the room, probably damning her with every thought. Herself feeling somewhat deprived of his company, she gathered her things and returned to the apartment, aware now that her feet had been pushed through slippers.

At her laptop, she flicked up the lid and among the list of Jeffrey Canes she saw a newspaper caption dated 13th August 1979. That looked interesting.

50-year-old Jeffrey Cane, a senior gerontologist working on a revolutionary cure for senile dementia, committed suicide after shooting his wife and her lover. Neighbours were stunned at the tragedy that destroyed a well-respected member of the community. Detectives were last night investigating the killings, which unfolded after Cane had a blistering row with his 40-year-old wife and senior lab technician at a private function held by Sir John Harcourt of Harcourt Pharmaceuticals based in Cambridge. Detective Chief Superintendent Andy Spruce, who is leading the inquiry, said, 'I would ask anyone who spoke to Mr. Cane yesterday who hasn't yet spoken with the police to contact us.' This came shortly after Cane's assistant Helena Vale was stabbed by a mugger outside her home and later died in hospital.

Was this the Jeffrey Cane with whom Ruben Stone admired, the man with a revolutionary cure for senile dementia? Thirty something years on and in a world of free information, a network of interconnected events, no such cure or talk of such cure had emerged. So, what contribution did he supposedly make to the scientific community?

She yanked a coke from the fridge, dismissed Jeffrey Cane and concentrated on what she had; apart from a wet pair of slippers and two dates added to her list, absolutely nothing.

1980 Ruben Stone born, parents dead.

2009 Amy Pots inherited house.

2009 Charles Stone sold out to Michael Fuller.

2009 Lenard Green signed up on life policy, died one year later.

2011 Amy Pots sold out to Michael Fuller.

2011 Peter Tudmoor signed up on life policy, died one year later.

CHAPTER 7

For days the customary cloud of rain continued to hang over the east. The river was rising and the town was awash in its gutters. Everybody was grumbling and said it was bad for the nerves. Of course, this never helped in the deliveries of seasoned wood and quality furniture bound for the shop with a magical window display. The luxury new gradually replaced the shabby old until all signs of poverty had been snatched away.

Unhappily, this reignited the idea that Ruben Stone killed for a million pounds, a notion initially spawned by the opportunistic Michael Fuller who now owned one less house in his wilting property portfolio.

But Ruben was more troubled by Grey's absence. Subsequent to that tempestuous encounter where each word drew a line between them, none had seen her save for the leading authority on gossip who swore blind the grey raincoat jumped out of a moving taxi. It was not until much later did he reason quite rightly that scares belonged to something else. Even so, when the sky abruptly darkened, he began looking for brooms.

'I see Mel is closing up early.' Charlie was sharing his view with Ruben, reminiscent of former days when stormy weather kept shoppers indoors. 'The last time it rained like this wus in 1964. Ted's farm copped the worst of it, lost his pigs.'

'Has the witch returned, I wonder…if so, she's keeping a very low profile?'

'George Buncombe, yew won't remember him, had a run in with some gypsies, thought they'd gone until he turned his tractor the following month, saw them parked behind the old cow shed. So that night he rolls a few barrels into the shed. Next morning he bounds in and says, *yew know them gypsies, Charlie, I saw them on Counsellor Thorn's turf. Shame about that* and gives me a wink. He's not going to be too happy, I says, to which he replies, *especially when he finds out they drunk all his wine.*'

Ruben smiled; him the submarine and Charlie his periscope. 'Marge rarely gets things wrong.'

'That woman has the eye for detail and the ear for a keyhole. If she saw Grey duck out of a taxi then I reckon she's seen an opening, just like George Buncombe.'

'How so?'

'Six weeks after that do, the gypsies were nowhere to be found and he got planning permission to build a house where his cow shed used to be. Go figure that one out, Ruby.'

'I have no leverage.'

'Yew could tie her to the bed post.'

Ruben wickedly grinned, quite liking the idea of tethering a witch to his bedpost. But it was becoming clear their relationship, which occupied no dimension whatsoever other than verbal ambiguities, had no life outside this particular time and space. He let his gaze fall back upon the outside world. If there was reason to hate, it would be levied at Michael Fuller who was in transit with a blond, frolicking in the rain. One wrong footing and he went headlong into the gutter and through the excretal remains of a dog. The realm of Michael Fuller was beginning to implode.

Grandfather and grandson doubled up, could not speak for laughing. They would find little left of the Estate Agent. His tale-tale shape angrily stomped into his premises. A happy scene.

'Ohh,' and Charlie dried his eyes on his sleeve, bringing an end to the mirth. 'Thass got to be the talk of the town fer a good while to come. Fate, Ruby…fate yew and me wus here to see it.'

'Serendipity is overrated.'

'It wus serendipity that brought Grey here.'

'It was by my actions that brought her here.'

'When yew thought this business had no future, she made yew see it had. Never once did it enter our heads to find a major outlet. She wus meant to come like we wus meant to watch a plasma screen from a leather armchair.'

Ruben nodded. There could be no argument against that. 'Are you going to see Betty?'

'Not tonight. She's heving her hair done.'

'Good. The plumber's coming so remember to give him the layout.'

The shower head changed from scalding to ice-cold at the slightest touch and after wiping the fog off the mirror Ruben looked like a bright red prawn. He shaved with the thought of growing a beard, brushed his teeth under a dripping faucet and returned to his bedroom, now immunized against suspicions. With earlier thoughts of strapping Grey to his bedpost, he sprung up and down on his new mattress glad he bought a double. If fate had brought her to his door, then fate would surely be kind enough to get him laid even if it took just ten minutes.

Expecting to be drowned outside, a chilly wind had suddenly replaced the thick veil of rain, dribbles and drips from gutters as he turned the corner and swung into the Green Dragon with many a jolly talker. Their heads turned, their sinister doors opened in their brains, their eyes were enquiring then lightened with the sparkle of good humour when he motioned with his chin.

'Can a man at least have breathing space?'

They grumbled but rarely obeyed.

'What's it to be?' Amy asked.

'His usual.' The soldier was parked next to Bill, a great shaggy animal guzzling down a pint. 'Thought you got lost, Ruby.'

'Charlie wanted a hand in moving the sofa so he could reap a better view of the television. Move the sofa, you move the armchairs and next we were discussing where to put the chimney. I should stuff him up the chimney. Cheers.'

'I'm hearing all sorts of rumours, my man.'

'It's all untrue, Ding.'

'So, you're not loaded?'

'Would I lie to you?'

'I met this Iraqi, daft as a toilet brush, said he could tell my fortune that I would leave with a bullet in my leg, and what'd you know, here I am because of it.'

'You made that up.'

'Would I lie to you?' They laughed. Both had their red jumpers looking like book ends. 'Seriously, Ruby, what's going on? Mick said you topped Peter to get hold of his life insurance.'

'I shall tell you what's going on,' and the nearby drinkers just got nearer. 'I'm trying to run a business without him poking his nose into my affairs. Since the day he took over that agency he's done nothing but turn people over.'

'Careful,' Tom Hutton growled, 'you're close to accusation. His mother's a solicitor.'

'So let her sue me. They took advantage of Charlie, like they took advantage of some others around here.' Turning with a flourish to the shaggy animal who was still glaring at him, he said, 'You, Bill…you sold your house so tell me if the money he invested on your behalf came up trumps.'

'We live in austere times, Ruby.'

'Huh, he knew damn well the market was crashing.'

'What we'd like to know.' Everyone held their breath at Amy. 'How did he manage to fall into that pile of shit?'

And the room exploded into laughter. They knew about Fuller's lot and referred to his mother in personal terms. But there was also a frank attitude to Bill's plight, which no one accused or pardoned.

Among friends in a lively reek of streaming life and no doubt about their sincerity, or their curiosity, Ruben drank pints by the dozen. Come ten-thirty, he had suffered his fair share damage at which point a familiar sound fell behind him. There, talking to Amy, smiling and laughing, her hair loose and wild, was Grey.

'Ruby, isn't that the girl you danced with?'

And would dance again. He swayed towards her, a near-empty glass in one hand, the other tucked in his trouser pocket, the nonchalant Ruben Stone observing her as she observed him. 'Are you here to see me?' He watched her donkey nod. 'Best we find a place to talk.'

They fell silent as they carried their drinks through the crowded bar, dodging little pockets of dangerous conversations, and settled in a snug where the air was less contaminated.

'Thanks for Amy.' Ruben felt generous.

'I did what any decent human being would do in my position…are you decent, Ruben?'

'My clean underpants prove it. Would you like to see them?'

'Not at this particular point in time.'

'So why are you here?'

'My broom needed servicing.'

'Did you sweep any dirt?'

'Actually,' she said, opening a packet of crisps, 'I found some remarkable titbits, coincidences perhaps or not as the case may be. Did you know a chap called Lenard Green?'

'Err…' Ruben made noises, not sure how to respond and completed his sentence. 'No, never heard of him.'

'He left a remarkable legacy to his dog, which, by happenstance died shortly after its master who, like Peter Tudmoor sold his property before going to heaven. The interesting part is what happened to the money.'

'Perhaps the dog ate it.'

'Or perhaps someone misappropriated the funds.'

'How do you spell that word?'

She leaned forward. 'Very carefully.'

Temptation was there to justify his position, but any defence was likely to be grim, so he just watched each crisp enter her voluptuous mouth, touching every cell in his body.

'Strange,' she continued, 'he should take out a life policy through Michael Fuller.'

'And what does that lying bastard have to say?'

'That you knew Lenard Green.'

'Well whoopee do. Am I to be the fault of every person who died leaving an insurance legacy to their dog? Look at me. Do I wear expensive clothes? Do I travel in a Rolls Royce? Do I own my own home? Not even my grandfather owns his own shop thanks to the turd residing in this town. No to these questions because what you see is what I am.'

'And what are you if not a thief and a murderer?'

'You would not be confronting me if you believed that to be true.'

'I have always been more curious than cautious.'

'Then let me take you to bed.'

Her eyes fell to her ankle length boots. It was almost ten seconds before she picked up her feet and walked off without a backward glance.

And it left him feeling pretty much empty and alone. So, he returned to the bar and ordered neat whisky. From glass to glass in trackless movements, it licked down his throat and mapped his brain stuck fast in dreams.

The soldier, also three parts to the wind had an eye on a target. 'Give us a kiss.'

Amy burst forward, shooting from the lips. 'I don't kiss twats!' Then she looked down at Ruben slumped on the floor. 'It's your own fault, Ruby. All you had to do was be nice but you had to act the idiot.'

'He had to act the idiot.' Ding echoed.

'Here, take him home before Tom charges for overnight accommodation.'

Outside, the bookends broke into a song. 'I can't smile without you…I can't laugh and I can't eat…I feel glad when you're glad…If you only knew what I'm going through…'

Shut the fuck up! Someone called out.

Ruben never remembered how he got home or who put him to bed, just a voice in the wilderness telling him to get up. Blurry eyed, he rolled off the bed, hiked up his underpants and walked into the wardrobe door. His next few venturous steps found him sharing the toilet bowl with a plumber.

'I'm Bob.'

'I'm asleep.'

The plumber nodded and zipped up his flies leaving Ruben to squint at his mirrored face, thanked God it was Sunday then slid into a trance of last night. There was little doubt Grey belonged forever. She refused to tolerate any thought of deflection in her case as though she had a perverse streak of nature that was stimulated by the challenge of adversity. He was on a perilous emotional ledge. The threat of his own death troubled him far less than the threat of being discovered as Jeffrey Cane.

With hair stuck up like the arched back of a hedgehog, Ruben stifled his sighs and plodded to the bedroom only to find the tanned skin of his friend sat on his bed drinking a cup of tea.

'Like old times, Ruby.'

'Thanks for getting me home.'

'Hey, don't mention it.'

'Got anything planned?'

'Nope, why, do you need a hand?'

'I need a favour.' Ruben struck into his jeans. 'When you're ready, we'll talk in private.'

In the kitchen the air was warm and filled with the smell of tobacco. Charlie was at the table, one hand to his whiskers and the spoon beating time with the other.

'Wat happened to yew last night?'

'I met the witch.' Ruben stuck his nose in the teapot and made coffee instead. 'She's latched on to Lenard Green.'

With that, the old man went to the door and jerked his head in the hall, looked about then brought his voice down to almost a whisper. 'Things are getting out of hand, Ruby. Bob doubled his quote. He thinks we're millionaires. Hev yew told Ding?'

'No. But I intend to.'

'Why?'

'Because he's my best mate and can help. And, Charlie, do I need help. She's like an unstoppable force.'

'Then come clean and tell her.'

Ruben rolled his eyes to the battered cream ceiling as in consequence of this lunacy would be the immediate descent of the roof caving in.

A second later the soldier entered and looked back at the old man leaving, the air in the room went with him and it took a few seconds to realize there was purpose in being left alone with Ruben. He cracked a few thick knuckles and said, 'You want me to work Mick over?'

Ruben pondered the comment for a second and shook his head. 'I need to know everything there is to know about Miss Grey.'

'How about asking her?'

'Your speciality is surveillance, yes?'

'You want me to listen in on her calls?'

'And tap into her computer if she has one.'

The soldier rotated his muscled bound arms then stretched his spine before swinging on to a chair to face Ruben. 'Talk to me.'

'Grey is not a Financial Consultant. She was sent by Fair Life Assurance as a Trojan horse to target me. Now she's dangerously close to learning the truth and I'm worried shitless.'

'And what's the truth, my man? Did you have a hand in Peter's death?'

'I facilitated Peter's death; there is the difference. Do you remember when we were kids how I clung to the name of Jeffrey Cane?'

'Strange you should say that. Amy said Grey took an interest in your school days, especially the part where you shoved me off the bridge.'

'It was an accident.'

'You were sodding angry because I called you Jeffrey Cane.'

'I was Jeffrey Cane.'

Dingle looked understandably bewildered. For a moment, neither of them spoke as if they were standing on the edge of a cliff.

Then, 'It's true I was him, a gerontologist who spent a good portion of his life studying the aging process. I made a discovery, a way to cheat death and taxes if you like, live again with past memories intact, except mine happened to be all over the place. And because of it, I worshipped a man I once was only to realize later in my stages of puberty that I had actual been Jeffrey Cane. You okay with this?'

'Jesus, Ruby, the brainiest sod in school and weird as a flying saucer, of course I'm okay with it. Yeah, it's starting to make sense. You gave Peter another life and why not, the poor bastard was losing his sight.'

'Except I never knew he covered himself for such a huge amount. He told me at the last minute, said half a mil wasn't enough to take care of inflation let alone give him the security he needed in case he was born into a family of misfits. It was no good making him see reason. The damage had already been done and I was left to pick up the pieces.'

'So how does it work, Ruby? You bury his money then he makes contact when he remembers who he was?'

'That's just about the gist of things.'

'Hell, I can see why you chose carpentry. What made you do it in the first place?'

'Like everything else it starts off with good intentions, give a second chance to those with incurable illnesses and then when it's too late you go figure the consequences. This must be kept tight. If Grey figures me out as Jeffrey Cane the floodgates will open and my life, Charlie's life, everyone connected will suffer.'

'Not helping with Mick Fuller spouting his mouth off. Okay, I can tap into her cell phone, also her computer but only when she logs on. What am I looking for?'

'A case gone wrong, back handers, anything to give me leverage.'

'Blackmail?'

'She prefers the word coercion.'

CHAPTER 8

Wednesday 24th October

The manager's office with the autumn sun streaming through the window fell directly upon her face as she leaned back in Fuller's executive chair, seemingly quite unperturbed. Thoughts of Ruben Stone, and his plea of poverty while his tie dangled in his beer mug, amused her. And it was so tempting to take up that offer of sharing his bed. If only for a few short indiscrete hours she would have the feel of a man course through her body and take her to places she rarely went. But she left. If there was one lesson her mother had taught her, it was that impulsive actions led to misfortune, and misfortune could have dire consequences.

Then the call she had been waiting for came through on Fuller's phone. It was Godfrey Shilling. Like always, his smooth mellow voice carefully defined their legal relationship.

'I am inclined to agree, Miss Grey. Prosecution is out of the question. How certain are you he will play ball?'

'Obviously I would wish for more leverage but I feel confident the threat of exposing his activities to the press will do the trick. Of course, there is the possibility of him calling my bluff, in which case how do you feel about press involvement?'

'No press. It will make him a damn martyr. Let us say he accepts defeat.'

'Then it's very probable he will plead poverty and negotiate the amount. Are you prepared to take a loss?'

'How much of a loss?'

'Give or take a little, I think no more than three hundred thousand. Alternatively, you might wish to extend his credit and receive instalments on the difference. His business is picking up nicely.'

'Are you absolutely certain Tudmoor and Green are the only two cases?'

'Absolutely, notwithstanding others he may have conned through different assurance companies.'

'What has he done with the money?'

'Best guess, he's bought assets, appreciable assets, a painting or gold, something that can be easily sold when he's ready to spend it.'

'How does he do it?'

'I am hardly likely to get that information.'

'Quite. The man's an idiot. With such a talent he could have gone into the pharmaceutical industry.'

'Say that again?'

'With such a talent-'

'Yes, sorry, I did hear. What are your instructions?'

'Get what you can, put an end to it. Well done, my angel. You can now call me God.'

Every imaginable question had been asked, and all leads followed up, even some that seemed absurdly far-fetched, but none as far-fetched as the one now crossing her thoughts. Was Jeffrey Cane and Ruben Stone one of the same? It pigeon-holed Betty's anomalies and gave new insight to why these men trusted Ruben with their deaths. Idiot, she said to herself, it was right in front of me!

The door flung open and in walked Michael Fuller giving her the evil eye. She had no intention of removing herself from his chair.

'What did Shilling have to say?'

'Let's talk about Ruben Stone?'

'Sure,' Fuller said and reluctantly took the opposite seat, 'let's talk about him popping off Peter Tudmoor.'

'You seem very certain it was him.'

'I have my sources.'

'Would you care to share them with me?'

'Now why would I share with a blackmailer who cracked my nuts over Amy Pots and sits in my fucking chair?'

'Hardly eloquently put, but yes I think that sums up our present positions.'

'What did Shilling have to say?'

'You may keep your agency on the proviso you take your final exam and confirm in writing any action taken by your tenanted clients will be dealt with by you, and, if necessary, compensated by you.' She expected him to show some displeasure but he just sat there with a smirk on his face. 'Is there something I should know?'

'Look, sweetheart, there's nothing you need to know except piss off out of my office and tell Shilling he can stuff his proposal.'

Fuller was a man whose grotesquely overblown ego never ceased to amaze her. So just to annoy him, she spent a while at his desk smearing on lipstick, took a further few seconds to powder her nose then stood on the spot to slip on her grey raincoat, very slowly indeed.

'Are you done?'

'Our business is concluded.'

The lowly sun was replaced by a freezing fog that drifted down almost casually, draping itself around the town when Grey came from the direction of Fuller's place with her hands tucked in her raincoat pockets, a gloomy expression on her face. Friends were rarely made in her line of work. And now she had met her objective with Amy Pots, she felt somewhere within the walls of that amazing shop there might be something to cheer her up.

'Ruby's gone out, my woman.'

'It's you I came to see.'

The old man removed his leather-bibbed apron, flipped the sign to close and took her upstairs into the lounge where she now viewed a different perspective.

'This is very beautiful.' Her fingers ran along a leather sofa. 'And you have a plasma television.'

'Why hev yew come, my woman?'

'Charlie, if I may be so familiar, I have a terrible confession to make.' She pulled from her bag a packet of cigarettes and sat down. 'Do you mind?'

The old man, who rarely indulged, reached for an astray and helped himself to one of hers. 'The last time I smoked one of these it wus white.'

'These are herbal. The pink ones are strawberry flavour, the green is menthol and the yellow is pear.'

'Why not banana?'

'Bananas do not grow in my garden.'

'So, yew make them yerself?'

'A recipe handed down by my grandmother.'

'Witches must grow in your family.' Choosing pink, he leaned to her lighter and inhaled. 'Lord!' he exclaimed, 'it tastes like strawberries, well, well, thass a new one on me,' then sat deep in a luxuriant leather armchair looking like a gentleman tart. 'Wat be your confession, my woman?'

'I am not a Financial Consultant but then I expect Ruben has already informed you.'

'That he did.'

'I expect he also told you why I was here?'

'That he did.'

'I do not wish for further confrontation between us and almost certainly I think Ruben feels the same. So here is my offer. If Ruben returns the money no questions will be asked. The matter is forgotten, the case closed and I shall be out of his hair.'

'He has no money.'

'Did you just make that up?'

'I make a lot of things, my woman, and one of them being a future fer my Ruby.'

'Why did he choose carpentry instead of chemistry?'

'Ah, there's a reason fer that.'

'Would you care to elaborate?'

'Only to his wife.'

'I never knew he was married.'

'Thass exactly wat I mean, he needs a wife.'

Grey smiled, reminding herself the last time she encountered Charlie Stone that she should check her words.

Appreciating a curious equality of friendship which originated between them, the old man spoke in a spirit of confidence. 'You're the only woman thass caught his eye and I don't say that lightly. His problem, he suffers the same trait as his father, stubborn as a mule, afraid to put a foot forward in case he has to take two steps back. And he's been doing a lot of that lately since yew came on the scene.'

'Oh, Charlie, I wish my father had been like you. He took everything for granted that I often wondered if he ever stopped to consider the ones who loved him.'

'Hev yew got a mum?'

'Alas, both my parents are gone.' It was a lie, but lying was part of the job. 'Look, I'm still at the Abbey Hotel. Can you speak to Ruben about my offer and let me know his answer?'

The old man stood. 'Come with me.'

They went downstairs and a further set of treads leading to a cellar, her hand feeling the damp wall, swallowing, delighted and scared. In the cobwebbed corners, the old man drew upon a large wooden chest, tossed back the lid and delved inside like diving into a pool.

'These are his things,' he said, tossing them aside, 'so don't yew be saying I showed yew. Jigsaws, he loved jigsaws, would spend all day doing the hardest he could find.'

'And books on chemistry.'

'He could teach them a thing or two.' A bit more rummaging, the old man dangled a thick gold chain upon which suspended an oval shaped locket, slightly dulled by age. 'This holds the key to his life. Take it fer now.'

'I cannot possibly take it.'

'Think of it as part payment.' The old man fed it about her neck. 'Cherish it, my woman and when yew hev a mind to think well of him, give him a chance fer some happiness.'

Grey opened the locket, held it closer to the light bulb. *When this you see remember me* was engraved on one side, opposite a picture of a man that neither looked familiar nor unfamiliar, just posed ordinary as people might have done before the invention of digital cameras and desk-top printers. There could be no misapprehension of the truth, no illusion that in his unspoken words the old man had given her the face of Jeffrey Cane and the life of Ruben Stone.

'Where is he, Charlie?'

'He had trouble with the motor. He went to see Jim, doubt he'll come back in this fog.' Charlie switched off the cellar light, shutting the door behind them. 'If yew had your time again, would yew choose a different life?'

'I would certainly choose a different profession.' She took a few steps towards the window display, picked up a miniature cat and sighed. 'Nobody smiles or thanks you for rapping their knuckles. Enemies are not far behind. But I have Bobble, my cat, rather like this one. I found him aimlessly wandering about thin as a rake. He hates it when I go away.'

'Then why do it, my woman?'

She sighed hugely. 'Why, why, I so often ask myself why. Very simply, I was born with a sixth sense, like my grandmother who would remind gifts are given for a reason, and should be used wisely for they have a purpose in life…what else does one do with such a talent? Fifty years ago, a man shook hands on a deal and it was generally honoured. Fifty years ago, people used their brains for mental calculations, not so now with the introduction of technology.'

'How roit yew are, my woman. It's made them lazy, decreasing their level of intelligence best suited to a nine year old.'

'What would you choose?'

'I'd choose to be a kamikaze pilot and blow up the Houses of Parliament.'

'Charlie, you are a man of conspicuous loyalty but a lousy liar. I think if you had a choice, you would be here, making such beautiful things. You have a gift, a very rare gift. It would be a terrible tragedy to see such a gift wasted. Does Ruben like making things?'

'He likes smaller things, yew in particular.'

'Oh, I like him too, Charlie. But I have a duty to my client. I just cannot walk away any more than you would walk away from a door hanging off its hinges.'

'Then yew take wat yew hev in your hand if it reminds yew of Bobble.'

She went on tiptoe and kissed him fondly on the cheek. 'Thank you for being so kind.'

Scarcely noticing if it was safe outside, she left in the fog which had settled in thick, malevolent silence. When, at the end of it all, she was faced with a decision, should she take the proffered locket? It was just too tempting not to and therefore had willingly hazarded herself, so could hardly complain if she was now to suffer the consequences.

Elsewhere, consequences were not too far to hear. The southern boundary of the river was echoing with an eruption of sound lasting for a number of screaming seconds. Noise and shapeless anarchy prevailed in the fog. Much later, as voices crept into the nooks and crannies of the town, the restaurant was drowning in muted exclamations where Grey struggled to catch the drift. Though she understood it, she did not agree with it, but neither could she leave it alone. After dining on cold chicken and even colder broccoli, she drank her coffee and returned to the Abbey Hotel.

The apartment was cold. The two radiators were barely warm. She slipped off her coat, dived into a heavy knit jumper and made a cup of hot chocolate, weighing the pros and cons of Ruben Stone. On the one hand, he was a product of Jeffrey Cane, a man who murdered two people. Anarchy was no stranger to him. Clasping the locket tight in her hand as though carbonizing the metal into her skin, she now felt very uncomfortable. That she believed she could act independently was perhaps a slight miscalculation and picked up her mobile to confide in her fearless defender.

'No,' she told him, 'he really lived before as a gerontologist. I just find it hard to accept he killed Michael Fuller.'

'You sure you heard right?'

'Yes, absolutely, I heard right.'

'Get out while the going is good, let me handle this.'

'I can handle this, really I can.'

'Sounds like it.'

'Look, I feel certain he will settle.'

'Does he know you know?'

'No. I gained the impression his grandfather would prefer to settle this quietly, but instinctually, I think Stone will be disposed to ignore me.'

'Or take the easy route out. What's he got to lose? Not much. He's sitting on a pile of money, bury that and come back happy.'

Grey smiled, laid out on the bed, her eyes to the ceiling. 'Betty said Peter would come back happy. Maybe he will. Maybe Stone is genuine.'

'The man killed his wife and her lover, does himself in, comes back to knock off two more in an assurance scam…most likely killed Fuller to keep him quiet.'

'But why kill Fuller in open hostility? It makes no sense. I honestly feel there are wider implications. Anyway, enough about me, what are you doing?'

'Eating a bag of crisps; or I was.'

'Are you at home?'

'Yeh, I just finished gluing the fin on the B52 bomber. By the way, Gran said Esmeralda needed cleaning.'

'And how are you going to do that?'

'Well, I did think about offering her my body.' He made her laugh. 'When do you plan to finalize?'

'I shall give Stone a day, failing which I shall make my move and confront him.'

'Ring me, ring if you need me.'

'I will. Speak to you later.'

Closing down on the conversation, Grey felt much better and glanced at her watch. It was a quarter past eleven and sleep was hard to find. Perhaps adding another two dates to her list would help.

1979 Jeffrey Cane died.

1980 Ruben Stone born, parents dead.

2009 Amy Pots inherited house.

2009 Charles Stone sold out to Michael Fuller.

2009 Lenard Green signed up on life policy, died one year later.

2011 Amy Pots sold out to Michael Fuller.

2011 Peter Tudmoor signed up on life policy, died one year later.

2012 Michael Fuller killed.

CHAPTER 9

Thursday 25th October

At eight the following morning, Ruben sat lingering over his breakfast, the newspaper lay ready to hand. Sometimes pausing to glance with an air of tranquil satisfaction, he smiled when Charlie presented himself in a home-spun jumper, one sleeve shorter than the other.

'Betty,' the old man volunteered, 'lost count in her rows.' He then pinched a morsel of bacon off Ruben's plate. 'I heard yew come in about six this morning.'

'The fog was too thick to drive home.'

'And that makes yew happy?'

'Our Miss Grey is an intuitive maven,' Ruben mused, dallying lazily with the teaspoon. 'Do you know what that is, Charlie?'

'Let me see now. Would that be someone who has a sixth sense?'

'Yes, she has a sixth sense using it to operate a business from who knows where. People like Shilling hire her as a last resort. Unfortunately, that's all Ding managed to get off her computer. I wager Grey is not her real name. She's very cute in holding on to her secrets.'

'A bit like yew then.'

'The difference, she knows more about me than I know about her.'

'Son, it's not rocket science. Yew only gets lift-off if yew press the right buttons.'

'Then where is her control panel?'

'At the Abbey Hotel.'

'Meaning what?'

'She came round yesterday afternoon to offer a deal. Pay back the money and it all goes away.'

'It's not my money.'

'Can't yew just borrow it?'

Ruben picked up his paper and buried his head in the newsprint, suddenly amused at his situation. 'If she's looking to broker a deal then she's on a sticky wicket.'

'Do yew intend to read that?'

'Yes, why?'

'Best yew turn it the roit way up.'

Attempting to appear unruffled, Ruben folded the paper and passed it to Charlie. 'How was it left?'

'I wus to let her know your decision.' The old man thrust out his hands, the ever-ready envoy. 'See these, Ruby. She said I had a rare gift, a gift to pass on and treasure. You hev a greater one and refuse to acknowledge the good yew can do. I'm no scientist but this much I do know. Your genes will flow through to the next generation but there shall be no next generation unless yew confront your demons.'

Although Ruben was someone else in another life, those memories still rose up and swamped him until it was almost unbearable. Even now, he still found it hard to talk about, to go back over those last dreadful days as Jeffrey Cane.

The abandonment of science in favour of carpentry was a side issue and sauntered to the workshop when Charlie rushed up behind and shoved the paper under his nose. 'Look here!'

The death of Michael Fuller was just another statistic added to a long line of statistics in Britain's failing capacity to halt the increase in crime. No more Michael Fuller, the venture capitalist playboy with a consumerist outlook and conceited nature.

'Who would kill him, Ruby?'

If distinction remained between black and white, Ruben no longer saw it. 'He made many enemies, including me.'

'Yew hev a sound alibi.' The old man saw a pulsating beat in the crook of his grandson's neck. 'Yew took her fer a spin and got caught in the fog.'

'I wanted to see how she ran.'

'So, yew slept in the car?'

'What else.'

'Who did yew see last?'

'Ding. I left his place round about four after picking up the motor.'

It was in such an emergency that Charlie displayed strength of mind and mental resource which rendered him the admiration of so many friends. After feeding his pipe with tobacco, he drew a little nearer to the stove. 'This is wat we do. Yew tell the police yew left Ding's at four and thass true, and yew had intention of taking the car fer a spin, thass half true, then yew say yew changed your mind heving a feeling the fog might get thicker so yew come back here. Now, if I roitly remember, Grey left the shop round about five.'

'So that won't hold water.'

'Listen. Yew say yew heard us talking and didn't want to intrude.'

'Talking about what? How not to go to jail? Can you see where this is heading, Charlie?'

'Listen, we talked of other things like her cat.'

'What about her cat?'

'She named it Bobble, all skinny and rubbing up against her legs.'

'Does anything else rub up against her legs?'

'Are yew going to pay attention before Ding comes here?'

'Okay, I'm listening.'

'Yew say yew spent the night here with me, listening to music, playing scrabble, the score wus 4 to 6 in my favour,' and the old man grinned at the knitted brows.

'It should be in my favour.'

'Yew wus drunk.' Advantage was still his to keep.

Ruben shook his head and tied a leather apron about his waist. 'If I never knew better, it would be her to kill Fuller to put the blame on me. So, okay, worst case scenario. I get rid of the lab, everything and anything that could tie me in with Jeffrey Cane.'

'Yew can't destroy your life's work.'

'This,' Ruben said, tapping his forehead, 'is where I keep my life's work.'

'Yew must hev written it down somewhere.'

'At the back of Cane's picture, the very reason it stays hidden in the chest.'

Charlie gulped. He had just given the locket to Grey so how was he supposed to explain that?

Thursdays were much the same as any other early days in the week, apart from Fridays when traders struck out their stalls. But with Christmas looming and the concept of flatpacks proving to be popular, the shop floor had its fair share of customers. Even to a blind man, it was becoming increasingly obvious that the shop, which was now no longer the main route to anywhere, had some future after all.

Then the day was supplanted by night and it grew suddenly quiet. Charlie sat drinking his tea by the cast iron stove drawing the damp-sweat out of his clothes while Ruben tinkered with a six inch carving of a witch that vaguely resembled the physiognomies of Grey.

'We did well today, reminded me of a time way back when I wus a lot younger.'

'I cannot imagine you young, Charlie.'

'Are yew going to see her?'

'What do you think?'

'Make sure yew hev a shower and put some of that aftershave on your chops. Speaking of which, wat happened to Ding?'

'He's tapping into Fuller's death.'

'That man has a talent fer spying.'

'Did I hear my talent mentioned?' Straight-backed and cheerful, the soldier waltzed in balancing three cartons on his head. 'I take it you're hungry.'

'Wat did yew get?'

'There's a choice. Pepperoni, cheese and tomato or ham and tomato…take your pick.'

Ruben swapped boxes. 'Pepperoni gives him heartburn.'

'Yew just made that up.'

'It makes you fart and you've been doing that all day.'

Charlie snatched it back. 'Then it makes no mind if I continue.' Out of sheer rebellion he allowed himself to break wind. But it was delivered unscented, at least, so it did not seem offensive and returned his affection to Ding. 'Do yew spy fer the government?'

'Everyone's a snooper now. Believe me it's not just the government that wants to ferret around in your texts and emails. We're all at it, a nation of keyboard gumshoes.'

Then their mouths filled up with quietness, their teeth tearing into deep-pan pizzas, the soldier prolonging his news until Ruben's curiosity emerged, asking, 'How was he killed?'

'They reckon he was killed at five-fifteen by a sharp bladed instrument, kitchen knife or similar. Until the autopsy they can't be certain. Did the police come round?'

'They sent a uniformed woman to question us both.'

'They questioned Tom Hutton. He was the last person to see Mick alive. Lulu told them that Mick was all stirred up after Grey left around three-thirty. He got a call and told her to piss off. As she was leaving, Hutton came in. He told the police it was business.'

'Tom wouldn't do business with Fuller.'

'He does business with his mother,' Charlie said.

'So why not visit her instead of him?'

'Anyway,' Ding continued, 'Hutton told the police he left Mick twenty minutes later. So, they worked out he shut up early for a meet by the bridge. They figured it was a woman because his suit smelt of perfume.'

'Have they questioned Grey?' Ruben asked.

'She told them after she left Mick, she came here to buy a cat, got talking losing time and left at five-fifteen, was certain of that because she heard a scream coming from the direction of the Abbey and looked at her watch. Then she told them she went directly to the restaurant and hung around for an hour before she got served.'

'Hev the police questioned yew?'

'Been a little busy, Charlie. Besides, I don't have a motive to kill Mick, and if I did it would be a clean kill.' The soldier ran a finger under his chin. 'Come up from behind, kick the body off and walk away.'

'So, a woman killed Fuller?' Ruben asked.

Dingle shrugged. 'Whoever did would be covered in blood, that let's your little witch off the hook.'

Ruben wiped his mouth with a handkerchief and stood to remove his leather apron. 'Ding, can you give Charlie a hand in putting away the tools. I want to see Tom.'

'Be careful how yew tread, Ruby. Hutton has influence in this town.'

Leaving with the old man's cautionary words ringing in his ear, Ruben rounded the corner with a sudden impact on the local gossip. They steadied themselves, readying for conversation.

'Did you hear about Mick Fuller?'

'That's why we have newspapers.'

'Do you know who found him?'

'No doubt I'm about to.'

'It was Father Dell, doing his usual walk. Fog never deters that holy man.'

'Good,' and Ruben resumed his gait with the assumption Tom Hutton would be at the Green Dragon, certainly Amy who was rodding cold ashes in the grate. 'Where is everyone?'

'Tom closed out of respect for Mick.'

'So why was the door open?'

'He's not that generous.'

'Is he about?'

She turned from her less favourite chore and pointed in the direction of the stairs. 'He's up there,' she said, 'with April Jones.'

'Who?'

'Mick's girlfriend.'

'Is she applying for a job?'

Amy sent a tale-tale smile and returned to her duties, which rather formed a narrow picture for Ruben. So, he crept upstairs and bent to a keyhole. There they were, groaning half crippled on the desk. Hutton with his trousers down, rocking fiercely between white thighs, and April with her matchstick legs wrapped round his neck, bucking electrically. In the absence of Fuller, Hutton found his girlfriend to shag!

When Ruben returned, he crouched beside Amy and lent a hand in lighting the fire. 'Is Josie aware of what he gets up to?'

'I don't understand it, Ruby. Tom's never been the sort to go this far, if he has, he's never dirtied his own doorstep.'

'And she was Fuller's girlfriend?'

'If she wears that wide-eyed wonder face for very much longer, she'll do herself a mischief.' Amy sat back on her heels, wiping her forehead with the back of hand. 'I know there wasn't much love between us, especially lately, but I wouldn't wish him dead, not really, might have thought it. Did you do it, Ruby?'

'Why must everyone assume I'm the culprit around here? There are others who loathed Fuller.'

'But most of them are too old to lift a fork handle. The bookies are offering 2 to 1 on it being a machete and 5 to 1 on it being a sword.'

'Are bets being placed on the killer?'

'Well,' she said, dropping her voice confidentially, 'rumour has it, Tom placed a bet at 5 to 1 on it being you, and 10 to 1 on it being Grey. I think Bill was given 50 to 1 on it being Father Dell.'

Warned by the laughter generated from above, they stood sensing Tom Hutton had finished his business with April Jones. Amy adjusted her mini-skirt and went to the bar as she was naturally expected to do and Ruben felt bound to stay where he was, warming his hands by the newly lit fire.

Then down came a pair of six inch heels, one methodical step at a time. Legs unadorned by hosiery, legs for men to admire, everything superbly starved but the ridiculous breasts. April Jones was gorgeous and thin, but not stupid. She gave miles of sensuous flesh without revealing everything. As her right foot landed on the floor, her gaze fell on Ruben, stayed on Ruben for several seconds before she made her exit leaving behind a pungent brand of perfume.

'She's something, isn't she?' Amy remarked.

Ruben never answered but thought if Jones stood sideways there would be no shadow. He went directly up the rickety stairs, rapped a knuckle on a half-open door and walked in. They played what's-the-latest for a few minutes then it was down to the nitty-gritty.

'I hear you laid odds on me killing Fuller.'

'Come on, Ruby, it's just a bit of fun.' The big man rolled up his shirt sleeves as if he was about to go in the rink and poured two neat shots of whisky. 'I understand how you feel, of course I do.' Then he kicked back in his reclining rocker and put his size ten on the desk. 'The way I see it, us being businessmen, we can help each other out. Have a table on me.'

'Will April Jones be serving the meal?'

'Fancy her yourself?'

'I fancy telling your wife.'

Hutton near choked on his whisky.

'The way I see it,' Ruben said, 'you and Fuller were in each other's pockets, which makes me wonder what a happy duo you made before he got topped.'

'Hey, you're on the wrong track, Ruby. I know what you're thinking. You're thinking Mick had me in his pocket. Well, forget about it. I walked out of his office and that's the last time I saw him.'

'So why go there?'

'It was business.'

'I hear Josie owns the land on Chapel Lane. Do you think she would be happy to pass it over in a divorce settlement?'

Hutton went quiet for a moment looking into his glass. 'Alright,' he capitulated, 'and not a word of this to anyone else. He had spare monies after Amy paid him off, so he says, fancy selling the land at Chapel Lane. Forget about it, I said, that amount is peanuts to its real value. Anyway, what does he want, a guaranteed view, pointing out the chance of me getting planning was like taking a slow boat to China. I couldn't disagree so I asked for six hundred grand, just to be snotty and sod me if he doesn't say okay. Next, he goes to his safe and hands me half in cash, tells me to get the deeds by the following day because he was picking up the rest that night.'

'Did he say from whom?'

'If I knew I wouldn't be sitting here wondering how the fuck I'm going to explain it to his mother.'

'Did you telephone him?'

'No. Why do you ask?'

'Lulu said he got a call before you went in.'

'It wasn't me. We bumped into each other at the bank, said he wanted to see me before he closed up. What have we got here, Ruby, a blackmailing Mick? Why would the stupid prick do that? Was he blackmailing you?'

'Me?'

'He said you topped Peter for the insurance money.'

'Am I likely to be sitting here asking questions if he was blackmailing me?'

'Then it has to be the witch. He had something on her.'

'Like what?'

'How the hell should I know.'

'Have you told the police any of this?'

'Nope, and don't intend to.'

Ruben slugged down his drink. 'You wasted your bet, Tom. The witch, you remember her. She never killed Fuller.'

'How do you know?'

'Trust me, I know.'

Hutton was a mixture of simplicity, shrewdness, and amiability though it took no great analytical skill to conclude he was a man of incorrigible folly.

A corner away was the Abbey Hotel. Indecision was there, uncertain if he should see the intuitive maven who called herself Grey. No unforgivable remarks had been made but many unforgettable ones, a good number by him he was sorry to recall. Now he felt utterly confused as though he might be on the brink of being quiet out of his depth with an element of sheer disappointment. Home was safe. Home was decidedly kinder.

CHAPTER 10

Friday 26th October

A window was hauled up suddenly, the sashes squeaking, and a gangly young man clambered out through the opening, the net curtain covering his face like a bridal veil before he emerged into the street.

Grey dismissed it as one of those crazy things young lads do and looked back at her mobile resting on the bedside cabinet. She led a reclusive life, often misunderstood but her primary objective was to solve cases. But she would never solve this one unless Ruben Stone was willing to co-operate on her terms.

Rocking into her raincoat and boots, she grabbed her shoulder bag and headed for the Lemon Tree Café. Here, she sat at a table near the front window, watching the world go by, consoling herself with the fact that at least Godfrey Shilling was still in the dark about Jeffrey Cane.

In the background, the long-legged April Jones was in conversation with the owner who seemed visibly shaken beneath his nervous chatter. In campaigns of gossip, a brutal lie always spoke more eloquently than any truth.

In the end Grey felt obliged to say, 'When did you become an authority on the man next door?'

Nick went about his business as April Jones approached her table. 'Mick told me all about you, Mizz Grey, ready to blame anyone else except your post-shag Ruben.'

Grey blotted her mouth sedately with a paper serviette. 'The scent you wear, I recognise it. Perhaps it rubbed off your Prince Charming after he disengaged himself from dog poo.'

April raised a pencilled eyebrow under her bleach-blond hair then carried herself outside. As she coasted across the road, Nick nimbly apologized. 'Sorry you had to hear all that.'

'It seems I'm your only customer.'

'She scared them away. Can I get you anything else?'

'No thank you. Your breakfast was very nice.'

At that moment a man came staggering in with a huge packing case on his shoulder. 'Where do you want this?'

'Over here.'

While the case was dumped behind the counter and being unpacked, Grey made a call as a last ditch attempt to pin her quarry down.

'Ruben Stone speaking.'

'Are you certain it's not Jeffrey Cane?' She heard the sharp and quick intake of breath and followed it up by saying, 'Ten minutes in Fuller's office.'

Grey paid for her meal then picked her way across the road and swung into the building, nodded to Lulu who struck open her mouth, signalled her intent and walked in the office.

For Ruben, it was difficult not to panic when the chance to salvage something from the mess was gone. The police had drilled him. Grey had discovered him. And the only shit shed was that which he tasted in his mouth.

The door slammed shut! 'Damn you, Grey!'

'Would you like a cup of tea?'

'I'm not here for a tea party!'

'Who killed Michael Fuller?'

'You shall get no false confession from me.'

Strange, Grey thought, how in the hour of defeat one could be so defiant. She left the comfort of an executive chair and walked round the desk to close the distance between them.

'You were an impenetrable mystery to me,' she said folding her arms, her eyes tilting up looking into his. 'The more I probed, the less I understood what made you tick then I realized that perhaps your hostility was not directed at me per say but at the company who facilitated Michael Fuller to accommodate his own ends. And that rather brought about the wider issue of whether or not Peter Tudmoor was the only one. As it so happened my hunch proved correct. Though in the case of Lenard Green, his policy was for a much lesser amount, three hundred thousand pounds I do believe. Whether or not there are others, one can only speculate. Your victory serves as a shining refutation of the ancient dictum, *ignoramus – ignorabimus,* we do not know and we shall never know. So, it leads me to say that Fair Life Assurance is looking for the return of their one million, three hundred thousand, which would close the case nicely and make God a very happy man.'

Ruben hesitated, lip-biting, tongue-tied and avoiding the eye until finally submitting. 'Let us say, for argument's sake, that 60% was to land up on his desk. Would it close the case nicely?'

'Would that be 60% of its current value?'

Clever, clever girl, Ruben mused. Beside her level of intelligence, she had another quality that made her a formidable negotiator. She had quite rightly assumed that one million, three hundred thousand was sitting in gold, a steeply rising commodity. Ruben now calculated at 60% of its current value. 'Am I to assume one million might close the case nicely?'

'And what is left will just have to work harder before your clients call in.' They smiled at each other, dignity intact and Ruben was at the door when she added, 'I am not your enemy, Ruben.'

'Neither are you friend.'

'I would like to be.'

Again, he found himself hesitate and slowly turned round. 'You would offer friendship to a murderer?'

'The image that emerges reveals a man who has a unique talent, but in all the more ordinary aspects is quiet clearly dysfunctional. As a friend, I would say it was Fair Life's duty to take Michael to task. I do not consider you corrupt but a man seeking justice, and perhaps in so doing gave others a second chance.'

'There were only two, Grey. It would not have come to light if Peter's policy was of a more moderate amount.'

'But you never knew, did you? That was why you two argued on the day he died.'

Ruben smiled at the irony and travelled his gaze over the gold links that disappeared into the channel of her V-neck sweater. Oddities and enigmas, it was a sight to wring fright from even the driest rag of imagination. 'Is God aware of Jeffrey Cane?'

'Only Him,' she said, pointing upwards. 'I suppose as a man of science you do not believe in a higher authority.'

'A true scientist keeps an open mind.'

'Would a true scientist like a cup of tea?'

'Thank you, yes.'

In her absence he drifted towards the window drawn to a cat sleeping on the wall. He could never have imagined such a contrast, both in surrounds and position. Not that many moons ago he was taking Celia to lunch without much of a future, ghosts his companions, burdened by his sense of right. Now he was standing in a dead man's office having brokered a deal and made a friend of his nemesis. No more would he take such chances in the holy grail of life or feel the iron frost of destitution. He now felt fairly unrestrained and a shade more relaxed when she came in with two cups of tea and a plate of chocolate biscuits.

'It seemed not to bother him,' she said kicking the door closed. 'He was at risk of his agency being taken away and it seemed not to bother him.'

'Is this why you occupy his office, to solve another mystery for God?'

'Have we not passed the point of mistrust?'

'I gave a lot; you gave a crumb.'

Grey hiked herself up on the desk, crossing her legs at the ankles. 'Here was a good place for us to meet and here God asked me to pick up some files in case Michael's tenanted clients look to Fair Life regarding their situation, which is, I have to say, on shaky ground.'

'How so?'

'Ironically, he told a lie regarding his position as a Financial Consultant. He was not fully qualified to give advice and this should have been checked by Fair Life Assurance. As your friend, I would recommend the easiest route is via his mother. No doubt as a practicing solicitor she would be more than pliable to negotiate the return of their properties.'

'How did you find out?'

'By intuition and a little delving, reason why God wanted Michael to take full responsibility for his actions, but as I said, he just fluffed it away like a piece of used cotton wool.'

'You are a witch.'

'A good one, I hope.'

'Is your hair by design or by accident?'

'Well now....let me see.' She sipped tea with her little finger extended as if born into gentry. 'I could say I was six and mightily curious when a thief broke into the family home on Christmas Eve, frightening me half witless or I could say, which would be less dramatic, my hair lacked pigmentation from the day I was born.'

'My guess would be that you say a lot but nothing at all in case someone discovers your weak points.'

'I go along with that. In your case you harnessed the good and recycled it.'

'Peter was losing his sight and Lenard's wife died in a care home. He had first-hand knowledge of what it was like to be spoon fed, years trapped in an ailing body, afraid to die in an ugly state and sordid way.'

'Can you be certain of a new life?'

'Charlie always says he might be born the ugliest sod on the planet but it can't be any worse than having your arse wiped by an immigrant.'

'You are the dumbest, cleverest person I know. Why covet such an incredible discovery when so many are labouring with incurable illnesses?'

'Look around you, Grey. Look at the elite who run riot like handfuls of diamonds thrown up in the air. The rich and powerful would transcend into Gods, and the deserving would trail into utter insignificance, as many already do. The world then was not ready for such a discovery nor is it now, probably never will.' Ruben finished his tea and placed the cup and saucer on the desk, aware his discovery had been the boat in which most of the things in his life had happened. 'Tragic irony or poetic justice, the man who made the discovery was naïve to think he could make a difference and suffered the consequences, unlike the man of today who was born a lot wiser.'

'So, this discovery, such that it is, someone would kill if they knew who you were?'

'You think Fuller was killed because he knew?'

'He knew you called yourself Jeffrey, he told me so but then how on earth did such a moron manage to fill in the gaps…unless someone told him and why not? It would answer the question why he felt so inured to God's threat.' Her features bunched together and sparkled. 'I say God, not in the literal sense but in the Shilling sense.'

'He received a call shortly after you left.'

'From whom?'

'Not Tom, you know, Tom Hutton. He said Fuller offered to pay him six hundred grand for the land at Chapel Lane in order to keep his view. He gave half of it in cash and told Tom the other half was being collected that night. Tom reckoned he was blackmailing someone and that someone killed him.'

'Who had such a large secret to pay out such a large sum?'

'That rather puts me back in the frame.'

'Tell me about your other life, Ruben?'

'My other life is of no consequence.'

On impulse, Grey removed the gold locket from her neck and placed it about his. 'Perhaps there may come a moment in time, hopefully sooner rather than later when you might wish to share your past?'

But not at this moment and closed his fingers lightly on her hands. 'Do you have another assignment?'

'Presently, no, but free board and lodgings will be sufficient to retain my services, cheap at half the price.'

'Best you fly in then.'

Grey watched him swagger in the clarity of passion, knowing without having to be told that he would, when ready, unveil Jeffrey Cane. Her next cast was made at the peaches and cream complexion looking up from the filing cabinet, a part knowing, part questioning smile that drew her towards the nineteen-year-old.

'How long have you worked here, Lulu?'

'Since leaving school,' and buried her auburn locks in the files. 'Is Mrs Fuller selling up?'

'Who knows what a bereaved parent might do in times like this. How well did you get on with Michael?'

'We had our moments.'

'Would they be moments in bed?' Grey caught the silent sigh. 'Is it true to say he was quite the acrobat in the sexual arena?'

'He was a useless tosser!' Screech-slam went the file cabinet drawer. 'Not that I want to speak ill of the dead, his mother thought the sun shone out of his backside. But he wasn't all bad, just went off the rails at times.'

Conversation was interrupted when Amy popped her head through the door. 'Is Ruby here?'

'He left about five minutes ago.'

'If you see him, tell him Quasimodo is on the loose.'

Grey stared blankly at Lulu who explained, 'The hunch back of reporters,' and pulled from her drawer a box of tissues. 'He works as a freelance journalist, always looking for the *big* story. Mick used to feed him with stuff until he read about himself shagging the Councillor's wife.'

'Hardly newsworthy.'

'Oh, it was. Mick was pulled over by the police while she was doing his thing down there.' Lulu burst into tearful laughter. 'Outside,' she said, gulping for air, 'he fell into dog poo! He came in smelling awful, had it all down his trousers and on his hands, and that blond he was with, she held her nose.'

'April Jones?'

'That's her, right madam, thought she owned the place and him…stupid, stupid, prat! I shouldn't be talking like this, whatever must you think of me.'

'I think,' Grey said, wiping clean Lulu's runs of mascara, 'that you liked Michael. Tell me, Lulu. Before Tom Hutton came in, Michael received a call. Do you know from whom?'

'The police asked me that.'

'And what did you say?'

'Nothing much because I didn't know but I think it was a woman, not sure. I think I heard him say *honey* or it could have been *money*…he was all over the place that day. One minute he was full of himself, next he was uppity…definitely uppity when you were occupying his office.'

'Did he say anything that sounded odd?'

'I know he had it in for Ruby, thought it funny he scammed Peter Tudmoor…come to think about it, that was odd when he said Ruby was going to be his meal ticket.'

The door swung open again and in came the greatest threat to mankind. All of six foot five and would have been taller but for the stooping gait, Jack Winkle, a name most apt in his profession, swooped on Lulu for a story. But finding his look unreturned, he focused upon Grey, at whom he came to stare with remarkable intensity.

'Hellooo,' she said, waving a hand in front of him.

'You're not that lady he had working here, are you?'

'How right you are, I'm not.' She watched him write that down. 'Make sure you spell my name correctly.'

'Terrible business his murder, what do you make of it?'

'Do I look like a detective?'

The corners of his mouth tipped up slightly. 'Are you staying now he's gone?'

'Actually, I was thinking of selling dollhouses.'

'Ah, fraternising with the enemy.'

'Your words, not mine.'

'Well, what have you got to say?'

'The exit is that way.'

The day was no stranger to assumptions or queries or even the state of confusion. Equally, a morbid couple from Norwich walked in asking where the body was found.

And the weather had been so variable from when Grey made her first steps into Wymondham. Rain soaked skies, warm pavements, foggy nights, autumn blusters and now the Abbey bells pealed to a crystal fair evening.

Deciding that the only tactic likely to succeed was to offer her services to Ruben and frankly hope he would indulge her curiosity, she picked up her suitcase and laptop, saying goodbye to the modest apartment and hello to the shop with a magical window display.

'Come on, my woman, let me take those. Ruby will show yew our workshop while I tidy upstairs and put clean sheets on your bed.'

'How very kind, thank you.' She sent her gaze at Ruben. 'Did you encounter Quasimodo?'

'I sent him to you.'

'Ta very much.' She walked on beside him, said not a word until reaching the yard and bent to caress a rose defying the cold. 'It smells lovely.'

'I grew that from a cutting.'

'And it survives the frost?'

'We're sheltered here.'

In the workshop, she gravitated to the cast iron stove, her coat slipping from her shoulders as she sat down drawing the warmth on her legs.

'Are you hungry?' He asked.

'I had a sticky bun for lunch.' A plate of doorstop sandwiches sank in her lap. 'Oooh, well, there is always room for more, I suppose.'

Ruben pulled up a stool, his knees almost touching hers. 'Hamburg, a small pond and one thousand dead toads, burst with such an explosive force, their entrails landed several feet away. Nobody could make it out. Then it spread to a nearby Danish lake. Now we come to the interesting part. The crow, a member of the raven family, likes to eat nuts, so it drops them on the road for the motorist to crack the shell. We ask how the crow collects the inside of the nut without being run over. Believe this or not, it drops the nut on the pedestrian crossing and waits for the traffic lights to turn red.'

'Really?'

'Yes, really, and we come back to the toad. In all the corpses, the liver was missing. With a liver missing and without a diaphragm, the toad just swelled and exploded. The crow knew exactly where to peck a hole to get at the liver, the liver being nutritious. The skin is poisonous to them. How did the crow gain such knowledge?'

'Perhaps it was trial and error.'

'As were my experiments which rather took longer than it did for the crow.' Ruben saw her labouring to raise a question, so continued to fill her in by flipping the rear casing to his pocket watch and tipped a red capsule on to the palm of his hand. 'Swallow one of these and your death is assured; your life experiences survive to a greater extent. One only has to summon their courage and embrace tomorrow's wishes.'

'Appealing to those who want to live again.'

'Appealing to those who need to live again.'

It was only a matter of time for Grey to grasp the crux of the matter. 'Damn you, Ruben! This is what comes of such a discovery, take a pill when threatened, live again and leave behind the people who care?'

'What other alternative? Fuller is dead. Who will be next? I put you in terrible danger.'

'I should be flattered but I assure you I feel very disappointed in your attitude. Has it not occurred that by killing Michael, this person has alerted you? Indeed, they would be very foolish to kill me for they put at risk the very thing you are thinking of doing.'

Ruben stared at his feet, his bottom lip coursed over his top. It was not as if he expected anything less than her stubbornness, not an earth-shattering revelation. He drew a hand over his face and smiled awkwardly. 'I never gave it much thought.'

'That is because you have this hidden agenda to commit suicide.' She gave him the plate to hold then scraped her stool to get closer still, their legs interlocking. 'Now, let's be sensible and look at the facts. Lulu, unwittingly, offered a valuable piece of information. Whoever telephoned Michael was the same person who killed him. That is a fact. He also knew of your history. That is a fact. Much more importantly, he sought for revenge in a meal ticket. That is a fact.'

'Wow, and you gained this from Lulu?'

'Actually, I gained this by logic. But I have a problem, Ruben. Unless I know your past, how can I put the pieces together?'

Now he was ready to extrapolate on his other life, talking in the third person as though to separate himself from the man he once was, the man who killed two people. 'Jeffrey Cane's father was a good person. He had two sons, one of whom died of pneumonia. The other graduated from Oxford and went on to be a highly respected gerontologist.'

'May I make notes?'

'Is your memory that bad?'

'Often the smallest detail can be overlooked.' She reached forward and stole the pencil lodged behind his ear. 'I left my handbag with Charlie. Paper?'

Ruben provided. 'Private funds were sourced from Sir John Harcourt, a man who had a fascination with death. Jeffrey worked at nights in Harcourt's private laboratory and by day he would come home to his unfaithful wife.'

'Why not get a divorce?'

'Because she was a scheming bitch,' the old man interposed and drew up a stool. 'They lived in his family's home left to him by his good father.'

'If I remember correctly from the newspaper cutting, she was ten years younger than Jeffrey.'

'That she wus, all sweet and innocent until that ring went on her finger.'

'Who is telling this story?' Ruben asked.

'I'm here to see yew get it roit…carry on.'

'There came a time for trials, human trials. Harcourt found a donor, someone who had prostate cancer. His name was Erik, a Swede, unattached, intelligent. The arrangement was simple. Harcourt was to maintain a private line, a number for Erik to contact after his rebirth. Jeffrey administered the dosage.'

'Was Harcourt in possession of the formula?'

'No. The formula would only be released if the trial proved successful. And six years later a young boy, nine months less of those years contacted Harcourt, demonstrating three fundamental issues in the experiment. One, a same sex rebirth due to the encapsulation of energy formed at time of death. Two, the subject's memory was enhanced at the stage of early puberty. Three, birth was localized.'

'Localized?'

'Energy is drawn to the most frequented area a person lives out their existence.'

'So, Erik was reborn in Sweden?'

'Correct. Now we approach the most complicated part of Jeffrey's demise, a year of untold misery. When Harcourt refused access to the test subject, Jeffrey refused to divulge his formula which caused a small rift in the relationship. Further, Helena Vale came on the scene one year prior, a student gerontologist predicting dreams could be turned to reality, Harcourt's idea to place a different perspective on the programme. At the same time, his wife was having an affair with Harcourt's right hand man, a physicist, the credentials of scientific creativity he possessed easily satisfied Jeffrey's scrutiny. However, it mattered not because Jeffrey had the onset of dementia and was planning a different future.'

'Ah, he found a way to tie up his assets for a new start. His wife found out. She told her lover. And when they tried to stop him, he shot them and took his own life along with the formula.'

Charlie was alerted. 'Ruby never shot anyone.'

'I did,' Ruben argued. 'I wanted them dead.'

'Wanting and doing is two different things.' Not to be outdone, Charlie referred to Grey, tapping a finger fiercely on her notes. 'Yew put this down. All he recalls wus returning home angry from that banquet John Harcourt arranged.'

'The evidence was indisputable,' Ruben claimed, inadvertently referring to Cane in the first person. 'I was overheard arguing with my wife, powder burns on my hand, my fingerprints on the gun.'

'Can you remember what the argument was about?'

'What our arguments were usually about, money. She discovered I had mortgage the house to the hilt and emptied the bank accounts apart from our joint account. It was damn stupid for the bank to write directly to me rather than as instructed to my solicitor. She opened the letter, that I do remember and all hell broke loose.'

'Dementia…' Grey chewed contemplatively on a sandwich. If it was mystery and wonderment they required, she had certainly provided it in that unfinished statement.

'Hev yew gone into a trance, my woman?'

'Yes, no, I was considering the severity of normal mental ability associated with the elderly yet Jeffrey was only fifty.'

'In my case it was never acute, just the odd patch of memory loss.'

'Then it's strange how the formula survived in your transition to another life.'

'Not so strange.' Ruben fondled the locket resting between the breastplate of his heart. 'It was my mother's given to me when she died, rarely removed, and never removed after a picture was inserted with my formula on the reverse lest I forgot in my transition. Even so, there was no guarantee I would remember anything, let alone where I might find my locket or the proceeds from the house and bank accounts.'

'You bought gold and buried it.'

'Come now, surely you can do better than that.'

Indeed, this was a challenge. Grey tugged thoughtfully on a lock of her hair, wrapping it around her index finger. It was one thing to come back from the dead, another to beat the taxman. 'Do you bury it? If so, how can one be certain of knowing where lest the memory fails entirely, and then, of course, there was nobody to help as in the case of Lenard and Peter? I'm not asking for answers, just sending my thoughts to the cosmos…but there again what did it matter if you returned without memories. Obviously, we all do that, unless of course some bright spark like Jeffrey Cane proves otherwise. You would be just like everyone else, a life to be lived, work and play, death and taxes…but yet, within us all there are dreams and premonitions, a pull to things we cannot explain, a gift, yes, a gift like Charlie has, making beautiful dollhouses. And you, your heart lies with chemistry, questioning the world around you. And better still you would be drawn to your family home. Was your wife on the deeds?'

'No.'

'Then you instructed your solicitor to purchase your family home in trust. The bank would be repaid upon your death, your wife would have what little proceeds were left and the new owner would be you by another name, proof given upon receipt of a locket which you previously buried somewhere…in the garden, a place where you always played as a child, maybe in your bedroom under the floorboards. No, not under the floorboards, there was no certainty of the house still standing so it had to be in the garden, or in a place of…sacred, yes, no, not in the garden but in your mother's grave, if not in a coffin but in her buried ashes. Mother or father, you put the locket in the urn. Am I right?'

'Told yew she had brains, Ruby. He wus eight when he told me, can yew believe that, never wanted to claim wat wus his, only the locket.'

'So let me get this straight. The locket was claimed but not the house. I don't understand, Ruben. You struggle financially, yet you could lay claim to a house that could be sold to invest in this business.'

'It held bad memories,' Charlie spoke again for Ruben, demonstrating once more the love and loyalty he had for his grandson. 'Sure enough, that house left him with bad memories, too scared to face his demons, my woman, scared if he lay claim to his fortune he would be found out.'

'So, what was the point of it all?'

Ruben was on his feet. In the corner tucked by the breast of a chimney he worked his hand behind a loose brick to reveal a secret gateway to a smaller chamber. Here, porcelain dishes, stoppered bottles of solutions, tripods and laptops, specialized equipment humming in the journey of discovery, detailed knowledge of atomic structure plastered on a wall, modern physics was having its apparently solid foundations undermined.

'This is the point to it all.' Ruben flipped the lid to his laptop and brought up a website called DID, his total triumph, a voice crusading for the legal right to Die in Dignity, thirty thousand and counting signed up for a debate in the House of Commons. Doctor Hope wrote the first chapter in this campaign.

'I have seen this,' she surprised. 'In fact, I signed up. I'm sure far more would if they knew your website existed.'

He closed down. 'Word of mouth is far better than any preaching advert.'

'Then what we need are your memories, and John Harcourt's if he's still alive.'

'I cannot see Harcourt! It will expose my position.'

'Then take back your pencil. It needs sharpening like your brains.' Suddenly her eyes widen as she looked beyond him. 'The gold is here?'

'Where else, besides a lot less to worry about when God gets his share.'

'Ruben,' she said turning a bar over, 'these seem not to be stamped.'

'I'm hardly likely to buy on the open market, what with the tax man wanting their cut.'

'Well how on earth are you going to off load so many to pay God?'

'Peter sold his shop to a fireman who has a licence to deal in gold. I don't ask any questions. He doesn't ask any questions. I get a fair rate. He gets a fair rate.'

'So, he will give you cash?'

'And it shall be one million to land on God's desk to close the case nicely. As you said, what gold is left will have to work harder for Lenard Green and Peter Tudmoor.'

Grey sat down on a pile. 'You must have felt very bad when you discovered Charlie had raised money from Fuller, knowing full well you had a fortune in property.'

'Bricks and mortar are no substitution for the security and love Charlie has given to me.' He settled beside her. 'There are secrets worth keeping, once revealed would change everything. This may not seem much, the shop, the plasma screen, the Sunbeam Rapier but elsewhere there is far more, customers, people, the friendship they give, the stories they tell, the troubles they share, all cannot be weighed against what we sit upon. If I had a choice, I would choose this life because here we can be who we are, not what we think we should be. Do you understand my meaning or does money play a significant role in your life? Perhaps you remove your grey colourings for something that glitters when not on a case.'

'My grey colourings are an extension to my nature, I like to think. Not always can we see things in black and white. If that were true, I would not be sitting here on a pile of gold having accommodated my client's wishes without revealing the truth behind Ruben Stone.' She sighed, pulling the pins from her hair. 'Oh, Ruben, it's true to say the definition of poverty is not having an iPod, so yes I can understand how you feel, wish that friendships grew on trees for me… it has been such a long day and so much to take in, I badly need my sleep. This is my secret I can afford to be generous with. Sleep is my restorative potion. Without a good dose, I'm useless at analysing a problem, even right down to a simple crossword.'

'How much sleep do you need?'

'It varies,' she replied in an extended yawn, 'it varies upon the intensity of the case. Sometimes a catnap or sometimes a full ten hours and so deep I could sleep on a linen line…'

Right now, sleeping on gold looked attractive. As her eyelids closed heavy, she slumped against his shoulder with primitive casualness. Not that he found this alarming, Ruben picked her up in his arms and nodded to Charlie. At some stage she would find herself on the bed, still dressed in jeans and sweater, with a duvet keeping her warm.

Narcolepsy, a condition marked by sudden episodes of irresistible sleep. It certainly answered a few questions. Why she became so secretively beautiful and alone. Why she travelled on public transport. And why she faced the devil that dogged her. Ruben toyed with the idea of how her life would take shape if she were to live with him. He smiled. The idea was very appealing. For Grey, she had never regarded herself as a victim of her condition but rather considered it as a gift to aide in the matter of solving cases. But no amount of sleep would solve the mystery of Jeffrey Cane unless she had Ruben Stone's full co-operation.

CHAPTER 11

Saturday 27th October

Less moderately expressed concern to Mick Fuller's death was mounting in the local rag. There existed a vocal group ready to explore the view that bed-knobs and broomsticks resided in Wymondham, more specifically in the shop with a magical window display.

Local interest was high, as was obvious the moment Charlie opened the door on what would in the normal course of events have been an ordinary day. He was greeted by Quasimodo and later by other inquisitive visitors and spent a tedious morning making light of the situation while Grey sold flatpacks by the dozen. At one point the crowd became so dense that she was overcome by the heat, slipped to the floor and had to be ushered upstairs. At the end of it all, a good day's trading but still no further in the case of Jeffrey Cane.

'Dearie me,' Charlie said, sat contented drawing on his pipe, letting the smoke drift from his nostrils. 'I can't imagine where that came from.'

Slouched in a leather armchair, Ruben stared sleepily at Grey making her way in from the kitchen and at the tea pot held in her hand. 'Perhaps our little witch has the answer.'

'At least he spelt my name correctly. Are you feeling rested, Ruben?'

'I feel the world has descended upon me. How are you feeling?'

'I was hot, not ill. Charlie, try to avoid dunking your biscuits in tea.'

'I've been dunking biscuits before yew wus born.'

'But you leave half in the cup.' She tentatively eased on to the sofa and kicked off her shoes. 'I am now consciously aware how hard it is to work in a shop, especially a busy shop.'

'Wat yew need is a long hot soak in a bath. Ruby can give yew a back scrub.'

'Charlie,' she said returning his smile, 'you are a very mischievous grandfather. Out of interest, who approached who in the case of Lenard Green?'

'That wus me. Ruby did it out of kindness.'

'Of course, how else, I should have known, no other way for them to believe such incredulity. I suspect one day someone, somewhere, will come across the same discovery, make a fortune and live off it forever. Will you be there to greet it, Ruben?'

'I am disappointed with life,' he told her. 'I had so much hope for an improved future, thought the width of the world would expand into knowledge and sensibility. Instead, I grew up to see ignorance and insensitivity. If money is to dictate our way of life, then the human race shall only survive by the workhorse majority propping up the affluent few.'

'Gosh, that sounds very depressing.'

'Pay no mind to him, my woman. He gets like this when he slips on a chisel.'

'Yes,' Grey confirmed, recalling the earlier sample which Ruben had shown her, of the knotted rag wrapped round his thumb. 'I think I will go for a bath.'

The moment she left the room, Charlie voiced his concern. 'Would yew care to tell me wat yew just achieved?'

'She firmly believes the architect of Fuller's actions and demise requires what I have.'

'So?'

'She wants me to see Harcourt.' Ruben left his seat and went down on his heels to stoke up the fire. 'I am betwixt worlds. One side there is Grey who leads blindly into danger and the other is a greater temptation to let events run their course, that perhaps by some divine intervention this will all go away and what I have left is a future.'

'Listen, Ruby, that girl has second sight, no two ways about it. If she believes this is about your formula then yew hev to see it through. Face your demons and find who's behind this.'

'And when I do, then what? Go to the police?'

'Thass a good question.'

'Do you intend answering it?'

The old man looked at him with intensity now, trying to gauge his reaction before going further. But Ruben just stared and waited. 'This is war, Ruby. Yew must decide whether to lay down your arms and surrender that formula or fight fer wat yew believe in. Make no mind to me if one less evil is wiped off this earth.' After gathering his pipe and tobacco pouch, the old man got to his feet. 'I've said me bit. I'm off to see Betty.'

The veneer over the old man's worries was nowhere near thick enough. For the first time Ruben observed the fatigue and weariness in his face, the fear and uncertainty that walked hand in hand with loyalty. He looked at the silver framed photographs resting on the mantelpiece, a life story waltzing across varnished wood which only added to both the melodrama and the tragedy. Chance could have taken him on to a track quite different from that of a carpenter, but what chance could now no longer do was alter his character.

On the way to the kitchen, he made a diversion and placed a listening ear to the bathroom door. She was splashing about and singing. That was a good omen. He ran his fingers through his hair before shoving a shepherd's pie in the oven. By the time he laid out cushions on the floor and uncorked a bottle of wine, Grey was in her room, still singing. When she finally emerged in jeans and fluffy sweater, his ardour was dampened by the tin cans in her hair.

'Do you sleep in them?'

'With great difficulty.' Her eyes then wandered over the arrangement keeping warm by the hearth. 'Why are we eating on the floor?'

'It was quicker than laying the table.'

'Was it quicker for Charlie to eat at Betty's?'

'Ah, you noticed his absence.'

'And you can be a very strange man. I almost felt like killing myself.' She knelt by his side and picked up the serving spoon. 'Tomorrow is Sunday.'

'So, you only wear rollers Saturday night.'

'Stop avoiding the issue, Ruben. These happen to be heated rollers and don't you dare say they will frazzle my brains.'

'Where do you live?'

'In a ruin.'

'A ruin?'

'Where else for a witch to live?'

'And where is this ruin?'

'Discreetly located.'

'I see.'

'No, Ruben, you don't see. In my line of work, I have to be careful. If my address got into the wrong hands I could lose my home to arson.'

'Do you live alone?'

'My circumstance is different from yours.'

'Well, what may I know of your circumstance other than wearing rollers?'

'I do not divulge my circumstance to anyone, especially to clients. Already you know too much.'

'Friends generally know a lot more or are you my friend until the case is solved?'

'There shall be no solving of cases if you keep your head in the sand.'

It went quiet for a few minutes, only the crackle of wood could be heard and the forks scraping their plates before Ruben summoned the courage to speak his thoughts aloud. 'If my memory did return, how am I expected to live with that horrible picture?'

'Charlie believes you never killed them.'

'The facts speak otherwise.'

'We all make mistakes, Ruben. That's why we have rubbers on the end of pencils.'

'And what mistakes have you erased?'

With her meal hardly touched, she set the plate aside and picked up her wine glass. 'There was a girl in my school, had a long golden plait, came right down to her waist. She used it as a tickling stick, fiddle with it mostly. Being of a curious nature and, of course, completely mental I stole into her room one night and cut it off. The end result was my immediate departure from boarding school which afforded me the companionship of a tutor who resembled Tom Cruise.

After my heart was broken, I bumped into absolutely gorgeous Angela who had no hesitation in telling me I did her a favour. I lived with that guilt, thinking I destroyed her life. All I had to do was find the courage to see her, say sorry but instead it was easier to put my head in the sand.'

'What happened to Tom Cruise?'

'He married someone else.' Grey removed her rollers one by one. 'You know what we should do?'

'Make love?' He grinned and she ignored him.

'We should go to the spot where Michael was killed.'

'Why?'

'To see how he was killed.'

'He was knifed from the front.' She looked surprised, he could see that. 'Ding's speciality is surveillance, homed in on the police radio. His suit smelt of perfume so they figured the assailant was a woman.'

'Show me,' she said, grabbing a knife and wiping it clean on her serviette. 'Show me how.'

Placing the tip of the blade against the lower part of his rib cage, he indicated its progress. 'It travelled upwards and pierced the left ventricle, suggesting he allowed his assailant to get up close.'

'The perfume?'

'Has to be.'

'Then we shall demonstrate.' Now holding the knife, she stood in front of him, a foot apart. 'Let us assume she is my height.'

'But I am not his height.'

She went on tip toe but this was not enough to level peg and waved it away. 'We don't know the height of his assailant so we must improvise. The money, we presume is in her hand and she has the knife in the other. You make the first move.'

Spurred on by her encouragement, he pulled her into his arms and made a discovery. The blade was at his waist line.

'You see, Ruben. It doesn't add up. Even taking into account different heights, we really need to visit the crime scene so I can get my brain in gear.'

'I can get your brain in gear.' He drew from his pocket a pill box. 'Take one each night before bedtime and your condition is cured.'

'My condition is a gift.'

'Your condition is narcolepsy.'

'Is that what you were doing, making me pills to become dependent on you?'

'Are we not dependent on each other?'

'Your dependency on me stops when the case is solved. I go back to my little world and you go back to yours.'

Those words wounded him as deeply as any he had ever heard. She had just placed their relationship in a forbidden zone, his mouth twitched with the thought of it. With such anxiety, he left the room, going directly to the bathroom as though he was angry with his own inability to accept such finality, angry with her for leading him into this dangerous wilderness. After splashing cold water on his face, he took a long hard look in the mirror with little to show that he lived at all. He sighed in resignation, towel-dried his face and returned to the living room.

'Okay, we visit the crime scene.'

'And tomorrow we visit Sir John Harcourt.'

'No.'

'Why?'

'He has senile dementia.'

'That's very odd. He sounded very lucid to me.'

His brows met. 'Have you been in contact?'

'He wants to see you, Ruben. He can shed light on your past.'

'And what if you're wrong?'

'You want me to be wrong because you cannot face your demons. And why is that, Ruben? What else is there to remember which makes you so afraid?'

'Quite frankly, I'm terrified of reliving a nightmare, for that is what it shall be, one long, continuous nightmare.'

'Is the man in the locket the same man I see before me? I think he's the same with good reason to do what he did, not what he wants to do now.'

'You have no idea what I wish to do now.'

'Like I told God,' she said pinching his cheeks, 'we must think above the waistline. I'll just get my coat.'

God preserve me.

They walked in the light of a cold moon retracing Michael Fuller's steps, by-passing a hungry couple looking for love among gravestones. No treason here and no confusion. But still he closed tight her hand when it ran through the crook of his arm. They never paused or diverted, continued down Becketswell Road, towards the bridge, the very same conduit on which Ruben played in his younger days.

'The river is very shallow,' Grey commented, peering over the side. 'Is it always like this?'

'Generally speaking, the depth is not significant to worry about drowning kids. The day I pushed Ding, he went feet first and landed over there, slipped on some weeds and went face down in the water. Fuller sat on him, making it hard for Ding to get his breath.'

'Why would Michael do that?'

'Six months prior or thereabouts, Ding borrowed his bicycle but he ran to mummy and told her it was stolen. Since then, they only tolerated each other because we mixed with the same crowd.'

'Where was he found?'

Ruben squinted into the darkness, adjusting his focus before guiding her on a path to the river bank. It answered the fundamental question that Michael Fuller died on the spot. 'This used to be our main play area.'

'So, it goes like this,' Grey extrapolated. 'He cuts through the Abbey grounds and Father Dell spots him as he turns into Becketswell Road. Then he walked to the bridge, and the voice called out, enticing him to this spot. As he made his way down the assailant takes him by surprise, using momentum and leverage to force the blade upwards, certain fatality. And fog, we must remember it was foggy. A motor would be out of the question so the assailant had to live or lodge locally.'

'The only new face in town is that woman he was dating, April Jones.'

'Can you ask Sam to check her out?'

'Sure. Are we done?'

'Do you notice how quiet it is? No houses to speak of and…what made Father Dell look down there? You did say he found the body?'

'It was Marge who said Father Dell found the body from his usual stroll…let's go this way.' Guiding her to take the river walk, he said, 'Fuller strikes past Father Dell, himself leaving the church for his usual stroll. Fuller, more in a rush and knowing exactly where he was heading, got sucked into the spot, the knife goes in, there's a scream and Father Dell goes hunting.'

'That certainly ties a neat bow. Ideally, I would like to speak to his mother.'

'What would she know?'

'Probably everything there is to know about a one and only son. I question the money, half he gave to Tom Hutton and half to come that night, how odd. If he was blackmailing somebody, then surely a dark and lonely spot is the last place an extortionist would pick.'

As they strolled arm in arm time was uncounted while the river path was silent and near freezing, smelling of old wood and rotting leaves. The dead sticks on the ground were easily seen, glittering with the night's new frost. As Ruben picked one up, his hand began to burn with the cold.

'Was your discovery by accident?'

'Not really,' he said, throwing the dead stick in the river. 'As a young Jeffrey Cane I was fascinated with the unexplained feelings of human experiences. So, I began with the fundamental principal of life, the indestructible atom of which all things are made.'

'So, you were a scientist?'

'Chemistry is science. What is that which keeps our hearts beating? What is that which keeps our feet glued to the earth? Everything is made up of atoms and atoms are active and dynamic, expressing various forms of life and energy, in particular the drive of existence that floats within us and around us.'

'So why study the brain?'

'Since the brain is different and immeasurably more complicated than anything else in the known universe, I thought I should challenge some of our most ardently held ideas. For instance, in the neurons the signals are electrical, but across the gaps they are chemical. Thus, the transmission of nerve signals is electrochemical in nature. Each impulse is of the same strength, but the intensity of the signal depends upon the frequency of the impulses, which may be as high as one thousand of a second.'

'And your formula taps into these signals.'

'Yes, in a way, it does precisely that. It taps into the neurotransmitters diverting the chemical signals at point of death. Think of it like trapping a fish then returning it to the water. Sometimes the fish has been out of the water for too long and consequently returns weak, so weak it dies, fades away or eaten up by bigger fish.'

'Now I understand why you felt so aggrieved not to have spoken to Erik. You don't know whether Erik is retarded or what?'

'Precisely. Our active memories hold several billion times more information than a large contemporary research computer. And similarly, there is no telling, like the computer, the brain could shut down from overload.'

Grey could listen to him forever and never get bored, probably confused but certainly not bored. 'I did go to the museum and discovered in Victorian times there were many shopkeepers on this street.'

'Alas, a vanished world of close knit families and older relatives living together. The cluster at the Market Street end is a far cry from the golden age of shops that were once here.'

'I really don't know how people survive in this part of the world. Lulu's wages are terribly low and petrol prices are astronomical. Unlike London where transport is good, people need to get to work…or do most of Norfolk work for the Council?' She smiled at the back door and walked in. 'I was being facetious.'

'When are you not?'

'When we see Sir John Harcourt,' and waltzed right by him. 'And you will see him, Ruben, even if I have to tie you up and drive you there myself.'

'You have no motor.'

'I shall drive yours.'

'Nor do you have a licence.'

She swung round on the third tread, her eyes squeezed into sparrow feet. 'You presume I have no licence.'

'Where is your car then?'

'Alright, give me the pills.'

'Remember, one each-'

'Yes, okay,' she said proceeding upstairs, 'one each night before I go to bed.'

'Do you play chess?'

'Yes.'

'Fancy a game?'

The offer was just too irresistible, presenting a perfect solution. 'If I win,' she said as casually as she could, 'we will see Sir John tomorrow.'

'And if I win?'

'You can ravage me.'

What Ruben failed to appreciate that Grey had intense powers of concentration as well as an intellectual mind and whilst they talked conventional nonsense, his ability to focus waned in the light of getting her into bed. She was, in effect, using this to advantage her position and further strained his attentiveness by sucking her thumb. By ten o'clock he had sacrificed a bishop where she had only sacrificed a pawn, and by ten-thirty his queen was now at risk.

'Did I mention that I was a virgin,' she said and he looked up astonished. 'Of course, a man of your experience would know what to do.'

'I find that difficult to believe.'

'Does it worry you?'

'Not in the least.' He entered another brief period of analysis and then took her castle. 'I would have thought you to have experienced love, if not sex.'

'Tom Cruise destroyed my illusion.' She took his queen.

'Are you an only child?'

'Your move, I believe.'

'I'm thinking.'

'Try not to think too long.'

Her fidgeting was exhausting and he moved a piece in a state of fever, falling into check mate. 'Have you ever considered settling down?' she asked.

'I was settled before you unsettled me.'

'It's my job to unsettle.' She leaned back on her heels, somewhat sad over her victory. 'As much as it pleases me to be in your company, I can only extend a hand of friendship.'

'Are you married?'

'Every time you ask a personal question you force me to lie and I don't want to lie.'

'Why lie? What is said between us will go no further.'

'But talking about it will not alter my situation.'

'How do you know unless you try?'

'I know, trust me, I know. Now can we put away this foolishness and resign ourselves for tomorrow?'

Ruben picked up the remote and switched on the plasma TV. 'Goodnight, Miss Grey.'

CHAPTER 12

Sunday 28th October

The Sunbeam Alpine drove its wheels over a never ending drive, its windscreen wipers blipping angrily from side to side beneath skies of sleet. And Ruben knew he was past the point of no return, the games of make believe were at an end. He was here to greet an old friend, a once vibrant patron of the sciences, now a pallid octogenarian who would no doubt stir ancient memories he cared to forget.

Sir John Harcourt resided in a white colonnaded mansion, lying on the western side of Bury St. Edmunds. Home to the Harcourt family for more than six generations, they had created a sizeable property in grounds of fifty acres. The rooms were large with their customary patterns, the largest being the tropical house where Harcourt was shadowed in this sleet-darkened room. For the most part, his sullen despondency matched the leaden drops streaming across the grounds, hope drowning for the return of Jeffrey Cane. Indeed, hope barely swam at all. Now he appeared to be on the verge of tears, keeping his gaze fixed upon the man who called himself Ruben Stone. It was a moving moment.

'Is that really you, Jeffrey?'

'Even driftwood may be salvaged.'

The greeting was one of friendship, the encounter planned earlier that day. Sir John Harcourt was frail in body, had the hollow cheeks of a skeleton, thin lips that hardly fed an appetite. He came to wheel in front of Ruben.

'My God you look damn good.'

'For my sins a better face and body.'

'For your sins you should be keelhauled. I see you still like to wear a three piece suit, and a pocket watch.'

'Old habits die hard.'

'Then why forget our friendship?'

'It's a long story.' Ruben sidestepped behind the wheelchair and brought enduring Grey into view. 'This is the woman to thank. Without her obstinacy, tenacity and single mindedness, I would be resting on my Sunday laurels.'

'Nice to make your acquaintance, Sir John,' she said with an almost faint curtsy. 'Ruben has told me so much about you.'

'Good things I hope.'

'Is anyone good these days?'

'Like her already, Jeffrey.' Harcourt wheeled thirty degrees and addressed the penguin suit standing in the shadows of potted blooms. 'Be a good chap, Windsor and ask Mrs G to make us some tea.'

'Very good, sir.'

'Good man Able Windsor,' Harcourt said, 'doubles up as my driver. Now, Jeffrey, who's trying to kill you?'

'Not sure *kill* is the right word.'

And so it was over tea and biscuits that Ruben went on to describe the complexities of his second life, the muddle-headed child that grew to follow in his grandfather's footsteps, as if that mattered to Harcourt who drew a few astonishing runs on his eyebrow. Even more astonishing when Ruben went on to explain his duplicity in defrauding Fair Life Assurance and what followed thereafter, the appearance of a witch and the demise of a bastard. A giant chain of events told, supported by Grey to seal the conclusion that someone had their own private agenda to steal the formula.

'A sad state of affairs,' Harcourt said and with a near soundless lament, the sleet faded away, light flooding rapidly through the colossal panes of glass. 'Shortly after that terrible ordeal I contracted pneumonia, was left with some drawbacks as you can see, eventually gave up my position on the board. But in spite of everything I was forever in hope of your return.' Then from the underside of his blanket that warmed his spindly legs, Harcourt revealed a stack of photographs and passed them to Ruben. 'This may serve to remind what you left behind.'

There were pictures the size of postcards without people, without explanation, a lamppost painted yellow and a red telephone box with its windows smashed in. But mostly they were of people, the white coats of lab technicians, a man with a clip-board in his hand, and a beautiful young woman smiling broadly into the camera.

Ruben looked at each in turn and when he was finished, he stacked them all in a neat pile apart from one. This he would keep.

'Yes, Helena Vale,' Harcourt said, gesturing at Ruben's choice. 'Excellent mind…had a dope of a husband. He thought he could cure her troubles by taking her to Canada.'

'What troubles?' Grey asked.

'Him,' Harcourt pointed to Ruben. 'The moment he clapped eyes on her he was besotted, followed her around like a lap dog. Right, Jeffrey?' There was a brief, embarrassed silence before he went on with a smile that was intended to engender contriteness. 'If I have said something out of turn, please forgive this old fool.'

Ruben sat paralysed, desperately wondering how to respond. His first impulse was to pretend to be insulted then he saw Grey's expression. Anything less than the truth would be taken as an affront. 'We had an attachment,' he told her but this was not enough to please her. 'Dementia does not happen overnight. In my case it mildly lingered for a good few months with Helena covering for my mistakes.'

'Obviously she covered a lot more.' Upon that terse reply, Grey produced her notepad and pen with gusto. 'Sir John, would you have any objections if I asked a few questions?'

'No, my dear, you carry on, anything to be of help.'

'Were you aware Jeffrey had the onset of dementia?'

'No, I did not. Had I known, and I am sad to say this, Jeffrey, I would have pressed you further.'

'Then you were unaware of his plans to leave this world?'

'I agree.' Harcourt rang for Windsor. 'Let us continue this conversation in the library. I need to show you something.'

'Yes, sir?'

'Windsor, tell Mrs G we shall be lunching in the library.'

'Yes, sir.'

'I am a recluse,' Harcourt continued, leading them through the halls of history. 'My wife died of a stroke, and my son went his own way. We have barely spoken to each other in nearly thirty years. I spent my life apologizing then discovered that having children is no guarantee of love. So, what do you call yourself, Jeffrey?'

'Ruben, Ruben Stone.'

'I am still calling you Jeffrey.' In a library full of serious tomes, Harcourt wheeled in the direction of a mahogany desk. 'Jeffrey and I have always seen eye to eye, Miss Grey. He came to me as a man with phenomenal ideas, ideas that conflicted with the laws of this country.' From out of a drawer, he slapped a file on the desk and foraged for his rimless spectacles. 'I am partly obsessed by death, but I am neither morbid nor senile. You mentioned you needed a copy of the police report, well here it is. Detective Chief Superintendent Andy Spruce led the investigation. There was no doubt Jeffrey shot his wife and my right hand man, Neil Pembroke.'

'Did he ever find Helena's assailant?'

'Do they ever? It's all in here.'

'Did you ever gain access to his formula?'

'It was the one stipulation Jeffrey insisted. He refused to share it with anyone.'

'Who else knew about the experiment?'

'Only Neil Pembroke and Helena Vale, each with different assignments…let me explain. Due to the illegality of the research, it was imperative to keep things under wraps, so Jeffrey used my facilities in the evening. When he was ready for human trials, I employed Neil Pembroke. His assignment was to locate a suitable subject, reporting directly to me.'

'I understand you refused Jeffrey access to the subject upon his return?'

Harcourt smiled modestly. 'The boy was barely six years old. His memories were not fully developed. I guaranteed his parents their child would not be subjected to tests until he was ready. I told this to Jeffrey but he refused to accept my reasoning.'

'Then you hired Helena Vale. Why?'

'Jeffrey was on to another discovery, an off-shoot from his first.'

Silence fell when the penguin suit wheeled in a trolley full of home-made goodies. Cold pork and ham, prawns and salad, hot new potatoes, a selection of pastries and cheesecake, everything laid out to mouth-watering perfection.

They talked a lot, and laughed, poured each other drinks and Ruben felt comfortable, good and real, relaxed in a leather armchair roughly the size of Mount Etna. Talking about Helena roused those intimate moments, moments he once tried to forget because forgetting made it less painful.

'What now remained,' Ruben told them, 'was to choose the subject for her thesis. It was to be the most important decision of her scientific life. I tried to persuade her that her talents could be infinitely better used elsewhere. But she insisted on staying, realizing my discovery held many other possibilities.'

'Sir John, what happened that night, the night of your banquet? Were you witness to the argument?'

'Not in the beginning, most certainly after the speeches were made. Earlier there had been friction at the table between Jeffrey and Neil, we could all sense it. And Jeffrey's wife, as fast as she sought to rebuild her defence, he pulled it apart. Money, I believe was the bone of her contention and cozied up to Neil, deliberately goading Jeffrey into submission. My God, that was a row and a half, never forgot it. The whole thing was a damn mess from start to finish.' He wheeled round and pulled a book off the shelf, its cover worn and faded. 'Do you remember this, Jeffrey, the Undertaker's Nightmare by Frothy Lemon?' To which Ruben shook his head and Harcourt passed it over. 'You should do. Helena wrote it, a piece of hilarious fun. You were waving it under their noses, shouting something to the effect *damned if you ever have it* and then all hell broke loose. A scuffle ensued between you and Neil, and your wife Geraldine got hold of the book and ran off. Neil went after her and you ran after them. Do you remember that?'

Ruben went into his own internal distance, the ghostly fragments of remembered actions. So much history, so much argument, so much pleading, and it had come to that. 'I neither remember the book nor the argument, although I do remember the disquiet at the table.'

'Sir John, what about Helena's husband, was he there?'

'Yes, most certainly, sat at our table.'

'And after the kerfuffle between Jeffrey and Neil, was he still there?'

'I have no idea. You must remember I had over two hundred employees, along with their spouses. It drew quiet a crowd. I was drawn to the mayhem as much as anyone.'

'Ruben, as Jeffrey, did you believe your wife and Neil were behind Helena's death?'

Ruben looked at the photograph. Her hair was as he remembered, cut short with a heavy fringe and he wondered if she was alive today what story would she tell about her assailant. 'I have vague memories of that crossing my mind.'

'Why?' Harcourt asked. 'Why would Jeffrey think Geraldine and Neil were behind Helena's death?'

'A week before she was attacked, I understand that Jeffrey's wife was told the house had been mortgaged and bank accounts emptied. Did you not think it suspicious, Sir John?'

'I had no reason to be suspicious of anything. As far as I was concerned, Jeffrey and I were in crisis over his formula. He refused to honour his part of the agreement which left my investment in his work rather vulnerable.'

'So, when Jeffrey died, you took the view the formula died with him?'

'Most certainly.'

'Then would you care to tell me why your shares jumped astronomically in the following years?'

'Do you doubt my honesty, young lady?'

'There is one thing I have learnt in my short life, Sir John.' Grey folded her notepad. 'Honesty is not always synonymous with the truth. Ruben honestly believes he shot his wife and her lover because the facts speak for themselves. I, on the other hand believe the jigsaw would fit much better if it were someone else.'

'I understand.' Harcourt used sense to blanket his octogenarian displeasure. 'Your attachment to Jeffrey clouds your judgement. My interest in his work was purely selfish. It could never be used on the open market for reasons expressed.'

'A high price to pay for just one pill.'

'Yes indeed, I would agree, a very high price but a price worth paying to live another life time.' Harcourt transferred his gaze to Ruben. 'You knew this, Jeffrey. Many a time we discussed this yet you failed to honour our agreement. Further, you withheld your situation and plans for leaving.'

'It seems so, doesn't it?' Ruben stood, slid his hands into his trouser pockets and went silently to the long-case window. 'I had a choice to make, a hard choice in whether to give you my formula or chance we would meet again, here, as we are now, or perhaps sooner. The fact that I had no need to discuss it made it all the sweeter, like it was a given, like it was as natural as a cup of tea or a shared cigarette.' He turned to look down at the man who had given him everything. 'If it had held the remotest possibility that my formula would get into the wrong hands, I chose the latter.'

'Surely a pill would have sufficed?' Grey asked.

'Not possible. The solution weakens the longer it's kept, and John knew this, himself a chemistry major.'

'I had a dog,' Harcourt said. 'Called it Bob, damn ordinary name to be sure. When he died, Shirley, my wife, went out and bought me another. It was never the same. No matter how hard you try to love them, it's never the same.' The grin made for a selfish pity. 'So where are we at, Jeffrey, a point of no return?'

Bringing his pocket watch to the open, Ruben flipped the rear cover and gave Harcourt what he most desired. It had not gone unnoticed by one other.

'Do not take it until I have finished my enquiries,' Grey told Harcourt who quickly squirrelled his prize under his blanket. 'Life is complicated enough let alone figuring out two lifetimes.' She went to the trolley and poured a cold cup of coffee. 'This world has accomplished very little under the jurisdiction of men.'

'Thankfully we have women to remind us.'

'Sarcasm does not suit you, Ruben. I know your heart is well meaning but what seems reasonable at three on a Sunday afternoon might not stack up in the cold light of a Monday morning. It is our destiny to make room for others in this untainted cradle of the universe.'

'A moment ago, it was tainted by men.' His smile brought her near to him. 'Are we ready to go?'

'No!' Harcourt protested. 'Stay a while longer.'

'If you will excuse me, gentlemen, I need to make a call.' Grey picked up her bag and coat. 'Ruben, I shall see you in the car. Sir John, it was a pleasure meeting you.'

'Windsor will see you out.'

'I'm fine. I know where to go.'

'Damn if she's not persistent, Jeffrey. Not sure about the hair, reminds me of my grandmother.' Harcourt wheeled to the drinks cabinet. 'There are too many of us, Jeffrey. This country cannot cope, nor can the government get out of the EU. Drink?'

'I'm driving.'

'I noticed you still drive a Sunbeam Alpine.'

'Motors look too much like modern shavers. There's a great chap, owns a garage, keeps my wreck ticking over very nicely.'

'Do you buy your friends, Jeffrey?'

'I cannot deny my road was hard. Charlie was the only one with whom I confided and school was so bloody boring. What do they teach nowadays? Half of them leave wanting to be pop stars, the other half are left to search for a secure future in an insecure world. What is the point to it all, no point to make a difference.'

'I shall make a difference, intend to travel the politician route, might make PM.'

'By the time you're ready to branch into the social scene, I doubt the Houses of Parliament will be that attractive…John, I should be going. We have another call to make.'

'I wish you luck in your endeavours.'

It was not as if Ruben expected anything earth shattering but he did expect a good proportion of his memories to return, but the only memories that came flooding back was that of Helena Vale. Before stepping out into the cold night, he drew his hands over his face coming to the conclusion his troubled heart will undergo further anxiety in company of Grey.

'Was Helena aware you had the onset of dementia?'

'Yes.' He turned on the ignition. 'She covered for my mistakes.'

'Were you planning to go together? Of course, you were. She was the reason why you tried not to come here, the reason why you chose to forget. And the locket, *when this you see, remember me*, it was for her to wear your picture.'

'Look, I'm sorry I failed to mention my affair. It wasn't something to feel proud about. Helena was married and much younger than me, vibrant and hard to ignore.'

'When you hankered for sex last night, whose face would be there, I wonder.'

'Not Helena's.'

'That wasn't a question.'

'It sounded like one. Who did you call?'

'Nobody. It was an excuse to read the report before we got to your house.'

Ruben drove on with despondency. Having to face that type of questioning was one thing, having to face his *old house* was not something he relished, and asked the only question he could muster. 'Find anything interesting?'

'The neighbour heard three shots, the latter delayed by a minute or two then he telephoned the police. The autopsy report made for thought-provoking reading. Neil Pembroke was shot twice in the back. You had gun powder residue on your right hand. Odd, considering that you are naturally left handed.'

'I was right handed as Jeffrey Cane.'

'Then we must assume your left hand never knew what your right hand was doing.' They briefly looked at each other and smiled. 'Also, the Medical Examiner claimed the acid in your stomach had a depressant effect on your central nervous system which caused your death. He put it down to some form of barbiturate poisoning.'

'My formula was designed to create death.'

'So can you tell me why this was missed in Peter Tudmoor's autopsy?'

'I kept up with the times, refined my formula.'

'What about the book?'

'Helena had a weird sense of humour.'

'From how Sir John described the argument it appeared to hold weight.'

'Obviously the book was all I had left of Helena.'

'If your wife ran off with it, then how did Sir John gain possession?'

He had no idea.

Jeffrey Cane had lived in a house that rose out of the lush green estates of Newmarket's wealthiest district, several miles west of Bury St. Edmunds. The property was a restrained, dignified and well-proportioned building being of the late nineteenth century occupying grounds of two acres, or thereabouts. The land interspersed with trees, overgrown in places was in a state of maturity and decay.

Ruben pulled up on the soft verge of a country road. It was almost six, and both stared at a lamp post, starlets of snow lightly dancing to its dim yellow light. 'One of the photographs John passed over was taken from here,' Ruben said. 'And over there used to be a telephone box with its windows smashed in.'

'Does it hold any significance?'

'In as much they were taken too long ago.' Then he switched his gaze to the property. 'I always loved that house. Now I feel nothing but dread.'

It took a few moments to realize Grey had gone on ahead. Ruben followed her because he had no choice, because he was already committed.

The house was dead, tatty and shabby, in need of updating. From the monumental masonry cracks as soon as Ruben opened the door, to the crumbling handrail and dodgy stone steps leading to the garden. Now accustomed to the dark, he tracked through the rooms, his sense reaching ahead and pricking for memories. That was the problem. Over time the house had been left to deteriorate, the central staircase creaked and groaned, the smell of damp and the freezing atmosphere, nothing felt familiar and nothing seemed the same. There was a moment when the grounds lit up. Reflexively, he crouched low then it went dark, the sound of a vehicle parking into the adjacent drive.

'What are you doing, Ruben?'

'I got scared.'

She grabbed his hand. 'Come on, this way to the crime scene.' It was where he needed to be, in the study, dank, dark and miserable. 'Now,' she said, 'from the police report your desk was somewhere about here. You were found slouched over it, gun in your right hand. Your wife's body was on the floor near the window and Neil Pembroke was face down by the door.'

Memories crowded in.

'You're a damn fool, Jeffrey, if you think I'll give you a divorce, have that slut take what's mine.'

'It was never yours in the first place.'

'Don't make me laugh. This house might be in your name but the law is on my side.' Geraldine looked down at the papers shoved in her hand. 'What's this?'

'The house belongs to the bank.'

'Bastard! You're not getting away with this!'

'I already have.'

Ruben could see it all now, the final farewell, kissing the lips of Helena Vale after her expiry in a hospital bed. Then quickly the scene changed into that night, the imagined shots, one after another, two blindly crawling or staggering until stilled by death, their freedom short lived. He retraced his steps through the house, had no interest in dwelling on the arguments, the anxiety of his nightmares no longer burned. The past could not compete with a rewritten future. Rather than return to the motor, he disappeared into the undergrowth, vaulted over a wall and pressed the neighbour's chiming bell. It took a number of seconds before the hall illuminated the coloured glass and a smartly dressed woman came to the door.

'Sorry to bother you,' he gestured, 'but do you know if anyone has showed interest in that property?'

'Are you a developer?'

'I was looking to buy in this area.'

'As far as I know it's never been up for sale. Mr. Johnson resides opposite. He might be able to tell you.'

'Thank you, and once again, my apologies.'

By the motor, Grey extinguished her herbal cigarette and sunk into the passenger's seat. 'What did you ask her?'

'If anyone showed interest of late, just a thought that's all.' He happily turned to face her, his hand on the steering wheel. 'I never killed them.'

She smiled with such girlish pleasure that if she had to sum up her endeavours in three words it would be *a blessed relief.*

'I am convinced,' he continued, driving off on a road which now lay deserted in its thin coating of snow, 'when one goes through the transition their memories are joined with hopes and fears. My hopes were to put the past behind me and start a new life. My fears were equally balanced by the thought of returning with no memories at all. In consequence, my recollections resulted in a jumbled affair.'

'Why did you go next door?'

'I wanted to know if someone had been nosing around. Logically, someone such as yourself who traced my history as Jeffrey Cane would no doubt make enquiries. For instance, Fuller, how did he work it out? Okay, you say someone told him. But how did that someone know where to look? Do you see where I'm going with this, Grey? If you're right, that the architect of Fuller's actions and demise is wanting what I have, then how were they able to latch on to me?'

'Maybe we have to give him some credit. The day I arrived, he spoke that name, Jeffrey, and maybe something twigged. Maybe he did what I did, went through the nuggets of Google…and maybe he contacted Sir John.'

'Did you get a feeling he was truthful?'

'He was holding back. He must have known you were planning something. The row alone would cause an intelligent man to think twice. So, tell me, what happened that night?'

'My actions were not planned, only the sobering thought of leaving my wife with nothing, nothing at all except misery, the same misery she had bestowed on me over the years. I was convinced she had conspired with Neil Pembroke to get rid of Helena where in truth Helena had met her fate by an unknown hand.'

'Why so certain?'

'Because Pembroke was with me in the lab when Helena was attacked, and I doubt very much Geraldine would dirty her hands. So, okay, we could say they hired someone. I think that would be too dodgy. I was not angry about my wife's affair, only angry to discover Pembroke had told her about my work. That's why we argued that night. It came as a complete shock. She threatened to expose me if I took the death-dive and Pembroke backed her up.'

'And the book?'

'Indeed, the book held relevance for within those pages Helena left a clue to where she kept her capsule, one of her little jokes. I was there at the hospital, thought there might be a chance for her recovery but she died, her effects were given to her husband.'

'So, he had the book.'

'There was more than one copy. That was the point of it. She got this agent to put her story to a publisher, thousands were printed. And somehow Pembroke knew but never told Geraldine until the row blew up at the banquet, that's why she ran off with it.'

'And you ran after her.'

'There was no point. Helena was dead. My life in tatters so I drove home, the house was empty. I poured a scotch, took a capsule and the world ended.'

'Then it was staged. Your wife and her lover killed to keep them silent, and you take the blame leaving the murderer free to find that capsule.'

'It would have done them no good.'

'Can you be more specific?'

'Each capsule is individual to the recipient, so keep that close to your chest.'

'Gracious! Am I to assume Sir John will not be returning?'

'But he doesn't know that. As individual as a fingerprint is to each human being so too would be their capsule for how else would the nuclei of the cells in our body respond gladly to a foreign invader.'

'I have no idea what that means but it sounded extremely intelligent.'

Ruben smiled. 'It's the suit.'

'It now means whoever may have found and taken Helena's capsule is dead, never to return and if they killed Geraldine and Neil we shall never know for certain, only assume. I wonder if Helena's husband is still alive.'

'What motive would he have to kill them?'

'I need to sleep.'

'You were supposed to take a tablet.'

'It's when I sleep my subconscious works, puts things in perspective, shifts out details, dumps irrelevancy, switches on some lights.'

'Well go to sleep now.'

'Have you got a sleeping pill?'

'You really don't want me to answer that.'

CHAPTER 13

Remember, remember, the 5th of November, looming on the horizon. It kept tills ringing while Ruben laboured in pockets of sawdust.

But there was more than the business to consider. If Grey's intelligence was correct, then the flimsy theory of Helena's husband came into question. She had established he went to Canada six months after that fateful night, and worse, he died at the age of sixty-five. For this reason alone, it was back to the drawing board.

'On a scale of 1 to 9, how certain are you nobody else had access to your formula?'

'Ten.'

In a pair of dungarees, Grey squirrelled back to the shop with a late morning ruffled hair style. Thirty minutes later she returned to disrupt his work load again. 'Did Helena regain consciousness?'

'Yes.'

'For how long?'

'About an hour.'

'And were you there by her side?'

'Only after she died.'

'Okay, see you later.'

A lesser time than before, she returned and tapped him on the shoulder. He switched off the lathe and looked down into those enquiring grey eyes. 'What you mean to say is that you had no opportunity to speak to her before she died.'

'I told you, her husband took preference.'

'Pick up the receiver. Sam wants to tell you his latest.'

Shaking his head as she squirrelled back to the counter, he picked up the extension. 'What you got?'

'April Jones came on the scene a couple of days after I arrived home. Wendy told me she opened a current account and that money has been flowing in from guess where?'

'John Harcourt?'

'Bingo!'

'Thanks, Ding, I owe you a lot.'

'How about a new life?'

'No guarantee you would be better off.'

When Ruben replaced the receiver, he took the proffered mug of coffee from his grandfather, the bushy brows covered in sawdust.

'If yew don't mind me saying, Grey seems a tad interested in this Helena.'

'My fault,' Ruben admitted and stared through the iron-grilled windows, the semi-white darkness beyond, feeling apprehensive. 'The truth is, I kept back a piece of my history and Grey found out through John Harcourt.'

'Wat history is that?'

'We were having an affair.'

'Was yew now?'

'I had every intention of giving the locket to Helena, had it inscribed with my picture inside. Just one lie pressed upon another because it was too painful to remember.'

'Yew should hev told me, Ruby. I gave the locket to Grey to help yew, not stir an old flame.' The old man leaned back against the bench, placed his mug to one side and folded his arms. 'Wus yew two planning mischief or wat?'

'Indeed, *what* is exactly the plan we had in mind before she was taken from me, I thought, by my vindictive wife and her lover. That proved not to be the case when I realized Neil Pembroke was with me in the lab when she was mugged.'

'So, yew wus beside yerself with grief, no wonder yew blew your top. I loved Betty, always did, still do. My heart weighed heavy that day when I married her sister.'

'Why be unfaithful, Charlie?'

'Betty kept herself pure and it wound me up. Not that I'm saying it's an excuse. Lord, I felt guilty, made all the excuses I could to keep away but she kept sending her sister. Women hev no real understanding fer a man's need, not in that way, but her sister wus all about. Hev yew got any love for Grey?'

'It's more like a love-hate relationship. One minute she's my best friend, next I'm her worst nightmare. She's bright, brighter than me at times but somehow, she makes me feel guilty too, Charlie. Helena and I were going to share a new life together, and yes, one of us or both may not have made it.' From his back pocket, Ruben produced the photograph. 'She was a lot younger than me.'

'Yew wus lucky for an ugly sod.'

Ruben snatched it back. 'To men perhaps, not to women.'

'I tell yew this much, it helps none to hang on to her picture if yew intend to marry a witch.'

'Who said anything about marriage?'

'Well wat do yew want, Ruby?'

'To see Victor before he closes.'

Leaving his coffee untouched, Ruben strode on without an upward glance barely distinguishing one problem from another. No matter the times he apologized to Grey, she still left his dirty laundry hanging in the air. By-passing a few friendly faces, he quickened his pace and darted into the shop once owned by Peter Tudmoor, whose solid old walls racked a collection of second hand jewellery.

A weathered beaten face looked up from behind a newspaper. 'You must have read my thoughts, Ruby.' Victor shuffled the pages together and braced himself for business. 'I got the cash in fifty notes.'

'When can we exchange?'

'I'll come round the back. That okay with you?'

'Sure, give me an hour.' Just as Ruben went to leave, he made a conscious decision and removed the locket from about his neck. 'How much for this?'

The head bent into the hallmarks and then the piece was weighed. 'Say about four hundred.'

'Come on, you can do better than that.'

'Scrap value four hundred.'

'You can sell it on.'

'The inscription inside devalues the piece. Tell you what, how about an exchange?'

'For what?'

'Got a nice gentleman's pin tie.' Then the part-time fireman held up his finger as if he had something better to offer. He went to a glass cabinet, pulled out a gem encrusted music box and opened the lid for Ruben to hear its mournful melody. 'Circa 1800s, got it at auction last month, paid three-fifty, do you a swap, can't say fairer than that.'

'What are the stones?'

'Lavender Amethyst, a popular Victorian gem.'

'Do you have anything grey?'

Again, the fireman held up his finger and wandered to another cabinet laced with rings. 'See that one there, your namesake. The mighty *rubinus lapis*, the fiery scarlet everyone wants to love.'

'How long has it been unloved in that cabinet?'

'Ignore the cobwebs. It's been waiting for the right finger. Mozambique Ruby and Diamond 18 carat yellow gold and cross my heart if that's not worth a thousand of anyone's money.'

'Talk to the hand.'

'Eight hundred and it's a bargain.'

'Show me.'

Victor retrieved it from the cabinet and placed it on Ruben's little finger. 'Not that old as antiques go, but the gems are good quality, made especially for a Ruby wedding.'

'And you know this for sure?'

'The daughter wanted some cash, true enough, even gave me the receipt. Her father paid two and half thousand.'

Ruben went to the window and observed the stone burn with fire intensity. 'It looks too much like an engagement ring.'

'You want something grey, I give you red and a good price. How about a diamond with no inclusions?'

'I am not looking to go down on bended knee. I just want to give her something nice, something to show my appreciation. Now she likes wearing grey.'

Victor clicked his fingers and dropped out of sight, returning with a necklace. 'Tahitian Pearls, grey enough for you?'

'Now that's more like it.'

'And arguably the most coveted of all pearls, despite only being introduced to Europeans in 1845.'

'Five hundred and you got yourself a deal.'

'Are you stark raving mad? Do you know how much these are worth? I can get seven hundred, just by dangling them in the window.'

'You give me scrap value for my locket and want top dollar for the pearls. Five-fifty and a nice box.'

'It's already in a box.'

'Then your squids in.'

'I need my head examining.'

'Can we square up?'

Victor, of the meticulous kind, reclaimed from the underside of his counter a small black book, licked his finger and turned the pages while Ruben detached his picture from the locket.

'How's your business doing, Ruby?'

'Making a profit.' In spite of this, £150 left him broke.

Now encased in a blue satin box, Ruben hit the cold rush of air and returned via the shop entrance where Grey had her head buried in Helena's book. They were just about to acknowledge each other when a man walked in with two rowdy kids.

Far from that maddening crowd, Ruben wandered upstairs and had a shower. Wiping the fog off the mirror with a hand towel, his reflection gave him an unwanted glimpse of indecisiveness. Should he take the bull by the horns and ask her to stay or should he wait? Decisions, decisions, he then went a step further, creating a vision of himself and his future. The husband, inspiring, his ambition could be focused on the business making money, enough to buy a house like Betty's by the river. What he would give to have a home like that, to face a burning grate in winter, to look upon coloured glass in spring, to sweep leaves in autumn and to pluck weeds in summer. Happy pictures played out and simply disappeared when he thought he detected a sigh.

'What's up, Charlie?'

'Better put some clothes on. Victor's brought his motor round.'

'Charlie, do you think Grey was annoyed because she was jealous, jealous because she thought I still loved Helena?'

'Look, son, I get jealous thinking about an erection but it doesn't mean I love my dick. It just means I love the thought of heving an erection.'

'Gee, Charlie, that's very helpful.'

'Glad to be of service.'

Ruben looked blank, considered when he got an erection, he had nowhere to put it. This and other things stayed with him as he dressed warmly and went downstairs to help load the gold into the boot of Victor's motor. One million in fifty pound notes enclosed in a leather worn suitcase given in exchange.

Few knew what went on behind the shop with a magical window display. Even as a hidden yard, it not always shrank from the outside world, the predictable habits of Ruben who routinely caressed his roses and grinned at the thought of those pearls round her neck. He would choose his moment and make it count.

By six the heat was trapped within the sheer walls of the kitchen which shuddered and shifted with life, falling in talks with one another.

'Pass the salt, Charlie.'

'Salt isn't good fer yew, my woman.'

'Why do you have it?'

'I'm past my prime.'

'My, my,' she said, tying her hair in a knot, 'how well you look for your age, now pass me the salt before I hide the apple pie.' Her gaze then fell upon Ruben. 'At least we know Sir John's messenger. He may appear fragile but not without influence though it's quite possible now that you made his day, he will call off his long-legged blood hound.'

'Made his day?' Charlie asked.

'Ruben gave him a capsule. Well meant, I assure you, but still, I thought a rather foolish gift when clearly, he thinks of returning as Prime Minister.'

That set the old man off. 'Ah! See! Thass exactly wat I mean. It's people like him who put this country on a state of welfare dependency. In my day yew laboured no matter wat, postie or mucking out pigs, it made no mind. A man carried his pride in his work. Our nation's habit of living beyond its means has run out of road. The state sector is much too expensive and far too many take more out of the pot than they put in, leaving productive people like me and Ruby to bear the tax burden.'

'When last did you pay any tax?'

'Thass not the point, my woman,' and carried on eating with his eyes screwed to the plate.

After a quiet prelude, they began to converse on the histories of their time together, the townsfolk and changing scenery of commerce which sacrificed the welfare of communities in the name of progress.

'We are not alone,' spoke Ruben softly. 'Other towns and villages have the same problem, some have become virtually extinct. The wrong people are being voted in, trying to be clever when in reality they are the legacy of a spoilt generation that saw fit to exploit the human wave of capitalism. Among us are businesses that have been trading since 1875, survived two world wars, one great depression, several recessions, and a three-day working week, catalogue and online selling, a one-way system and parking charges.'

'Yew fergot the supermarkets.'

'Yes, they too have contributed greatly. In a way, you are right, Charlie. But you only have to look in the mirror to see who's at fault.'

'We need a culture change,' Grey suggested. 'We get rid of the House of Lords and put Liam Neilson in charge of security. He has a particular set of skills that make him a nightmare for yobs. Of course, it does not do to threaten Sir John's leggy minion who might have a preference for kidnapping. What do you think, Ruben, or are you asleep?'

Ruben's expression was almost serene. She had made the table come alive, elbowed Charlie without spite, and stirred the atmosphere with her deranged sense of fun. To let her go would be catastrophic. 'Okay,' he said, after swallowing, 'on the premise he still wants my formula, his long-legged minion kidnaps Charlie.'

'I'm too close to the knacker's yard.'

'Charlie,' Grey asked, 'what happened to the money Michael gave you for this property?'

'Why do yew ask?'

'I was just curious, especially since that seemed to kick off everything else which has happened in the last three years.'

'See, it wus like this, my woman. Amy got her nan's house and it needed updating. Ruby helped out and gave her the money he wus saving to buy a new microscope. When I heard wat he done, and without him knowing, I sold this property to Fuller thinking it were a loan. Anyways, damage done, and then I had another idea when I heard Lenard wanted to do himself in.'

'You are incorrigible, Charlie, and so hard not to love. I suppose you used the money to fully equip Ruben so he could refine his formula.'

'That I did, my woman, all the best intentions in the world and we hev yew at our table.'

'Did Ruben tell you there is a way to buy back this property without due concern?'

'He did but we hev no money. Ruby refuses to take anything fer his troubles, not that it wus offered.'

'The business is picking up nicely, and I'm sure Mrs Fuller will be more than obliging to take into account all the rent you have paid, ergo far less to find, and let us see where that may come from.' Grey referred to Ruben, stealing a runner bean off his plate. 'Are you selling your house?'

'Is there anything you don't know?'

'Not really,' and carried on eating. Yet beneath the fabric of wood, her foot found its way to his crotch, forcing him to smile.

'How did we do?'

'Good, up by thirty per cent compared to last week. It slowed just after lunch which gave me time to read bits of Helena's book. And that makes me wonder what kind of person becomes an author? Is it rampant egotism or an unswerving belief in their talent? The kind that can write, you would imagine, although the shelves are littered with examples which shoot down that theory.'

'I take it yew wusn't impressed with hers?'

'No, Charlie, to be frank it quite sickened me. Sorry, but that's my honest opinion. Her story was very crude and obvious, the undertaker having intercourse with dead bodies. Did you read her book, Ruben?'

'I was too busy reading my journals.'

'I best be reading it,' and they looked astonished at the old man who quickly thought to cover his lust. 'Just like to help out, find where she might hev hidden her capsule.'

Apple pie later, the old man left his trail of crumbs as he toddled off to visit Betty while Grey pushed those guarded boundaries that kept Ruben a little remote over supper. 'Are you still in love with Helena?'

'Jeffrey was in love with Helena.'

'You are Jeffrey, the same man rolled into one.'

'I spent the last of my memories in not wanting to be him.'

'But he was a good man. Why not take that truth into your heart?'

'The system doesn't reward the truth. To leave one life in the hope of something better was the greatest disenchantment a man could have. Nothing is better. Nothing has changed.'

'Rubbish. We have greater choices in life.'

'Choice is an illusion created between those with power and those with not. I'm not sure whether this makes it better or worse.'

'That sounds like a prognosis for loneliness.'

'Stay?' The moment it was said Ruben knew he had made an ass of himself, watched as she took a deep sigh, her eyes averting to her watch. 'Or not,' he added quickly.

'It would never work between us. And do you know why? Apart from holding a lasting torch for Helena Vale, we live in different worlds, and you know this to be true.'

'What world is so different when both stand on the same soil, eat the same food and talk the same language?'

'Would you give this up? Leave your world of magic, your grandfather and friends, to live with me?'

'Why not you live with me?'

'Then you have answered your own question. Maybe we are here to serve as intended to serve and that man in all his egotistical glory cannot defeat their destiny.'

'And what is mine?'

'To listen to my theory while you make tea.'

Ruben waved his hand as a concession to his thoughts and switched on the kettle. 'Okay, fire away, I'm listening.'

'We have established April Jones is not who she purports to be, and neither has Sir John been entirely truthful. But I cannot visualize a stick insect with silicon breasts stabbing a man in the chest. Nor can I visualize Sir John ordering a hit job on Michael Fuller, although I can visualize a younger Sir John following Jeffrey Cane home that night, dismayed to find him dead. And who should walk in, Geraldine and Neil, they too dismayed whereupon an argument ensued. Them threatening to go public and Sir John solving his problem by shooting first Geraldine and then Neil in the back as he tried to make his escape. The third shot came later, the gun placed in your right hand, the trigger pulled in order to leave powder residue on the fingers. Why not, he considers, why not let Jeffrey Cane take the blame for their murders? And so, he picks up the book, the book I shall have tested for blood spots and goes home safely in the knowledge that somewhere in that story he will find where Helena Vale hid her capsule.'

'But he never found it.'

'And that makes it all the more intriguing and very necessary to plant April Jones behind your counter.'

The arc of his brow rose. 'Can you back-track on that statement?'

'Ruben, it's the only way to get information. The fact that she is working for Sir John is evidently enough of an incentive to do this.'

He kept his eyes peeled to the floor so they would not betray his exasperation. When he looked up, she was smiling. 'This is no laughing matter. She seduced Fuller then hopped over to Hutton. How do you think my reputation will stand if I ask her to come and work in my shop?'

'You don't ask. You tell Marge, the quickest route to let April know there's an opening. I think this was their gambit, to get close to you, gain your trust but I got in the way.'

If he had to sum up his years on this earth it would amount to 83, almost two thirds more of her lifetime and yet he felt far less wise. Perhaps love had something to do with it.

Grey prodded her teabag in the mug, her voice sounding almost apologetic. 'I'm sorry, Ruben.'

'What the hell, I make lousy tea.'

'No, I'm sorry to put you through this.'

'So, you think she may know who murdered Fuller and this I am to obtain by what method?'

'You have a brain, so use it.' Grey looked at her watch. 'Where is the case full of money?'

'In the shop, next to your things...I'm curious. What did you do with the dollhouse? Give it away?'

'Absolutely not, I just love it. No, I had it sent to my home by courier.'

'Dare I ask again where you live?'

'You have my mobile number.'

'So, I can post your tablets.'

'I might just want to pick them up.'

As a last ditch effort, Ruben pulled from his pocket the blue box. 'I exchanged the locket for this, not intending to buy you favours but to show my appreciation for all you have done.'

Grey sat motionless beholding the pearls and then at Ruben, trying to look into his eyes but could not see out of her own. 'Why, Ruben? Why sell your mother's locket?'

'It just seemed the right thing to do. No, correction, not the right thing, but the best thing to do. It doesn't hold sentimental value, not any more. I only kept it because at the back of my picture was the formula.'

'If I take this-'

'As a friend,' he interjected, and placed them about her neck. 'Consider it a bonus, and, who knows, you might fancy a shoulder to cry on if Tom Cruise returns.'

'I may just do that. Ring me on progress.'

'She could be here for weeks.'

'I know, it's a bummer, weeks spent looking at Venus. Make sure Charlie behaves himself.'

He wanted to extend the conversation, anything, just anything to keep her longer in his company but a car horn raised the alarm. Ruben drew back the net curtain and observed a black limousine half-way parked on the pavement. When he looked back, Grey was gone.

The silent wonder of a cold starry night appealed to Godfrey Shilling as he sat stoic in the rear of his chauffeur driven limousine. He was overjoyed by the success of Grey and mightily amused within himself to have overseen the receipt of funds outside the shop with a magical window display.

'Do you wish to be taken home?'

'No,' said Grey, who had her share of vanity, obstinacy and love of power but in so doing she furthered the ends of justice in a very uncommon degree. 'Drop me off at Liverpool Street station.'

'Liverpool Street, Grange.'

'Yes, sir.'

'Did he kill Fuller?'

'Ruben Stone is not that stupid.'

'He was stupid enough to get caught.'

'I was clever enough to back him in a corner. There was no evidence, only supposition and supposition holds no weight in a court of law.'

'I wish to retain your services.'

'Why?'

'His mother, Susan Fuller feels her son's death is connected to your investigations and since you were employed by my company it seems only right to do the decent thing.'

Grey understood him perfectly. 'The decent thing would be to make up the difference on the bond yields her unqualified son sold on your company's behalf to her tenants when she bought their properties thirty per cent below market value.'

'Even so, I see no reason why you cannot make enquiries, unless it worries you.'

To say Grey was worried would have little meaning. She was extremely worried of Ruben Stone's true identity becoming exposed. After meditating for a long time, she said, 'I just feel your money will be wasted. The police believe it was a woman.'

'Give me a figure.'

'The suitcase you just received.'

'One million is a high price to pay.'

'If it ever gets out her son was unqualified to give advice, her tenants will not only take her to court but they will drag your company into the process and ask for more than a suitcase.'

'I hardly think it likely she will tell them.'

'No, and shall I tell you why? Because she has agreed to take full responsibility on the condition you give her the name of her son's killer. Correct me if I'm mistaken.'

Not so much as a slight wagging of his chin, the Chief Executive remained a perfect desert in the broad map of his face while he eyed her during this brief negotiation. 'The suitcase is yours.'

So much money, she thought, and lazed against the smell of cream leather that threatened to rock her into convulsion. She felt an eerie upwelling in the pit of her stomach like a massive locomotive straining to reverse direction and took a deep breath.

'Are you alright?' Shilling asked.

'To be truthful, I feel a little sick.'

'Grange, stop the car.'

Just past a strategic bend in the road, the chauffeur pulled on to the hard shoulder and Grey got out, the cold rush of air quickly supplanting her sickness. It was not the warm and silent vacuum that back seat passengers usually enjoyed but the abandonment of Ruben Stone, leaving him in pursuit of knowledge and primarily for her own sake.

A taxi swung into the layby. Perfect timing, and at her insistence sent God on his way. Then her fearless defender grabbed her things, dumped them on the front seat while she crawled into the back and closed her eyes. Images of dancing cheek to cheek with Ruben Stone came flooding in, the memory carried like an echo from the past into the present.

'Are you okay?'

'God wants me to identify Fuller's killer.'

'Don't go there. Let me handle it.'

'I have no choice,' and she shrugged. 'I'm already committed.'

Then she went on to explain the facts of Ruben Stone, why her curiosity led her on a road of discovery, the visit to Sir John Harcourt and his involvement with April Jones.

'He asked me because he knows I can deliver his company from a pack of law suits. Susan Fuller wants to know who killed her son and in return she's prepared to take full responsibility for his actions. And the best part, he offered a clear million.'

A cool whistle and a pack of herbal cigarettes flew over to the back seat. 'How did you get him to cough up so much?'

'He knows the law suits would cost his company far, far more in damages, and I see no risk once Ruben gets his head round April Jones. Mind you, I need him to see Susan Fuller. I also need forensic evidence off a book.'

'I can do that.'

'Also, Sir John's place should be watched. It never rang true his reasons for holding back on Ruben regarding the test subject. If April Jones never killed Fuller then the only lead I have is this Erik from Sweden. Find him and I get more pieces to fit in this very confusing puzzle.'

'You think Harcourt wants the formula?'

'I think everyone involved wants the formula. As Ruben said, the elite would transcend into Gods and the deserving would trail into utter insignificance. He would far rather kill himself than give it up, and that is really terribly sad.'

'He's sad full stop.'

'Actually, he's extremely intelligent and very dismissive toward those who gain their wealth on the backs of others. And that's been our problem in this country. Hard to imagine him choosing to be a carpenter when he has the brains to give people a second chance in life.' She sat forward looking into his eyes that were looking at hers through the rear view mirror. 'If you had a choice to come back, would you come back to me?'

'Hell, yes.'

And then she felt the pearls round her neck. No doubt about it, Ruben had surprised her to the point of tears. The picture he painted in a very small way was a future by his side which, in truth, was no future at all.

'I need to give him a ring.' Grey sat back, grabbing her mobile. 'By the way, what did the vet say about Bobble?'

'He's old.'

'What's that supposed to mean?'

'We just need to keep him on a chicken and rice diet.'

'Ruben,' she said when he picked up, killing two birds with one Stone, 'it was most absent of me not to say thank you for the pearls. I do apologize. I never even said a proper goodbye.'

'Four hours later you seem to be saying hello. Is it my magnetic personality or something else, I wonder?'

'I shall come straight to the point. I want you to see Susan Fuller, ask what she knows of her son's activities.'

'I hardly think she will talk to me.'

'She will, Ruben, and I shall tell you why. For the name of her son's killer, she's prepared to give God an undertaking that his company will not be held liable for her son's dodgy dealings over the bond deals. Now, for all intents and purposes, God hired me to find that out which means it can work in both our favours.'

'Let me get this straight. Not only do you want me to invite trouble into my shop, you also want me to play detective for Susan Fuller while you do what? Get paid for sitting on your laurels?'

'As we speak the book is in transit for examination.'

'Whoopee do.'

'Ruben, I cannot return to Wymondham. If I do, April Jones will not make contact and you really do need her to make contact. Now, I'm prepared to split the fee God is paying me, which is only fair.'

'How much?'

'Fifty thousand,' and bit her lip.

'Is that 5% of what I just gave him?'

She should have known better and groaned down the line. 'The truth is-'

'Yes, how do you spell that word? With difficulty I should imagine. You take 5% or come down here and finish off what you started. I have a shop to run or had that slipped your mind.'

'Before I was so rudely interrupted, I was going to tell you the truth but why should I bother. Your head has returned to the sand.'

No reply.

'Ruben?'

'What is the truth?'

'It was either me or someone else and if it was someone else there would be a risk of your past becoming exposed. I thought it fair to offer fifty thousand because my brains are worth more than yours.'

'So how do you expect to use them when you're there and I'm here using mine?'

Grey looked at the receiver and poked out her tongue. If she thought she could pull a fast one over Ruben Stone, she was very much mistaken. 'Okay, fifty-fifty.'

CHAPTER 14

'Come on, Charlie!'

The old man came trundling down the stairs in his mothballed suit, grabbed his overcoat and donned a cap shadowing his white whiskered face. 'Wat yew done to your hair?'

'Combed it.'

With the wind playing spitefully about their legs they ventured to one of the finest historic churches in all of East Anglia. Its confident bells, being a mixture of indulgence and discipline tolled to the funeral of Michael Fuller.

At the entrance, a few stragglers, locals who had given their shops to the sign of close, now gave their friendship to the bereaved mother who looked secretly mysterious behind her black-netted veil. She lifted her head and straightened, observed their oncoming. It would have been unseemly to appear uncontrolled.

'We're sorry fer your loss, my woman.'

'Thank you, Charlie,' and referred to Ruben in harsher tones. 'Have you come to gloat?'

He took that with a pinch of salt. 'Are the police any nearer in their enquiries?'

Mrs Susan Fuller never responded, turned and walked away, a loan divorcee more successful at both making money and keeping it. She remembered being temporarily unhinged after the shock of learning her son was dead, the stuttering incompetent ripple of a police investigation and the most apocalyptic example of gossip by Marge Dingle, and what she saw could, by those with a mind for it, be turned into financial ruin.

The Abbey was filled to half-capacity in the pews confronting the delicate golden Altar Screen, a masterpiece designed by Sir Ninian Comper. A string quartet played *it's my life* to give the bobbing and nodding audience time to reflect, to ponder on those words.

Then Father Dell held up his hands. The music ceased and talk subsided. Like others before him, he was solemn, the gravity and dignity of a priest with a caring heart and a serious disposition. Shortly after his literary sermon which he had hired from the ecclesiastical library, he genuflected at the altar and sauntered to the pulpit, closed his religious tome and looked up to deliver his speech.

'We are here today to say farewell to Michael Fuller, beloved son of Susan Fuller.' He let his gaze fall upon a silver urn holding precious ashes. 'In life and so in death, his remains will feed the ground upon which a tree shall grow. I cannot think of a more befitting gesture, giving something back to God's own world. It has ever pleased Him to prosper all Michael's undertakings, and I feel confident he has His blessing in this most perplexing time. Although Michael rarely attended mass, he never forgot the church. Christmas, he would provide our Lord's manger with straw and a complimentary session at his mother's practice. Let us pray.'

His proclamation complete, they knelt in silent communion. It was time for prayer and reflection, for the community to make their final farewells. And this they endured for five minutes, before the priest came down from his pulpit and gestured to the bereaved parent to take her position behind a shiny brass lectern made in the traditional form, the word of God carried on the wings of an eagle.

For the sake of her son and the course of business, she would have her say. It was the art of survival. Not a man coughed or created sound, not a woman rustled or sneezed. She lifted her veil. 'No parent should attend their child's funeral. No parent should attend their child's funeral with headlines and sub-headlines, with pictures and, above all, with accusations in which news now takes precedence over truth. My son may have been many things but he was not a crook as some would have us believe. What happened was cruel and meaningless.' She paused, dabbing her eyes with a finger, a dramatically different version from the one presented as the official image of the family. 'Whoever you are, and wherever you are, I will make you pay for the misery and senseless murder of my son.'

Some wept easily, sniffing, and healthily flushed as if they had been mourning the death of a dog, and others to the accompaniment of a string quartet performing *every breath you take I'll be watching you.* It was the oddest of funeral dirges and no expense was spared.

After a gawky period, people melted away through the exit point, separately, in opposite directions. Within minutes they would be spreading through the streets of Wymondham, putting the word out, throwing open their doors to a different kind of conversation.

In the background was Ruben, solemnity ruled as he watched a few idle feet gather round the bereaved mother, a combination of indulgence and sympathy.

'What a terrible tragedy.' It was April Jones seizing the moment, her sultry voice coming from behind. 'I understand you're looking for a shop assistant.'

Ruben turned to face her. 'May I ask why you're enquiring?'

'I'm at a loose end, could do with the money.'

'Your outfit costs more than I can pay for a week's work.' Play it cool, play it smart and turned his back on her. 'Try John Lewis, the pay is better.'

'I'd prefer to try here.' Her six inch heels side-stepped in front of him. 'We've never been formally introduced,' and proffered her hand. 'April Jones desperate for a job.'

'Ruben Stone desperate for someone who's not a five minute wonder.'

'Yes, I heard your last girl had to leave rather abruptly… sort of left you in the lurch.'

'Wait here. I have to pay my respects.' Ruben walked off in unshakeable confidence now that he had her interest and came to a halt in front of Susan Fuller. 'May I have a quiet word?'

Clutching the silver urn, she nodded and broke away from her fan club. 'What is it?'

'You want justice, I can provide it.'

'Come to the house, say about four.'

Ruben nodded in a farewell gesture before returning to April Jones. 'Walk with me. Give me your background.'

Wrapping her fur collar against the cutting wind, she kept to his pace. 'I used to live in London working for a PR firm in Cavendish Square. I was dismissed because the boss's wife thought I was a threat on their marriage.'

'Were you?'

'You should've seen what she looked like. Anyway, the whole bloody thing got sordid and messy. My flat-mate gave me notice so I decided to get away.'

'What made you choose Wymondham?'

'I went to Norwich and met Mick at his squash club, moved in with him for a bit until Tom Hutton gave me a room over his pub but he can't give me a full time job…'

April continued with her plausible lies, covering all the angles until they reached the shop with a magical window display. Here, her nose ran unchecked, sniffing a porthole to the rooms upstairs before Charlie arrived. He shook her hand as if she had the plague and between all three it was like a war game; identify threats, develop counter-strategies, and the entire time stay one step ahead.

'Charlie, I need to pick up those nails.'

'While you're out, buy a loaf fer Betty?'

'See you there then?'

After that coded message Ruben departed, committed to covering his tracks. He went to Clements and picked up the nails that were not really needed, bought a crusty loaf as if that mattered and wended his way towards the home in the dip by the river. Using Charlie's key, he pushed through the house tempering his atavistic response to Betty, dropped off the nails and loaf, and left via the back door.

Now scouring his surrounds, he wended his way along the river path then crossed the valley, arriving at Fuller's house just gone four. The smudge of mascara beneath her cinnamon eyes told him she had cried before he came here. But her voice was possessed by an indestructible barrier and she poured tea with an elegance of manner as though her approaches to life were bred and nourished from birth.

'I do hope this is not some kind of elaborate hoax to feed more lies to the press.'

Ruben leaned forward and took a biscuit. 'True, I've never been a fan of your handy work, using your son to gain an armful of properties but we do have one thing in common. Whoever killed him did so fearing he would alert me.' Ruben saw no immediate surprise and figured the only way to gain her confidence was to spill a little of himself. 'Let me say I am a keeper to something important.

Until recently nobody was the wiser, then someone walked into your son's life, or perhaps he walked into theirs to make economic sense.'

'Miss Grey?'

'Most certainly she turned my world upside down and also your son in parts. Yet it was she who pointed me in the direction of his latest conquest, April Jones. Did he mention her?'

There was a brief silence before her poise deserted her, assuming a friendly, avuncular tone. 'She met my son at his squash club and within two days had taken over this house, drinking champagne as if it had gone out of fashion. But I knew my son. He would never plant a girl in this house unless there was something in it for him.'

'Did you find out what?'

'Truth was far short in coming until that Grey woman dug her heels regarding Amy's house, stupid fool. So, I asked again, why open your door to a slut. He owed her for information provided about you. I never heard such poppycock in all my life. Or am I wrong, Ruben? Were you once a man called Jeffrey Cane?'

Ruben uncrossed his legs. This was going to be painful. 'How confidential is this?'

She took from her bag a packet of cigarettes, smoke drifting over the weary discoloured bruising beneath her fifty-year-old eyes, her face drained white with a dark red mouth, had all the mournful vulnerability of a clown. 'If I had wanted to penalize you for the death of my son, your name would be splashed across the nationals. Your one saving grace is that I knew where you were at the time of his assault. I'm past caring, Ruben. We had a terrible argument. Regretful things said. Even so, I told him at the time, it was no business of ours who you were or what you did, that to stir things up could bring both our reputations into question, especially with the Grey woman nosing into our affairs. Could he see it? No. He was an angry child who wanted revenge for the black eye you gave him. Worse, he was besotted with April Jones and refused to get rid of her. She shed no tears for his loss, had the temerity to tell me I could send her things on to the Green Dragon.'

'You saw me?'

'I was to see my son that night, on my way from London when the fog came down heavy, and there you were right in front of me turning off into a layby. I carried on a hundred yards and stayed at the hotel, too nervous to do anything else.'

'Has Tom Hutton been in touch?'

'I shall honour my son's agreement.'

'You might get planning permission.'

'I might get justice.'

'What do the police have to say?'

'Try ringing the station for incompetence. I understand there was a call made to his office before Tom arrived. Do you have any idea who that might be?'

'Same here, no idea, only possible thought sat with April Jones. Why would your son trudge in the fog to meet her when he could meet her at this house? I do feel, however, she knows who, ergo, reason I hired her today to serve behind the counter, not sure if my business will survive on that legacy. Did your son mention any new name, or someone seen with April Jones?'

'I never lived out of my son's pocket, Ruben. And most certainly I wanted nothing to do with that slut. Damn fool. He had his father's brains.'

'He wasn't at the funeral.'

'His real father died leaping from a plane, both of them fools. I divorced my second husband ten years ago. He thought he could waltz in and make comfortable by my efforts.' She felt the pot. 'Would you like more tea?'

'I would like my grandfather's shop.'

She paused at this and sat back down. 'I suppose it would be fair to give you an opportunity to buy it at present day value.'

'Less thirty per cent and the rent paid.'

'I see no reason to be generous.'

'You want the person who killed your son?'

'I shall have the person who killed my son.'

'That rather depends how generous I feel toward Miss Grey.'

'What has she got to do with it?'

'Shilling hired her to get you the name. That was the deal, wasn't it? You had to make a deal, Susan. You had Shilling by the balls. Fair Life allowed your son to sell bonds without checking if he was qualified. The day he died, Shilling told him he could keep the agency providing he took the FSA competence exam and full responsibility should his clients take action. Interestingly, he refused to do both, expressing greater value on his ego than on the business.'

'Who else knows this?'

'Well obviously Miss Grey.' Ruben placed his empty cup on the coffee table. 'If the incentive was there, I would work with Grey in order to identify the killer or I could pension Charlie, give you the property and disappear off this planet.'

'What makes you think she's incapable of doing it alone? After all, she caught you.'

'Have you seen her? Has she called? We are dealing with something more than a case of fraud.'

'Do you have the money?'

'I will do.'

'Then I shall draft up the papers.'

'You know, a person can only sleep in one bed, sit in one chair and eat at one table. Why need so much when things that matter slip through your fingers?'

The distress was written on her face, miserable with the horrible beginnings of tears. Nothing was ever quite what it seemed, Ruben mused and took his cue to leave. She was a skilled player in the art of legal and business matters but she was also a despairing mother grieving for the loss of her son.

Close to the museum, in a small terrace, Sam Dingle was dressed in his soldier's uniform and packing his bag. He had shown unimaginable bravery and resilience against Iraqi insurgents. It was a miracle he had survived and one that would need to be repeated.

'Ding.' Ruben entered, closing the door softly behind him. 'Going back?'

'Got the call an hour ago.' He bent to pick up his lucky coin off the floor. 'Remember this, Ruby?'

'You were reluctant to tell me you were joining the army, a penny for your thoughts, yes, you kept it all this while.' Ruben brought out his pocket watch and flipped the cover. 'I don't need to give you another penny for your thoughts.'

A capsule passed from one hand to another. It could be a land mine or a grenade, its trajectory and source unseen, or it could be a merciless siege among burning wreckage, left alive long enough to reach inside and liberate the capsule. Nemesis indeed followed hubris. It was within his grasp, sat in the soldier's open palm. There were many who would not be partaking in a second chance at life. He closed his fingers upon it and wordlessly embraced his friend.

'Never saw you at the funeral.'

'Hell, I see enough where I'm going.' The soldier back wiped a tear. 'Was the sex kitten there?'

'She was, not out of respect but to get a job.'

'Ah, she took the bait then, seems Grey was right after all.'

'When is she not? How you getting back, train, I'll walk with you?'

'Not going for a bit, have to deal with Mum, the usual don't-forget-to-wear-clean-underpants and eat-your-sandwiches.' They smiled. 'Did you go see Susan Fuller?'

'She said the Jones woman fed the dossier on me to her son, which makes me think he had me sussed all along.'

'Why say that?'

'It stands to reason he contacted Harcourt, how else did the old man know where to send April Jones.'

'How was it left?'

'A bit dodgy seeing she knows who I am.'

'You watch your step, my man. Like mother, like son.' Zipping the bag, the soldier donned his cap and gave a salute. 'Write me.'

'You write me, lazy sod.'

Ruben travelled on with the wind in his face like a fresh baptism, reached the worn out path leading down to the house by the river where his grandfather was there to greet him.

'Betty's heving a nap on the sofa.' A cold beer escaped from the fridge. 'Our customers are going to hev a heart attack if she keeps bending down with no knickers.'

'No knickers?'

'I had an erection lasting longer than it takes to smoke a pipe.'

'I daren't ask what you did with it. What's for tea?'

'Cheese omelette, alroit?'

Ruben nodded. 'Ding got called back for duty.'

'Shame, yew shall miss him. How'd it go with the Fuller woman?'

As Ruben went on to explain the events of his meeting with the bereaved parent, Charlie darted about the kitchen leaving an awful mess, followed by the drudgery of cleaning it up while Ruben sometimes ate standing up, tearing crusts off the loaf with his fingers, a hand-to-mouth feeding that expressed his hunger.

Sometime later he poured himself a sherry, made comfortable on a chair in the hall and telephoned Grey. It was so good to hear her voice.

'Hello, Ruben. Good news I hope.'

'Jones took the bait at the funeral.'

'How did that go?'

'Odd, very odd, string quartet in dicky bow ties and a sort of multi-vitamin strike at the press coverage by Susan Fuller.' Ruben paused to the sound of a male voice. 'Are you with someone?'

A door closed. 'There,' she said, 'we can talk. So, she took the bait?'

'Of course, I played it cool.'

'Naturally.'

'I also had a word with Susan Fuller.'

'Great. What emerged?'

'Two things emerged. Fuller made me as Jeffrey Cane, contacted Harcourt who sent April Jones to fill him in. And she knew nothing about the deal he made with Tom Hutton.'

'Then we must assume he was blackmailing someone else.'

'You got it in one.'

'Was it her who telephoned that afternoon?'

'No. The police told her the call was made from a public telephone box, so no luck there. Where are you?'

'At home.'

'Who with?'

'Bobble, he's not been very well. So how was it left between you?'

'She has no interest in exposing me.'

'Did you speak to her regarding the shop?'

'She went for the deal.'

'Oh, that's great.'

'But not so great for others, Grey. If we don't come up with the goods, I can't see her feeling as generous with them.'

'We will, trust me. We're on the right track. There were tiny particles of blood on the back cover of that book, confirming my theory. Sir John did shoot Geraldine and Neil.'

'Who's the bloke in the background?'

'The vet.'

'Making home visits?'

'He's devoted to his job. I must go. Speak to you later.'

Ruben slowly dropped the receiver on to its cradle, not entirely convinced a cat existed at all. His hand clenched hard around the glass, his knuckles rising hard. *How the hell did I get in so deep?*

Rather than spend a night with the old folks, he grabbed his coat and walked home with a feeling of being followed. Such alarms were neither threats nor prophecies. Above, a pigeon flew low and landed on a concrete sill pecking at a pane of glass. The window shot up and out popped the head of a great shaggy animal.

'Watcha, Ruby.'

'Fancy a pint, Bill? I'm buying.'

'Say no more.' The bird was grabbed, the window shot down and ten seconds later Bill thudded his size nine boots on the pavement. 'That was a roit ol' do at the funeral. Did you go? I never saw you.'

'I was there.'

'Here, I had a funny call from Mrs Fuller. She asked if I wanted to buy back my house.'

'And what did you say?'

'I have no money.'

'Did you tell her why?'

'That I did, Ruby. I said her son sold me a duff bond and blow me down if she didn't offer to forego the rent until the markets picked up. Now what do you make of that?'

He made of it as *covering her arse* and swung into the Green Dragon with no surprise shown. 'Quiet tonight, Amy. Where's Tom?'

'Upstairs in his office, I think. What can I get you, the usual?'

'Make it a whisky and a pint for Bill.' Ruben turned into the room and leaned idly against the bar, spying two locals cutting cards for crib.

But few cards were played that night. The door flung open and in marched a face contorted in rage. Tom Hutton and his floosy had been found out. On his wife's lips was only one word, in her mind a single thought. She swept through and ascended the stairs, bent on punishment. And what followed thereafter was an outburst of unspeakable language, divorce a certainty, poverty most likely, and a lifetime of fragile trophies flung out the window. Everyone craned their necks and watched the decent of a cricket bat plummet to the pavement, crash and trash, followed by silver cups, small and large, ping and pong, the sweetest and most sacred of music. Gradually her blazing tongue weakened, the spasm was over and everyone rushed to their places when she came downstairs, being composed of all that had fashioned her long past.

'Amy,' she said calmly, 'when you see whore face tell her she's welcome to that shit.'

A few seconds later, shamed faced Hutton made an appearance to retrieve his things. Ruben was already outside collecting them.

'I can't figure you out, Tom. Josie is a good looking woman, good mother and faithful by all accounts yet it's not enough to keep your dick in your pants.'

The fool shrugged and went upstairs, part laden with his broken past. Hutton had no intention of returning home, a home now out of bounds. There were his own affairs to consider, his own skin to preserve. 'I know I've been a bloody fool,' he admitted and placed a battered trophy on the shelf with a deep sigh. 'Sex with Josie is pleasant, but with April, well, it's nothing I've ever known. I can ask for anything I want. There's no fear of being judged, of being thought dirty, or perverted, or selfish.'

'Not much of an excuse.'

'What I did was unforgiveable, I know that.'

'How did Josie find out?'

'Someone tipped her off, don't know who. I saw you chatting her up, taking her back to your place.'

'She was asking for a job.'

'I used that one on Josie.' Hutton smiled, though he had nothing much to smile about, and poured a couple of neat whiskies before sitting down to face Ruben. 'The way I see it, you can give her a bed.'

'The way I see it, she can keep the one here.'

'Are you serious in giving her a job?'

'She says she needs the money and I need a girl behind my counter.'

'Look, she's a freeloader, Ruby. Just after Mick copped it, she came here. Who was I to complain when she told me she worked a bar, discovered she was better at working on me. It's not an excuse, just a stupid move. You want my advice, take what you can and give nothing back.'

'How did you break the news to Susan Fuller?'

'Now there's a noble woman, Ruby, every bit decent and understanding, honoured the transaction. Now I have to figure out how to get the money from Josie.'

CHAPTER 15

Ruben swung round with a start then turned off the lathe, looking down at a pair of liberated pink nipples jutting tightly against silk, defying any man to remain unaffected.

'I know this cool little sushi bar,' she said.

'Not into uncooked fish.'

'What are you into?'

Truth would be helpful. 'Customers, or have you forgotten they exist?' Daring her to return to the counter, the sex kitten grinned wickedly, spun on her six inch heels and left. 'We're in big trouble, Charlie.'

'Best yew feed the cat some sushi before she eats our customers alive.'

It was true. On each occasion when April Jones served a customer, she tested their patience, made no concessions for the youngsters and too frequently powdered her nose, attaching enormous importance to her pretentious self-image and the ability in which she successfully used it to attract men.

So, in an attempt to crush her vanity, Ruben found her in the throes of polishing her nails with infuriating gusto. 'Had a thought,' he said and she looked up in shameless seduction, 'they do terrific barbeque ribs at the fish and chip shop.'

'We eat with our fingers?'

'We eat here with instructions on how to serve customers.'

'Oh dear, will I have my botty smacked?'

Leaving tainted with the spoils of sexual inferences, Ruben would keep Grey in mind, as a refuge, in event of weakening, or, at worst, succumbing to his natural instincts.

An unwanted glimpse in the mirror and he briefly caught the face of Jeffrey Cane, love-struck over a younger woman capable of opening a man's senses to physical pleasure and producing a certain sexual besottedness in their behaviour. That sounded so familiar and not too dissimilar to the views expressed by Tom Hutton who was not such a fool to mistake his feelings for love, or anywhere close.

In the workshop Ruben withdrew into his asylum and became ever more hopeful that perhaps the last episode had scared her into thinking she might be given the sack. Maybe she would just simply confess, and he could continue along his happy path of building a business on the cusp of success.

But when the shop closed at five, and unbeknown to Ruben who was on his way from the fish shop, April Jones went to the Green Dragon and returned with her things.

'I just couldn't afford to stay there,' she said easing her suitcase down, 'unless, of course, you wish to give me an advance on my wages?'

A layer of sweat broke across his forehead. He never foresaw this and was instantly mute.

'Can I stay, please, pretty please, just until I can get myself sorted?'

Or until I can get you sorted, he thought and picked up her suitcase, dumped it in the spare room and walked back to the kitchen gathering his wits. Here was poise and audacity, the gravity of his situation now weighing heavy. There was every possibility of her seducing him in the middle of the night and with no Charlie to keep him in check, the outcome could be disastrous. Flinging back a cupboard door, he foraged for survival and dissolved three of Charlie's sleeping tablets in her wine.

She came in smiling, dimples forming perfectly, her bleached-blond hair falling a few inches below her shoulders. 'It seems like only yesterday when I first saw you.'

'It was yesterday.' He ripped two ribs apart, slinging sauce into his eyebrows. That just about summed up his situation. 'What did Tom have to say?'

'He wasn't there. I expect he'll be glad to get rid of me, especially since his dopey wife disapproved.'

'You were having an affair, how disapproving could she be.'

'Is it my fault I was flat broke? So, what, I paid in favours, what you would do in my situation.'

'In your situation I would have stayed in a job until I could afford to move.'

'Far be it from me to stand on a moralistic high ground but you did the same with the witch.'

'Far be it from me to educate your mind but she acted like a lady and served our customers well.'

In the short silence that followed, and the reason why she was so thin, April left her ribs untouched and turned in her chair, crossing her mile-long legs. 'Why did she leave?'

'Her business was concluded.'

'Mick said something about her coming down here to investigate an insurance fraud.'

And no doubt said a lot more. He licked his fingers before wiping them on a paper serviette and held the glass to his lips. 'I'm curious, why shop work?'

'To be fair, this job is only temporary until I can find something more suitable for these assets.'

'Assets?'

'Do you think I was blessed with these looks? They were bought and painfully received for the reason why men don't look at frumps.'

Brains would be less painful. 'Tell me about Mick Fuller?'

'I met him at the squash club.'

'So you said yesterday I believe.'

'You have a funny little habit of meeting your brows when you get annoyed. Did you know that?'

'I can keep them knitted together if it helps.'

'Oh, this is boring, so what, I shagged Mick because I like sex. He never had any complaints, only his prig of a mother complained. I can't say I blame her, after all it was her house.' She inspected the wine label. 'Have you got anything decent?'

'Champagne is beyond my reach.'

'I'm not.'

'I am.'

'You're not much fun to be with, sweetie. Are you gay?'

Unable to think of any response, Ruben grinned like an idiot, like he was about to fall asleep and glared at the glass he was holding. Oops!

It was perhaps a subconscious act due to the level of anxiety in her company, or perhaps he had totally under-estimated her guile. His one thought now was to protect his castle from ruin. Fighting the almost irrepressible need for sleep, he picked his way to the workshop and snuck into his secret room. There, he closed himself in like a cosy over a teapot and slept among its treasures, comforting, frightful and familiar.

He dreamed of days long ago, of a time when his socks slipped down to his ankles and before that as a fifty-year-old gerontologist called Jeffrey Cane, all promises, lies, love and truth. What else mattered but the woman frantic for his touch? The visions were crude but jaggedly vital, for in them they revealed the psychological motives of the individuals involved. And then, with startling clarity, the features of Helena Vale curved into the features of April Jones, no two people were more alike.

Midnight passed and the early hours of morning progressed towards dawn. He woke to the smell of wood smoke, rolled off the cot, washed his hands over his face and drew into the workshop where the old man was smoking his pipe by a warming stove.

'Come and hev a cup of tea, Ruby.'

'What time do you make it?'

'Just gone seven and before yew ask, she's fast asleep.'

'How did you know she was here?'

'Hard not to when she snores like a cow.'

'Charlie,' he said and took to a stool. 'She's Helena Vale.'

The old man blinked comically a few times and scratched his head. 'Forgive me fer saying but didn't she die from a stab wound?'

'There was a slim chance of recovery but she had access to her capsule. It's the only thing that makes sense, why I keep getting this feeling she's familiar yet unfamiliar. Helena had a sexual appetite though I wasn't complaining at the time and a sick sense of humour.'

'Are yew telling me she hid her capsule up-'

'Yes.'

'I racked my brains all this while and the answer wus in front of me when she bent down.' The old man tapped him fondly on the arm. 'Tell me, Ruby, and mind yew say the truth. Are yew still in love with her?'

Emphatically, Ruben shook his head. 'I've been an utter fool, Charlie, a complete and utter fool. As Jeffrey Cane, I was a fool and up until this point an even bigger fool. Grey knew…she knew it was important I discover this for myself.'

'It seems to me that Harcourt fellow planted a sex bomb under the laboratory bench, yew not being Mr. Universe might just part with his formula.'

'But fate deals her a raw straw. There she is, in hospital waking up to a prosaic husband in an uncertain future so why not take a new future? And where does that leave Harcourt?'

'With a man heving the onset of dementia, and so desperate is he, follows yew home and finds yew dead. We know that because Grey had that book tested for blood. Now where does that leave him?'

'Years in hope, perhaps…my guess April returned to blackmail him. She had to have looked up the past, what happened to Jeffrey Cane, and figured out who murdered his wife and her lover. He keeps her in luxury, probably paid for her facial reconstruction and-'

'Well! I never, fancy that! Just goes to show yew wat money can buy.'

'It can buy almost anything, Charlie, except love, the kind of love some people are lucky enough to find. I was like Tom, if truth be told, my ego boosted by her flattery. I know this to be true because if I had loved her, I would have trusted her. Instead, I blamed myself for her death, experienced a kind of delight in torturing myself. I have often asked myself whether this wasn't simply a device which I used against myself to give me the right to forget.'

'But yew remembered, remembered it all, sound the better fer it.' The old man chuffed and ruffled his hair. 'My grandson found himself. I read somewhere each generation fulfils their destiny by the product of others so when a child chooses to take a leap forward, it makes distance by acting the rebel. Your road, your choice, my Ruby, I shan't question your plan.'

'What plan?'

'Yew must hev a plan. We can't hev her here wreaking havoc fer much longer.'

'No, I agree but what?'

Within the secret walls of his laboratory, Ruben closed himself in and rolled up his shirt sleeves. If nothing else, he needed to be smarter, preferably a lot smarter and applied the science of his mind, recalling Amy's words long ago; *if you could make someone dead with your mind, would it be Mick Fuller?* Death, of course, in the physical sense was out of the question even if shown the demise to be brought down by the vicissitudes of fate. No. He had to be a hell of a lot smarter.

As the daylight hours elapsed in the putrid smell of chemicals, the future of Ruben Stone was still not certain. He leaned idly on his elbow, a clenched fist supporting his chin, his left hand working the keys of his laptop. Beside him, a plate of ham sandwiches curled at the edges, forgotten.

Quietly the old man emerged having suffered his fair share of damage. 'She's had more visits to the toilet than I've had hot dinners and nagging me stupid to see wat you're up to.'

'Then let's not keep her waiting.' Ruben stretched, his fists knuckling childishly on each side of his head, his gaze held at the screen which petered to a gloomy vagueness. Then he pocketed a small phial and went into the adjacent workshop.

Removing his sculpting knife off the rack, he pulled up a stool by the iron-cast stove and began to whittle, absorbed so rapidly on Grey's facsimile that April Jones was hardly noticed as she stood in front of him.

'Why are you here?'

'To earn money.'

'Money can be earned other ways.'

'At present it's here.'

'At present you lie.' He glanced up. It would be his pleasure and her agony. 'You spend more time on the throne than you do in the shop.' And then he carried on whittling. 'Should I have a camera installed to find the truth?'

'I'm not cut-out for shop work.'

'Tell me something I don't know.'

'I would if you'd just stop twiddling and look at me.'

Already he could hear the suppressed irritation in her voice, let the silence lag before setting aside his work and stepping up to the kettle. 'Coffee?'

'Black, no sugar.' She sat down crossing her legs, giving him a tantalizing glimpse of a lace stocking top. 'Have you ever been sky-diving?'

'I prefer to keep my feet on the ground.'

'And waste your life carving witches and hob goblins, fairy tale creatures to sell over the counter. Neither will count when you're dead and buried.'

'Is that what you do, live on the edge of reason?'

'Ha!' She held back her bleached-blond head and laughed, making a mockery of his statement. 'Do you know what they say around here…Ruben Stone, the boulder to shoulder the misfortunes of others.'

'What is so wrong in helping your fellow man?'

'What you do is buy loyalty and silence of this town.'

'Who buys your loyalty and silence? John Harcourt?'

'Do you know who I am?'

'Have you forgotten your name already?'

Again, a short burst of cheerful bliss to accommodate his humour and licked her lips like licking juices from an orange. Then she looked into her mug, suspiciously. 'What happened to you last night....could it be you drank from the wrong glass?'

'Could it be you drank from the right one?'

She stepped up to the sink and threw her coffee down the drain, made another from the hot water left in the kettle. 'You always were so damn predictable, Jeffrey. I presume you still remember who you were.'

'Did you ever love me, Helena?'

'You were a misguided fool, took everything so fucking seriously.'

'So, everything was a lie.'

'Not everything. I did so enjoy our late night romps in the lab. You were correct in your analysis. The memory develops at puberty, although I gather you had a little problem with yours.'

'I remember a woman willing to take her life in preference for a new one with me. Or was that too a lie?'

She looked at him over the rim of her coffee cup, trying to read his reaction but Ruben sat rock still and waited. 'A doctor's wife wasn't the life for me, and glad John Harcourt made his proposition after a roll in the hay. All I had to do was get the formula and I would be swimming in the Bahamas. No. That was not going to bloody happen because you were a sanctimonious old fart refusing to part with anything other than your mistakes. It was me who guessed your problem, yes, the onset of dementia…oh God was that a miracle in more ways than one.'

'Did you tell John?'

'Wake up and smell the bacon, did I tell John his prize was rapidly going downhill, nothing I could do about it…until…' Her gaze alighted on the grilled window, rubbing her left arm, watching the winter cold night as if the answer was somewhere out there.

'Until?'

'I thought we could make it, kept thinking of the possibilities. You said it never mattered who we turned out to be, we could always do it again. I even wrote a book for the sheer fun of it and next I'm waking up in a hospital bed with my dope of a husband asleep in the chair.'

'You took the capsule.'

'Had no choice, sweetie. I looked a mess.'

'And returned to blackmail John Harcourt.'

'I was born into poverty, nothing was said about that or having a mother spending her money on fags and boyfriends, lazy cow…things are different now, Jeffrey, they can be different for both of us, together, like you said, a new life with lots of money. We can-'

'Who killed Mick Fuller?'

'You did, sweetie.'

'Would I be asking if I did?'

Abruptly, and to Ruben's horror, she toppled off her stool in a short burst of piteous cry and collapsed in a heap on the floor. The mug found its resting place in two parts at his feet. One could die for any reason. It might be liver poisoning, cancer of the breast or even one drop too many in the kettle. Sudden death syndrome had done for April Jones - stress caused a fatal arrhythmic attack.

Elsewhere, the old man stood in the shadows of the shop stroking his beard, content to linger with his thoughts until a tap on the shoulder and a gesture to follow.

'Her heart collapsed.'

'Do I take it she's dead?'

'That's what happens when you got no heart.'

'But she has a habit of coming back.' The old man knelt, placed his ear to her chest and just to be certain, looked up her dress. 'She's dead alroit.'

'Glad we got that sorted.'

'Wat happened?'

'I made her a coffee, left enough hot water in the kettle for another, slipped in the truth drug and the double bluff worked. She sang like a baby.'

'Who killed Fuller?'

'She thought I did.'

They looked at each other, nodded then attacked the malt, speaking without raised voices, moving smoothly over old ground and never tripping over the body that lay as an obstacle in their wake. Sometimes they heard mysterious sounds, the fire sank and died in the stove, as did the fire of stupidity.

'The way I see it,' the old man said, 'there's but one thing to be done. We bury her.'

'Where, when we have no garden?'

'Betty has a garden.'

'She also has nosey neighbours.'

'Then the cemetery.'

'And let it be shown a disturbed grave?'

'How about posting her to China?'

Ruben just crackled and stared at the cold stove as though he had an ace up his sleeve. 'Why not use someone else's garden…a very big garden.'

'Whose do yew hev in mind?'

'The man who sent her to me.'

With dog-like grins they set to, wrapped the match-stick body in a sheet and accommodated the boot of the Sunbeam Alpine. It was Ruben who took the wheel for the journey ahead, leaving Charlie to rest for the dig. They reasoned, quite rightly, that Sir John Harcourt's disquiet would be swallowed up by his larger anxiety on finding a make-shift grave for the body under his compost heap.

Bury St. Edmunds appeared in a starfish of light dilating in a pool of distance. It was at this point they went over the details. Ruben would keep Harcourt busy for no less than an hour giving Charlie time enough to find his way, would probably work slightly out of breath, aided by the odd puff of oxygen.

So, in keeping with the plan, the motor stopped half way along the private drive. The old man gathered his spade, and shouldered the body, disappearing in the undergrowth. Ruben carried on, parked outside the main entrance of the white colonnaded mansion, and was dutifully greeted by Windsor who showed him to the library. For it was there, silhouetted briefly against the light of a desk lamp, Sir John Harcourt sat, drowning in his own malt as if he had been waiting for this moment.

'Drink, Jeffrey?'

'This is not a social call.'

'It was never my intention for this to happen.'

'Is that the line of a politician bidding farewell or the line of a murderer?'

'I see you have pieced it together.'

'Whatever happened to the man who was satisfied with exploration, content in the wisdom of science?'

'He fell into the company of Helena Vale.'

'Both it would seem with a gift for corruption and a penchant for betrayal.'

Harcourt drew further into the light. 'Forgive the deception, Jeffrey. I was merely seeking to put you in her direction when last we spoke, and yes, omitting the foolhardy part I played all those years ago. I was besieged by madness, all for the want of that formula, to make a new life in wiser capacity. The formula was never in question for general consumption, this I so swear.'

'Yet still you sit alive.'

'I sit alive to atone for my sins. When Helena returned, she was born into poverty, money her motivation to keep safe my secret. True, our arrangement altered when a gentleman by the name of Michael Fuller contacted me. Chair bound, I was hardly in a position to seek you out. All I wanted is what you have given. All Helena wanted was the formula. I did not condone her actions but that is her way, a risk taker, agent provocateur.'

'Did you have Fuller killed?'

'We assumed it to be you.'

'What possible motive would I have?'

'Then all three are none the wiser.'

Ruben changed his mind and poured himself a stiff brandy. It was not so much keeping the chair-bound octogenarian busy but rather quenching his irritation. 'My life is like a cartwheel, rolling down a road of your making. You should have paid Helena off, anything, done something to shut her up. Instead, you pay her to waltz into my life knowing what she is capable of doing.' He watched the face, saw his words bite deep. 'Whether by design or accident, she must have told someone else about me. She got Fuller killed, has alienated decent people against one another but some good has come of it, perhaps. Who else knows of my history?'

'It occurred the fatality of Michael Fuller may have been to protect you. If Helena divulged your history to Michael Fuller, then it goes without saying he would have you by the balls. I understood when last we spoke you expressed yourself as a thorn in his side.'

'What benefit would it serve them?'

'Perhaps to keep a loved one safe?'

Or perhaps to keep the secret safe. 'Who was the test subject?'

'I cannot say.'

'Cannot or will not?'

'What does your Miss Grey think?'

'Her interest has waned in light of completing her task to the satisfaction of God.'

'Then you have no fall-back position.'

'It's a price worth paying.'

The octogenarian was so gaunt, so ashen grey it was possible he had remained alive for reasons other than those stated. He pulled out a drawer in a quivering state and brought to the desk a small pouch laden with five carat diamonds. 'Let me make amends.'

'And be in your debt.'

'Not for long, Jeffrey. Now that I have confessed my sins, I shall leave with a clear conscience.'

'I would far rather be given the test subject's name.'

'To do what? To pry and question, to stir what should remain unstirred? You think he stands alone with just himself to consider? You think I would not betray a trust if I believed it would do some good? If there is one thing left to say before I die is to wish you well. Now please....take this and let us part on good terms....who knows, I might just look you up after my rebirth.'

It just seemed so final, so immoral to be bought off by a handful of diamonds and let a man think he was returning with his memories. 'If there is one thing left to say before I leave is to wish you reconsider being Prime Minister.'

Harcourt smiled and kept on smiling even though it was no smiling matter. 'Wit has never left your side, Jeffrey. I so missed those days. Come, indulge this old fool and take his parting gift.'

'I shall put it to good use.'

'In that I have no doubt.'

The smile from Sir John Harcourt was weaker when Ruben walked off with his thoughts dwelling on the intrigue of Fuller's killer, his steady pace carrying him on to the motor. Kill for the sake of protecting a loved one, or kill for the sake of keeping the secret safe? He swung the motor round and stopped half-way along the drive.

Charlie dropped in as if he had just licked the cream off the top of a milk bottle and sat back closing his eyes.

'Everything okay?' Ruben asked.

'As good as it gets, boy.'

'Charlie, did you kill Fuller?'

The old man cocked an eye half open. 'Has Harcourt been messing with your mind?'

'He put forward a notion which I hadn't considered. Since Helena confirmed she did not know, and neither did he, it stands to reason Fuller's killer acted on their own, either to keep me safe or keep the secret safe.'

'Hev yew fergotton I wus with Grey when Fuller got killed.'

'Grey had already left the shop.'

'Hev yew asked her the same question?'

'No.'

'So, wat makes her different from me?'

CHAPTER 16

In the great metropolitan city of London where people fused like a patchwork quilt, Grey was wending her way to a glass and chrome bar on the corner of Petticoat Lane.

Up until now, she had been hard pressed to locate the elusive test case *Erik*, convinced that he fitted somewhere in Harcourt's plan, and this being the case, theoretically, sooner or later, contact between them would happen. It was a long shot, the only shot she had. But watching Harcourt's mansion was a tiring and time consuming business. Cold drinks, rubbery sandwiches, and go-behind-the bushes, the whole situation had an abandoned air of farcical practicality until a change in Harcourt's daily routine brought results.

From point of sale, a woman's hands were full of care, laden with coffee and secret dread. Hardly an inch above five-foot, this mother of two came to rest the tray in a quiet corner. 'Not sure if you wanted cappuccino or ordinary.'

'This is fine.' Grey slipped off her gloves and unbuttoned her coat. 'Am I correct in assuming your husband is in the dark?'

The nod of a head and Mary slipped off her scarf, tucking it inside her bag. 'You shook me a little when you mentioned the name Jeffrey Cane.'

'Yes, I rather gathered that from your tone of voice over the telephone. Let me just say this is between us, I promise.'

'What do you want from me, Miss Grey?'

'Please, call me Grey. Basically, I just need information. Are you aware of a gentleman called Ruben Stone?'

'No.'

'Were you once Erik from Sweden?'

'Are you a reporter?'

'Heaven's no. Simply put, I'm a private investigator looking into the background of Ruben Stone...or rather to be more precise Jeffrey Cane.

They're one of the same, actually.' She waved it away, brought out her notepad and fell into a quiet melancholy, sipping her coffee and remembering when last they spoke, how he sounded so bleak and despondent, herself unable to convey her thoughts but wishing she could.

Mary broke the moment. 'You were saying?'

'Yes, confusing, because Ruben gave a second chance to an Erik from Sweden, born again a Swede and here I am looking at a very lovely and educated woman with a distinctive English accent. I take it you were born again?'

'I was never a Swede, a boy, yes. John Harcourt had his own reasons to keep my identity a secret. My then father was his closest friend…and me…well a sickly fourteen-year-old who never quite cut the mustard.'

'Who was the Swede?'

'I have no idea.'

'So, who administered your dosage?'

'John Harcourt's best friend.'

'Can you be more specific?'

'Neil Pembroke.'

Grey sat back, amazed. 'Neil Pembroke was your father?'

'I don't wish to sound rude but I feel very nervous talking to you. You said very little over the telephone and I'm not sure if I want to continue this line of questioning unless you tell me what this is all about.'

Having intuitively sensed Mary was genuine Grey felt the explanation was long overdue and sat forward, lowering her voice. 'I was sent to investigate an insurance fraud, to wit Ruben Stone was my quarry. It soon transpired it was not he who defrauded my client but rather the men with whom he assisted in death, perhaps a little misguided but nevertheless he did what he did on compassionate grounds. Sadly, during my investigations a profoundly nosey local estate agent was murdered. Now my job is to find out who murdered him.'

'Look no further than the reincarnation of Jeffrey Cane. Did you know he killed his wife and my then father?'

'As a matter of fact, it was Sir John.'

'Don't you think I looked into that? Cane's fingerprints were on the gun. His wife was having an affair with Neil Pembroke and-'

Grey held up her hand to refrain her from going further. 'Trust me, Mary. Jeffrey Cane was already dead when Sir John found him. I have irrefutable proof to show he planted the evidence. You see, Jeffrey was caught in a love triangle, deceit and betrayal by the people he trusted, and then as Ruben Stone, his nightmares continued, recent events have been a harrowing experience not knowing who's after his formula. If I could just get a handle on your background, it would be really appreciated. Can you tell me why you met up with Sir John?'

'He telephoned out of the blue, said it was to my advantage we meet. He told me he had followed my career with great interest, that he was now leaving for a new life and gave me a few uncut diamonds by way of a thank-you for keeping things quiet, not that I want to shout about it.' Only pausing to take a sip of her coffee, Mary continued. 'I've been so lucky, Grey. I had wonderful parents second time round, still do. Without their love and support, things could have been so different.'

'This Erik,' Grey said and flipped back to her notes. 'Do any of these dates ring a bell…1973, the year of the so-called trial, and 1979, the year of the so-called arrival?'

'1973 was the year I died and 1979 was the year when my parents made contact with Sir John. Not all my memories returned but I had this number buzzing in my head, pictures and names, very frightening and very confusing.'

'What do you remember of your other life?'

Mary sighed. What should have been a minor infraction proved a major catastrophe. 'My parents were separated. At least I remembered not having a mother to take me to school. And I can't say I was a happy child. And I can't say I felt loved. I was a thorough disappointment then it got worse when I contracted Tuberculosis.'

'Can you tell me what happened?'

'He, that is Neil Pembroke, took me to see John Harcourt, and together they explained my only cure was in a capsule, that I would have a new life, a healthier life and that when I was old enough I would return and be reunited with my father. What was I supposed to know at fourteen? The next stage of my new and early life was mostly lived in nightmares. I had horrible dreams, awful headaches, cried a lot but then what else can one expect. Setting aside all that, things became a little clearer by the time I was five, not entirely clear but enough to cause concern to my parents. They went to see them and from what I gathered, Neil Pembroke tried to buy me like bidding for a Rembrandt. But my parents stuck to their guns and threatened to expose them if they tried anything on. That's why I felt so loved and protected. I was never out of their sight.'

'But eventually you met Sir John.'

'Yes, I wanted to see him. I was curious as to what happened to Neil so he showed me the newspaper article. God forgive me, I was overjoyed.' Mary shrugged and glanced at her watch. 'I told my husband I was Christmas shopping.'

'What happened afterwards?'

'That was it. Never saw him again until yesterday then your note was pushed through my letter box last night.'

'It was a gamble. I followed Sir John and thought it strange he would meet a woman at a petrol station, so I followed you but when I saw your house I thought it was odd, a little cottage in the country with fresh bread cooling on the kitchen sill. That never rang baddie.'

'Strange, very strange, I don't feel up tight talking about it. I thought I would. I thought bringing up old memories would stress me out. In fact, I feel quite relieved.'

'I know someone who would feel relieved if you would consider meeting him.'

'Why does he want to see me?'

'He's a scientist as well as a carpenter…the truth is, Mary, Sir John fed him false data regarding the test subject. If he could get genuine feedback, it would help him to comprehend more about his discovery. Such as the nightmares you experienced, how you felt about remembering your past as a male, what your thoughts were to a new life. His was not exactly a trip on the carousel but rather on a big dipper.'

'Do you know what I do? I'm a doctor, and I shouldn't be saying this because it's against our code of ethics but there's been many a time I would gladly pull the plug on some of my patients. It's very wrong that a person should be discriminated against. The ability to decide when and how they want to end their life is a basic human right. It troubles doctors, I know, but imagine living for years in a useless body, praying every day that someone could find the courage and compassion to take them out of their misery.'

'The argument is we go down a slippery slope.'

'That is utter nonsense! Let me be clear, there are a number of self-interested parties who don't want this to happen and I'm not talking about the bigoted few and religious camps. There is big money to be earned, especially out of hopeless cases, known as test cases for new drugs.'

'The pharmaceutical companies, like Harcourt?'

'Oh, much bigger than Harcourt, I can assure you. The NHS is an open cheque book for them, a fortune to be made in those types of medicines. We haven't progressed, Grey. We have digressed in this age of enlightenment. This Jeffrey, or rather Ruben, has he patented his formula?'

'No.'

'Then what's his objective?'

'I'm not sure if he really has an objective. He feels the world isn't ready, probably never will be. For myself, I'm in two minds. On the one hand we give people dignity in death and a new life coming into the arena with wisdom and knowledge. On the other hand, do we really want six year olds telling their parents what to do?'

'Obviously you have no children. If you did you would know they try to do that anyway. I could read and write when I was three, play the piano at two. I qualified to be a doctor way ahead of my time because of it.'

'How does one choose who to save and who not to save? Do you give a pill to an ailing bomber serving his time in jail or do you-'

'People who take a life should forfeit their own. It's as simple as that. I make no apologies for my views and feel very angry of being afraid to express them, especially in my position as a doctor. Apart from it costing us a fortune to keep these horrible people locked up, we are sending the wrong message. If someone took my child's life I would make pretty damn sure they would pay with their own.'

'I feel no differently. At times I have to watch my tongue in case some liberal do-gooder starts giving me the third degree.'

'There, you see, we think the same. They would stand in the freezing rain to uphold the rights of a vile person and yet when it comes to those who really matter, they become sanctimonious imbeciles.'

'Tell me about your family, how did you meet your husband?'

Instantly Mary's face glowed. 'We met at a fete. I was nineteen going on twenty, love at first sight.'

'Ah, I understand. You wanted to see Sir John before you got married, to make sure Neil Pembroke never turned up to embarrass you.'

'I would love to continue this conversation but I really must be going.'

'Look,' Grey said, quickly writing down Ruben's number, 'if ever you feel like talking to the person who made it all possible then give him a ring.'

'Where is he based?'

'Norfolk, a town called Wymondham. He has a wonderful shop full of dollhouses and related items.'

'He makes them?'

'His grandfather makes the dollhouses and he makes the miniature furniture. If not, if you feel you need an intermediary, telephone me.'

'You really like him, don't you?'

'Is it that obvious?'

'I shall tell you what's obvious,' said Mary grabbing her coat and scarf, 'a person doesn't walk alone out of choice.'

'I'm sorry, I don't understand.'

'Ruben Stone, he walks alone so he must have an agenda for his formula.'

'Have you ever seen the website by Doctor Hope?'

Mary instantly sat down. 'Oh, bless the man. Is he behind the campaign for euthanasia?'

'Yes. I signed up, long before I knew it was him.'

'I signed up too, last year. I heard about it through a patient of mine. Wish that I could spread the word, but my hands are tied.' She looked at her watch again and stood. 'I must go. Tell him to keep up the good work.'

When, at the end of it all, Grey believed she had most likely established a new friend, they shook hands and parted company, doubtful they would see each other again.

Outside, the sky was a pastel blue and the air icy thin. She flipped up her collar, crossed the road and fell into a waiting taxi. 'Let's return for more surveillance.'

Partly convinced Erik may be out there and still to make contact, she returned to the skirts of Bury St. Edmunds with her fearless defender to cast another thoughtful gaze over Harcourt's empire.

By the time they arrived, shopped at Tesco, parked up in the same side road and spent three hours peeled on the gated entrance, it was 8.30pm and the night was getting colder. It had snowed massively all along the north-west coast of Scotland with the weather men predicting parts would drift east.

A motor appeared, its headlights making fast down the road. At first, they could distinguish only the outline then distance closed and sharper focus came. The Sunbeam Alpine slowed at the entrance, its lights disengaged and then turned into the drive.

Leaving Grey in the motor, her fearless defender darted across the main road, quick on his feet, disappearing like a ghost. It was now a matter of waiting, biting nails, and listening to the radio or telephone the vet who sees the good in every animal, even homicidal crocodiles.

'How's Bobble, Mr. McCloon?'

'Bobble, Bobble, ah wee Bobble. I had to let him go, lass. Up, up and away to wee heaven.'

'But he was fine last week.'

'Awk no, he was in pain.'

'I'm in pain. I never had a chance to say goodbye.'

'Now listen, lassie, the wee creature had a cuddle and a kiss before leaving, that I know because ye was fretting some. D'ye want me to put him on hold so ye can give him another kiss?'

'No,' she said wiping a tear away, 'I cannot bear the thought of seeing him dead. Can you put the ashes in a jar?'

'That I can.'

'Thank you, Mr. McCloon.'

She pulled a picnic blanket up to her chin and huddled in on herself, reflecting her current situation. She was cold. She was tired. She missed her home. She missed her cat. But most of all she missed Ruben Stone.

A good hour passed when she saw his motor cruise from the entrance, the headlights bucked and swayed as he turned in the direction of Norfolk. Then five minutes later her fearless defender dashed across the road and jumped in.

'What did you find out,' she asked.

'You're never going to believe this. Half way up the drive, the old man gets out and throws a body over his shoulder then the motor carried on and parked outside the house. I followed the body which got dumped in the compost heap, later picked up by a penguin suit and taken inside.'

'Did you get a look at the body?'

'Female, blond hair, about thirty, tattoos on her backside and great tits.'

'Honestly, why can't men say breasts?'

'Do you know her?'

'Certainly, the silicon, manufactured in France, so no worries there now she's dead. I cannot imagine Ruben killing her and to then dump her on Sir John. You say the butler took her in?'

'I won't speculate what impulse he was trying to satisfy but there is definitely something serious going on in his head.'

'Can you be more specific?'

'He was getting off on her tattoos.'

Quickly, Grey plucked out her notebook and skipped pages back. 'Was this what you saw?'

'Yes, I think, sort of.'

Grey said nothing, added one more date to her list of dates, and by far it had increased to almost confusion. Yet between the lines in the early part of Ruben's other life she could see a story emerging.

1973 Test subject Erik? Mary?

1979 Test subject arrival. Erik? Mary?

1979 Helena Vale died in hospital.

1979 Jeffrey Cane died.

1980 April Jones born (was Vale)

1980 Ruben Stone born (was Cane), parents dead.

2009 Amy Pots inherited house.

2009 Charles Stone sold out to Michael Fuller.

2009 Lenard Green signed up on life policy, died one year later.

2011 Amy Pots sold out to Michael Fuller.

2011 Peter Tudmoor signed up on life policy, died one year later.

2012 Michael Fuller killed.

2012 April Jones (Vale) died.

CHAPTER 17

Ruben threw open the door. The road was silent and white. As he bent to grab the morning paper, an incoming missile whizzed over his head and struck into the shop with calamitous excursion. Guilty and giggling, the newspaper boy made for a hasty retreat in the counter-attack. Within seconds both were engaged in a snowball fight, no rules and nothing but snow. Winter had come, total winter, millions of tons of the lovely stuff which nobody owned.

Ruby!

To the call of his name he went inside as the old man shook the paper portentously. 'Listen to this,' he said, 'Sir John Harcourt, forefather of Harcourt Pharmaceuticals was found dead in the cold arms of his mistress by the long-served confidante and friend, Able Windsor. It is believed thirty-three-year-old April Jones suffered a heart attack hours before he overdosed on his medication. Now wat do yew make of that!'

'I make it in our favour.'

'But who put her there?'

Unconcerned, Ruben picked up the pieces of a broken roof. 'This needs to go back to the workshop.'

'Here, yew look after the counter while I make us a cuppa.'

Not that a stampede was visualized, Ruben brushed himself down then picked up the paper skipping through news, turning pages in a land of coats and brollies rather than hope and glory. His real interest lay in the tectonic plates of politics shifting on the issue of a failing euro and the gold prices, both inextricably linked. He smiled. Gold was up and still rising in a confusing economy managed by a group of confusing idiots. It was making his yellow pile of glitter shine even brighter.

The door opened and closed to the weight of Tom Hutton, briefly allowing cold air to flood in. 'Have you got down to the obituary column?'

Ruben glanced up a few inches just above the paper and looked directly at the publican. 'You were correct, work wasn't her strong suit.'

'Josie thought the same.'

'Have you kissed and made up?'

The grin was tight, conspiratorial, yet filled with gleeful satisfaction. 'Come round later for a drink, got a proposition you might like to hear.'

'Will it bankrupt me?'

'Not unless you're bloody stupid. Where's Charlie?'

'Not dead yet,' the old man said and coveted his mug of tea. 'How's business, boy?'

'Good, Charlie, going good, considering the turmoil of late and this weather doesn't much help.'

At which point Marge blustered in, clutching a stack of envelopes. 'Never guess what,' she said dishing out Christmas cards, 'Susan Fuller is going to move back and run the agency.'

'Is that so,' Charlie said.

'And she promoted Lulu as JFC.'

'Do yew know wat that is, my woman?'

'No, Charlie.'

'Neither do I. Got any more news?'

'Well, Father Dell slipped in the river and sprained his ankle, though goodness knows why he thought it necessary to throw a twig in the water. And we all know about Bill losing his pigeon, poor man. He did love that bird.' Then her nose fed around them and between them. 'Where's Miss Jones?'

'Ruby gave her the sack.'

'She never wore any knickers, you know.'

Held by the silence of her comment, they looked at each other in turn.

'And of course,' she continued in all fairness, 'the weather hasn't helped. They say this is going to continue right through to Christmas.'

'Thass how it used to be, always had snow fer Christmas, thass wat winter's fer, a good lot of snow to kill off the flies. Hev yew heard from that brave son of yours?'

'Oh yes, thank you, Charlie, for asking but yet to receive the same question from Tom.'

Hutton was about to apologize when the door blew open to a gust of snow and a camel-hair coat with the collar turned up strode in, the face shaded by a brown fedora. It brought the conversation to an end, friends departing in see-you-later goodbyes leaving Ruben to handle the customer.

'Are you okay looking round?'

'For the moment.'

The man continued to loiter, browsing and picking up pieces then another customer staggered in, a boy no older than twelve stamping his feet on the mat, immediately followed by another. Such outbursts were often contagious and led to a wave of others, hands deep in their pockets, shivering.

'What we goin' to hev, then, eh?'

As they buried their cherry pink noses in a pile of flatpacks, Ruben watched the fedora leave with a smile of far deeper meaning than ordinary.

'Wanna know summat?' An urchin said, and Ruben looked down into a cheeky squint. 'I's only got a tenner.'

'And you want a Native American tepee.'

'Core, can I hev one?'

'What does it say on the price tag?'

'Aww, I's only got a tenner.'

Negotiation took time. In the end the lad scuffled out with a wigwam, and the rest followed with their pockets full of Indians. Children could bring out the generosity in any man.

He watched from the window as they trooped flat-broke across the white-driven road then focused his attention on the familiar figure lurking nearby, Able Windsor forgotten in the wider scheme of things.

Ruben gestured him in. 'What's with the get-up?'

'I come incognito, sir.' Removing his hat which left a red tram line around his receding hair line, the well-groomed Windsor stood very much at ease in front of Ruben. 'I shall come directly to the point, your time being of the essence. It was me who facilitated the problem, sir, and as such it comes at a price.'

Ruben gave him a sharp clear look and uttered not another word, leaned back against the counter and folded his arms.

'Oh dear, is there somewhere we can talk?'

Considering the till had to be manned, Ruben picked up the receiver and buzzed through to the workshop. 'Charlie, can you look after the shop, I need to iron out a wrinkle.'

'Roit yew are.'

To the painted mushroom Ruben did go, bent low into an underworld of magic behind a green-baize door. Here among the *little people* reflecting nursery rhymes it was convenient to sit on the old sofa and converse in a windowless room.

'Much better,' said Windsor and sat on the protruding spring, oblivious to anything but his reward. 'There is little not to know when one serves an old man bound in his chair, the comings and goings. Though I have to admit to the difficulty in understanding what lay beneath his anxiety…that was until your name came into question. My, my, I can tell you, sir, I was quite taken aback by your discovery.'

'Did you kill Fuller?'

'Am I likely to confess if I had?'

'Carry on.'

'Well, sir, there is not much else to say other than the sight of your grandfather blundering across the grounds with a white sack over his shoulder. It made perfect sense to tie the whole matter up when Sir John took his pill.'

'And if I refuse?'

Windsor considered the question as if it was the subject of original sin. 'In my possession is a very interesting journal which I rather think might add as an inducement.'

'What if I kill you?'

'Come, sir, we are forgetting our brains.'

'It is you who forgets their brains!' Ruben challenged Harcourt's long serving confidante and lowered his voice so there was no misunderstanding. 'Listen to me well, Able Windsor. One word in print and I will kick your sorry arse all the way to your grave.'

'Believe me, sir, you have the wrong end of the stick, I assure you my intention was not to threaten but to enjoy a little security for my old age, keep my position in service to Sir John's son.'

'Edward? Edward has returned?'

'He made contact in response to an advert Sir John placed in the Times shortly after your first visit. But then a fortune is thicker than water.'

'Where has he been all this while?'

'When you left Sir John, I had to inform him you dropped off Miss Jones in a rather sad state. He gave instructions what to do and told me his son had been living in Brazil, that he would arrive when probate had been finalized and I was guaranteed my job as chauffer. He told Mrs G her position was guaranteed as cook. Truthfully, what he gave to you was meant for us but you rather put a spoke in the wheel.'

'Windsor, you do fully appreciate blackmail is a serious business. Fuller was killed because of it.'

'From a lay person's point of view, I consider your achievement a truly miraculous discovery, sad it should be lost in the human jungle.'

'It's the human jungle that deems my discovery a ticking time bomb.'

'Had that thought not occurred before devoting your time into making the discovery?'

Ruben gave him a displeasing look. 'I was a scientist, not a philosopher.'

'And now you are a carpenter with an academic brain seeking the truth.'

'If you must know, I once believed in the pacific might of science, lived for the search of truth, that one day it would make its contribution to easing life and the peaceful progress towards physical, moral and intellectual well-being. Naïve words, but they were naïve old words of impossible idealism. Today, science develops in political machinations. Passion, compassion and integrity are no longer the by-words of this century, predicting the turmoil of what could happen should my discovery be exposed.'

'I am surprised your discovery has thus far escaped exposure considering your endeavours over the last three years.'

Ruben made no effort to reply. It was the crowning circumstance of his grandfather.

'I knew of a young woman battling a rare and debilitating condition that was turning her into a human statue, *fibrodysplasia ossificans progressiva*, a condition in which her muscles changed into bone. Her neck was locked and she could not move her head. She had restricted movement in her jaw and was unable to raise her arms above her head. She told me, without a cure, she would soon become locked in her own skeleton. That was five years ago, poor soul. Nobody knows better the feeling of hopelessness, to see a life stripped away all for the want of a cure. And you know, sir. Those who will return with such grateful memories of your effort make a far better crew than the likes of Helena Vale.'

Ruben instinctively laughed. But it was a nervous laugh. There appeared something so very candid, so very truthful and yet so very opportunistic. At length, he returned his gaze at the man who knew how to wheel a trolley. 'How long have you been in the employ of Sir John?'

'Almost twenty years, sir. I arrived at a time when his poor wife died.'

'So, you never married?'

'Not for the want of trying.'

'You see where I'm going with this, Windsor? You waltz in my shop, tap me up for the diamonds, and then lecture me from a moral high ground. How do I know you will keep your mouth shut? Edward could offer you an inducement far greater than diamonds and where does that leave me?'

Windsor brought to his lap a journal and opened to the first page. 'Do you recognise the hand writing, sir?'

Ruben studied it for a while and then all became clear. 'It cannot be.'

'Shall we look upon this as a fair exchange?'

At best it would prevent further exposure if Ruben obtained it, or at worst it might hinder and throw further hazard in his wake should Edward obtain it. The latter was a disturbing thought, a grimly evolving one. Making haste to his secret chamber, Ruben grabbed the bag of diamonds, kept a few back and returned to the windowless room. The exchange might have been called off, but desire for knowledge substituted the resentment toward Windsor.

'Is this the only one?'

'Yes, sir,' and donned his fedora. 'You are more than welcome to come and search for yourself.'

'I might just do that.'

After Windsor's transition into the white world beyond the shop, Ruben left his grandfather standing and made haste to his lair to read Harcourt's journal, giving no other signs of life than putting a glass to his lips. Beginning with the early stages of Jeffrey Cane's undoubted challenge to prove his theory via the introduction of a test subject whose symbolic gesture and acceptance of death made for a great deal of mental anguish. Pursuant six years later, Harcourt left no doubts in the mind of those who would read his journal as to what work he could lay claims for himself and the follow-up observations on Mary. When he closed on the last chapter Ruben set aside the journal and held his head in his hands. None of what was written had changed the situation but it had shifted the balance of thought. Who the hell was Mary?

'Did you know,' and Ruben looked up. 'The British people are degenerating into a bunch of half-wits. Technology has made their brains lazy, decreasing their level of intelligence best suited for a ten year old. Everything stops for two inches of snow. I mean, is it beyond the wit of man to notice this island is close to the North Pole? Next, we shall be getting a hose pipe ban.'

Somewhere along the way he managed a nod and stuffed her carved facsimile under his jumper. Love impulse required no sense.

'Leave you alone for five minutes and the place goes to pot, Mr. Stone.'

'Hard put to find the staff, Miss Grey.'

'Now,' she said, and came to sit opposite by the belligerent heat of the stove. Her pearls shone so beautifully about her neck that to look at them against the grey of her jumper was quite breathtaking. 'What did the butler have to say?'

'That he was Able and Windsor.'

'Can we be a little more specific?'

Smiling, he went on to explain the events, regulated by a moral law of gravity, which, like the physical one held him down to earth. 'I'm not sure if it was John Harcourt's last wishes I receive his journal and used it in a shrewd attempt to get the diamonds.'

'Villainy wears many masks, none so dangerous as the one of virtue.' She picked up the journal. 'I so missed our conversations but I had to leave. Am I forgiven?'

'No, that's okay. It nearly led to self-slaughter.'

'Charlie,' she said laughing, 'told me he put her under the compost heap. No two guesses as to whose idea was that.'

'When did you arrive?'

'I popped my head in earlier but you were busy reading. Are you peckish? We could go next door for coffee and cake, loads to tell.'

Ruben looked at his watch. Where on earth had the time gone? 'I need to see Tom about a business proposal.'

'Okay. How about I see you at the Green Dragon, say about six?'

'Six is good. Six gives me time to change. Are you staying at the Abbey Hotel?'

'Yes.'

Barely a second passed without reminding himself this was business, this was a kind of twisted fate that brought her back. Changing into black jeans, he chose a blue polo-neck sweater with a holly-leaf motive, filled his pockets with notes and change, slipped a comb through his mop and then went into the kitchen and tortured Charlie.

'Why didn't you tell me Grey was here?'

'Yew wus busy,' he replied, flourishing the bread knife in the air. 'Besides, she helped me to operate that card thing.'

'We're eating at the green Dragon.'

'Good fer yew. Don't forget to ask her.'

'Ask her what?'

'If she killed Fuller.'

Ruben took a deep breath, gave a roll of the eyes and moved on, now wondering what insane impulse triggered Grey to return to Norfolk. Was it the death of April Jones mysteriously found in bed with Harcourt or was it something deeper? On the upside, she was here with loads to tell. On the downside, she took the journal.

Amy appeared across the bar and began with a friendly, 'Hi, Ruby, what's your poison, the usual?'

'Make it a half.'

'Make mine a whisky.' Hutton checked out the sweater but refrained from comment. 'It occurred to us, us being keepers of profit and loss that we should round up the rabble and put this town back on the map.'

'Mmm,' murmured Ruben, unsure where this was heading. 'Rabble as in locals?' and threw some peanuts into his mouth.

'Robert Kett, you remember him, led a protest against injustices. Now, the way I see it, it's an injustice our livelihoods are threatened and the council raking it in from parking fees.'

'Correct me if I'm wrong but didn't 3000 of his followers die at Dussindale?'

'No democracy in those days, Ruby. The trick, of course, is to get up a petition and request a reform, call it Oak of Reformation part two.'

'Oh, I love sequels,' Amy interjected, and typically followed up with her ignorance. 'Who's Robert Kett?'

'He had three acres of land around the Tiffey Meadow,' Ruben said. 'His tanpits were probably located somewhere in that area.' *Now there was a thought.* 'Tom, did you by any chance remember that when you sold off your parcel to Susan Fuller?'

The publican grinned, no flies on him. 'What do you think, Ruby? We muster up the rabble and demand a reform…be all we can be in these times of austerity.'

'Sure, I'm in for the count. How many signed up?'

Hutton slowly raised one finger, turned it around and prodded Ruben. 'You, my good man, can lead the rebellion.'

'Me! Ohh no, not me.'

'Nice voice, nice face, not sure about the jumper.'

'Or the haircut,' Amy shot in.

'Do you see this?' Ruben pointed to the floor. 'This is where my feet are kept, firmly planted on wood. Your idea - you lead the good fight and Amy can be your press secretary.'

'I hate ironing shirts,' she said.

To this tragedy, the tort reformer breathed on, his face mobile with the spectre of desperation. There was one who would not be participating in his rebellion.

'So…what's on the menu?' Ruben asked as a group descended upon the bar, and there, weaving her way to his side was Grey removing her coat.

'Have you ordered?' she asked.

'Not yet.'

'How about steak & ale pie or chilli…yes, chilli for me, I think.'

'Why did you take the journal?'

'For a very good reason,' and they retreated to a corner where no one could hear them. 'I needed to check a few things out to the benefit of your case.'

'Did you kill Fuller?'

Lightly, she deployed a hand on his forehead. 'No, I don't think you're running a fever.'

'I had to ask because the latest theory is that whoever did was protecting me.'

'Oh, I so agree, you definitely need protecting. Now what do you want to eat?'

He was tempted to say, *you,* instead he went to the chalk board. Amy came hobbling along bearing a crate of bottled beer, wispily grinning and taking the order with a limp. After that, they settled upon a table near the fire and wedged themselves in before reigniting the conversation.

'Ruben, what did you make of Harcourt's journal?'

'Confusing, very confusing…it speaks of a test subject, male, aged fourteen and the subject returning nine months less of six years as a female. Either the journal was a deliberate attempt to alter the facts or it was written to lay claim to the discovery.'

'Hard to lay claim when no formula is shown?'

'Is that what you were looking for?'

'Yes. Now tell me what you need from a test case in order to make a capsule specific to them?'

'Simple really. I just need their DNA.'

'Blood?'

'Or a strand of hair, like I took from Ding.'

'You gave a capsule to Sam?'

'Am I going to have my hand smacked for giving my friend a safe passage?'

'Actually, I think it was a lovely thing to do. Now where was I? Oh yes…exactly when and how did you administer the capsule to Erik?'

'The same day I met him, nice chap. We spent more time talking about his country than his condition. He allowed me to examine him then I discussed the risks involved, which to him, he felt was no risk at all. We were both in agreement the trial should continue so I took him to a room set up for the event. Harcourt was there to witness the crossover. After Erik undressed, he sat on the bed with a glass of water and then he swallowed the capsule.'

'A capsule prepared that day?'

'No, it was prepared a week beforehand. Pembroke gave me samples of his blood.'

'And then you and Sir John watched Erik die?'

'No, we left to give him some dignity.'

'Who returned to the room, Sir John I wager. What did he say? I shall take care of the corpse? You go home and get some rest on this auspicious day?'

Every thought took him back to that time, to the easy smile fastened on Harcourt's face, to the close of that door and all those wonderfully nebulous words that hid everything else.

After the meal arrived, Grey kept her voice down to almost a whisper. 'I can paint you an interesting picture.'

'Do so.'

'Sir John paid Erik to act a part, not necessarily feigning his cancer, no, it wouldn't work, the cancer had to be real so money was the inducement to pretend to take a pill, which in turn was given to Sir John. Now, instead of an Erik from Sweden, we have a capsule which you prepared earlier from the DNA of a sickly lad who was manoeuvred into your experiment by a disenchanted father. The old dreams are forgotten. Nine months later a mother gives birth to a baby girl and life resumes ordinarily until dreams become real. The parents pay a visit to Sir John with a degree of concern for their troubled little girl. Of course, all politeness ends when the ex-father wishes the return of his child. That's the reason why Sir John refused you access, Ruben. It was Neil Pembroke's son.'

'You're kidding.'

'I kid you not.'

'Why would Harcourt go along with it?'

'Because Neil Pembroke and Sir John knew each other way beforehand, were the best of friends but that friendship was sorely tested when Pembroke overstepped the mark by having an affair with your wife, or rather Jeffrey's wife.'

'I was never made aware Pembroke had a child. In fact, I never knew he was married.'

'No, you wouldn't because when he came on board to be Sir John's right hand man, it was already in their minds who to test. Remember, you were told Pembroke was employed specifically to locate a test subject, reporting directly to Sir John.'

Ruben gave his fork a rest and looked around as if others were lurking. 'Should I ask how the hell you found this out or should I ask where she lives?'

'Ask me anything but not that. Mary, her name is Mary and she has a family. If I can offer you any consolation it would be to say she has your number and she's terribly proud of your work, especially of your website on euthanasia. She signed up.'

'She did?'

'Oh yes. So, let's keep it that way, okay?'

'Okay. How's your chilli?'

'Hot.' Grey drained her glass and smiled when he promptly filled it. 'Carry on like this and I shall be out for the count of ten.'

'How did you find her?'

'By a little luck and thinking outside the box. At the time I could understand Sir John's reluctance to divulged Erik's new identity but when April Jones involvement came to light, I was inclined, like you, to consider this Erik might be part of Sir John's gang, might have killed Michael Fuller. In which case, this Erik had to be in contact with Sir John.'

'You watched his place?'

'Had to.'

'How?'

'From a vehicle.'

'In a taxi?'

'Well, it certainly wasn't a bus.'

Ruben threw down his utensils, the reserved Miss Grey, highly selective of what to say and what not to say. 'Don't play semantics with me, Grey. You packed your bags and walked away leaving me to deal with a tarantula, and that I can understand but to withhold your thoughts again when clearly, we agreed to work this out together. Why did you keep this from me?'

'Why did you keep your affair from me?'

'I was another man for Christ sake!'

'Different penis, same mind.' Grey looked apologetic. 'That was a really stupid thing to say, and very much regretted. I'm in the throes of confusion. It comes with the territory. Don't let your meal get cold.'

Obediently, he resumed eating with a need to know exactly what did come with the territory. 'So…this taxi came with a driver and then what?'

'We watched the comings and goings of Sir John, which happened not to be coming or going anywhere until the day before he took his life. I cannot say where he went but rather who he saw and why they met for a brief exchange at a petrol station. Leading on from there, we followed her, a piece of luck really because I took a gamble and popped a note through her letter box…*ring this number if you please*. And she rang the following morning, and we met for coffee in London. The meeting had to take place in secrecy because her husband is completely in the dark. Sir John advised he had intention of taking his life and gave her some uncut diamonds as a fond farewell. She knew nothing of his crimes or you as Ruben Stone.'

'Do I take it she's off the suspect list?'

'Yes.' Grey dived into her handbag and brought out her legendary notepad. 'After seeing her, I resumed surveillance thinking Erik might still be in for the count, but of course we spotted your car to drop off April Jones, which confirmed you were completely off your rocker. Anyway, set that aside, I delved into the Harcourt family. The son, and at a guess, cognizant of skeletons in the closet, broke family ties and somehow disappeared off this planet. I would probably do the same.'

'He lived in Brazil.'

'Really?'

'Yes. Harcourt put an ad in the Times and Edward answered the call to money. It fits. I came on the scene, gave him a capsule, he makes a last ditch attempt to make up with his son. The son takes the bait, all the money goes to him and daddy ties everything up quite nicely to come back happy.'

'Ruben, you gave him a capsule on the pretext of coming back happy.'

'If those who wish to end their life just for the sake of another then I shed no tears of remorse. Harcourt wanted to return and be Prime Minister so I did the world a favour, probably the son a favour.'

'The son will inherit his father's wealth, not least a substantial holding in the company. Would you be tempted to join forces with a better man?'

'What do I do, Grey? Flush my formula down the toilet, notch it up to experience, or put it to good use?'

'It depends on what you wish to be. Do you wish to be a carpenter or do you wish to be a scientist?'

Ruben rolled an elbow over the table and rested his chin upon the ball of his palm, directing his eyes at Grey. As beautiful as she was remote, his true wish was to be with her for a zillion years. Since that was out of the question, he said, 'Let me see now. You pose a very interesting dilemma. Do I wish to play the Good Samaritan or do I wish to carve wood into little people? Since I have been playing these roles simultaneously over the last three years, which have resulted in the threat of exposure by a very tenacious witch, a one million pound pay out from monies held in trust, the entry into flatpacks that by no means qualify for expertise, my house being sold for peanuts to keep Charlie happy, and a killer after my balls. Gee, that's a hard dilemma. Daddy or chips.'

To that extraordinary account, Grey turned the corners of her napkin, and smoothed out the wrinkles, silent as Ruben. After a long pause, she said, 'My cat died.' A hand closed about her fingers. 'He looked so much better when I left, Ruben. The sad thing, I wasn't there to say goodbye.'

It was ungallant to think of himself. Instead, he dwelt on her pussy. 'I'm sure Bobble knew you loved him.'

'I don't feel like getting another.'

'Neither do I.'

CHAPTER 18

To the early dark light of a winter's morning, Grey waltzed in smelling of perfumed witchery. Her hair was tied up like cotton candy and a pyjama top was all that covered her. She placed a cup of tea on the bedside cabinet, swished back the drapes, which were so not her colour, and looked at Ruben snug as a bug in bed. He was in that place of magic where reality could not reach him, where flying high on a witch's broom was preferable to waking up. Three glasses of wine and sympathy for Bobbles, that was not Grey then, but the revealed unknown, a labyrinth of naked flesh, binding her body with his.

'Come on lazy bones, wake up.'

'No,' he muffled under the bedclothes.

'Yes, we need to hit the road.'

Ruben stirred, grabbed his pocket watch off the bedside cabinet. It registered too early. 'Would this be the road to Windsor?'

'We ask the fundamental question how far he would go to protect his master's interests.'

'Hop into bed and rape me again.'

'Rape you?'

'So, I imagined you tearing off my shirt?'

'Well,' replying a little contrite, 'I may have been somewhat exuberant but that is not to say it should happen again.'

'Oh no, we mustn't let it happen again,' he conveyed with mocking amusement.

'I wish you would take things seriously.'

'I do, Grey. I do take things seriously, that's why we need the pyjama bottom to marry the pyjama top.'

'What we need,' she said laughing, 'is to see Able Windsor and follow the trail to Michael's killer, thus collect one million pounds. You don't need to sell your house. You can buy the shop with your half.'

'My half is returning to the pot.'

'That's crazy, Ruben. With what you have and gold rising exponentially, there is more than enough for their future. Use the money to buy the shop and invest in your business. Keep your house in Newmarket. Do it up, rent it out as an investment. You have no need to sell it for peanuts.'

He placed his empty cup aside and watched her wriggle into jeans. Her shape was like an hour glass, virgin breasts filling the cups of her bra, every bit a woman to have and to hold. But who was having the holding?

She smiled at him watching her. 'Penny for your thoughts?'

'I gave Ding a penny for his. He told me he had joined the army.'

'Did it upset you?'

'In a way I was slightly relieved. His talent would have been wasted if he had stayed.'

'But you missed him all the same.'

'Yes, I did miss his company, rather like I missed yours. Tell me, what did the taxi driver do other than keep his meter running?'

That gave rise to her leaving the room. They had weathered many disagreements and a hundred other things but the inconsistencies for delving into her private life had touched on principles that made him aware he was on shaky ground.

Not this time and whooshed back the covers, stalking her strutting steps. 'Okay for him but not for me.'

'Stop being ridiculous,' she said at the sink, 'it was the vet's voice you heard. Notwithstanding the current problem, obscurity is my safety net.'

'No, Grey, anonymity is your warm blanket. I know because I had one myself. You keep to your designated patch marked out by windbreaks and picnic baskets then dipped your toe in the sea and now you're scared of drowning.' He swung her round, waited for a reply but there was only her breathing. 'Hard put to acknowledge the truth?'

'I'm adjusting my heart if you must know. I have never argued with an escaping penis.'

Ruben looked down at himself. The madness befitted the moment. Muttering obscenities, he picked his way back to the bedroom while Charlie's smoke filled the air, the sitting spectator.

'Oh, he's impossible.' She felt a cold teapot. 'I should have returned to the Abbey Hotel, instead I drank myself silly and now I have a rebellion on my hands.'

'Best yew go-'

'Good idea. I shall do exactly that.' Leaving the old man with his mouth hanging open, she trotted off to bully Ruben. 'We need to talk.'

'You need to go home. I can handle Able Windsor.'

'Sulking is not the answer.' She picked out a tie, turned up his collar and initiated a knot. 'Ruben, aside the fact that someone is after your formula, you would expect me to take you home when you cannot even decide what you wish to be.'

'I wish to be with you.'

'Are we not together?'

'Is that why you returned?'

'I returned to sort this out. We make good on our agreement, together we go see Able Windsor, find out who killed Fuller then I get the money and we split it right down the middle.' She stood back. 'What do you think?'

He drew close to his mirrored self and adjusted his tie. She was very *Able* at making a good *Windsor* knot but not very able in confiding her secrets. Catching a glance of her reflection as she stood to share his mirrored view, he saw the image of a strong and vibrant woman who could be beautiful one day, wilful the next. It would need more than a hammer to crack open her shell and turned to face her. 'To see Windsor with you in tow would ring his alarm bells.'

'That's the whole point, ruffle his feathers.'

'He never killed Fuller.'

'But he may know who did.'

'Exactly, ruffle his feathers and he clams up. He offered me, not you, carte blanche in Harcourt's library.'

'Okay, and if you discover he killed Fuller then what? You slip a capsule in his tea?'

'That was the gist of things.'

'So, you made yourself another, the ever contingent Ruben Stone.'

'Actually, I didn't.'

Eying him suspiciously, she said, 'A moment ago you wanted to handle Windsor on your own so at what point would you find time to make one?'

Bollocks! Would there ever come a point when he could win an argument? 'Dishing out capsules like confetti opens the floodgates to police enquiries.'

'You never thought that when you gave away five.'

'Five?'

She counted them off her fingers. 'Lenard Green, Peter Tudmoor, Sam Dingle, Sir John, and two for Charlie in light of Betty's dementia.'

'That's six.'

'Making your point irrelevant,' she wonderfully replied. 'Shall we ask Charlie for his?'

Double bollocks!

With this treaty, they went into the kitchen seduced by the smell of freshly ground coffee and mounds of hot buttered toast sitting comfortably with the white whiskered face spooning ginger nut dregs from his tea.

'This is nice, Charlie,' said Grey and pulled up beside him.

The old carpenter made no reply, just filled their cups, passed over the jam and took off his watch. He laid it smack bang on the table then returned to his dregs.

Ruben and Grey looked at each other, gave a shrug and swung into action, making light conversation between bites. Yet all was clearly not going well.

'Are you okay, Charlie?' asked Grey. 'You've hardly said a word.'

'Thass because I'm waiting fer yew to ask.'

'Oooh, you were eaves dropping!'

'Yew wus in my bedroom, not that I hev a mind to covet my bed, it would help to hev my slippers.'

'Sorry, Charlie,' Grey apologized and flashed him a marvellous smile. 'I sort of got carried away last night…leading on from there we need a capsule just in case we discover Able Windsor murdered Fuller.'

'There is no *we* but me,' Ruben insisted.

'I can read a lie as easily as reading a book so it's vital I go with you…and besides I can make sure you drink from the right glass.'

Ruben frowned at Charlie. 'Traitor.'

'I wus telling her how it came about, thass all.'

'Well try telling her why she has to stay here.'

The old man stroked his beard, mulling over the residue of their ridiculous situation, not wishing to take any side. 'Marriage is fer life,' he told them and they blinked. 'Yew, my woman, if yew intend to lead an invisible life Ruby won't see yew. His bed will grow cold and old, wishing he were dead. And yew, Ruby, if yew intend to push a cart load of wood, her flame will die long before yew carve a nest. I said me bit, make of it as yew will.'

Bewildered, doomed by ambitions, they sat looking at each other in wordless confusion as the old man left in his socks to search for his slippers.

'Did Charlie just divorce us?' Grey asked.

'He gave us a reality check. I don't know who I screwed last night and you don't know who you want to screw next.' Acknowledging her winning smile, he picked up Charlie's watch off the table, flicked open the rear cover and procured the capsule, handing it to Grey. 'Be absolutely certain he killed Fuller. Now how do you want me to play this?'

'Be candid about me.'

'Hit the sack, candid?'

'No, not hit the sack. He listens at keyholes so he knows my interest in the case. Try to get an invitation for lunch.'

Ruben put his hands in a prayerful grip and bounced them off his chin, twice. Then he got to his feet, grabbed the telephone and dialled Able Windsor. An answering machine picked up. *Please state your name and nature of your call after the tone...beep, beep, beep...*

'It's Ruben Stone, thinking about a tour in the library sometime today. Give me a-'

'Here,' Windsor picked up. 'Come for lunch, sir.'

'Good idea. Make it for three.'

'Three?'

'You remember Miss Grey?'

'Indeed I do. May I enquire her interest?'

'She's looking into Fuller's murder. Unless you killed him, there's nothing to worry about.'

'She is most welcome, sir.'

'Look forward to it.'

Grey never moved until Ruben replaced the receiver then she crossed her legs and sipped warm coffee, bidden to her thoughts.

'Why not consider Harcourt was right. Whoever killed Fuller did so to protect me?'

'Then that would mean someone close to you. I never killed him, and besides I have an alibi and so does Charlie. Who else? Sam? What alibi did he give?'

'He was at home. I know because I left him there and his mother can vouch he stayed in his bedroom listening to rock n roll music.' He rolled up his shirt sleeves. 'I'll wash, you wipe.'

She grabbed the teacloth. 'When we did a practice run the knife entered at your waistline yet it entered his left ventricle. Suggesting someone was equal in height.'

'He was short, remember.'

'But he wore three inch heels. Have I missed a possible clue? Under the bridge the land slopes so it could have been a woman.'

'You amaze me, Grey. You missed that out?'

'I just felt April Jones was too slight in build to wield a knife into a man's chest. If it was her, then she must have been hidden, waited until he came down the slope near the water's edge, turned as she came at him but then why not come at him wielding the knife as if wielding a hammer. Instead, she came at him with an upward thrust.'

'Why back to her all of a sudden?'

'Because I cannot get my head round anyone else. I just think Fuller was killed because of two reasons. One, he was blackmailing someone, and two, he knew too much. The only person who had money to burn was Sir John, and the only connection to him was April Jones.'

'Why would April Jones meet Fuller by the bridge when she was damn well living in his house?'

'You make a very valid point. Even so, if it was her, she had to get the money from somewhere, someone, and telephoned from a call box.'

'Able Windsor?'

'Why on earth would a butler-'

'Confidante,' he corrected.

'Okay, confidante. Why would a confidante take such a risk? He has nothing to gain except his job. No money was left to him in the Will. And you said, he was promised the diamonds but Sir John gave them to you. Understandable he should feel a little aggrieved and thereby took the journal as a further incentive to get what he felt was rightfully his.'

'Jones thought I killed Fuller. In fact, those were her last words before she keeled over.'

'Every time that woman opened her mouth out came a lie.'

'You forget I gave her a truth drug.'

'Well maybe part of her subconscious mind couldn't help but tell a lie.'

'Okay, if it was her how do we prove it?'

'No need to prove it. God will take my word for it. And no, before you ask, I cannot live with myself if I took money on false pretences.'

Pity.

Pausing only to don on their coats, they made their way to Jim's garage gulping perishing air and treading new snow as if it came to defeat the gritters.

'It seems your car spends more time at Jim's than in your yard.'

'That's the price you pay for ancient relics.'

'What was wrong with it this time?'

'I cracked an axle after dropping off the body, just about got home. Jim's a good bloke, good mechanic. When the money comes through from the sale of my house I thought about buying a Volvo.'

'And when you get the proceeds, how will you handle Susan Fuller? The bargain came with justice. If Able proves a dead end, I would like to pop home and no, before you ask, you cannot come with me.'

Disappointments were too numerous to mourn, the snow too cold to allow for delay. He had been so close, had tasted her flesh then fate conspired to snatch her away. The marital bid was short-lived.

The motor was ready to go. Jim tossed Ruben the keys and touched his forelock at Grey. *Square you up later* and they were on their way.

The snow cleared long before reaching the skirts of Bury St Edmunds leaving the roads wet and slushy. But it gave them freedom to drive in the shortening length of the sun. Then, on the change of a downward gear shift, they swung into the driveway that stood against the course of history.

There was no certainty this property held any connection to the Fuller murder but in the cold light of a winter's day it seemed to advertise a shadow of doubt when Windsor materialized on the front step, his wardrobe considerably improved. Gone were the marks of a man servant, he bounded up in brown flannels and a paisley cravat. If there was any tale-tale sign of his former life, it presented itself with a long-suffering smile under a slick centre parting.

'Miss Grey, indeed this is a pleasure.'

'I trust not an inconvenience.'

'Not at all,' and swung his sight at the Sunbeam Alpine. 'How does she run, sir?'

'She has her moments, sometimes expensive moments. I will probably shed a tear when she goes but I'm thinking of buying a Volvo.'

'A good choice if one needs a tank.'

Leaving cold air behind, they were taken through a marble-laden hall and onward to the garage, Windsor citing difficulties with out-dated motors, point-scoring the benefits of new. The Aston Martin, superbly comfortable, featured a luxurious interior and packed a potent V12 engine. Ruben would have whistled, but the moment called for restraint. He was playing it cool, giving Windsor a wide berth, and listening.

'Both engine and transmission are well proven, so major faults should be rare.' Windsor showed a full set of capped teeth. 'Sir always preferred the Bentley Continental.'

'Not sure if you're aware of this but I don't have the garage that goes with a car like this.'

'What a pity.'

'Yes, pity.' Ruben licked the dribbles off his chin and sighed. He turned to Grey whose lips were parted as she hung on their every word. 'Do you have a decent garage?'

'No,' and paused, her manner unruffled. 'Why not take it for a spin and leave me to bore Windsor?'

'Good idea, sir. I take it you are insured.'

Ruben needed no other encouragement. He climbed in and took instructions before turning on the ignition and grinned like a Cheshire cat. If this was a bribe, there was no better inducement.

Grey slipped her hand through the crook of Windsor's arm and steered him inside the main building. 'Tell me, when did you discover Sir John was leaving the Aston to you?'

'The night of his departure, although, I must admit it came of no surprize. The diamonds were guaranteed, a promise instantly undermined when he gave them away. I assure you the transaction was legal. I have the log book and his signature can be verified.'

'Oh, I don't doubt your claim, Windsor. But if he gave you the Aston in recompense then why call upon Ruben?'

'It was a matter of necessity, madam. The Aston serves as a depreciable asset and costly to run. The diamonds serve as an appreciable asset. Mrs G was also promised diamonds but they simply never materialized, given to someone else, all plans gone to pot when his son made contact.'

'The son, Edward I believe lived in Brazil.'

'There is a family archive which he occasionally fondled. Would you like to see it?'

'Yes please.'

Where the Harcourt family tree grew across the library shelves, Grey remained mute, leafing through the pages of history. Men assumed the trait of slant-hooded eyes, women not always recognised in their shaded bonnets. It provided a comfortingly gradual introduction to new styles and new values. The first professor of industrial chemistry was Sir John Harcourt, aspiring to the loftier riches in the pharmaceutical industry. His bride had a thin face and body, and sad eyes gave her a delicate appearance. Edward, the son, took after his father but had a rather large nose that tended to dominate what would otherwise be a roughish form, typical of men before they wore deodorant.

Grey looked up when Windsor re-entered the library. Bone china cups and saucers with sugar lumps were so typically English. 'How old would his son be?'

'Fifty, Madam, fifty is an educated guess. I do remember Sir John telling me his son left in 1980, the time of Jeffrey Cane's death. One lump or two?'

'One please. Of course, you never knew Sir John then.'

'I was employed in 1992 after the death of his wife. Prior to that, I was a librarian with books for company.'

'You never fell in love?'

'How sensible you put things. People usually ask if I was ever married to which I would reply, no, failing to disclose an unrequited love which caused my transition from librarian to confidante.' He sunk deep into a winged-back chair, overlapped his legs and lit a cigar. 'When, after trying more gentle methods, she told me the brutal truth, the unhappy constant lover resigning myself to a future without her. It has entered my mind I still have some good years left and if fate smiles again without a frown I would like to enjoy the fruits of a woman.'

'Well, you certainly have a lot going for you. A bagful of diamonds, currently living in a mansion, charming, intelligent, and the babe swinger, the Aston…wow, a great catch.'

A smoke ring blew her way. 'What are you doing here, Madam? Protecting Mr. Stone's interests?'

'Mr. Stone is not my client.'

'May I know who is?'

'No, you may not, though I will say that whatever contrivance happened under this roof, it calls into question Edward Harcourt's validity.'

'Let me make my position clear. Whatever claim which may or may not be levied upon this estate, his wishes take precedent in any court of law. His son was made sole beneficiary, his signature witnessed upon a valid document drawn up by a public notary shortly after his wife died.'

'Then why risk your position?'

'It suited me to do so as it suits you to meet the challenge of the moment.' The smile was a cushion to his warning. Neither Grey nor Ruben would alter his predicted course. 'One invader affects another in a carpenter's life. You raid his heart. I raid his brain.'

'Both are allied to common sense.'

'Common sense rejects a DB9?'

'If you want to sell the Aston, even at a reduced price, Ruben is not in a position to buy. You have his diamonds, remember.'

'Not all of them.' Again the smile. Inversely proportional to the enthusiasm with which he greeted Grey's doubt. 'I see he withheld that information.'

'I am not his keeper.'

Windsor turned his head towards the library door and in so doing the cravat displaced, unveiling a large blemish on his neck.

'She runs like a beauty,' said Ruben. 'What's a car like that to tax and insure?'

'Have we changed our mind, sir?'

'Put it this way, don't sell it yet.' He tossed the keys to Windsor and strolled over to the desk where Grey had her head buried into the past. 'What you got there?'

'The family photographs. Did you ever meet his son?'

'Sure, a few times at the annual banquets.'

'What was he like?'

'I remember him being young and enthusiastic over my jokes.' He bent over her shoulder and pointed. 'Yup, that's Edward with a big nose.'

Grey closed the album. 'Thank you, Windsor. It was most informative. When do you expect to see Edward?'

'I fear legal matters drag for the purpose of irritating the recipient.' Windsor stubbed his cigar in the ashtray. 'Shall we withdraw to the dining room?'

Their discussion continued over lunch. The silver and napery arranged in order, a set for each separate dish. Cold cucumber soup, duck a la orange and chocolate cheesecake, all cooked and served by the competent Mrs G.

'Are you politically ambitious, Windsor?'

'Call me Able.'

'I call you that anyway.' The mere thought of him being anything less was foolish. 'With all this wealth you can encourage Edward to buy into the Labour party, get a complimentary bumper sticker for the Bentley.'

Grey tittered.

'A bumper sticker, yes, quite amusing, sir. You appear to be a man with his feet stuck firmly to the ground with the unenviable position of walking backwards.'

'Explain?'

'Well, sir, considering your past history one would expect a man to live for the future, capitalize on his achievements. Instead, you seem to be a veritable doomsday machine.'

'He is forced to be so,' Grey went in defence of Ruben, 'because he guards the most precious thing on this earth, and in light of recent events I cannot say I blame him. You should know this by the actions of your master who sent a vile creature into his world and virtually turned it upside down. Are you prepared to acknowledge this or remain silent to a dead man's wishes?'

'You believe I know who killed this Michael Fuller?'

'I believe you must know something. You smoke his cigars for goodness sake.'

'Any man between masters would do no differently, take a holiday and live for the moment.'

'And Sir John?'

'He was not a man who wept. He would always keep a steel grip on his emotions for fear of damaging his image. But after Mr. Stone made contact, he struggled to keep the tears at bay. I think he blamed himself for sending Miss Jones to his door and that she was instrumental in Fuller's death.'

'Were your ears tuned when he made contact,' Grey said with her notepad open.

'He requested payment, if payment is the correct terminology for keeping his mouth shut. That is the extent of my knowledge regarding Michael Fuller. In regard to Miss Jones, there was a creature of considerable discomfort to Sir John. To put it mildly, money was his saving grace to keep her amused.'

'Were you aware of any liaisons with other men?'

Windsor walked over to a Queen Anne sideboard and robbed a gold toothpick from the top drawer. To the next drawer down he robbed something else and returned to the table. 'I do have her diary.'

'May I have a look?'

'No, she may not have a look!' Ruben picked up his glass. 'Does it hold any valuable contribution toward science? I think not, so get rid of it and say thank you for lunch.'

'Ruben.' Grey interjected. 'It could hold valuable clues.'

'Like what? She screwed me, screwed Harcourt and had sex for brains.'

'That is the point, she had sex for brains. If anything was untoward, she capitalized. Shortly after your death, Cane's death, Edward left and never made contact. We assume it was due to his father's transgressions but what if it was something else. Do you know, Windsor?'

'How would he know? He was a librarian.'

'Ruben, why must you work against me?'

'You want to know what she did to me.'

'I want to know who killed Michael Fuller.'

'She's hardly likely to write that down.' Ruben snatched it out of her hand and threw it in the burning grate. 'Now ask Windsor who killed Fuller.'

Fuming, Grey pushed back her chair. 'You are an imbecilic moron,' and left the room in a deathly hush.

Five or ten seconds later it was Windsor to break the awkward silence by striking a match and lighting his cigar. 'It was her financial records, nothing to indicate any sexual liaisons.'

'I feel I should apologize.'

'I feel I should send my condolences.'

Ruben smiled. 'Yes, she is rather a handful.'

'Take a piece of advice and park your heart elsewhere. Women like that are destined to scramble a man's brain.'

'It depends on the man.'

'Since she already has one what does that make you?'

Ruben looked blank, his heart up by several beats per minute.

'You never knew she was married?'

'And you know this because?'

'Sir John asked the Fuller chap to check her out.'

'I tried to check her out.'

'You never looked in the right place.'

'Where is the right place?'

'In there.' Windsor gestured with his eyes to the handbag resting on the floor. 'From what I gathered he installed her things in the Abbey Hotel and although there was nothing to identify her name, he found a wedding ring lodged in her purse.'

'Perhaps there is need to wear a ring on certain undercover operations.'

'Then we shall leave it at that, sir.'

'Must you keep calling me sir?'

'Force of habit, one not to be dropped in company of a new master unless otherwise instructed.'

'Do you hanker to be in the employ of his son?'

'I have led a solitary existence in company with a man I very much admired. He had his faults, as do I, as do we all. But what shall I do with myself having led such a life? I shall be lost without Mrs G and her cooking.'

For Ruben, all manner of possibilities sprang up and stood when Grey entered the room with their coats draped over her arm. 'Thank Mrs G for the meal. She made a handsome effort.'

'I would like to lay claim to the dessert. She allowed me to sprinkle the chocolate.'

'Do you have any objection if I pinch a slice for Charlie?'

'Please, be my guest, take what is left.'

'Thank you for a superb lunch,' Grey said and pushed Ruben's coat into his chest. Forgiven he was not. 'Tell her I thought the meal was scrumptious.'

'I shall give her your sentiments, madam.'

'Oh, must you call me madam. It sounds so archaic.'

'Here,' Ruben said, giving her the plate to hold. 'I'm driving.'

'What may that be, I wonder?'

The Sunbeam Alpine still had some life, even though it lost a wheel hub. Two miles on Ruben made a predictable statement. 'I should have bought the Aston.'

'Why refuse in the first place?'

'Because it would make me feel bought.'

'He wasn't buying you, he was bribing you.'

'Bribing me?'

'You only gave him half the diamonds.'

'Ah.'

'Ah indeed.'

'Why do you wear grey?'

'It matches my hair.'

'Do you ever wear colour?'

'When I'm off the case, yes, I wear grey.'

She went quiet after that and Ruben shot a glance to his side. The plate sat at her feet and her eyes sat on her notepad as if any moment she would fall into it. The signs were never wrong. She surrendered to sleep.

What an opportunity. He pulled over, rounded the passenger side, and laid her on the back seat then rummaged in her handbag. Every guilty squeak was a bandit, every puff of wind a ghost. But he had to know. For his own peace of mind, he had to know. It was almost a relief when he found it tucked in the small crease of her purse and aside the capsule he had gave her earlier that day. But relief was quickly supplanted by doubt and just as quickly by misery. Had she not told him, many times over, they had no future? Had she not said this morning it should not happen again?

Instead of an easy ride home, the foot went hard on the gas, three cameras sequentially clocking a Sunbeam Alpine. Then, as Ruben turned into Wymondham he sensed a change in the ambient murmur of the town. Tentatively he slowed, instinctively knowing what it was, hoping it was not. And Grey, somehow, feeling it too, clambered over the front seat, instantly switching into the liveliest state.

Picked out by the drifting smoke, accompanied by the ever-diligent firemen, pin-pricks of light blazed their story, tracing the charred timbers. It had been four hours of hard fighting, beating back flames with water and axes, no retreat, protect the adjacent assets at cost to the shop with a magical window display. Even the brick-built workshop had been annihilated to prevent further spread. It was a sight to render any man speechless.

Emerging from the thinning crowd of onlookers was a soot-blackened face, the shoes making puddle tracks on cindered ground. Ruben embraced his grandfather.

'I'm alroit, lad, don't yew be fretting.'

'What the fuck happened?'

'Kids climbed round the back and let off some fireworks, thass all.'

'All! We got no bloody home!'

Elsewhere, Grey attached her interest at a fireman reeling a hose. 'Have you found the seat of the fire?'

'Now there's an intelligent question.'

'Do you intend to answer it?'

The part-time fireman removed his hat and wiped the sweat off his brow. 'What's your interest?'

'So, it was started deliberately?'

'I never said that.'

'It was written on your hat.'

Victor transferred his gaze to Ruben. 'You got a smart one there, Ruby.'

'Tell me about it. What's the verdict?'

'Kids,' he confirmed. 'The governor reckons a couple of rockets smashed through the first floor window round the back.' Victor leaned close to the ear. 'I felled your stash through the floorboards.'

'Anyone notice?'

'Not a peep.'

'Thanks, Victor, I owe you one.'

'Children are not allowed to buy dangerous fireworks,' Grey interposed. 'And most certainly not well after the 5th of November.'

'Well, they get them somehow,' Victor said.

'Even so, they should be found and their parents punished. Any likely suspects?'

Victor stood uneasy, casting his blackened eyes at Ruben. 'Just a thought, take it how you want but those rockets are not sold over the counter.'

CHAPTER 19

The night had been so profoundly lonely and so profoundly still that he believed his was the only heart beating in the house by the river. Sleep was impossible when the mind raced.

From a trading point of view, and Christmas being the most lucrative time of the year, stock and shop destroyed, he might as well call it a day. From a personal point of view, he was left pretty much homeless with just the clothes on his back and an urgent need to hide the gold. Disregarding who was behind this, the fight to regain a piece of territory in the community was gone. In its place was something much different, a pair of trauma-strained eyes washed by the faint radiance of dawn.

Standing by the open back door as if pneumonia would be a blessing, a scented presence came from behind, brushed soft against him.

'It may not be the right time to say this but fate now charts a positive course.'

'Gee, that's comforting. For a moment I gained the impression I was charting a negative course.'

'Ruben, I will forgive your sarcasm because things look terribly bleak, so terribly bleak and God knows it cannot feel much bleaker but if you were to keep hold of your house in Newmarket, you could-'

'I could do what?' He turned angrily at Grey. She too had hidden agendas. 'Reinstate my memories of Helena Vale? Relish moments of being screwed to the ground? When will you get it into your witch's head the only thought I wish to carry of Jeffrey Cane is the formula.'

'A good man lost in the scheme of things.'

'He was an imbecilic gerontologist who thought he could change the world when in reality the world changed him. What has been done to me and those around shall not go unpunished. I shall rip the heart out of that bastard and sleep very easy in my bed…when I get a bed.'

'You have a bed here.'

'And you have one at the Abbey Hotel. So why are you here?'

She touched his face. Her hand was warm and soft, sweeping back his dishevelled hair. 'You feel so cold, Ruben. Come inside and close the door, have something warm to drink.'

'I wish to drink the blood of my enemy.'

'Do you know your enemy?'

'The bastard who burnt down my home.'

'Oh, Ruben,' she sighed, 'it's you that is your worst enemy. You took on the liabilities of Lenard Green and Peter Tudmoor knowing the thought of your own death troubled you far less than the thought of being discovered.'

Whatever was left of his guard had crumbled away in the candour of her words. 'I just lost the plot, Grey. When Charlie told me he sold out to Fuller, I had this crazy notion Fair Life Assurance should pay. If anything, maybe subconsciously I wished for exposure, in particular the need of data from someone who could relate their findings. I don't know, life went on, becoming clearer our days were numbered in a business that saw fewer footfalls by the week. Charlie was happy to plod along, the shop his life. This will be the end of him.'

'Go make tea, my woman.' The old man stepped up and placed a shielding arm about his grandson's shoulder, his eyes misted with recollection and regret. 'We reap wat we sew, Ruby, so pay no mind to my losses. Lenard Green, a suffering man, like Peter, and yes, this foolish old man locked your future in their travels.' He back-wiped a tear from his eye and stepped outside. 'Do yew see that rock, lad?'

Ruben sauntered to the boulder that had his name chiselled at birth. As a young lad it had given him a seat to ponder, provided anchorage in the many confusing memories of his past life as Jeffrey Cane.

'Rising as the tallest of towers, and my feet never touched ground until I was six.'

'I lived fer yew, Ruby, and wat I had in my power to give. If yew want to continue in my footsteps thass fine by me but I shan't be turning a lathe no more. I shall be turning over this boulder to shoulder their gold.'

'Not on your own, not without me.'

'Look, lad, make use of wat years I got left. I shall be here to answer the door, give yew chance to sort yerself out.'

Ruben nodded in understanding. There would be time to handle the details later. For now, he needed to get warm. 'Come on, Granddad. Let's have a cup of tea.'

They picked up their feet and trekked into a Post-it-Notes-on-the-wall kitchen, drawing round a teapot and chocolate cheesecake.

'This looks good,' Charlie said, cutting himself a slice.

'Harcourt's cook made that. Grey, do you want a piece?'

Wielding a pen, she twizzled round on her heels and made a definitive statement. 'Able Windsor is Edward Harcourt.'

They looked at her as though about to give utterance to some majestic statement.

'I think,' she said, 'he underwent plastic surgery, returned in the guise of a chauffeur, leaving his father none the wiser.'

'It makes no sense. Why go to that extreme? Why not return as the prodigal son?'

'Okay, I agree, it sounds bizarre.' She pointed to a date. 'What exactly happened in 1980 between him and his father we can only hazard a guess, but he left and bought a new identity, a new face and returned in 1992 shortly after his mother had died. Now, all he had to do was wait for a sick old man to pop his clogs then off with the masquerade and ta dah, Edward Harcourt reveals himself as the rightful heir to his father's estate.'

'Why not mention it when we were there?'

'Probate first, Ruben. After probate he can sing all his songs.'

'April Jones? He never bargained fer her.'

'No, Charlie, quite right, he's in a sticky situation like this Post-it Note,' and flicked it from her fingers, 'if she ever found out, hello blackmail.' Referring to her notepad, she said, 'Present day, when Michael Fuller contacted Sir John, he sent April Jones on a mission and we all know what resulted in that little fiasco. What a stroke of luck, April Jones no longer a problem thanks to Ruben Stone. His father no longer a problem thanks to Ruben Stone and the entire fortune lands in his lap.'

'And when the real Edward Harcourt comes on the scene, then what?'

'He is Edward Harcourt.'

'John would know his own son.'

'He left at twenty years old, in 1980, had twelve years to grow up and change his face. But the one thing he failed to do was obliterate entirely a birthmark on his neck.'

'That was no birthmark. It was a love bite.'

'Ruben,' she said annoyingly, 'Edward had a pronounced birthmark in the same place as Windsor. I saw it in one of the photographs.'

'So, what you're saying is that he killed Fuller and burnt down the shop while we were dining at his table? Does that sound logical to you?'

'Of course, he never burnt down the shop but it's possible he killed Fuller.'

'Why? Why would he kill Fuller? He was obscure, irrelevant, unknown you said to his father and likewise to April Jones.'

'I admit there are some minor cracks in my theory but-'

'I shall tell you my theory with no cracks at all. April Jones killed Fuller and the bastard who razed the shop is sitting behind her desk rubbing her hands.'

'Susan Fuller?'

'Yes, so go tell God and get my money.'

'She has no motive to destroy your home.'

'What is clear to the common man is as unclear to you even in sleep. She sought revenge, blames me for her son's death and nothing is worse than a woman who loses the one thing that matters in life. Unless you had children, you would know this. But in doing so, she stripped Charlie of his property because she holds the deeds to a blank space in a prime position in town. Now tell me if that doesn't make more sense than Edward masquerading as a damn butler?'

'I gained the impression he was holding back.'

'Of course he was holding back. He had you snapping at his heels, prodding and probing, looking for someone to blame. What else makes you think Windsor is Edward?'

'He was too protective over the Will for one thing and he talked as if born to education.'

'The man was a librarian so he would know long words.' To her smile he took the notepad out of her hand, comprehending it was more precious to her than to him. 'Why write things down when you have a computer?'

'For the same reason you keep the formula in your head. The notes get burnt when the case is finished, client confidentiality protected.'

For Ruben, he considered the case closed and passed the notepad to Charlie under her watchful eye. 'Do you remember what you told me? That we live in different worlds; that when the case was solved you would go back to yours and I would go back to mine?'

'Oh, Ruben, please don't do this.'

'Give me one good reason why not?'

For a character with such a blustery personality and intuitive qualities, Grey was secretly afraid of being wrong. Or was she afraid of closing the case and losing Ruben Stone? She looked up into his eyes and for a thousand silly reasons said, 'I cannot find one.'

'Charlie, burn it.'

While sentence was executed Ruben walked on, a sadder person could not be found. He had weathered many storms but to weather the storm of Grey would tip him far beyond the reaches of sanity.

The streets were empty of life, like the shop that was no longer a shop but a gaping void between two other premises. Part of the staircase still remained, winding upward from a great mound of ashes. Fragments of broken steps offered an insecure footing and then were lost again. Beyond these charred ruins, ghostly fragments of a carpenter's life could be seen, broken bottles and corrupted walls that once held the truths of Ruben Stone. The axe had made its mark on all but the smallest of things and buried under a pile of rubble was untouched gold caught in the tangle of splintered wood.

Elsewhere, destruction amplified the memories. No longer would he sit by the stove sculpting a piece of wood or nursing a whisky at the end of a day. No longer would he watch the sun filter past the grilled windows or smell the fragrance from his potted blooms. Picking his way through the debris he came across the carved facsimile of Grey. By some miracle the witch had survived unscathed.

'Hello? Mr. Stone?' Clambering over and in between the burnt-out mayhem was a uniformed officer with a toothbrush moustache, his walkie-talkie broadcasting a yelping voice. 'Sorry about that,' and turned the volume down. Introducing himself as PC Muddy, he went on to say, 'Hard to imagine such damage in so short a time, sir.'

'These buildings carry old timbers. Would you like me to show you where-'

'Just need to ask a few questions. Then I can be on my way.'

'Let me save you some time. Yes, the fire was started deliberately. No, I was in Bury at the time. Do I have a witness? She is presently staying at the Abbey Hotel. Do I have any enemies? Only if you count the arsonist who failed to leave a calling card, and where shall I be in case you need to question me further? Down the road, turn left and it's the third house on the right.' There was no response from the wax-blue image. 'Have I missed anything out?'

'How about insurance for a Sunbeam Alpine registered in your name?'

Oops! 'I can explain.'

'Let me save you some time, sir. You were in Bury and could see these premises on fire. So you jumped into your motor accompanied by your witness presently staying at the Abbey Hotel and put your foot to the floor, ignoring all speed limits and safety of others in the hope of rescuing the insurance policy which is currently out of date by two days.' The smile was artificial. 'Have I missed anything out?'

'The bit where you get to tell me how I stand.'

'Without a licence, sir.'

Perhaps there was chance to melt the heart behind the uniform. 'All I have left is my motor. Take away my licence and I can't do business.'

'Sorry to hear it.' One click to the biro, Muddy was far from sorry. 'Do you have your licence?'

'Let me see, do I have my licence.' Ruben patted his suit pockets. 'No, it's not here,' and then stamped his foot through the carbonized remains of a dollhouse and proffered a handful of ashes. 'The address needs changing.'

'Oh, very good, sir, we are a comedian. Perhaps you would like a bed at the station?'

'Am I likely to find an officer that can investigate a crime?'

Muddy shifted on his feet, balancing to savour his dictatorial role when suddenly he dropped through a hole, parting with his walkie-talkie.

In a manner unruffled, Ruben craned his head. The plod was sat on his derriere gathering his wits, soon to establish his losses.

'Are you okay down there?'

'Yes, fine.'

'Should you get bored, there's a jigsaw puzzle in the chest.'

'If you lend me a hand, I can pull myself out.'

'That's a novel idea, lending a hand to someone in need. Did I happen to mention I needed my car?'

'Yes, sir, you did. But you broke the law and it's my duty to enforce the law.'

'Then why are you not catching criminals?'

'I'm a traffic cop, not a detective.'

'You detected my insurance ran out.'

Nursing his traffic-cop cap, the image of being left down a hole was becoming more real. 'Don't make matters any worse than they are.'

'How worse can it be? You're down there. I'm up here. And oh look, you left your radio behind. A fascinating dilemma, one which I'm sure we may overcome with tact and patience.'

'I can do nothing about your speeding fines.'

'How many did I clock up?'

'Nine points on your licence.'

'I can live with that. Can you live with that?'

For the sake of his health and sanity, and perhaps for the sake of his job, PC Muddy sighed resignedly, victory denied. 'It appears to me there was a genuine misunderstanding between you and your insurance company. I shall let you off with a warning this time and ask you not to drive until you get adequate cover.' Now that Ruben had clawed back what deemed to be another loss, he stooped and seized the hand in a simple rescue. When all said and done, courageous fireman had risked their lives in a spiralling inferno, here a traffic cop had only his pride at stake. He slapped the dust off his uniform, picked up his walkie-talkie and went on his way to find another poor sod to taunt.

Energized by victory, Ruben gripped the wooden facsimile of Grey in contemplation of a lucky charm and headed for Fuller Estate Agent across the road. No doubt Mrs Susan Fuller would be counting her gains.

Dressed smart in a red suit, she was mulling around Lulu's desk in a friendly exchange then turned her head with a weighted and worried look.

'We need to talk.'

'Talk, yes, in my office.' Closing them in, she came straight to the point. 'Who did this, the same person who killed my son?'

'Have the police been in touch?'

'Police notch it up to vandalism.' She went to the coffee-maker and poured two cups of decaf. 'Do you still want it?'

'Now why should I pay for a hole in the wall?'

'The insurance company will make good.'

And I pay double its original valuation. That would suit her very nicely. 'Bought any fireworks lately?'

Her sleep-starved mind barely registered the inference. 'Victor told me those rockets cannot be bought over the counter. Are we looking at the same person who killed my son?'

'April Jones killed your son and I killed her.'

The grieving mother sipped her coffee, trying valiantly to appear composed. 'April Jones,' she uttered and then her features took on a satisfied glow. 'How did she die, painful I trust?'

'Grey will fill you in with the details.'

'Maybe it was kids, Ruben. Victor said you can buy those rockets as easily as you can buy a gun. You just have to know the right person.'

'So,' Ruben said a little unsure if he had pegged her right, 'you're happy with the result?'

'Ruben, I cannot thank you enough. Justice you promised and justice you gave. If you want our agreement to stand, I shall do all I can to make sure you get that shop rebuilt as soon as possible.'

'At the price agreed?'

'What makes you think I would renege on our agreement?'

'I had this crazy idea you set fire to the shop.'

'You need your head examining.'

Alone he would agree. 'If he just kept his mouth shut, he would still be alive and I would be working the business.'

'Not without Charlie.'

'Why say that?'

'The spokes in the wheel that worked the business was never at any time more than a peculiarly reticent grandson to a white haired grandfather who shared his workload for many years. But the hub of this wheel and its hard driving force was indisputably Charlie. Everyone knows it, and I understand it. We want our offspring to follow in the same steps, as if we require a residue of ourselves.'

'I was hiding from myself.'

'And Charlie was giving you cover. Like that time when you pushed Sam Dingle off the bridge. He kept you at home instead of school.'

'It served a purpose.'

'What must it be like to have so much knowledge in a child's body, hard I should imagine?'

'I never handled it well, too much going on in my head. Amy and Sam were the only true friends at the end of the day, still are. The place needs boarding up.'

'All arranged.'

'You're on the ball.'

'I cannot afford some idiot breaking a leg and claiming damages. Is there much to salvage?'

'The fire took everything except for the workshop and that sits in a heap of rubble.' He finished his coffee. 'Keep an eye on Charlie for me.'

'You're not coming back?'

Ruben regarded her question rhetorical. What did he have to come back to? Outside, his gaze briefly snagged on Grey, frantically waving from across the road. There would be no further discussions or long goodbyes and made a dash to the car park before she could offer food in her honey voice. There had been a fragile tendril of intimacy between them but even so his resume read like a graveyard and was still in working progress. He was off to see Able Windsor, had no idea what his future held or if his honourable pursuit for justice would fall in tattered shreds.

Wymondham shrunk steadily in the rear view mirror, a town that had given him invisibility. He stopped off along the way, grabbed a sandwich and considered over coffee to do a recce of the grounds before stepping up to the door. Although checking things out in the daylight struck as a dumb thing to do.

In the motor now, parked in a side road opposite the colonnaded mansion he found an apple in his glove compartment and rubbed it clean. He then brought out his chiming pocket watch, looked at the time, flicked open the rear casing and discovered a headache pill. Huh? His first thought was Grey. Was this in retaliation to searching her handbag or was it Charlie taking back his safety net? Either way he was fucked.

When the light subsided, replaced by a darker sky, he left his motor to abandon one fire in order to enter a furnace. Moving stealthily between the undergrowth, he belly-crawled across an exposed part of the rear garden then braced himself flat against the wall. It was risk reduction, electing not to buccaneer into the open. Edging towards a light source, he peered round a column to gain a clearer view of a heavily lit patio set in flagstones and potted conifers. For a while, he listened for noise, for conversation but there was only the crackle of winter yet through it came the clarity of a single truth. He was bloody freezing.

Now that Ruben had acquired new reason to move on, he ambled up to the patio doors and quietly let himself in. No one was present, just a visible light from the lapping tongues of a coal fire which sent heat and shadows around an unfamiliar room that preached a lordship's comfort. After helping himself to a brandy and a cigar, he wandered to the hearth, sat in a wing-backed chair and loosened his tie. And suddenly the world seemed at peace.

Not even Windsor's entrance disturbed the moment. 'Have you returned for the Aston?'

'Actually, I returned for my wheel hub.'

'That might explain why your suit is dirty.'

Despite the seriousness of the situation, neither of them could help smiling.

'Grey thinks you are Edward Harcourt.'

'Her thinking is correct.'

In response, Ruben blew a smoke ring, watched it drift into the ether then allowed his gaze to settle on the centre parting. 'What made you leave the family home?'

What indeed. 'On long walks he would explain nature in terms of reason. Why should human behaviour not submit itself to similar logical processes? But the most interesting about this educational pastime was his ability to bed everything in sight. What better method of procuring a son. I found her, you know, my true Mother and took her name.'

'I wondered if, by your father's actions regarding the deaths of Cane's wife and her lover that you left because of it.'

'The final nail in the coffin so to speak.' Windsor gave a tug on the bell rope. 'We can talk in the morning. Zoe will show you to your room.'

Not that his smouldering dissatisfaction was visible, Ruben shifted his weight off the chair when she bounced in like a cat on a hot-tin roof. Eyes heavily blackened, plump red lips, needle sharp hair and a midriff open to view, the only indication of propriety was in her voice.

'Come, you must be exhausted.'

In her upscale leggings, she ascended the marbled staircase with Ruben falling behind and somewhat working the windmills of his tired mind. A million questions to ask with nothing but mud and puddles in between.

'I must say, you're handsomely conservative, which is not surprizing for someone who came back from the dead.'

'I wouldn't put it quite like that.'

'How would you put it?'

'At the back of your mind.'

If her intention was to engender closeness then she was on a sticky wicket. Grey was all Ruben could think about, silky grey hair tumbling over his face as she rocked on his loins, laughing, panting, breasts bouncing elastically, fast, slow, she took him to the moon and back. A smile played on his lips.

The door opened and brought a vision of copious luxury. Feet disappearing in a thick piled carpet upon which stood a four-poster bed with all its swanky trimmings. He popped his head round the bathroom door. The shower looked inviting, the bed more inviting still. It had been such a long, long day, such a confusing and harrowing day that he had little mind to extend the conversation.

So, when Zoe left, he gave a sigh of relief and took from his pocket the carved facsimile of Grey. She had been right all along. Those intelligent, watchful eyes, the dark centre parting combined with a changing persona suggested Able Windsor was a man who could destroy him.

CHAPTER 20

'Did you send Zoe to destroy my home?'

'Abu Manu destroyed your home.'

In the dumb silence that followed, Windsor served breakfast in bed. Poached eggs on toast, grilled sausages and tomatoes, a newspaper tucked under his arm. 'Your grandfather takes a good picture.'

True enough, page 4 and caught on the hop, the old man shared the limelight with a firework arsonist who was captured last night by PC Muddy, a Traffic Cop that dished out more than a speeding ticket.

Well, well, well, Ruben mused and closed the paper feeling a little contrite but not enough to warrant an apology. 'Was this one of your usual duties, serving your father breakfast in bed?'

Windsor slipped his hands into his trouser pockets and sauntered to the window, looking upon his estate but not really looking at all. 'I was with him that night, at the banquet. Mother, as I thought her then, declined to listen to his pompous rhetoric, how science would alter the world.' Glancing back, he briefly added, 'Never understood his ideals.'

'Were you with him when he shot Geraldine and Pembroke?' The absence of a reply had already informed him. 'You were an inquisitive lad if I rightly remember.'

'It was too tempting not to leave the car when shots were fired. My fault was being seen at the window.'

'Your mother never guessed?'

'Barely comprehending the horrors, she enjoyed her privileges. I try not to dwell on those times.'

Ruben set his tray aside and went to the bathroom, leaving the portal open. 'So,' he called out, 'you up-sticks in search of your real mother. I presume the current one never tried to stop you.'

'We were never that close.' Windsor appeared in the doorway. 'The real argument began when he caught me reading his journal. It suited him to get rid of your wife and Pembroke. He was about to take credit for your work but the problem became clear. He never had the formula.'

'Even so, his position with the law would make it impossible to lay claim to such a discovery.'

'You forget his many influential friends, men willing to open the debate on euthanasia. But it remained unanswered. Through his frustration we locked horns and I learnt the nature of my bloodline. The road not taken, the word not spoken, his sins were casting long shadows. And damned if his fortune was going to be left to some whore he picked up along the way.'

'You got a new face.'

'And returned as the redoubtable Able Windsor.'

'I take it you still parade willing and Able?'

Windsor slapped his back, sending the razor blade wide. 'I always liked you. At the table you spoke your mind, never held back, and sometimes cracked a good joke. I wanted to be like you, but alas, my misguided youth travelled on a separate path. How long did it take Grey to work it out?'

'Most likely during my spin in the Aston.'

'Does she believe I killed Fuller?'

At present it suited Ruben to nod and wiped his face on the towel. 'Fuller was blackmailing you.'

'He was blackmailing Jones.'

'So, she killed him?'

'She was convinced it was you.'

'It doesn't add up.'

Windsor shrugged. 'I had your suit cleaned, your shirt washed and ironed. When you're ready come downstairs.'

The bathroom had been filled with sense and reason now looked forsaken, abandoned by Windsor who had quite literally dashed out the door.

Not so much a home from home as an exercise in living stylish. Ruben showered under a foot diameter head, dried off in a thick cotton bath robe and combed his wet hair with a silver-toothed rake. He then slipped on a starchily iron shirt, donned his three piece suit, chained his fob watch to the waistcoat pocket and stuck his feet through polished shoes. Standing back to observe his mirrored reflection, he looked the part and spoke the right words.

'Enter.'

'May I make your bed, sir?'

As the shadowy little smile came and went on the maid's face, Ruben nodded, unaccustomed to the attention he was given, though indeed was now enjoying.

Familiar in part to the layout of the colonnaded mansion, he wandered aimlessly like a floating cloud until he came across Zoe in the gym, exercising her perspiring figure on a treadmill.

'Looking for Abe?'

'Yes.'

'He took the Bentley. There's coffee in the drawing room.'

'How many servants run this place?'

'Just two,' she puffed, 'Mrs G and her daughter.'

'What do you do?'

'Try to look fantastic.'

Lip-biting, tongue-tied and avoiding the eye, Ruben took a cursory glance at the weights then followed his nose to the drawing room. Here, he poured from a silver coffee pot and asked himself why Windsor was so accommodating. Maybe he felt no threat because he never killed Fuller, and most certainly he never caused the fire. And Zoe, she was too prudent to say anything of merit.

'Don't get me wrong,' she said walking in, flushed from her exercise. 'I like older men. They usually lose their adolescence by the time they reach thirty and come into full maturity at forty-something. I suspect you past your adolescence before puberty.'

Ruben finished his coffee. 'It has been pointed out in a much complimentary way.'

'Grey?'

'Yes.'

'You admire her?'

'What's not to admire.'

'Then Abe was right. You have a thing for her.'

'Are you related to Windsor?'

She drowned a glass of water then picked up her mobile, playing some stupid game. 'You think because I'm half his age I must be his daughter.'

'Are you?'

'Vale was almost half your age.'

'We had something in common.'

'Sex,' interposed Windsor, his steps quickening into the room. 'Off you pop, sweetheart, keep company with Mrs G.' Reaching for the coffee pot, he said, 'I want to offer you a future.'

'By killing off the one I had.'

And here Windsor sighed, shook his head as men do when their minds are full. 'I admit I could have made contact, warned you about Jones but I had to protect my interests.'

'As I see it you could have lived off your own efforts and leave daddy alone.'

'We all make our choices, my friend. For you, is there not more to life than selling dollhouses?'

'Like dignity in death?'

'Yes.' He gestured to sit. 'Politically, the Chancellor is sitting on an elderly time bomb. We are living longer and many live long in a nursing home, costing the NHS a fortune. The Government is trying to address this matter by introducing another reform of National Insurance, forcing people to pay for their future care. You need not think any further to know that those who live out their lives in good health do not get their contributions refunded. In these austere times it is doubtful this proposal will get off the ground. From cradle to grave, this has been our fundamental right, reason why National Insurance was introduced.

Yet it fails to meet its objective. And palliative care is no guarantee of quality care. Price to obtain dignity in death from our nearest European neighbour is ten thousand pounds. A solution if you can make the crossing alone.' Then for some seconds Windsor looked very hard into his coffee before saying, 'It will happen. Sooner or later, it will happen. Parliament will be forced to debate euthanasia and if the law passes, I foresee an opportunity.' Windsor looked up in the pause. 'So, the question I must ask, do you wish to finish what you started?'

Ruben sat forward to look into the eyes of an older face. Behind those altered features was evidence of pain, the bridges crossed to regain a foothold in his father's empire. But there was also an element of senseless conceit. 'When it becomes law, only then shall I consider using my formula.'

'Lenard Green? Peter Tudmoor?'

'And because of them my life turned upside down.'

'Then we shall say no more about it. Your feelings are too strong to alter your perception.'

'You do realize your father's company feeds on the misery old people endure, especially in long-term illnesses.'

'As a sizeable shareholder I would hope to add some weight in the direction it takes. Would you consider working there?'

'What on, my formula?'

'Ruben, my friend, you have a fixation about your formula. Surely, with a brain like yours, there must be a nugget or two that could aid in the welfare of others.'

'It just so happened, I had genetically modified a strain of wheat intended to limit the age of the population.' That held Windsor in awe. 'Realistically speaking, death at seventy would save the country trillions. But then the population would stop eating the wheat once they figured it out.'

'And you did this recently?'

'No, I did it in your father's time, while waiting for Erik to turn up, but huh, it was not a Swede. Did you ever meet Neil Pembroke?'

'He was at our table that night. That's all I remember of him.'

'Did you take your father to meet a woman at a petrol station?'

'Yes. She was Mary, the same Mary you read in his journal. I do not know her address.'

'What did she look like?'

'Petite, elegant, soft in her movements…she wore a head scarf, appeared nervous.'

'Did he ever guess you were his son?'

'Odd, wouldn't you say, my friend, a father not really knowing his son's voice. I shall never forget when he hired me, a stroke of genius on my part. He looked at me with those far away eyes and asked if I knew how to care for a cripple. There were times I felt very compelled to reveal my identity. One day, I kept telling myself, one day you will die old man and I shall dance on your grave. Of course, when it came down to it, I never danced. I felt sad in a way. The death of Jeffrey Cane had become the death of him and in turn the death of his family. Nothing else mattered except that capsule. He thought if he could crack the code in Helena's book, find where she hid her capsule he could break it down. Do you know, he never even asked where I was going, just stood, watching me open the door and leave with suitcase in hand.'

'Tell me about Zoe?'

'Zoe,' he laughed gently. 'My Zoe is a cure for the cynical romantic. We met between the fishcakes and frozen peas. I cannot remember her exact words when we both went for the same packet of carrots but I do remember her asking if I came there often to which I had to answer in the negative. Mrs G normally orders the food in. Needless to say, I found an excuse to go again. How does it stand with you and Grey?'

'I left rather abruptly. You were right. She had a wedding ring in her purse.'

'What shall you do, my friend? Rebuild your premises, make dollhouses?'

'Charlie made the dollhouses. Now the fire has determined he will make them no more. And me, well, I do have a house in Newmarket, and most definitely a garage to take the Aston.'

'I have a confession to make. As no doubt you ponder my reasoning to ask for the diamonds when in reality, I have all this. I wanted to make contact, give you his journal to help in some small token. Yet I was apprehensive in giving away my identity.'

'How then will you explain your position with Harcourt Pharmaceuticals?'

'When probate is final, I will become Edward.'

'Some may recognise you as his confidante.'

'Nobody looks at a servant, they are second class citizens. When I walked in your shop, did you recognise me as Windsor?'

'You're right, I never recognised you, not until I saw you hovering outside.'

'You were his only visitor in the last ten years of his life which made my future more tenable as Edward Harcourt returning from abroad.'

'It seems you thought of everything.'

'Time on my hands there is not much else to do but think of everything. Would you like the Aston?'

'Do I get my diamonds back?'

Windsor smiled, rising to his feet. 'Help yourself to a drink. I shall not be long.'

Ruben sat back to work it through. He would cancel the sale, do up his house and get a hell of a lot more as Grey suggested. Notwithstanding potty Betty who could tax any mind, he would leave the gold buried in her garden, rebuild the shop and make flatpacks by the dozen. That would give Charlie an incentive. So often when a man retires, he retires his brain. At length, he got to his feet, poured a whisky and picked up the telephone resting on a Queen Anne desk.

'Hello,' the old man answered.

'I'm not selling my house.'

'Then yew need a carpenter.'

'I am a carpenter.'

'Yew wus a detective when yew left.'

'Yeah, right, is Grey there?'

'She's gone, Ruby, gone after seeing Susan Fuller. Yew will hev your money, she said, coming to this address. Wat do yew want me to do with it?'

'Take whatever you need then go see Victor and dig a bigger hole.'

'Here, did yew hear they caught who burnt down our shop?'

'I read it this morning. Charlie, liaise with Susan about the new building, tell her how you want it.'

'Yew better not be doing this fer me, Ruby.'

'Did you take back your capsule?'

'Grey gave it to me.'

'You know sometimes I cannot fathom her out. She replaced it with a headache pill. What was I supposed to do with that when I'm confronting Fuller's killer.'

'Has she come back again?'

'Who?'

'April Jones thass who.'

'I was not referring to her but to Windsor.'

'He killed Fuller?'

'No.'

'Ruby, make up your bloody mind.'

'I don't know who killed Fuller. Who does Grey think it is?'

'She told me if yew asked, I'm to tell yew why she should hev to put up with your antics. Now tell me boy, hev yew got the Aston?'

'As we speak, I get the Aston and my diamonds.'

'There yew go, it can't get better than that. Just yew remember to send me and Betty a Christmas card.'

'Since when do we send cards to each other?'

'Since yew now live in Newmarket.'

It was instantly a different world for Ruben Stone. In his crispy shirt and combed back hair he looked upon the glistening lawns, took a long pull on his whisky and figured it was time to get on with his life. Grey was out of the equation so wept not for her, because half a mil was coming his way. He had a DB9 and nine points to match on his licence.

CHAPTER 21

The oak door to the Chief Executive's office sounded to the knock of a woman. His secretary entered and approached to speak in a whisper.

Godfrey Shilling nodded, and, while his secretary retreated to perform her duties, once more addressed the small gathering. 'I think that just about concludes our meeting.'

While the double-breasted suits ventured beyond his office, he nonchalantly walked across the spongy carpet and poured two decafs. Not every executive believed he could pull it off. Some had their doubts. Rutherford, he mused, was privately patronizing. But no matter how critical he was of Grey she had come through and was here to collect her suitcase.

'Do you know,' he said and swung his head round with a plastered grin. 'It was four months ago when you slipped into this office and bowled me over.'

It felt like a lifetime for Grey. She slid out of her full length raincoat and dropped it on the chair. 'You would have me twiddled my thumbs in front of your secretary.'

'Force of habit, my angel…or I should call you my guardian angel. Susan Fuller happy, I now have her signature to a document exonerating this company of her son's wrong doing. Who killed him, she wouldn't say. Still, it matters not...'

While the Chief Executive was detailing his courageous battle to protect his company, Grey was looking out of the window. People were slipping into a white layered city like children getting lost in a circus, impatient, at last, to do their Christmas shopping. There would be no counter sales in the shop with a magical window display and sipped her coffee with aching regret.

'For reasons obvious,' Shilling continued, 'do you have a man standing by to escort you home?'

'Yes,' she said simply and turned to look at the suitcase resting on his desk. 'Half is all that should be paid and sent to Charles Stone.'

Shilling gestured to sit, his face composed of apprehension. 'Speak to me.'

'Can I be assured what passes between us is treated in the strictest of confidence?'

'You have my word.'

'Ruben Stone,' she began, 'had lived as another man in another life, a gerontologist who made a wonderful discovery. But the world in which he lived proved to be the same world in which he lives now - deceit and avarice by those with whom he trusted before. I cannot shed names or go into detail, but what I can say that he now has a new road to travel and, in his travels, I hope he finds what he's looking for. In doing so, I refuse to put further obstacles in his way and therefore decided to choose a victim that deserved to take the blame for Michael Fuller's death…'

To her tale, Shilling remained rooted to his seat, the symbolic acceptance of something beyond his entire understanding, and bathed in the contradiction of life and death. Incredible as her tale was, he kept his feelings under control with the absolute certainty she was telling the truth. At the centre of it all, visibly malicious, was April Jones who received her comeuppance through the accidental hand of Ruben Stone.

'For this reason,' Grey finished off, 'it suited to tell Susan Fuller that April Jones killed her son.'

'Do you know who did?'

Expediently, Grey shook her head. 'Ruben took the matter into his own hands and informed Susan Fuller it was April Jones. And since she is satisfied with that answer and can now move on, your problem has been solved at the same time.'

'Have you eaten?'

'I'm not really hungry.'

With that, the Chief Executive pressed the intercom button to his secretary and placed his order then transferred his attention to Grey, sending a bleak confession. 'I wish my Mother dead. Lost her marbles years ago, now confined to a nursing home costing me a fortune.'

'You should be ashamed of yourself.'

'She was an independent woman, always advocated euthanasia than sit all day staring into a void with dribbles running down her chin. An interesting scenario if that discovery becomes legal, people returning to visit their loved ones. Can you foresee the Government allowing it?'

'Ruben said the human race is not ready for such a discovery, and I tend to partly agree. Like all good discoveries, there are the opportunists. The internet is a prime example. I think some of us do live again in some small way, ever evolving. For Ruben, his mind is so fixated upon death that I wonder if he will ever divulge his formula. Still, I consider my task is complete and business concluded.'

'Take your half. I am satisfied.'

'On principal, I refuse.'

'I shall not argue with a stubborn woman.'

Grey gathered her coat. 'If you want to find use for the rest, I suggest you look through your files and find a way to compensate the losers. Susan Fuller is not exactly that generous with hers.'

As his secretary knocked and entered, Grey shook his hand and left an edifice which soaked the legendary power of Godfrey Shilling. Her life would start again with the same indefatigable nature that had led her to this point.

But the face of Ruben Stone haunted on. She had stood at a tricky crossroad, to leave or not to leave, and the intellectual challenge to put the blame on someone else. Then regret won out again when denying herself the finder's fee. The grey shroud of distress was conspicuous only by its absence. She wandered lonely as a beggar through the cold streets of slushy London, stopping occasionally at window displays. There was something so magical about Charlie's shop as if he too was a wizard conjuring up fairy tales for the cast of little people sculpted by Ruben, so beautifully enigmatic and suiting the role they should play.

'Tempted to buy?'

Grey turned sad at her fearless defender. She had every reason to love him, every reason to love the face that was no longer the face of her brother but half a distorted face, cracking his scarred skin. And she started to think about that time all over again, a dozen horrible images looming up like monsters, gasps rushing in and out of his bleeding mouth, gasps of air struggling to reach his smoke ridden lungs.

She squeezed her eyes shut to rid the horrible images then opened them again so what she saw was the face she now loved. 'What do you want for Christmas?'

'For you to be happy, but you're not happy, sis, are you?'

'Ironic,' she sighed, 'dead people cannot talk, not unless they take a capsule and live again. I wonder if she had taken another and was later discovered to have lived as April Jones would she be charged for the death of Michael Fuller.'

'You refused to take the money, didn't you?'

'I refused my half because it never felt right to take it,' which seemed an appropriate end to a bad day and fell into tears.

Instinctively, his arms curved protectively around her. 'Come on, sis, money isn't important when you have me?' His words passed from her mind like breath from a polished mirror. 'Tell you what. Let's do our Christmas shopping, get that out of the way then we go home and with any luck we can get our skates out. What do you say?'

With a lighter heart, and eyes the brighter for the tears that dimmed her, she resumed the dialogue. 'Do you know what they want?'

'Buy the same then there can be no arguments,' and walked on with his hand in hers, taking them into a book store. People stared, tried not to show they were staring but they stared all the same, at the two of them, all through their journey, choosing books. Two hard-back titles were purchased. Gallows Humour for their mother because she enjoyed quirky ghost stories, and Giddy Midnight for granny who merely cherished blood and gore.

It kept on snowing, spotting endlessly into the ground, blanket layers building over blanket layers that all one could see of a land and a lake was wavy lumps and stiletto humps where half a fortress rose. The years ran back through its pattern of confusion, almost shamefully blighted by a sinister history. But it drew Grey's family together in a web of secrecy and cut them off almost entirely from the outside world.

There were the usual hugs and kisses and then a stumble into silence. The dog barked, a door slammed and Grey pulled on a pair of jeans, joining her brother William dressing the tree.

'Are we skating or not?'

'The ice is thin in places,' Granny Martha said without looking up from her knitting.

'Is that true?' Grey asked.

'If I say it's true then it's true.' Martha spoke no more after that, the unbending grandmother with a straight back and strict features.

That there were now occasional sounds of feet and voices, three of the occupants of this odd country seat lazed in a convivial lounge proud in the light of a Christmas tree. William sat reading the paper, and Grey remained mute like a scarce-breathing parcel of flesh while granny hummed gaily to her clacking needles. There were moments when Grey was almost moved to more tears and rounded the polished oak floor like a prowling tiger, looking for something to do.

'Not long now,' Granny said, her silvery head slightly tipped to one side. 'Not long before we eat. Put some flesh on your bones.'

'I have flesh,' and poked her nose in a vase. 'Do we ever put flowers in this?'

'What on earth are you wanting, girl? Your body arrived but not your mind.' Granny dropped the knitting into her lap with some uneasy glances and shouted at the dog. 'Doodle! Give that to me!'

Doodle the poodle ignored the reprimand and shot behind the sofa with a stolen ball of wool. His behaviour had worsened since the death of Bobble.

'Dinner ready,' Mother cooed.

They picked up sticks and travelled to the feasting table like a plotted strategy. William escorted Granny Martha in her beaded choker after she kicked the dog and Grey followed on from behind, smiling. She was almost certain her brother had bought her a cat. Why else would there be one less present under the tree?

'For what we are about to receive may our ancestors make us truly grateful.'

After granny's dictum they all sat down in their designated spots. Granny Martha had the most bulbous chair at one end of a table that was as long as a yacht. The other end sat widowed Silvia, eyes of orchards, a jewelled mother unconscious of her beauty. Brother and sister, born three minutes apart, sat opposite each other, and in between the large voids the dog roamed free to pay duty to each one.

'Sweetheart, why the long face?'

Avoiding the question, as she always avoided awkward questions, Grey told her mother, 'I was just thinking of my next assignment.'

'Do you have a next assignment?'

'No, I was just thinking *when* I might get my next assignment.'

'William, what was her last assignment to make her so cheerful?'

He lifted the fork to his face and said, 'Ruben Stone,' just before the meat reached his mouth.

But it was Grey who started to repeat herself, telling a tale she had told to Shilling earlier that day, even briefly covering the website drawn up by Doctor Hope. 'If euthanasia is made legal, then his discovery can be put to good use,' she ended.

'Sis, that product is a licence to kill. Anyone who wants to rob a bank or do away with his next door neighbour, they come back again with impunity. Life suddenly has no meaning, risk is no risk at all and in the end anyone who doesn't feel comfortable with their lot will take pot luck in the next life.'

Brushing a wisp of hair behind her ear, Grey formed a different opinion. 'Controls will be put into place.'

'What controls? They cannot control the use of Class A drugs let alone control the use of a mind-blowing reincarnation.'

'Harcourt Pharmaceuticals could administer the drug.'

'Do you really think Ruben Stone is the only clever man on this planet? Someone will get hold of his product and dissect it, piece by piece until they have his formula.'

'In that I have no doubt, which goes without saying if it isn't Ruben, it will be someone else. Surely, it's better to get this out in the open, control it the best way we know how. Think of the good it can do.'

'Think of the bad it can do.'

'Surely the good outweighs the bad.'

'If nature had wanted us to keep our memories, don't you think we would be doing that now?'

'To be fair,' her mother entered the debate, 'some people do claim they are the reincarnation of another life.'

'They never claim to be a chimney sweep or a muck spreader. It has to be someone of notoriety and bandy names such as Queen of Sheba or Lord Nelson.'

Granny spoke. 'I believe there is something more than us mere mortals. In fact, I know there is something more.'

'I believe there is nothing more frightening than a woman who believes they are right.' William generated smiles at the table. 'Sis,' he said in a more affable tone, 'are you in love with this Ruben Stone?'

This was uncomfortable as it was uncomfortable refusing her fee from God. 'Just because I admire his work does not mean to say I want to bring him home for tea. And besides, men like him take women to bed and leave in the morning.'

'He can leave in the morning and come back at night,' Granny said.

'Martha!' Mother scolded. 'How can I instil propriety when you make comments like that?'

'Shut up, Silvia. She knows what's she's doing, don't you, my girl?' Without pausing for a reply, Martha used her fork as a pointer. 'See that face. It has the markings of rejection. He spurned her counsel for want of his sanity.'

'Is this true?'

'Shut up, William. If I say it's true then it's true.'

Knowing the mocking eyes of the world were upon him, he failed to respond because only women in the family tree gained second sight.

'I'm not going to have children,' Grey said in defence of her brother.

'You may have no choice,' and at last Granny had everyone's attention, her crooked finger illustrating a circle. 'You stepped into his ring of destiny and made it your own, fused by the flames of his ardour.'

'Is this true?' Silvia asked and warned Martha. 'If you say it's true, Martha, I shall tape up your mouth.'

'I was in an emotional crisis due to losing Bobble.'

If this voluntary confession had a purpose, her diamanté mother showed no trace of wavering. Her lips compressed with deep and settled purpose.

'It was just a dip in the water, Mum.'

'Then you used him like the pearls round your neck, nice to wear on the right occasion.'

'I don't know why I should justify my actions. I'm single and entitled to sleep with whom I please.'

They all shook their heads, remaining mute in the afterthought of her statement. And then, as if there was nothing left to say, they took up their eating. The only consolation, if there was consolation to be had, she made two hundred grand in the original case of Ruben Stone.

Her appetite had diminished. Against propriety, she left the table and took a few sedate steps to the door, then quickly left to venture outside. Muffled up to the eyeballs, she crunched snow across a white silent lawn. The lake nearby was stiff and black but in parts was icy thin yet not for a moment did she feel the cold. Steadily she worked her way around the lake, sometimes collecting dead sticks and throwing them away, reminding herself of the time she walked the river path with Ruben Stone. To prevent him thinking that he was the only man seriously to have twisted her heart, she told him a precautionary tale from her past, of falling in love with her private tutor, which was untrue. And somehow it seemed wrong, a feeling it was wrong to push him away, a premonition or a warning, something she missed.

Fifteen minutes passed by when she found herself looking at the crumbling tower, once a tall round narrow structure forming part of the larger, lower building. Through its entire history no one cared to rebuild it, no one cared to tempt providence. It was a stone wreckage, more ghostly than ever, a former site that had seen weapons drawn, the rages of desperation, the sharp end of holy war that played to a baying crowd. A final settling of historic scores.

Her gaze alighted on Willam kicking his feet through the snow, red scarf, orange bobble hat, yellow jumper, his wardrobe malfunction on this occasion. 'Gran is right, the lake is not completely frozen solid.'

'Gran said to tell you that I never bought you a cat.'

'Oh, why must she always read my mind...that wasn't a question by the way. So, what did you buy me?'

'I hid it because you always guess before you open it.' He patted her on the back as if he was about to throw her a biscuit and nudge her into a basket. 'You got to have kids, sis. I want to be an uncle.'

'Great, just summon me up a man who wants to live here at his peril.'

'You don't believe in the curse.'

'It's a curse putting up with Gran.' She looked at the forsaken remnants of that tower, once built of stone, had hand-carved windows, moss-flaked tiles and walls so thick they kept a damp chill inside them whatever the season or weather. 'Odd, really odd that Ruben is a carpenter and his name is Stone.'

'Has he asked you to marry him?'

'No, silly. I was just wondering if it was a sign for us to rebuild the tower.'

'We don't tempt fate. You know the rules.'

'Rules are meant to be broken.'

'Is that why you slept with Ruben Stone?'

The thought of it made her light headed with a twinge stirring below but she told herself it was only sex, a natural bodily function she normally took great pains to avoid. It was entirely likely she would never see Ruben again. In fact, it would be a miracle if she did.

They walked into the house, the dog following at William's side. Grey continued straight ahead, down a long and wide hallway to the kitchen. The hard wood floors creaked underfoot. Her mother was returning the lid to a hot tea pot, her poise as steady as a gymnast.

'Mum, I'm sorry.'

'Sorry is for a penitent man seeking absolution.'

Grey sat down and put her hands in her lap, under the table. 'His father died in a car crash, his mother slit her wrists three days after he was born. He's very easy to talk to and we talked a lot.'

Her mother stopped pouring tea. 'I married your father because I loved him. You went to bed with a man you neither married nor loved. What will you do if you find yourself pregnant?'

'We could talk about baby clothes and cute names, go browsing round Mothercare, make jokes about epidurals, except that I'm not pregnant and if Dad was here, I would be in a position to love someone.' The moment she said it, she regretted it. 'Oh, Mum, I never meant to say that.'

Instead of words in the kitchen there were screams, memories of the cries of people dying but not dying quickly, shrieks that conveyed the intensity of their despair in a train crash. The terrible day he died. Holding his hand in hers, leaning over him to hear his final whisper *look after them* and then his hand going slack. She had kissed his forehead, his rough cheek, held fast to her dead father's hand, the world unthinkably hard without him.

SIX MONTHS LATER

CHAPTER 22

June 2013

After a few minutes, the noise of an echoing rasp quietened again. Ruben laid his saw to one side and lifted the worktop into position.

A taxi drifted into the road, its engine clacking loudly, drawing his attention. The door opened and a couple spilled out. The woman was not Grey. It seemed so fresh in his mind, even now, six months later and thirty miles away. He just remembered her waving, those moments of frantic waving. When he stood back to admire his latest achievement, the plumber walked in with his bag full of tools.

'Can we square up?'

'Let me see now. The boiler and rads came to sixteen hundred, including pipes and fitting, make it two and a half grand. Three days connecting two bathrooms and the cloakroom downstairs, for cash let's says an even three grand.'

Ruben, with his wad of cash stored in a teapot, counted out fifties and gave them to the plumber who squashed the notes in his back pocket. No sooner had he left someone else hobbled in on crutches.

'Call yourself a carpenter?'

'Call yourself a soldier.'

'Hell, shit happens.' Sam Dingle swung on to a chair to rest his plastered foot. 'Got my arse peppered with shrapnel, dived into a ditch and snapped my ankle.'

'How did you get here?'

'A mate dropped me off. Charlie said look for a bloody fantastic dark green DB9 on the driveway and here I am. Take me back in that any day of the week.'

'She runs like a beauty.' Ruben pulled two cans of lager from the fridge. 'How long do you reckon before going back?'

'Depends how fast it heals. Cheers.' Glug, glug, and the soldier came to the point. 'What the fuck are you doing here, man?'

'Is that Ding speaking or Charlie?'

'He's worried about you. Hardly a call, never a visit and everyone's asking why you left.'

Ruben leaned back in his chair with eyes so sunken and so shadowed by his brows that he remained silent for a short time and then said slowly. 'I have to finish what I started.'

'Here? You have to finish it here by doing up the place. I can't see it and neither does Charlie. Doesn't this place give you the creeps?'

'Sure, it's creepy. But this is where it all started for me, Ding. And this is where it ends.'

'You're not thinking of doing yourself in.'

Ruben sighed, leaned forward and rested his elbows on his trouser-dust knees, rolling the can between his palms. To himself he would admit there had been moments, tempting moments but they were fleeting moments of despair from a man who walked alone. 'There was nowhere else to go but here, and besides it was pointed out that I was crazy to sell this property for peanuts, so why not do it up and get a good price.'

'Charlie said you were keeping the house.'

'Charlie gets his knickers in a twist.' Ruben would say no more about that. 'You want to stay awhile?'

'I was hoping for an invite.' The soldier grabbed hold of one crutch and said, 'Come on, show hop along Cassidy round.'

'Well, as you can see, I'm nearly finished in the kitchen. I just have to fix the worktops, wire in the ceramic hob and electrocute myself.'

'I can do that, no problem.'

'I'm glad you're here.'

'No hanky-panky in bed. I have a reputation to consider.'

Hardly a smile from Ruben, he showed his efforts to update a home that had fallen heavily into disrepair. The study, once the crime scene with blood splattered walls now accommodated a dining-room table and six chairs. In the lounge, glass bi-folding doors opened out to a sun-deck terrace, and under the heat of a mid-day sun, the soldier viewed it all and nodded. The mundane, which nearly always went with a four bedroom house, was skipped. It was the shed at the bottom of the garden that fashioned Ruben's world. Cluttered shelves, coloured bottles, high tech equipment, and in the corner, a single bed, recently slept. Habits rarely changed.

'I take it you don't bring the girls in here.'

'I don't take them anywhere.'

'So, you don't get your end away?'

'When did you?'

Two fingers up and Dingle sunk on the edge of the mattress, setting aside his crutch. A gleam of sun shone through a sealed window chequering the dark space with a broad patch of light. 'You remember Pat? She got a divorce.'

'Do you still fancy her?'

'Nah, she looks like a roly-poly pudding. Hey, you should see Amy, all dolled up and looking tasty. She asked about you.'

'I trust you kept her uninformed.'

'I kept her busy,' he responded with a big grin which faded to a non-responsive face. 'Have you heard from Grey?'

With a slight shake of the head, Ruben flipped the lid to his laptop and brought up his website. Over one hundred thousand, and counting, had now signed up for a debate. 'I revamped the website to push things along.'

'Are you going to sell your formula?'

'Good question.' Ruben came to rest beside his friend. 'Personally, I cannot visualize my discovery doing much good when man himself elects to live in a society of social inequalities.'

'So why do this?'

'Ding, if it brings about a change in the law, many people suffering from incurable illnesses will at least be given the basic human right to die in dignity.

Justice is not the only desirable characteristic of a society, kindness is also necessary.'

'Amen to that. So, what you got planned up your sleeve? Wait it out here until the law gets passed?'

'I have a plan.'

'I thought you might.'

As might he would and bent to pick up a cat. 'I call her Comeback.'

'Good name if she did.'

'A feral was living in these grounds and made nice company. But alas, riddled with nodes, I thought, why not. Then this little beauty turned up on my doorstep.'

'It could just be a coincidence.'

Ruben gestured to a local rag. 'Read for yourself, a six week old Persian leaving via a cat flap not half a mile away. I met the owner, nice lady and bought her, not the lady mind you. Comeback is very intelligent.' Returning the cat to the floor, he spoke to the animal in lighter tones. 'Where is your ball?'

The cat went meow and sat there looking dumb.

'So that's your plan, breeding illiterate cats.'

'My plan is to sell the house and make good a business in Wymondham.'

'Odd plan when you don't even visit.'

'Charlie is handling the layout.' Ruben looked down at the cat with a ball at its paws. 'See, it just takes a little faith.'

Dingle was unimpressed. 'Got anything to eat in that half-finished kitchen?'

A frozen pizza was shoved in the oven, cooking while the soldier spoke of friends they knew, like Tom Hutton, now a Town Councillor. Eventually they came circumspectly to the issue of Able Windsor.

'Probate came through a few weeks ago. He calls himself Edward now, offered me a job at Harcourt Pharmaceuticals.'

'And what did you say?'

'I gave it some thought. In fact, I'm toying with the idea of giving him my formula when the law is passed.'

'Charlie said Grey had him pegged as a liar.'

'Yes, he was lying out of self-preservation.'

'Have you spoken to her about it?'

'The last time I discussed anything with Grey was six months ago in front of Charlie, a keen listener to the conversation.' Ruben took the pizza outside and there they sat with the sun on their backs. 'In short, she felt very uneasy in forming a relationship and I can understand why. She had a wedding ring tucked in her purse.'

'You think she's married?'

'It suited my purpose to think so. On the one hand she was doing my head in. On the other, she was getting under my skin.'

The soldier quietly smiled. 'Doing your head in and getting under the skin amounts to the same thing.'

'I disagree. She was doing my head in because of April Jones.'

'What about April Jones?'

'She killed Fuller but could she see that? All she wanted to talk about was Windsor being Edward Harcourt.'

'She was right, he was Edward Harcourt.'

'Yes, but what difference does it make? He never killed Fuller and he never started the fire. Anyway, life moves on.'

As Dingle put his plate down, empty, on the deck, he glanced over the lawn with a worried expression. 'I hate to say this, pal. Running away isn't exactly my idea of finishing what you started.'

'Who said anything about running away?'

'You said-'

'I know what I said.' Little thinking of a plan for his happy settlement in life, Ruben wiped his hands feverishly down his jeans. As the weeks passed and as public interest grew, the results of sitting things out quietly began to show. 'If you want the bare facts, my mind is still in two places. Do I return to the life I had looking back with regret or do I press on with this crusade and go work in a lab? Grey asked me a similar thing and I didn't know then.'

'Fancy getting drunk?'

'I do that most nights.'

'Okay, here's an idea. We go to the Green Dragon, have a couple of quick pints and say you have to get back to the ruin.'

'What ruin?'

'Charlie told everyone you hitched up with Grey to spend time in her ruin.'

Ruben rolled his eyes. 'I told him to tell everyone I was busy doing up a house.'

'See, that never fitted too well because he couldn't say what house you were in. Come on, my man. It'll do you good to be with friends. If you like, I can get drunk.'

Ruben needed little persuasion. His life in which he lived had become a featureless desert where he talked to a cat, slept in a shed, ate when he remembered to eat and worked on a property that had no love.

The soldier, left alone on the deck while Ruben changed, continued to sit staring about him. He looked round and spied Comeback actively cleaning its white thick fur with a sweeping pink tongue. Was it at all possible this cat held memories of a life before? If so, how can one gauge the truth by a fetch of the ball?

'What's that?' said Dingle, pointing to the ball.

Comeback answered by an affectionate meow, submitted with an air of perfect indifference to be fondled, and turned a curious eye upon Ruben when he appeared in a pair of clean jeans.

'I shall be back late,' Ruben told Comeback. 'Are you ready?'

'Lead the way, my man.'

Closing the glass bi-fold doors, ensuring ground floor openings locked and leaving via the front entrance, there was no better sight than an Aston Martin ready to race the wind. Who could look on and see her lavish green lines, and not desire to own one of these? The accelerator was in greater danger of being put to the floor than a voluptuous woman.

Cracks in the road, signs on the side, and trees arching their branches, all these things merged into one another, although at the bottom of Ruben's every thought there was an uneasy sense of being caught speeding. He glared into the rear view mirror, indicated left, drove into a layby and just sat there while a blue peaked cap tapped on his window.

'Well, sir,' Muddy said, 'we have come up in the world.'

'And most grateful you allowed it so.'

'Please step out of your vehicle.'

In compliance, Ruben leaned against the bonnet, crossed his legs at the ankles and folded his arms. The outcome was palpable.

'Nice motor,' Muddy delightfully grinned. 'Pity you won't be able to drive for a long, long, long while.' He then went on to caution Ruben and added in utmost satisfaction, 'Should you get bored, I understand there's a jigsaw puzzle in your chest.'

'I don't suppose-'

'Not a chance. You were doing ninety.'

'Hell, that can't be right.'

'Why's that?'

'It's a bloody disgrace only doing ninety in an Aston.'

The policeman who had once been denied his victory deigned not a word in answer. If anything could have exceeded his joy on this occasion, it was thrusting a ticket into the top pocket of Ruben's shirt before rejoining his co-driver.

'It's odd,' Ruben said getting into the Aston, 'how man has allowed the development of the motor car, yet in a perverse sense disallows its pleasures. I never realized how slow my old motor until I drove this.'

'You still got it?'

'No. Fancy driving this one? I ask because I'm done, truly done. Nine points already on my licence which means I had a good run on the Aston and might as well let you drive it until you get yourself sorted.'

'Don't be daft. You pay a hefty fine and at worst get banned from driving for six months. You can put the Aston in the garage.'

'I have it insured for any driver.'

'Okay, you can get drunk and I'll drive back.'

The journey, being somewhat tardy owing to recent events, took twenty minutes. Parking in the town's car park – free after 6pm – they strolled towards the Green Dragon making a stop on the way. Ruben wanted to see the progress, if any, on the shop which once held a magical window display. Now, in sort of keeping with its past elevations, there stood the makings of a commercial property that appeared very much larger in floor area.

'It makes more sense,' Ruben said, casting his eyes over the brickwork. 'Charlie did mention some while ago the back room was a waste of space.' They moved on, passing the Lemon Tree Café. 'Have you seen Nick?'

'I popped in the day I arrived, told me his business increased due to the workmen.'

'When they go, what then, I wonder.'

'Mum still goes on about the greengrocers. We used to pinch his apples, remember?'

'I sometimes wish I had no memories. It's so sad to see this town losing its shopkeepers. What it will be like in twenty years, one hazards a guess; perhaps a struggling few against the might of a hand-held screen.'

'You still don't have a mobile, Ruby.'

'No need when I have a telephone.'

'But nobody knows your number.'

'Nobody needs to know when I can telephone them.'

'Yeah, right.' Sam Dingle, swinging little by little on one crutch, ventured first into the pub with Ruben trailing behind. Those who slumbered over their pints in a sentimental mood looked up, becoming increasingly aware he was not alone.

Ruby!

Amy shouted and darted round the bar, flinging her arms about him. 'You bad, bad, boy, where have you been?'

Here was a glimpse of happiness. Never were friends so glad to see each other, and more drew close to hear his tale. This better be good.

'As well you know,' he began with a pint, 'the shop burnt out, I wended my way to London in the midst of such immensity that Grey suggested I kip in with her. So…how have things been?'

'Is that it?'

'You might get more on my second pint.'

Now they all talked over each other, plebs and pensioners stuck in a double-dip recession, every indignity piled upon them in order to stay alive. It was not the full-scale reunion Ruben would have liked until another presence floated in, bearing a grin so large that the whiskers tickled his ears.

'Betty sends her love.'

'I see she's still knitting with one needle.'

'I'll hev yew know I knitted this cardigan.'

'Then what's with the holes?'

'Ventilation…now, wat do yew think to our Amy?'

Ruben passed his approval as she proudly gave a twirl. Silver streaks in the hair, light on the make-up, a neat figure slipped into a modest dress, the nails painted pink. Indeed, Grey's influence was far reaching.

'I have a part-time job, Ruby, working for Susan Fuller on my day off selling properties.'

'Does she pay well?'

'I get paid commission.'

'How many houses have you sold?'

'None so far but I sold three bungalows and two flats.' There were things about Amy that would never change. 'What's it like living in a ruin?'

'He don't live in a ruin,' Charlie answered, closing the portal to her curiosity. 'I told yew he was brave doing up her kitchen.'

'Figuratively speaking,' Ruben added. 'Sherry, Charlie?'

'Make that a whisky,' Dingle rejoined. 'Charlie can afford to get drunk now he's retired.'

Drunk or not, the three stood in the same spot and posture until the last patron had turned a corner of the street, then, they looked round as if to make quite sure Amy was not within listening shot.

'Tell me, boy, how yew bearing up? Yew look thin and pasty.'

'True, my body has seen better days. Ding is going to stay with me…but then you probably guessed that might happen.' Ruben passed a sceptical glance at his friend then back at his grandfather. 'Did you two write to each other?'

'Thass wat friends are fer, Ruby. Besides, he keeps blowing himself up so he might as well blow himself up with yew.'

To the sound of stuttering footsteps, Hutton's ill-timed appearance was not unexpected, a man who never loved his life so well. 'Where you been to look like shit, you soft bugger.'

They shook hands with extended smiles. 'How's Oak of Reformation part two coming along, Councillor Hutton?'

'Got in too late, Ruby, to make a difference.'

'What good would it do to have another empty shop?'

'Loads of people asked about yours, loads. You could have set up in Jim's garage, get you over the hump.'

'No, it was too much to take in.'

During the whole of this dialogue Sam Dingle and Charlie Stone had left to wait outside, exchanging information under a star peppered sky.

'He made a good job of the house but sleeps in a shed with a Persian called Comeback.'

'Dearie, dearie, me,' Charlie shook his head in dismay. 'I knew things weren't roit.'

'We got talking about that Windsor bloke. He plans to turn over his formula when euthanasia becomes law.'

'Not for a long while will that happen.'

'I wouldn't be so sure, Charlie. Ruby's drumming up support from his website. It'll happen and when it does, I think he'll pass over his formula.'

'Has he been in touch with Grey?'

'I wish he had. She's got more bloody sense than him.' Dingle slipped his foot out of the cast and gave it a scratch before slipping it back in. 'I think he's losing it, Charlie. He can't make up his mind what he wants to do and keeps going on about finishing off what he started.'

'No, I can't believe that.'

'Did you know he had six points on his licence?'

'He never said.'

'Well, we got done for speeding coming here. So, he says, I had a good run on the Aston and might as well give it to you. Does that sound like he's thinking of staying?'

A shuddering sigh paused the moment and the old man shifted his gaze, was plainly summoning his thoughts. 'Wat yew must do,' he said in damage-control mode, 'is to remove temptation. Take that capsule he keeps in his watch.'

That seemed a good plan. It needed stealth and precision, which a soldier had, creep into the shed and do the business where his best friend slept with his watch. But he also slept with his bottles around him, half or quarter full their chemical compositions would resupply his watch. Blowing up his shed might be a better option.

'Leave it with me,' he told Charlie and sent an exaggerated wink.

It was for a moment an overwhelming relief to Charlie who now forced himself to leave without a backward glance, clouds of smoke from his pipe trailing behind. He never heard Ruben's call, or if he did, he certainly never responded.

'He needs to get his head down,' Dingle made excuses. 'And that's what you should be doing, my man. Give us the keys.'

'In your condition?'

'My foot never drank two pints and three whiskies.'

'I lost my licence anyway.'

'Oh man, your senses are impaired. You could do damage, serious damage to someone else. Do you want that? At any rate, you said I could have her.'

'I must have been drunk.'

'You still are.'

Thirty miles of stepping on gas with a plastered foot was like a walk in the park for Sam Dingle. Injured or not, anything on wheels, it was another example of his physical ability to overcome problems. He knew the pressures on Ruben to take some definite action were at this point enormous. But there was a serious question at issue. Would Ruben ride the storm? Not only was he mentally broken, he was noticeably thinner. Amy noticed but did not say. Hutton noticed and he did.

When Dingle pulled on to the drive Ruben staggered out of the motor and into the house. In a combination of alcohol and the fatiguing occurrences of late so completely overpowering him, he fell head-long into the couch quite unconscious Dingle was observing from a dark corner of the living room door.

No better timing was now.

He threw off his jacket, slipped his foot out of the cast, sprang open the bi-fold doors and bolted across the lawn and into the shed. There he collected a laptop, discs and books and carried them inside the house, returning to raid the chemical shelves for an accelerant. Before lighting the match, he turned on the hose and dowsed the nearby shrubbery lest it burn to create further havoc. It was midnight. It was dark. And he was determined.

A match was lit and tossed inside. The shed caught fire easily. Standing well back, the eyes of the soldier were smiling as they absorbed the scene, sweeping from the crackling flames and on to the wet shrubbery close by, entirely unaware there was a methane gas bottle under the bed. He nodded to himself. All was going well. By morning there would be nothing but smouldering ashes for Ruben to tread. It was a friendship that knew no bounds.

While, for the moment, the soldier did not worry, the incendiary rage of the shed had finally ignited the bottle. Waamph Booom! Reflexively, he threw himself down to the ground, recovered fast, but by then the bed was already in flight along with the cat. Propelled upwards as high as they could manage, bed and cat careered over the bordered trees and made a crash landing into a greenhouse. In abject horror, Dingle dropped to his knees. He had already pissed in his pants.

Morning seeped through, hours had passed, and Ruben rose stiffly. But for the melodious chime of his pocket watch, he would doubtless have slept on, oblivious to anything. Before taking a step forward he felt the rubbing of Comeback between his legs and looked down. *What the fuck happened to you?*

With a scorched tail, half singed whiskers and blackened face but none the worse for her flight in the night the cat meowed on an epic scale, risen again, was back from the dead. She had acquired new reason to hate Dingle.

'She's okay,' the solider said emerging with a cup of tea and the cat hissed. 'We just had a little accident.'

'What sort of an accident?' As Ruben said this, he glanced to the outside world and wondered what was missing from his view. 'Where's my shed?'

'Oh man, it caught fire.'

'It caught fire?'

'Yeah, bloody shame. Here, have a nice cup of tea and a couple of aspirins.'

Ruben squeezed his eyes at something else more alarming. 'Unless I am mistaken, you seem to have made a remarkable recovery.'

'I was banking on sympathy.'

'You had it for a while.'

'Okay, hands up. Charlie was worried, so I took leave and sneaked in to get a handle on the problem. You would do no differently if the boot was on the other foot. We've always been there for each other, Ruby, so don't start fobbing me off. Tell me if you're not thinking of doing yourself in.'

'Did you burn down my shed?'

'Look, everything is okay, your laptop and stuff, I took it all out, even cleared up,' then apprehensively added while he scratched his neck, 'it's just the bed I left behind.'

This was no answer. With a stuttering heart, Ruben placed his tea aside and went to see for himself. The various ornamental shrubberies were severally singed, the concrete based was charred and cracked, and beyond that, in a gap between neighbouring trees, a greenhouse flattened. He peered again. It was flattened by his bed. Its damage had also shown the inevitability of total obliteration.

Dingle, sharing the view, half bending forward, kept his voice low. 'I don't reckon they've seen it.'

'I can see it.'

'Yeah, but you never heard it.'

'Would you mind telling me how it landed there?'

'You left a gas bottle under your bed.'

'You're a fucking idiot.'

CHAPTER 23

August 2013

Renowned as the bloodhound of current affairs show, Don Wadley deployed his arsenal of rough tactics, forcing the Health Secretary to admit a debate on euthanasia cannot be ruled out. Get ready for the fight of your life. Wadley asked, 'If you had a choice, would you prefer to die in dignity or live as a vegetable?' The Health Secretary exploded. 'Oh, come on, Don. You have got to do better than that.'

Grey had read enough.

In the coffee room of the Hilton Hotel, and in front of a new prospect, she sat back in her sleeveless dress and crossed her legs in shimmering nylons. The heel of her left shoe dug into a thick-piled carpet, the other precariously balanced on her toes. As cool as she looked in grey, her heart was beating ten to the dozen. The case of Ruben Stone had come back to haunt her.

'I saw the programme,' she said. 'Anyone doing the same would know Wadley spoke the truth. The Government is afraid of the medical profession, not least how to surmount their ethical views.'

'There will be a debate.'

'In that I have no doubt.'

'Do you get the feeling of it going well?'

'Mr. Tag, are you here to enrol me into politics or get a reading from my crystal ball?'

Ice-blue eyes, receding hair-line and a white shirt beneath a blue blazer, Robert Tag, Chairman on the Board of Harcourt Pharmaceuticals filled her in on the basics. 'I am here to seek your help in the matter of Edward Harcourt, primarily the man behind this crusade.'

'May I ask who recommended me?'

249

'A chap called Godfrey Shilling. We dine at the same club. He was telling me you cracked a difficult case of fraud, had utter faith in your abilities.'

Grey refrained from comment.

'Genetically Modified Foods,' Tag began, and paused in a weak smile, sat for a moment, drumming his fingers on the armrest of his chair then he unbuttoned his blazer and leaned forward. 'Prior to it going public, I was Head of GM division, an area not to be ignored with a growing population. More recently, the Government pledged a sixteen million pound grant for us to cultivate a strain of wheat which, in itself, has problems. The crop was contaminated by anti-protestors who nearly caused the cessation of the scheme. Be that as it may, earlier this year Sir John Harcourt's son wasted no time in making contact as a twenty percent shareholder of the company. He wasn't particularly bright. In fact, I thought he was damn ignorant about our work. Now I have a crisis on my hands. If the Government gets wind he's behind this crusade, it will threaten the company's long-term survival.'

'How so?'

'Death is painful, Miss Grey. Whichever way one views it. There are families to consider not least the implications for this company and its five hundred strong staff. We shall have demonstrations outside our door and irreparable damage to the company name. He must be stopped, and stopped quietly.'

'Then hire a hit man.'

'My good woman, if it were that simple, I would gladly dispatch him myself. You cannot fail to find him incompetently amusing and very dangerous indeed with his outspoken views on euthanasia.'

'You disagree?'

'We spend millions on prolonging lives.'

'And make billions in doing so.'

'Am I wasting my time?'

Grey uncrossed her legs. 'Would you excuse me for a moment? I need to powder my nose.'

On her mind a single thought. Had Godfrey Shilling imparted knowledge given to him in confidence? Checking the lavatory cubicles, she used her mobile to contact God.

'What can I do for you, my angel?'

'Mr. Robert Tag?'

'Ah, good chap who needs help. Far better from you than, say, the likes of Ben de Wit, don't you think?'

'He poured his troubles to you at your club?'

'The whole damn lot.'

'Please, please tell me you never confided in him.'

'My angel, you do me a disservice. What was said between us shall remain between us. Ask for half a million in cash.'

'That doesn't happen to be in the same suitcase?'

'I had a devil of a job finding a way to get rid of it. Now, if you ask for it in cash, I shall be able to assist him and be his best friend.'

'Gosh, he might even steer his employees to buy assurance from you.'

'Goodbye, my angel,' he said laughing.

She closed down, looked in the mirror and wiped the smile off her face. This was frightening. This was extraordinary. This was perhaps advantageous to Ruben, to the company, and to herself. She took a few steps back and viewed her mirrored reflection. Loneliness had never felt so lonely in the absence of Ruben Stone.

'What evidence do you have that Edward Harcourt is behind this crusade?' she asked sitting down.

'None, other than his openness in supporting the campaign and when one takes other factors into consideration, it has to be him.'

'What other factors?'

'About fifteen years ago Sir John was invited by the then Chairman, Duvall, to open the new facility of which I was made Head. He was attended by his aide Able Windsor. I never took much notice of the man except to remember an incident when Sir John required assistance to view a culture. Duvall went to assist after the aide disinclined by suggesting to a more pressing issue of returning home. Admittedly, Sir John was feeble in manner. The event, although forgotten was strangely recalled shortly after meeting Harcourt's son. So, I took it upon myself to delve into his background. He claimed to have lived in Brazil for many years yet I could find no evidence to support this. It stuck in my mind, couldn't shift it so I mentioned it in passing to the Company Secretary. A couple of days later he showed me an old photograph of Sir John's son when he was eighteen. I saw no remote similarity, even taking into account the lapse of time. I was, and still am, convinced Able Windsor is posing as Edward Harcourt. How that was made possible, I have no idea. The solicitors acting in Sir John's probate refused to discuss the matter but gave assurances he is Edward Harcourt.'

'Set all else aside for a moment are you aware of the publicity gained in 1979 surrounding the death of a man called Jeffrey Cane?'

A huge sigh and a lapse of five seconds, the verdict was not very good. 'Godfrey informed you would do your homework. I was not around at the time, but the event still resonates among the curious who have nothing else to do but tittle-tattle in their coffee break. It took a long while for Duvall to bring this company round.'

'He stepped in after Sir John became ill?'

'Yes. He advised Sir John to step down and capital raise by going public. By doing so, the company branched into the lucrative business of cosmetics and later expanded on genetically modified wheat.'

That certainly answered Grey's nagging doubt, how the company shot upwards after the death of Jeffrey Cane. 'Your concern is two-fold,' she said. 'As I see it, you cannot afford any more bad publicity. Edward Harcourt must not be exposed as parading as Able Windsor. I should imagine you and he both feel the same. The other is in conflict with your views. Where you believe he campaigns for euthanasia, the company would suffer a drop in its share values.'

'As we speak, Miss Grey, share values are dropping. It takes no financial wizard to see the future of this company if this law is passed. And I have this dreadful feeling it will.'

'Half a million,' Grey slipped in. 'Cash.'

'Not sure I can-'

'It's non-negotiable.'

'Very well, cash it shall be.' Tag lifted his brief case on to his lap, clicked the catches and passed over a slim blue file. 'You might find the contents helpful. I did consider buying time of a private investigator but Godfrey felt your route was more effective.'

'Am I to assume, you have authority of the Board?'

'You assume correctly. Apart from Norman Plaid, our Chief Executive, has been kept in the dark for reasons of palling up with Harcourt.'

'Do you know why?'

'The man is good at his job, no question about that but he shares the same views to a limited degree.'

'When was he appointed?'

'A year ago. He had the right credentials and charisma to sweep the other contenders out the door.'

'But you had someone else in mind.'

'This is why we live in a democracy, Miss Grey.'

'I had the pleasure of knowing someone who would disagree with your comment. There is no democracy, as there are no choices. Choice, he would say, is an illusion created between those with power and those with not.'

'He sounds like a liberal.'

'I hardly think so since they love Brussels, an entity in which our government bought into without our permission, without a referendum. They took our money, erode our sovereignty, tell us we must prostrate ourselves before psychos and criminals in the name of human rights, and make us give jobs and benefits to millions of johnnie foreigners.' She smiled and stood. 'I just gave my bit in case you had a mind to know my views.'

'You leave me speechless, Miss Grey.'

'And shall return to give you a voice.'

Business clinched and fee agreed Grey slipped outside and straight into a ticking taxi that expressed a secret agony of its own. 'The damn thing needs a service,' William said, a piece of information she could well do without. 'Where to?'

'Err, um.' Undecidedly, she lit a cigarette and wound down the window. 'I need Ruben to help me get rid of a problem.'

'Has he not been the problem?'

'I know, isn't it wonderful.' She smiled dreamily and drifted her eyes to the ones looking at her in the rear view mirror. 'I think a newspaper shop and then Wymondham to see Charlie.'

It was almost a year since she first stepped into this town and encountered Charlie Stone outside his magical window display. Between that and present day, the only other cases that came her way had been embezzled money from a company supplying surgical instruments and a sorry excuse for a runaway bride. But what she had done was to deliberately push Ruben aside because every time she thought about him, she would sink into depression and listlessness.

Outside Liverpool Street station she purchased a cross section of daily newspapers and read them on the way. Don Wadley and his rough tactics dominated the headlines. Not that his character was dislikeable. On the contrary he was everybody's best friend. His comments vindicated the views of the people and delivered a firm rebuke to the Health Secretary who claimed euthanasia was an open door for grasping relatives.

From the town's railway station she walked alone in the lengthening shadows of a late afternoon, bought a bunch of roses twice the size of her head, passed rows of houses built in the nineties, down to where the river ran low and ducked under bougainvillea trained into a canopy before stepping up to Betty's front door. Again, the sign was ignored.

'Who's that?' Betty asked.

'Is Charlie there?'

'He's at the shop.'

'What shop?'

The door opened by some unseen measure. 'I know that voice,' Betty said. 'You're that woman who can't make up her mind what to call herself.'

'Betty, I'm terribly sorry to bother you but I do need to see Charlie.'

'He's at the shop sorting things out.'

'Ah, the shop he used to have.'

'Now don't you be going all daft on me when I just said he's at the shop.'

'Thank you, Betty,' and thrust the roses into her chest. 'These are for you. Sorry to have intruded.'

From the house in the dip by the river, Grey wended her way along a street where once she walked with Ruben. He had spoken of its past, how families lived above their businesses, together and in harmony generating income. And it was to the end of this street that she stood in amazement. The shop which once had a magical window display would no doubt be again. The shell had been completed, the windows whitewashed over and when she walked over the threshold she walked into chaos. Wires dangled from the thick wooden joists, walls waiting to be plastered but the smell of scorched timbers still lingered. Beyond all this, a void in the stairwell and open back door showing the way to a yard where Charlie was bent over picking up bricks.

'I see no workshop, Charlie.'

The old man straightened, turned in his leather bibbed apron and smiled from his whiskered face. 'Thass because I can't make up my mind where to put the windows and door.'

'Surely in the same place?'

'Not that easy when yew disagree with the architect.'

Grey side-stepped around a cement mixer. 'Has everyone left off?'

'They gone next door for a cuppa,' and sat on a pile of bricks unscrewing his flask. 'We can share Betty's stewed tea.'

'So, have we become a bricklayer?'

'We hev become an overseer until this shop is ready to open.'

'And then it's business as usual?'

'Remember wat yew said? If I had a choice I would be here, making such beautiful things. Yew hev a gift, a very rare gift, yew said. It would be a terrible tragedy to see such a gift wasted.'

'You remembered my words.'

'Just because I look ancient doesn't mean I lost my marbles. Now tell me, my woman, why are yew here?'

'I need to see Ruben.'

'Not for a social call I should imagine.'

'Indeed, you are correct.'

'I doubt he will see yew, has it in mind you're married.'

'Yes, I rather gathered that too. The thing is, Charlie, something has come up which could solve his problem.'

'Yew wus his problem.'

'I know, but-'

'Listen, my woman, he moved into his house to do it up, slept in the shed talking to his cat until Ding sorted him out and blew up his shed. Then he got another shed.'

Grey laughed.

'Are yew married?'

'The ring belongs to my grandmother, nothing more sinister. If he had just kept his nose out of my purse we might have been able to say goodbye on amicable terms. But no, Ruben does what Ruben wants to do regardless. I must speak with him, Charlie.'

With that, the old man shifted to one side and dug in his back pocket for a mobile phone saying, 'Give me a minute to work this out,' but working it out first required his glasses and these he placed on the bridge of his nose, and then scratched his head after pressing the wrong buttons.

Grey took it from him. 'Here, let me. These things can be very frustrating if you're not used to them.'

'Hy, Charlie, what's up?'

'I need to see you.'

'Grey?'

'Yes. Can we meet?'

'Why?'

'I met someone today who is willing to pay a hefty amount to put Edward Harcourt to bed, so to speak.'

'Good for you. Go purchase another pair of sheets.'

The line went dead and she rang him again. 'So, what was your plan, to hide in a shed and talk to a cat for the rest of your life?'

'And what was yours? Shed or wind breaks, I see no difference. Who's the client?'

'Robert Tag, Chairman on the Board of Harcourt Pharmaceuticals.' Immediately she heard his intake of breath. 'Ruben, he knows nothing of you, trust me.'

'Trust is a pretty hard word when it has no name.'

'My name is Grey. I don't use my first because it's utterly ridiculous. Now, I suggest-'

'No, let me suggest you work on your trust skills and leave me to work in my shed.'

To a dead line, Grey sat like an owl on a limb. Be calm, she said to herself, I can do this, then tried again. 'Ruben, will you stop being so damn stubborn and listen to what I have to say?'

'I asked you for one good reason why I should not burn your notepad and you told me you couldn't find one. End of story.'

'Not end of story. We have to deal with Edward Harcourt.'

'I don't have a problem with Edward. You do. So, I suggest you find yourself another notepad and deal with it.'

The line went dead for the third time and she looked at Charlie a little more urgently. 'You must speak to him, make him see sense.'

'Is that to say yew hev no idea how to do it?'

Her eyes dipped. 'Well, yes if you must know.'

'Hev yew thought about inviting him home for tea?'

Oh God, must it come down to that? 'My family is obsessed by their history and there I shall be, cringing as they strip him apart and drown him in carrot cake.'

'He might like to see yew cringe.'

Grey smiled, pressed the redial button and said when Ruben picked up, 'Would you like to come home for tea?'

'I'm already home.'

'My home.'

'Your home?'

'Yes, my home.'

'I shall be there in thirty minutes.'

Grey returned the mobile to Charlie and rummaged for her own, contacting her fearless defender on the *qui vive*. 'I invited Ruben home for tea.' Upon hearing his chortle, she said, 'I'm serious.'

'Are you going with him?'

'Yes. I shall get him to park at the bottom of the lane to give you time to warn the others.' Closing down, Grey looked at Charlie who was looking deeply serious at her. 'That was my brother.'

'I wus thinking about my Ruby using the motor.'

'Oh, is it playing up?'

'He got the Aston, gave away his old one all in the time he lost his licence.'

'Can you be more specific?'

'Well, yew see, that day yew wus coming home from seeing Able Windsor he clocked up three speeding fines, thass nine points on his licence so Muddy said when he wus down the hole. Next, he goes back and picks up the Aston. He wus happy about that, had his life sorted, do the place up, sell it and return here, that was the plan but he never made contact so I wrote to Ding to sort him out.'

'By blowing up his shed?'

'Before that, he got him to come and hev a drink at the Green Dragon but on the way, Muddy caught them speeding.'

'Is Sam still there?'

'No, he returned after he got himself a Porsche. I reckon it was driving Ruby around in that Aston.'

'Was it a new Porsche?'

'As shiny as a new ten pence piece and I say, why not. The lad could do with spending his money.'

'I would have thought a property more desirable.'

'Thass because you're a woman.'

They were interrupted by the return of the tradesmen, so conversation was functional, where the counter would go and why the windowless room was no longer a windowless room, until, Ruben drove up outside and tooted his horn.

This was going to be interesting. She went to the driver's side and opened the door. 'Charlie said you lost your licence.'

'I couldn't find it in my drawers.'

She would wipe that grin off his face. 'May I suggest you let me drive?'

'Which is worse? You or me, the latter I think.'

'Just because I don't own a car doesn't mean I have no licence.'

'You told me you had no licence.'

'No, you presumed I had no licence.'

'You shouldn't have a licence in your condition.'

'My condition is self-imposed. I did tell you but it went in one ear and out the other.'

'The pills I gave you?'

'Oh, such a nice gesture,' and yanked him out of the driver's seat. 'I can assure you my driving is exceptional.'

Exceptional indeed. Ninety minutes of nail biting, fidgety chewing moments with a silver-haired woman at the wheel of a DB9, she was the worst damn driver he would most wish to forget.

Trying to manoeuvre into a space between two cars was comical and made all the more humiliating when Ruben stepped out and said, 'I can walk to the kerb from here, thanks.'

'There is something I must tell you.'

'You can't drive.'

She ignored his remark and slipped her hand through the crook of his arm, leading the way over a pot-holed country lane. 'A number of years ago,' she began, 'there was a terrible train crash. Father never survived, died instantly. I almost never survived, trapped in a carriage with a broken leg. My brother escaped with minor bruises…I suppose it all depends where you sit, some with hardly a scratch, others lying dead beside you…then, the realization of burning alive. He pushed me through a small opening before the flames engulfed him. People turn and stare…they cannot help themselves staring when they see the other half of his face.'

'He drives the taxi.'

'Yes, my fearless defender. His name is William, my twin and I love him to bits.'

'I shall not stare.'

'The other thing you should know is that my mother is a stickler for propriety…well they all are in a manner of speaking. Martha is the matriarch of the family. She can be blunt and what she says usually goes.'

'So, you take after your grandmother?'

'Yes, she is a true Grey.'

And then half a fortress rose, its daunting mass and the enormous portal made this building in its evening light as forbidding as the fortress that might stand between Heaven and Hell.

'It was part of a sixteenth century monastery,' she said. 'The system bred compliance and reinforced control before our lot pulled half of it down. I say our lot, meaning the descendants of Julius Grey. All that is left is those you shall meet.'

'Do they know my background?'

'Yes.'

'So, the bit where you burn your notepad for client confidentiality was a lie?'

'Ruben, I was just as much in a flux as you were that day. I could feel your pain and anger. But good has come of it. Charlie said you did up your house. By the way, have you put money behind your crusade?'

'I designed a new website.'

'What about Don Wadley? Did you contact him to take up the story?'

'No. Why do you ask?'

'Come, we shall talk later.'

With more windows than a lazy man would care to count, they entered through a large door made of oak, grotesquely carved, straight on to creaky wide floorboards. Grey slipped off her coat and hung it over a bear's claw.

'What in the name of Zeus is that?'

'A stuffed bear, what else.'

For a moment he looked about like a man who had been transported back in time. 'Was your father a taxidermist?'

'He was a salvage expert if you must know. I recommend you keep your mind focused on the here and now because it upsets Mum to talk about Dad.'

Instantly, Silvia came from out of nowhere and tore off her apron. Instead of shaking his hand she plonked a kiss on his cheek. 'My daughter has told me so much about you.'

'All good I hope.'

'No one is good.' Martha said. in her beaded choker and shawl, she was ready to obliterate his senses. 'Did you wipe your feet?'

'There is no mat,' he replied and followed her line of sight. 'That's a rug.'

'In this house, young man, that is a mat.'

William appeared. 'Pay no mind to Gran, her buns collapsed in the oven.'

Ruben never betrayed so much as a raised eyebrow when shaking hands with her brother. 'I hear you drive a taxi.'

'Can park anywhere with a taxi.'

After a few polite exchanges, Ruben was ushered into the dining room where goodness-knows-what to eat lay on the lengthy table. The cheerful china plates, the lopsided icing and the delicious dollops of buttercream icing, he chose to sit in the chair at the head of the table.

'Gran sits there,' Grey said.

'Let him be,' Martha scolded. Wrapping the shawl further round her shoulders the old lady pulled up alongside him. 'Pour the tea while I read his nature.'

'Martha, this is not-'

'Shut up, Silvia. It pleased him to come here now it pleases me to abuse him.'

Ruben smiled, helping himself to a piece of carrot cake. 'I can see who Grey takes after.'

'My granddaughter takes after Esmeralda Grey.'

Again, he followed Martha's line of sight and reasoned quite rightly why she allowed him to sit in her chair for there, under a barrelled ceiling was a gilt edged portrait of a woman who looked remarkably like Grey.

'Is she not my Granddaughter?'

'Indeed, the likeness is remarkable. Is that your name, Esmeralda?'

'Oh please, if you must, call me Esme.'

'With a name like Esmeralda, I could not bear to part with a single syllable,' and looked at the painting again. To surround anything with an air of mystery was to invest it with a secret charm and power of attraction which to him was irresistible. 'Tell me about her?'

'To know her,' William interjected, 'you must first know of Julius Grey, our first known ancestor.'

'Oh, must we bore him to death?' Grey said.

'No, I wish to hear. Carry on, William.'

'It began with a girl in service to the district magistrate. She fell in love with a priest called Julius Grey. In an act of contrition when learning his seed had bloomed in her belly, he confessed his transgression in the hope of being released from his vows but in so doing he had sealed his fate. His superiors had become his torturers and executioners. They beat him with wooden batons, at first on the soles of his feet to drive out the devil, and then on his limbs. Before dawn, a noose was tied round his neck and there he was left to hang from the tower. The girl, lifting her hands in wretched misery, her voice carried into the wind…those who cruelly take you, their deeds will not go unpunished for they will die at the hand of our son swimming in my belly or some such thing…so upon his last breath he vowed the daughters of Grey shall carry his gift of second sight.

The baby turned out to be a boy and when he grew into a man, he gathered an army, dispatched the lot and pulled down the tower, claiming whosoever rebuilds it will suffer a terrible fate. After that, he took a wife and lived in the remaining part.'

'Is that why the tower is still incomplete?'

'We don't tempt fate.'

'And Esmeralda, where does she fit in?'

'She was burnt at the stake for being a witch. All the rest escaped, kept their heads down. None of the males have second sight. All the females get born with grey hair. Martha is a true Grey, aren't you, Gran?'

A mischievous grin at Ruben and she thread her fingers through his. It felt like a small dry flame which he could neither hold nor throw away. 'You have a carpenter's hand.'

'Tell me something I don't know.'

'There are many things you do not know and should know if you intend to marry my granddaughter.'

'So,' Grey threw in, 'best we leave it at that. Have a cucumber sandwich.'

Ruben refused. 'To awaken curiosity, to gratify it by slight degrees, and yet leave something always in suspense, is to establish the surest hold that can be had…so what do you know that I should know?'

'There is nothing you should know other than my meeting with Robert Tag.'

Ruben cast an eye at Martha. 'What is she hiding?'

'A glow-in-the-dark vibrator.'

William choked on his tea, Silvia froze in absolute horror, and Grey held her head in shame. This was the worst possible outcome of his visit.

'William,' Silvia announced sternly, 'show Ruben the lake.'

'Good idea,' and whistled for Doodle. The dog skidded round the corner, sniffed Ruben's shoes, barked twice and wagged his tale with its tongue hanging out. 'Come on, boy, let's go walkies.'

Two more barks and the dog disappeared through the door. The men smiled at each other and followed its route.

'Gran,' Grey moaned, 'did you have to say that? It was embarrassing.'

'Yes, Martha, it was embarrassing. How could you do that to my daughter?'

'She brought him here under false pretence.'

'Is this true, sweetheart?'

'Shut up, Silvia. If I say it's true then it's true.'

'I thought you cared for him.'

'I do care,' Grey responded emphatically. 'I may appear disingenuous but I do care what happens to Ruben.' She paused and looked at her grandmother frowning. 'What else could I do, Gran? I needed his co-operation to put this to bed.'

The secret sniffles, the swollen eyes, Martha saw in a much wider sense how Ruben had affected her. 'You must let him feed off your knowledge and allow him to decide the way forward.'

'That could be a catastrophe.'

'A catastrophe if you believe him a fool. He did not come here at your persuasion. He came here to quell his curiosity.' Martha returned Silvia's stare. 'You got something to add?'

'He gave her the pearls.'

'What of it?'

'Esmeralda was given pearls by her lover. It was he who condemned her as a witch.'

'Mum, we live in the twenty-first century.'

Suddenly Martha went into a trance. Her old all-seeing eyes rolled back, lashes fluttering like butterfly wings. 'The pearls,' she wailed, 'the pearls were her doom,' and then came to her senses. 'But she wore them with vanity. It was herself who sealed her own fate, scorning the man she loved.'

Such alarms were neither threats nor prophecies but simply repetitions, being composed of all that had fashioned her long past. And Ruben was there to see it.

Silvia opened her arms and plonked another kiss on his already gleaming red cheek. 'Ruben, sit down and have a slice of carrot cake.'

'Thank you, Mrs Grey.'

'Oh, please, call me mother.'

Grey covered her face in apocalyptic doom. It got worse when the beaded choker stared at him again, her pink eyes glittering. Ruben in turn stared at her.

'You look young for 84.'

'You are mistaken. I am 34.'

Martha poked his forehead. 'In there is where you live and in there is where you stay at 84.'

'And you know this by looking at me?'

'I know this by listening to my Granddaughter. She said you were the same man. And she was right. Different body but the same man who can't make up his mind which to be, carpenter or scientist. William, sit down, you're making the place look untidy. Did he tell you he keeps an eye on his sister?'

'What did he do before that?'

'Before that he kept an eye on his sister.'

'I see,' Ruben said as if to himself and nibbled his bottom lip, first glancing at Grey, a woman who earned enormous sums of money, and then at her brother. 'At what stage will you not keep an eye on your sister?'

'When I find a man who can.'

'Hem,' Grey made noises. 'Ruben, would you like me to show you the house?'

'Some other time, perhaps.' He finished his tea and pushed back his chair. 'I should be making headway.'

'Ohh,' they voiced disappointedly and Grey added quickly, 'I shall get my things.'

Out of unreasoning loyalty and a fixed belief that he would let her stay with him, she threw a suitcase together, soared downstairs, picked up her shoulder bag, and flew out the door. Ruben was ambling down the lane with his hands in his trouser pockets, gazing up at the night sky.

'I do apologize for my family, especially Granny.'

He stopped. 'You are not driving my motor.'

'I shall do better this time.'

'Do you have a problem with understanding what I say or do you wish me to physically pick you up and hand you back to where you belong?'

'Fine! Go ahead, let Edward Harcourt ruin your dreams. Why should I care?' Grey turned on her heels and stomped back to the house. 'Why should I care he has your formula.'

'Excuse me?'

'Oh, do you have a problem with understanding what I say or do you wish me to physically pick you up and dump you in your DB9 so you can go kill yourself?'

Since Grey had simply stoked the fire, Ruben caught up and swung her round. 'He does not have my formula.'

'Yes, he does.'

'You lie.'

'Shut up, Ruben,' Martha shrilled from the doorstep, her finger wagging in the gloom. 'If she said he does then he does. Now go pick up her clothes and take her to where she belongs.'

Ruben glanced down at the suitcase she was holding, her clothes spilling out, her silk bra and panties down the lane, trampled into the dust. Bewitching and captivating Esmeralda Grey, hair dishevelled, dark lashes wet with tears, her whole self a hundred times more beautiful in this heightened aspect than ever she had been before. 'Okay, but I'm still driving.'

CHAPTER 24

'This is nice,' Grey said, letting her suitcase fall where it would and kicked off her shoes. 'Did you make the cabinets?'

'Yes. Ding wired in the hob.'

'Did you install a shower?'

'Take your pick, look around.'

As she went in search of her did-you answers, his mind wandered foolish and wide, between the sheets, in the grass or a quickie on the kitchen table. That was an interesting thought. Looking back to those months, his troubles then compared to those of the present seemed paltry. Would she leave his heart confined by cobwebs again? He was so intent upon his own musings that he was unaware of her approach and gave a start when she placed a hand upon his arm.

'Did you do the decking?'

'Everything you see apart from the plumbing and electrics.' Throwing a teabag in a clean mug, he poured hot water, hesitant in whether to speak his thoughts. 'Grey,' then changed his mind when she stuck her head in the fridge. 'Have you a motor at home?'

'No, not any more. With a taxi William can park almost anywhere, free to travel the roads with impunity. No one questions a taxi, not even when it's parked, round a corner such as keeping watch on Edward Harcourt parading as Able Windsor, not that I knew it at the time. Plus, there is room to stretch my legs and work off my lap.'

'Or sleep.'

'Yes, sleep sometimes. Where is your cat?'

'Right behind you, so don't step on her tail.'

'Oh, you sweetie,' she echoed. 'What's her name?'

'Comeback.'

'Come back from where?'

'Well, that's debatable,' and left it at that.

'You seem preoccupied, Ruben? Did my driving upset you again?'

'What upsets me is that you always get your own way.'

'Ruben, you would have gone to jail if you had been stopped by the police. Not only that, because you have no licence it makes your insurance invalid. What do you suppose would happen if you had been in an accident?'

'Gee, cut off my hand, why don't you. I had a dippy moment and got flashed three times for speeding. No sod took a blind bit notice on my appeal.'

'Perhaps leaving a police man down a hole never helped, another dippy moment I presume.'

'I just got my arse kicked by an arsonist or had that escaped your notice.'

'Well at least he was caught.'

'To be released on remand.'

There remained a lengthy pause as she finished off her cheese sandwich, only then to raid the fridge again for something else.

'Tell me about Robert Tag.'

'More recently,' she said bringing liver pate to the table, 'the Government pledged a sixteen million pound grant for the company to cultivate a strain of wheat which, in itself, has problems, but even more problematical is your campaign on euthanasia. He honestly believes Edward is Doctor Hope, mainly because he preaches euthanasia like a philanthropic entrepreneur. As Tag explained, it takes no financial wizard to see the future of the company if this law is passed. Worse, if a reporter starts probing, the whole lot could blow up, more likely than not the Government may be forced to withdraw its funding and hundreds of people will be out of a job.'

'I want this law passed, Grey.'

'As I told Tag, it will no doubt happen one day.'

'What makes you so certain he has my formula?'

'Before I stretch your imagination, just tell me one thing. When you returned to see Edward, did he put forward in part or in whole a business proposition or a suggestion to finish what you started?'

'Yes, he did in part suggest my formula would bring advantages to the company but I told him straight that only when it becomes law would I consider selling my formula.'

'And he pushed you no further?'

'He respected my views.'

'Did you tell him you were Doctor Hope?'

'No and he never asked. Our time together was very amicable, I felt. He spoke about his father with whom he disliked intensely, and without any pushing. He even apologized for not warning me about April Jones not that it mattered.'

'Yes, it fits very nicely. He never warned you about her because he had a different agenda.'

'And what may that be?'

Grey leaned forward tearing crusts off her sandwich. 'Sir John was no doubt preparing to end his life anyway, so it just made sense to put the body with him, plus, he needed an excuse to come and see you, just to be certain you were completely in the dark. And when you took the journal in exchange for the diamonds, he made it seem a plausible thing to do. With or without me he still would reveal himself as Edward Harcourt. He had no choice because he was the named beneficiary in the Will. Nicely, nicely, treads the crafty monkey. He's magnificently clever. If you took his offer, he wins. If you refused his offer, he wins. Either way, he wins. In or out, you would never know he already had your formula.'

'But how? I never let it out of my sight.'

'You know,' she replied coyly, 'when we made love that one and only time, you being fast asleep and me being somewhat naughty, I rummaged in your pockets and found a carved figure that looked a little like me, flying on a broom.'

'That's very deceitful.'

'Well, I saw you hide something up your jumper and I was curious, that's all. But it occurred…in a similar situation Helena Vale would do no differently. So, one must ask, did you sleep together, somewhere, and were you wearing your locket, and if so, by then had you put your formula on the back of your photo?' She reached for his hand and said, 'Please, Ruben, think carefully. You had the onset of dementia, stages of memory loss. Try and stretch your mind to this possibility.'

For a moment Ruben withdrew his eyes and looked at her hand caressing his as an inquisitive mother might do. Then he pulled back the curtain of his memories with Helena Vale. The night before she got mugged, they slept in a nearby hotel, laughed, drank, had ignominious sex and yes, he went out like a light, and yes, he wore the locket, and oh God yes, the formula was on the back of his picture. The fact that Helena had booked the room was a clincher. How naïve can one be?

Grey patted his arm. No more words need be spoken and left to take a shower.

If Ruben had to count on one hand the number of times she was right, he would admit to running out of fingers. She was right about him. She was right about John Harcourt. She was right about April Jones. She was right about Able Windsor. She was right about the formula. But was she right about Fuller's death?

He shot down the last of his tea, switched off the lights and went upstairs. The bathroom door was slightly ajar. Slowly he pushed it open and there she was, hair damp and bent over the basin cleaning her teeth in her nightdress. 'Did April Jones kill Fuller?'

She turned with a mouthful of toothpaste. 'What makes you ask that?'

'It crossed my mind I pushed you into the idea. I was wrong about Susan Fuller setting fire to the shop.'

'Ruben,' she said, repaying a visit to the basin, gargle, gurgle, spit, 'can we just concentrate on the current problem?'

'Yes, let's do that. Let's ask why you have a glow-in-the dark vibrator when you can have me?'

Flushed from the neck upwards, she viewed his mirrored reflection. 'Gran was being her usual cantankerous self.'

'She's as potty as my Great Aunt.'

'That may be so, the difference being I take her advice seriously. You, on the other hand, allowed Charlie to spin a line to Betty with the preconceived notion nobody would believe her.'

Ruben stepped aside and followed her into the bedroom, watched as she put her things away. 'So, Jones and Windsor were an item?'

'Of course not. He's far too clever to get mixed up with a nymphomaniac and she was far too stupid to know what to do with what she had. If that were untrue, she would not have stuck with Sir John all those years.' Grey then got into bed with her face cream. 'No, she busied herself in trying to work it out, distrusting Sir John entirely while spending his money. Then Fuller made contact, but I was in her way. When she finally got you to herself it was to her detriment and Windsor's benefit because he got the formula the day she died.'

'That's a leap in the dark,' he said removing his shirt.

'Not when she had it tattooed on her bottom.'

'When did you see her bottom?'

'What are you doing?'

'What does it look like I'm doing?'

'Sleep in your own bed.'

'This is my bed.'

CHAPTER 25

Silence gilded the patio table in the warmth of a rising sun. Cornflakes and toast, she crunched in jeans, he munched in shorts with his eyes glued on Tag's notes. If there was a bright side, and usually there was, it had been his turn to rape her.

'Grey, I'm sorry for last night.' Although she flashed a brilliant smile, he knew it hid a thousand words and went on to justify his actions. 'You should have known it was my bedroom, so what was I to think when you got between the sheets.'

'That the only glow-in-the dark you were likely to get was from your bedside lamp.'

'Secretly, you wanted my body.'

'Ruben, you took no precautions, which begs the question where does that leave me if I am pregnant?'

'I would look after you and the baby.'

'Brilliant, poverty and boredom in one stroke.'

'How much is Tag willing to pay?'

'We split half a million right down the middle.'

'Then that should be sufficient to buy a cot.' Again, that brilliant smile of hers, it was enough to put any man on edge. 'Well, what do you suggest?'

'I suggest you think above the waistline…now, the way I see it, we have to show Robert Tag a new dimension to this law. Instead of drugs to keep terminally ill people alive, why not consider the reverse.'

'Are you suggesting I give my formula to him?'

'It makes perfect sense.'

'Not to me it doesn't.'

'That formula has become so glued to your backside that sitting down becomes more painful by the minute. We are not talking about next year or the year after that but a long-term future and solution for your formula. You can actually finish what you started without sleeping in a shed.'

'I wonder if grey is the colour of wisdom.'

'I suppose William concluded his tour of the lake with the ghostly tale of Esmeralda Grey?'

'He mentioned she was born with grey hair, like you.'

'All the females born of a Grey share this genetic trait. And that's all it is, a genetic trait.'

'You do not subscribe to your history?'

'Yes, erm, well.' Her hand went to her face but her calm dexterity was still the same. 'I hear Sam blew up your shed.'

'The silly sod never realized there was a gas bottle under my bed. It catapulted in the air and crash landed on the neighbour's greenhouse.' Then he added with solemnity, 'Including the cat.'

'Comeback?'

'She certainly did.'

Had it not been so comical and well meant, Grey would have something to say. 'After the Cane scandal Sir John stepped down in place of Duvall who made the company go public.'

'Did you know Edward had a different mother?'

'No.'

'Whether it was by design or accident, John took his son after buying off the mother. Windsor said he knew nothing until they had a big row after John caught him reading his journal. So, he left and took his real mother's name.'

'It would therefore seem Edward had a distinct loathing for his father. Sir John's wife, how did she view it?'

'He said all she cared about was the manner in which she was accustomed to living.'

'How can a family be so dysfunctional?'

'You forget, it stemmed from John Harcourt who himself was obsessed with death.' Ruben returned to Tag's notes. 'There has to be a reason why Edward portrays himself as a philanthropic entrepreneur. It's almost as if he's willing the company shares to plummet.'

'You think he wants to destroy it?'

'Does he need it with my formula?'

'Did you see a Bunsen burner?'

'One doesn't need much space, only the right ingredients.'

'Perhaps he has a shed,' she said laughing.

'Is there a worthier contribution to make other than a dig about my shed?'

'Actually,' she said into a spiral of smoky mint, 'I'm fresh out of brains. Short of killing him, I have no idea how to stop him given the restrictions placed by Tag.'

Ruben removed the cigarette from her fingers and took a couple of drags in a shudder of ecstasy. 'Hell, this is potent stuff. No wonder you're fresh out of brains. Who makes these?'

'Granny grows them, William makes them and I smoke them. I assure you they are completely harmless.'

'Drugs are not harmless.'

'I was talking about my family.'

Having poured scorn on her cigarettes, he decided to have one himself. 'How did you know about the tattoos on her backside?'

'William was on Charlie's trail and looked the body over before Windsor took her in. I knew it was the formula because it matched what you had at the back of your picture.'

'You have my formula?'

'It was in the notepad Charlie burnt.'

'I knew a girl who had tattoos on her backside. It was quite off putting.'

'You do know why she put them there?'

'I never asked.'

'I was referring to April Jones.'

'Ah, well, err, no, I don't actually.'

'She liked to live dangerously, and stupidly. It makes one wonder if she was more mentally unstable than you as Jeffrey Cane. Anyway, we digress. Windsor has the formula. What does he propose to do with it?'

'We may know that if we can figure out why he seems unperturbed by his shares devaluing.'

'Perhaps by devaluing the company he is able to buy more shares at an affordable price. In effect your crusade is helping toward that end.'

'Okay, once he's finished buying then what? He needs to raise the share values.'

'He could do this by announcing your formula.'

'He cannot announce my formula, not before euthanasia became law.'

'So, we're back to the original question. Why does he promote euthanasia which is causing the share values to drop?'

'No, the original question is what does he intend to do with my formula.'

'Ruben,' she frustrated. 'Why must you be so pedantic? Are the two questions linked?'

'Ah, a third question. Are the two linked?'

Grey rolled her eyes. 'I suggest,' she said collecting the dishes, 'you work that out while cutting the lawn.'

'Why?'

'It's taller than your cat.'

As Ruben looked upon his patch of heaven, there was Comeback deep in the thick of camouflage, poised to capture her prey, pulling softly towards it. That was commitment. That was food.

Being, then, in a pleasant frame of mind, Ruben went to the garage and rolled out the lawn mower. Two pulls on the chord and it sprang into action for a therapeutic exercise to get his brain in gear. Except the only thing in gear was the lawn mower running amuck, spitting out oil and gobbling up grass until its bag burst free.

As sweat ran down his legs he wheeled it back to the garage and noticed the drive lay deserted. Where was his motor?

Then a bright shiny nose came swinging on the drive. It was Sam Dingle in his Porsche. They greeted each other in their shorts, grabbed lagers from the fridge and took the conversation outside.

'Hell, my man, what happened to your lawn?'

'Ask the mower.' They smiled at each other. 'So, you're not dead, you're not crippled, what's the occasion?'

Dingle scanned the horizon as though lulled into a sense of security. 'I left the army, Ruby.'

'Is this another one of your-'

'No, seriously, I thought what the hell, live a little.'

'When did this happen?'

'A couple of days ago…had a drink with Amy and went to see Charlie last night. He said Grey took you home for tea. No, better than that, he said she drove your Aston.'

'Drove is not the word I would use.' He took a deep breath and calmed himself. Perhaps she had gone home. For a moment, he was lost in the labyrinth of fragmented walls leading to the history of Julius Grey.

Dingle snapped him out it. 'You okay, my man?'

'I cannot say where or what her place looks like, but her family is a bunch of nutcases.'

'You fitted in then.'

'Yes, I did rather. I like her brother. Her mother is a belter, kept giving me sloppy kisses but the one to note is her grandmother. She has the same gift as Grey.'

'So, it runs in the family?'

'Apparently so.'

'Charlie mentioned you might be in trouble again.'

'Quite the reverse,' and went on to explain the situation with Robert Tag, his words sucked down in the privacy of a lawn that looked like a patchwork quilt. And somehow the sun seemed to have stopped in its progress across the sky, the steady heat baking his arms.

'You think this Edward guy is looking to turn you over?'

'He already has if she's right about my formula.'

'Are you okay with her around?'

'We have an understanding. She thinks above the waistline and I think below it. How's Amy?'

'She asked about you, still looks good. She works full time for Susan Fuller. Hutton wasn't very pleased about losing her but as I told him, the pay is better so what can he expect.' Then he spotted Grey. 'Ah, it's wonder girl.'

'Hello, Sam. Ruben, do you mind if I had a word?'

'It's okay, I told him the problem.' Ruben kicked out a chair. 'Tell me what you got.'

'A packet of Durex,' she said sitting down. 'I thought the medium rather than the large.'

Unsure if that was a deliberate attempt to embarrass him or an innocent faux pas, he squirmed in his seat and said, 'When I asked what you had it was in reference to information on the case.'

'I gave you all I had.' She glanced at the other book end in his sunglasses. 'What is your opinion?'

'Yeah, medium should do it.'

After that little light hearted banter, Ruben brought more lager to the table. 'We cannot make a plan unless we know which direction he's taking.'

'There I can help,' said Dingle, sitting back against the rib of cane. 'Conversations, anything and everything going on under that roof I can get providing I have the right equipment.'

'What do you need?'

'First off, a sketch of his grounds so I can work out where to plant an LBD…this will allow me to home in from a non-combatant vehicle geared up to cover a five mile radius. I reckon thirty grand should cover it.'

Ruben looked warily at Grey. 'Can we live with that?'

'We can live with that.'

'I also need you with me, my man.'

'It goes without saying.'

'We change our demographic position on a daily basis, be ready at all times to move off in case we meet trouble. We also stock up on provisions, no popping into the pub or supermarket. We treat it like a black op.'

'Then let's get started.'

The soldier stood, ready for war, ready to take a position behind enemy lines, but rather let himself down when he said, 'I better tell Mum I won't be coming home for tea.'

CHAPTER 26

Positioned in a side road half mile distance from the colonnaded mansion, Sam Dingle's idea of a non-combatant vehicle was a black transit windowless van with all the technical knobs and whistles to defeat an enemy at large.

It was 8.45pm, ten days into the operation and the scene in the dining room could be visualized through a pair of earphones; white table napkins, low lights, crystal glasses and silver spoons, ladies chin-wagging in their silk refinery and dickey-bow ties enjoying their little tricks and ambushes over brandy.

The side door slid back. Dingle jumped in, filling the van with sustenance. Against all his preaching, the fish and chip shop was too good to miss.

Ruben removed his earphones and washed his face with his hands. So far nothing of any consequence had materialized from this operation. It was intensely frustrating and intensely laborious, often giving rise to personal predicaments. Unwrapping his supper showing signs of frustration he said, 'Do you think she really bought a packet of rubbers?'

Dingle shrugged. 'Don't know, my man. She went out, came back and you never stayed to find out.'

Like hunger and thirst, a man's sexual nature was coded into the lingering compulsions of their primeval genes. Not so for Grey. It appeared her deepest instincts were buried in a quagmire of social conditioning.

'She once said we lived in different worlds, and maybe she's right, maybe we do and I just have to accept that.'

'See that's your problem, Ruby. Half your brain is living in the twentieth century. You can't expect her to stay at home baking fairy cakes. She does what she does and is good at what she does.' Dingle nudged him out of the doldrums. 'Come on, my man. How's the party?'

Ruben picked up the headphones. The men in the colonnaded mansion did a lot of talking. Sex, travels and politics, not necessarily in that order, and for the women it was shoes, make-up and how much money they could spend. Then, what seemed to be a boring social event had become a closed door event. The men moved into another room where a conspiracy took place. He listened intently, gathering more and more insight into how Edward had put his master plan together. Nice, Ruben thought, very nice.

At 11.45pm when the last guest left, Dingle shot into the driver's seat and swung the van round. It took them out of range but Ruben had heard enough and was anxious to see Grey. The tension built into a larger bunch of tension in every passing mile.

'Have faith, my man.'

'I can't because I'm not there yet.'

'Ever been in a sandstorm, Ruby, no, course not. I tell you it's a body of thick cloud wrapping around you like a sheet. Your eyes become sore and the grains of sand grate between your teeth.'

'Where was this?'

'Over the Mesopotamian desert in a helicopter a few months back. We all thought we were gonna crash before we got anywhere near the base. There was no point in racking our brains for some kind of solution, because there was no solution. Either we got there, or we didn't.'

'Did you feel tempted to take your capsule?'

'What the hell would happen if I took it and never crashed, you tell me.' For most of his life, dawn had carried the threat of an enemy assault or involved preparations for a raid. In Iraq that expectation was stronger still.

The house in Newmarket was swallowed in a haze of dark mist, and partly came alive as the headlights tracked the frontage. It brought no witch to the door or explanations.

Ruben switched on the lights, immediately hit by the transformation. Flowers on the table, coloured throws on the sofa, satin cushions, silk lamp shades and all the bits and bobs only a woman knew how to dress a home. A note was stuck on the newel post; *command centre is asleep.* He smiled.

In silent comment, they climbed the stairs. Ahead, white light impatiently squeezed under Grey's door and Ruben wondered if she was awake thinking about him.

The door flung open. 'Let's have tea,' she said and waltzed by in a pair of spotted jim-jams, her hair like a wind-blown tumble-weed. 'Sam, you are not invited.'

Behind her back, Ruben slapped fingertips with Dingle. Warmed by the conviction she had waited up for him, he followed her into the kitchen.

'Did you find anything out?' she asked.

'Why do you think I'm here?'

'You might have returned for a shave.'

'I like what you did to the house.'

'I was practicing on how to spend your money.'

'I'm not staying here, Grey.'

'But you will take your furniture, I assume.' After plugging in the kettle, she produced an agent's valuation. 'They have two clients on their list looking for a home in this area. If you sign the agreement they will send them along.'

'Wow, what happened to boredom and poverty.'

'Knowing you it will be used to top up Lenard and Peter's gold reserves.'

He stepped up from behind and wrapped his arms about her like a blanket but she moved to unplug the kettle, slipping from his embrace. Disappointed, he leaned against the sink. 'Tell me about Norman Plaid?'

'Norman Plaid?'

'Yes, the Chief Executive on the Board of Harcourt Pharmaceuticals.'

'Oh my, what has he been up to?'

'He intends to walk into the Board Meeting and put forward a vote of no confidence based on Tag's inability to stop the devaluation of the shares, lack of attack against Wadley and Doctor Hope's crusade.'

Grey sat down. 'He's in league with Edward.'

'Plus, two others who intend to second the motion. Kevin Smite, political columnist, the furtive driving force to up the ante on my crusade. The other is Gavin Frost, MEP, and useless tosser responsible for an EU treaty that locked our country into the immigration policy. Both have a place on the Board as advisors. Plaid intends to oust Tag and put Edward forward for a seat on the Board.'

'Not as Chairman, surely?'

'His father founded the company, what better credentials can you get?'

'Your formula, he cannot proclaim the formula, not at this point in time, it would need proof of life and in giving proof of life he would be giving himself a jail sentence.'

'He has no intention of going public, now or in the future. After they oust Tag, only then will Smite retract his support on euthanasia and back the Health Secretary on her anti-campaign, putting the debate back by years.'

'And the shares will rise.'

'Correct. Their intention is to use the company to advantage their positions, replacing members on the board with their own kind. Two questions are answered, why Edward wanted the shares to devalue and what he intends to do with my formula. You once asked if he had a laboratory, well look no further.'

'Oh, this is a complete omnishambles.' Miserable Grey padded bare foot and dumped her mug in the sink. 'I should have seen this coming. What on earth can Tag do? If I tell him, what defence can he put forward? Plaid will laugh at him. The Board will laugh at him.'

'We have the conversation taped.'

'Yes, no doubt you have and to use it means exposing the formula in a roundabout fashion.'

Ruben hooked his fingers into the corners of her mouth to force a smile. 'I can save Tag's position and put the company on the map.'

Now she smiled voluntarily and stood a little awkward fiddling the top button of her jim-jams, perhaps expecting him to make a move on her body or perhaps expecting further conversation. They opened their mouths, spoke at the same time, he said Grey, she said Ruben, it came out garbled and they said it again, staying remote but wanting to stay together.

'Ruben, the day Sam arrived I met up with William who wanted to talk to you, but, unfortunately, Sam was there and then you both left.'

'Talk to me about what?'

'He wants a new life.'

'Uh?'

'Do I really need to explain?'

'Yes, Grey, you do need to explain. You spent most of your time cracking my nuts about my vocation or lack thereof and now you're asking me to drive a sodding taxi.'

'Then why did you ask him to step down?'

'I never asked him to step down. I was trying to find out how he felt about me taking you away.'

'Taking me where?'

'To live with me.'

'Why can't you live with me?'

'Your place is falling down.'

'Your place burnt down.'

'Okay, I want you to stop working.'

A profound silence ensued before she fixed her eyes on his. 'It is said that blood is thicker than water. It's what defines us, binds us, and curses us. For some, blood means a life of wealth and privilege…for others, a life of servitude.'

'I shall never see you.'

'You will if you became my fearless defender.'

'I am your fearless defender, protecting your interests and making a nest, a new nest where we can raise chicks, pretty chicks.'

'Ruben, leaving home is out of the question. It's been in my family for over four hundred years. Every Grey lives there, with or without their mate.'

'I will not be your trained poodle.'

'You're nothing like Doodle.'

'Is Doodle your brother's mate?'

Grey laughed. 'Don't be silly.'

'I suppose I passed your grandmother's scrutiny?'

'She said I stepped into your circle and altered your predicted course.'

'We all step in each other's circle that's what makes us who we are.'

'No, generally we step in and out, like you step in and out of Amy's circle or I step in and out of my client's circle. I stepped in yours against your will and now you are locked into mine.'

Ruben took her hands, holding them close to his chest and imagined her life driven by the motions of the sun and moon, the stars and tides, by the forces of nature that made her so unique. It was as if the veil had been lifted from his eyes and he was seeing her for the very first time.

'Esmeralda.' He spoke her name. 'We stepped out of our circles and created one of our own. I'm sure your granny made you aware of this.' He paused to gauge what effect his words had produced. She only answered with a muted nod. 'Remember what you once asked. Do I wish to be a carpenter or do I wish to be a scientist?'

'You wish to finish what you started.'

'I *must* finish what I started. No more hiding in the shadows or wishing for a miracle. Edward cannot be allowed to use the formula and I must protect those who entrusted me with their future. The Board meets in six days, so little time to work things through.'

'Gran said I must let you decide.'

'Your granny is a very wise woman.' He cupped her face and leaned to kiss her. 'Do you trust me?'

'With all my heart.'

'I need a body.'

'You can have mine.'

'Later,' he said. 'I want an adult male no older than fifty, recently dead, preferably dead from a drug overdose and with a penchant for same sex.'

'Wow, that's a tall order.'

'Can you help?'

'Yes.'

'Excellent. I must go.'

'Go where?'

'To the shed.'

There would be no retreat, no alternative path or temptation to faint heartedness. Much was at stake. Significantly, Tag's position on the Board and the corrupting influence of Edward should he be voted in. That Plaid, Smite and Frost contributed to the plot was without question. Just as important was their determination to crush Doctor Hope's crusade and that was totally unacceptable to Ruben.

CHAPTER 27

The idea that materialized in some unexplored region of his brain had grown into manic preoccupation. For days Ruben had isolated himself and ignored any direct communication from Grey. Sam Dingle was his go-between, agent provocateur who bought a glow-in-the-dark vibrator.

It was the night before the Board meeting when Ruben stepped blearily from the shed. His cat was sprinting her way across the grass, her progress marked by the pigeon she carried. Then he saw Grey hot on her tail and shouted, 'What are you doing?'

Grey stumbled in fright and went head long into a clump of late bloomers. Picking herself up, she said, 'I was trying to save the pigeon.'

Smiling, he removed the green debris stuck to her face. 'The pigeon is dead, that is its fate, as yours will be if you foolishly think you can change the ways of Comeback. Did you get a body?'

'I got a Pole.'

'I asked for a body not a pole.'

'Ruben, what exactly have you been doing in the shed to make you such an imbecile?'

'Well, I…err, had a lot on my mind.'

'Was it below the waistline?'

'If you must know my equipment failed.'

'Well, that's what comes from using a vibrator.'

'Look,' he said, himself getting even deeper into the quagmire, 'it was the ideal tool to give the slow impulses required to coagulate the chemicals.'

'And the glow no doubt helped the chemicals to see in the dark.'

His gaze hung in the air like a dewdrop on a blade of grass. Was he ever going to get the best of the conversation? 'Where's Ding?'

'He went to get a couple of pizzas.'

Without further word, Ruben walked off and went inside the house. He grabbed a beer from the fridge and drank what he could on the way to the bathroom. Here, he quickly showered under a belt of hot water, wrapped a towel round his waist and used another to wipe the fog off the mirror. In two minds whether to shave or not, he decided against it and donned a pair of blue jeans and blue chequered shirt over a white cotton top.

Comeback gave a thunderous caterwaul and used her head as a battering ram against his legs. He picked her up and went outside to be with Grey.

'Is this the first time you ever owned a cat?'

'Yes, and I rather see the pleasure. They are quite undemanding and very self-sufficient.'

'I do miss Bobble.' A huge sigh and she looked up at the deep purple sky. 'Where I live, you can see a universe glittering in the dark, if the clouds stay away. Here, even without clouds it still looks very bleak.'

'Here, street lighting contaminates the sky.'

'What did you think to my home?'

'Well, I erm, thought it was drafty.'

'You never liked it at all, did you?'

'The lake was very nice.' Saved from further confrontation, Ruben veered his eyes beyond Grey, the approach of his friend, pizzas in one hand and a bottle of wine in the other. 'Where did you park the van?'

'It's okay. I parked it behind the sub-station.'

Instead of the house, it was the shed that came to life with mugs in preference of glasses, pizza boxes in preference of plates and fingers in preference of forks.

'Have you seen Charlie?'

Nodding, Dingle answered, 'Yes,' then added after swallowing. 'Amy sends her love.'

'So where are we at?' Grey asked.

'Here,' Ruben answered and floated a formula on to her lap. 'This is Tag's ammunition. We need to see him tonight.'

'We?'

'Is there a problem?'

'I just thought-'

'Grey, trust me. I know what I'm doing.'

'Well at least you had a shower.'

Ruben met his brows. Definition of a woman – they must have the last say. 'Your vibrator, does it come with three speeds?'

Colour spots rose to her cheeks, giving a simple account of her blushing and changed to a more constructive topic. 'There is a BBC programme tonight reporting on the views of Westminster.'

'No doubt it will be staged melodrama, liberally sprinkled with theatrical effects.'

'At least it keeps the topic of euthanasia in the public eye. Have you given thought to Smite?'

'Ask Ding, he wants to blow the lot up.'

'You two are incorrigible. Am I to know anything of your plan?'

'Yes,' Ruben said. 'After we thwart Plaid's attack on Tag, Edward will come here. While he tries to convert me, he will be consuming a drug laced with polymer to take effect after he's gone. Meanwhile, Ding drops the body in his boot and the police will arrest him. This gives us a chance to raid his wall safe, drop some dope, and we're home free to deal with his other three stooges.'

Grey sat transfixed, the pizza slice drooping slowly in her hand. It was the most ridiculous plan she ever heard.

Ruben gave her a nudge. 'Good plan, eh?'

'He will be suspicious of anything he drinks. Aside that, if he fails to get you on his side he will kill you.'

'I have his back covered,' Dingle said.

'Brilliant, two idiots working in tandem.'

'What did your granny say?'

'She never said play the damn martyr. How do you know Edward will come here?'

'He will because he wants the tapes.'

'What tapes?'

'Now who's lost their brains?'

Dingle spoke. 'He will figure out we bugged his place and made tapes.'

'After tonight, you hop in a cab and go home. There you will stay until I give you a ring.'

'Why can't I stay here?'

'I need to know you're safe.'

She moaned softly.

'Grey, I'm-'

'I know. You must act the idiot.' She wiped her fingers on a paper serviette and left the shed to contact Tag.

This gave rise for an opportunity. 'You want I kill the bastards?' It was the soldier who led from the front, who would enjoy nothing more than to tear them apart with his bare hands.

'No, we stick to the plan.'

'She might be right, Ruby. It's a loose plan. Any number of things can go wrong.'

'You see,' Ruben irritated. 'She's got you doubting about my abilities. We stick to the plan. It's the best plan we got. Are they still on for tomorrow?'

'Yeah, nothing has changed. They're preparing for a celebration.'

'A bit premature.' Ruben carried on eating. Then for some peculiar reason a notion popped into his head. Was it one of them who killed Fuller and not April Jones? Had Fuller discovered their secret? Was Fuller blackmailing one of them? 'Ding, when you said the police smelt perfume on Fuller's body, might it have been cologne?'

'You think Grey got it wrong?'

'To be honest, I'm not sure. She wouldn't have collected on the money if she felt she had.'

Just then, Grey popped her head inside. 'Are you ready?'

'How did he sound?'

'Like a man escaping a prison sentence.' On this humorous note she pulled from her bag the journal and hit him with a piece of good news. 'We see him at his place.'

'Where's that?' Dingle asked.

'Where the bed landed,' and smiled at Ruben. 'If you had taken the trouble to communicate, I would have told you.'

Ruben felt a collaborative hand on his shoulder, a silent gesture by his best friend to communicate more than his fair share of the blame. For Dingle, it was oddly comforting to do so, to think about what he should have said rather than what he did.

Where conical trees grew, marking the border at the end of the garden, they squeezed through a gap. From patches of deathly black their sight opened to a generous vista lit by solar lamps that squandered their light over well-manicured lawns and a new greenhouse. Their focus was now on a man who walked with determination, distance closing on the tailor-made blazer.

Impressions were crucial, especially to Robert Tag, thrilled at the prospect of snaring the culprit who annihilated his greenhouse. But what he saw was a man who walked in thick-soled boots, denim jeans and hair flicked over a forehead like the Victoria Falls and almost like a bearded giant the closer he came.

'Mr. Tag,' Grey opened up, 'this is Ruben Stone, your very apologetic neighbour.'

Ruben shook the proffered hand. 'With little excuse save for a moment of madness.'

'Madness is no compensation for the destruction of my greenhouse or lack of decency. What on earth went through your mind?'

'Edward Harcourt,' Ruben replied, putting Tag back in his box.

With a nod, Tag led them to his private den atop the triple garage, away from family and assets. Here was a man's world under a vaulted ceiling, smells of hide and whisky, and table lamps casting shadows over their faces as they sat with drinks watching the end of a BBC report spilling out from a fifty-inch screen.

...the snapshot of opinion at Westminster last night fuelled hopes that Britons will finally get a say on euthanasia. Seventy per cent of MPs from all parties in the Commons think the debate will be held at some point. With ever increasing demands on the British taxpayer to fund the NHS, euthanasia is becoming far more than the cradle to grave we joined. Nearly three out of four MPs believe a debate is in evitable, some even believe legislation will take place in the parliamentary term after the next election in 2015.

Tag hit the remote. 'Miss Grey tells me you are the answer to my problem, Mr. Stone.'

'And you to mine.' Ruben sat forward looking into his whisky. He could play this one of two ways. Begin with his life experiences or adopt a rather pragmatic approach. He chose the latter. 'Edward has a plan to oust you off the Board and hop into your shoes.'

'Tell me something I don't know.'

'It will happen tomorrow.'

Tag placed his drink on the table, stood up, squirmed out of his blazer, and sat back down. 'Go on.'

'What would you say if I told you that one could die in the knowledge of rebirth keeping their memories intact?'

Predictably Tag said, 'I would disbelieve you.'

'Then you disbelieve what you see before you, a man who took this transitional stage and because of it, has suffered a series of problems in order to keep his identity safe.'

Grey laid the journal on the arm of her chair, giving rise to Tag's interest. 'Sir John Harcourt gave a man called Jeffrey Cane licence to experiment in the company's laboratory but took credit for himself. In there you will read of a test subject, returned as Mary. I met her, a practicing doctor, and sympathetic to euthanasia. May I suggest you take it at face value so we may cover ground?'

Tag picked up the journal, flipped a few pages and nodded.

Ruben spoke. 'His aim is to gather influential people who intend to advantage their positions in this life as well as the next, and what will eventually become an elite society of intellectuals calling themselves the Apostles. This may imply there will be only twelve but I only know of three. Kevin Smite, a political journalist and Gavin Frost.'

Tag's face creased in disgust. 'Frost, a shit thrice over, sold this country to a new EU treaty at benefit to himself. You mentioned three?'

'Your very own Chief Executive, Norman Plaid.'

Tag showed no surprise.

'Tomorrow Plaid intends to challenge your position at the Board meeting. We know Smite and Frost will back him. As for others, he will try to convince them of your incompetency to halt the decline of share values, of which, your company makes millions prolonging life.'

'He has no argument. It's what our company does.'

'Then let me be more explicit. They want you off the Board so they can control the company while they build their army who will return to benefit under Edward's control.'

'How do they benefit?'

'When you know your time of departure you make financial provision for your return without paying any tax and this can be done through a company that is controlled by the very person who gave them a new lease of life. Think of it like the mafia laundering money.'

'I shall be laughed at if I challenge them, creating conditions beyond my control. The Board will demand an inquiry and next shall come publicity, sending shock waves across the country.'

'You do not challenge him. Before he challenges your position, you will announce a breakthrough on a new drug for use on terminally ill pets. In effect it is the same formula slightly remodelled and with it all the evidence that is required to substantiate the claim.'

'With this,' Grey interjected, 'the shares will rise exponentially, shutting out Edward Harcourt and his three stooges.'

'Were you this man Jeffrey Cane?'

Ruben was almost afraid to say yes. 'The truth of Jeffrey Cane would still be buried under a pile of lies instigated by John Harcourt had it not been for the admiral Miss Grey,' and thought he would leave it at that but Robert Tag's piercing blue eyes stared through him as someone sent by the Gods to lead their country into greatness.

So, beginning with the banquet held by Sir John and ending at the point of leaving Edward Harcourt to stew in his own juice, midnight had passed, they were on first name terms and Ruben had selected his next grenade.

'I want your company to progress on my original concept when euthanasia becomes legal in this country.'

'Life and death raise many questions.'

'Ah, but the one question which should be asked, do you still want your job?'

Tag went quiet for a moment, unruffled, in command of his universe then smiled. 'I most certainly do.'

CHAPTER 28

Edward Harcourt sat deeply in his leather winged-backed chair and stared blankly at the yellow flames darting up the massive chimney. He was immersed in angry rumination. How the hell did Tag pull it off? Why, it was Ruben Stone who assigned his friend to pry into matters outside his concern. One manoeuvre had been blocked, that was all. There were many ways remaining to achieve the desired goal.

He let his gaze fall on Plaid sinking his worried eyes into whisky, doubtless scratching for clues as chickens scratched for grain. 'We eliminate Stone.'

Plaid looked up, nervously aware what the boss had suggested. 'Eliminate Stone and Tag will sing to the police.'

'Tag knows he has no legal footing.'

'If they heard us, they taped us.'

'I shall get the tapes.'

'Even so he did a deal with Tag.'

'I know Stone. He's an idealist, a veritable doomsday machine. He won't pass over his formula, not until euthanasia becomes legal, if ever.'

'Can you bloody credit it, the clever bastard homing in on our conversations. No bloody restrictions or Government interference, just a damn long line of pet owners placing their order.'

'We can do the same. First, we get rid of Stone.'

Plaid swung forward in his chair, flourishing the glass he had emptied more than once. 'Get rid of Stone, how? You think getting rid of him is going to be easy when he has the soldier to get rid of us.'

Edward gave a curt smile and left his chair. He walked across the room, delved into his secret nook and returned with a manila folder.

As dozens of photographs splayed on Plaid's lap, he saw his entire career coming back on course. 'When are you going to confront him?'

'Not yet. Stone needs to be lulled into a false sense of security and the soldier sent back to his cubby hole.'

They discussed every option, a habit they started when their partnership began a year ago, and one they clung to with conviction. The world would be their oyster, shared by the few with their relative merits, beyond reach, above the law, creating a business empire dedicated for their personal prosperity and life eternal.

But there was to be no current life for Ruben Stone. When news of Sam Dingle returning home reached the ears of Edward, he walked to his secret nook and pulled out a Berretta. How cruel, how ironic, that he, the great Jeffrey Cane, a man who had taken his life for a better life, would now be taking it again. How many times would he engineer his fate so he could watch the world go by, powerless to do anything else?

Mrs G invaded his thoughts. 'Are you dining in, sir?'

'I shall be going out.' He found a cigar and stepped up to his desk. 'Where is Zoe?'

'In the gym, sir.'

'Inform her not to wait up.'

'Very good, sir.'

Edward made his way to the triple garage where sat his Bentley Continental. Things looked just the way he liked it. He rubbed an already gleaming bonnet, sat heavy behind the wheel, turned on the ignition and hit the remote. The garage door slowly rose as he tuned in to the news.

...Ministers were last night under pressure to halt British aid to India immediately after new figures showed the fast-growing Asian economy is set to outperform Europe for years ahead...

He smiled. Nothing was going to outperform Edward Harcourt, not this time. He would give Ruben Stone the option of changing sides, or the option of taking a capsule, failing that he would just shoot him.

The Bentley circled the area, Edward searching for signs, signs of being followed. A trap could be costly. When satisfied, he swung into the road where a line of expansive homes standing on expansive plots lived. How well he remembered that night so long ago, a young lad with a big nose travelling with his father, the opportunistic rogue seeking to get hold of the formula. He remembered pressing his face to the window after the first shots were fired and watching his father put the gun in Cane's hand, firing it off a third time at the man half dead on the floor, a man anxious to escape. Before rumour spread, before reputation was irretrievably blackened and before the company went public. These memories faded when he parked behind the Aston.

Invoking all the powers of mischief under a thick veil of brown hair, barefoot in jeans holed at the knee Ruben Stone answered the door. How prophetic Edward could be, he mused. 'Well, well, well, what do I owe the pleasure of your company?'

'You owe me an explanation.' Edward stepped in, drawing his interest to the transformation as a cat brushed soft against his well-creased trouser. 'Is that your test subject?'

'Careful, her talons are sharp.' Ruben switched off the television, grabbed an unopened bottle of whisky and two glasses. 'Playing God with my formula deserved a response.'

'It was business, nothing personal.'

'It was personal to me.'

Despite the animosity between them, they chinked glasses, stole seats, and conversed in civilized tones, although Edward, a nature prone to false enthusiasm and a vanity of being a leader used words like *caution* and *prudence*.

'I cannot change the world in which we live, my friend, nor would it be prudent to do so. But I can, with Tag out of the way, steer a greater vessel, change the crew into wiser men.'

'A wiser crew can leave an unwise captain.'

'I would be foolish to give away the one thing that holds sway over many.'

'I'm curious. When did you twig Jones had the formula?'

'When I fucked her arse.'

Ruben felt the need to say something but there were no words to match the enormity of the moment.

'Come now, did you think me a closet queer?'

'Please enlighten me.'

'If you insist,' said Edward, smiling so tight under his centre parting that both his cheeks lifted up to meet his eyebrows. 'The irony is that the old cuss couldn't make it out. He thought she was pulling a fast one, too far gone in the grey matter and she, in spite of her absurd little novels, was unable to prove it. So, we came to a nice little arrangement when he began limiting her funds. I got a piece of the formula every time I fucked her and she got to raid the old man's bank account. It took long term planning, which kept the relationship healthy and my identity a secret.'

'Have you worked it out?'

'Why do you think I bought Plaid?'

Ruben left his seat and waltz to the glass bi-fold doors that gave him a vision of the night sky. He wondered how screwed-up his life had become or, worse, how screwed-up it might get. 'Why?' Ruben said looking back. 'Why do you hanker for so much when there are others begging for food?'

'You are a dreamer, my friend. A visionary but none the less a dreamer if you believe the Government will applaud your formula. They will see it as a threat, you as a threat, a threat to the fundamental principles of death and taxes. The Church of England will caution them on such matters, and so too other religious sects will rise up to frown upon your discovery. Not in your present lifetime will you see your formula adopted, if at all. Here, my friend, here is where it ended for Jeffrey Cane. Here is where it can begin for Ruben Stone.'

'Not sure if you're up to date on things, but I went over to the other side.'

'Listen, my friend, you are a practical genius when you have to manipulate the elements but not when you have to manoeuvre the practical situation of life. Whether to provide facilities for your work, or to compromise the purity of your scientific ideals, Tag will mothball your formula. He cannot afford to do otherwise. The company is tied to Government grants and contracts. Your sense of values is the same as mine so be practical and change sides.'

'I am being practical. I saved Tag's position and in return I got a contract which just about gives me a division to do what I want with what I have.'

Edward fell silent. It was plain enough that this was mere talk on Ruben's part.

'Did you think I was going to hand over the formula for peanuts?'

Did you think I was going to let you? Basking in the smile of Ruben Stone, Edward pulled out his Berretta. 'Harsher realities shape your actions.'

'So speaks a son who follows his father's ways.'

'Come now, my friend. Let us consider the outcome of your demise. While you reside below ground, Tag will leave with a healthy bonus and the company will grow much stronger under my command.'

'Shooting me will only complicate matters.'

'Yes, I had considered that. An inconvenience to be sure but we can go for the alternative residing in your watch. Think of it as a third chance at life.'

'A chance I would use to kill you.'

Edward sighed. When, after trying more gentle methods he gave what even he had to recognise as the coup d'état. 'I have certain photographs in my possession that should you feel it necessary to pursue your vendetta they will be sent to the police.'

'Photographs?'

'Most inconvenient at the time, what with it being foggy but I had to protect my interests. You should get yourself a mobile. It comes in handy for the little things in life.'

'Who killed Fuller?'

'You really don't know, do you? It's quite unlike Grey not to solve a problem. But then you were her problem, always someone, somewhere ready to hire her services…still, let us get down to business. You give me the tapes and I give you another life, cannot be fairer than that.'

Edward's smugness was really starting to irk Ruben. His temper was dangerously close to reaching a level that he could not control. 'I give you the tapes and I lose my leverage.'

'I give you a bullet and you lose your life.' He swung his focus to the drawer Ruben motioned with his head. 'That's a sensible chap.'

About to retrieve the tapes, the firearm drooped and Ruben's hostility had reached its zenith. He lunged for the gun, but before he could grasp it, a bullet cracked through his thigh, and then the butt end of the Berretta's grip smashed down across his temple, sending him to the floor, dazed and bleeding. This was unplanned. Fingers clawed for his watch, the weight of a body bearing down. It rather put him in an awkward position but at least he knew the nature of his fate.

Edward bent close and spoke softly of the soldier who killed Fuller for the money. Ruben groaned in the revelation, and then his heart stilled. Murder and manipulation were then skilfully hid.

After taking the tapes, and wiping all traces of himself from the house, Edward created havoc about the scene, making it look like a robbery gone wrong. Before leaving, he looked back and let his sight drift across the room, the sum achievement of what man could do. Everything silent and blighted, he climbed into his motor and drove silently away, totally oblivious a cadaver was in the boot of his car.

Fleet of foot, forgotten in the fray, the soldier leapt through the bi-fold doors. With his left hand, he retrieved a syringe from under his tunic and pulled the protective plastic cover off with his teeth. Then he stabbed the needle into Ruben's neck and pressed the plunger, seconds for the stimulant to work.

But seconds approached a minute and time was now counting down instead of up. Ruben was in that far off place where thought belonged to the stars, a billion trillion memories flung into space, all finely tuned to make possible the development of life in a universe of wondrous beauty.

Come on, my man! Breathe damn you, breathe! Out of sheer frustration the soldier thumped the chest again, and again. *Breathe damn you, breathe!*

Consciousness returned, arrived with the impact of pain. Ruben groaned, aware that he still lived and opened his eyes, slowly focused on his friend.

'Oh man, you gave me a fright.'

'Why is the universe the way we see it?'

'Huh?'

'If it had been different, I would not be here.'

'Then wait there while I get a universal medical kit.'

Ruben pulled himself to rest against the sofa, bags of blood and bags of pain. His head was throbbing, the eye partly swollen and when he looked up his vision was slightly impaired.

'What possessed you to go for the gun?'

'I wanted to kill him.'

They smiled. That was acceptable.

Now, ripping apart the denim material, the extent of Ruben's folly could be seen. An in-out entry wound, the bullet had tracked through a muscle and lodged itself in the armrest of a chair.

'What's the damage?'

'The good news, you get to keep your leg. The bad news is the size of this needle.'

Ruben passed out on the first stitch and came round on the last. Then reaching out with his left hand, he took a sip of hot black coffee and swallowed a couple of pain killers. 'There are photos,' he said.

'Photos?'

'Yup, photos of you killing Fuller.'

The soldier sank back on his heels, his face drained white. Oh, would it were someone else.

'Was it Edward who telephoned?'

'Yeah, Fuller found out he wasn't the butler so I kept tabs on his phone. I heard the tape after you left me at Mum's and shimmied down the drain pipe. The drop took place by the old station so I waited for Fuller by the bridge. I did it for the money.'

'You did it for the money.'

'Yeah, shedloads of money.'

'You never did it for me?'

'The Porsche was better looking.'

Beginning to see the camouflage behind that smart arse grin, Ruben smiled resignedly. 'Okay, how did you make out?'

'No problem, package delivered. What about yours?'

'It was already in his glass.' Ruben picked up his watch. 'I reckon he will be well and truly out of it on the road to Bury.'

'Best we get a move on.' Dingle proffered his hand and pulled him upward. 'You get the cat. I'll lock up.'

Ruben hobbled across the lawn and met Comeback half way. He picked her up and tucked her under his arm. Gone was that man who hid behind a counter. Gone was that face which creased to the name of Jeffrey Cane. Carpenter or scientist, he had become much more and was finally going through the steps of something he had played over in his mind countless times. This was it, and it all seemed so easy.

The soldier was keeping an eye on the road, proudly taking his station at the door. They looked at each other, hung motionless like two ropes attached to an anchor, nodded, and then made their escape to the vehicle parked behind the sub-station. They floored it through the residential neighbourhood until reaching the open road that was a favourite haunt for traffic cops. If Ruben got his recipe right, somewhere along here they would see the Bentley Continental.

'I don't see him, my man?'

'You will.'

'He might have taken a different route.'

'There is no other route.'

That was true. There was no other route based on the assumption that Edward had a mind to go home. This part of the plan was crucial. They travelled a further mile before hitting jackpot. The soldier slowed, meeting a line of traffic reducing speed. Visible now was the Bentley parked in a layby, the boot lid up and serving a crime scene. Standing near were two police officers and a handcuffed Edward Harcourt looking more drunk than drugged. His attempted explanation of the body in the boot of his vehicle wilfully ignored a policeman's dedication to duty.

Ruben smiled, crawled to the back of the van and snuggled into a sleeping bag to keep warm. His cat curled beside him. 'Not long now,' he spoke softly. 'We get through this last bit then we're home free.' Comeback purred louder, evidence of complete communication in the moment.

Dingle parked the vehicle in a side road where once stood a taxi to view the comings and goings of Sir John Harcourt. He took to the headphones and homed in on a late night supper in the kitchen. The radio was blaring to a rap song. Despite what was undoubtedly a happy scene, Zoe would soon thank Edward for the worst night in her history. Late night supper never tasted more delicious.

In weather that was growing very cold, more secret and late condensation had formed on the inside of the vehicle, and the cat licked rivulets of water dripping to the floor bed.

Ruben had one hand poking out of the sleeping bag, enduring a siege of the shakes as violent as those that reportedly accompany malaria. Aware his best friend was looking at him, he said in all of a quiver, 'I'm fine.'

'You don't look fine.'

'Have the police made contact?'

'No.'

'What's the situation?'

'The cook went to bed. The other two are making out in Edward's bedroom.'

'Say that again?'

'Yeah, makes you wonder, doesn't it.' The soldier removed his headphones, slipped his knife in the thigh pocket of his army trousers and then grabbed a torch. 'You're going to slow us down, my man. Best I go it alone before the shit hits the fan.'

'I never went through this not to have my day.'

Dingle washed his face with his hands for a second time and geared them up with lip mikes and ear pieces. 'Okay, this is how it works. You slow me down, I leave you. You keep up, you get no thanks. We talk to each other in whispers. It's not a yelling contest or bed-time stories. Once outside you follow my lead.

If I make a fist, you halt. When I signal to move, you move. And if I look as if I'm poking two fingers in my eyes it means watch where you're going.'

Lo, that Ruben walk in the valley or some-such-thing, he dosed himself up with pain killers, shook himself free of the sleeping bag and followed the quick pace of his friend.

Unlike the time before creeping and crawling on hands and knees, Ruben was ducking and diving between shrubbery, mimicking the front runner who moved with speed and agility. When the clenched fist came into view, he stopped. When the signal came to move, he moved. The soldier was closing in, using the greenery as cover. At the servants' quarters, he extracted his knife and stuck the blade between the slit of overlapping wood, disengaging the window catch.

'Stay here,' he told Ruben then slid through the gap like an eel.

After a minute of standing under a cold half-moon, Ruben heard instructions through his earpiece. 'Move in, keep your head low and go to the door on your right.'

So, Ruben moved, working against his searing pains shooting through his left thigh, banged his head on a low slung ceiling light and froze. Oops! He clicked on his torch and went to the door on his right. There he stood a little confused. A hand grabbed his collar and pulled him through. It was good to be wanted.

The kitchen floor was tiled. Pots and pans, brooms and buckets, they were now in the belly of potential noise. One wrong foot and Mrs G would be alerted. Her quarters were across the corridor that ran to the marbled hall from which fed a giant staircase and a series of doors leading to essential rooms.

'Where to, my man,' Dingle whispered.

'Over there, the recessed door.'

'Stay here.' Dingle hit the floor, did a forward somersault, came up on one knee and said through his lip mike, 'All clear.'

Ruben shook his head, limped across the marbled hall and ducked into the room where he had once been before on a snowy night.

Silently and carefully, they began a methodical search behind paintings, an obvious choice to hide a wall safe. When that proved fruitless, their secondary search took them through the drawers of an antique knee-hole desk. There were papers of inconsequence, household bills and sales literature, a girlie magazine and old newspaper cuttings relating to the incident of Jeffrey Cane.

'There's nothing here,' Dingle whispered. 'We try elsewhere.'

'The library,' Ruben returned. Then he shifted his attention from the desk to a marbled statue of Icarus who flew too close to the sun. That was odd. 'Did you know his wings were made of wax?'

'Come on, my man, we don't have time for this.'

'On the contrary, I think we do. In true mythology, Icarus was a man who made wings out of wax. He strapped them to his chest yet these show to be growing from his shoulder blades.'

'You think it holds significance?'

'Exactly, but for what we may ask?'

The soldier drew close, tapped his knuckle in various locations and said, 'A safe place to hide things.'

They finger searched for secret controls, a pull at the hand or a press on the penis, even a tweak of the nose, both in danger of suffering an aneurysm.

'It's far too heavy to take away,' said Ruben, resisting the urge to smash it. 'Got any ideas?'

'We get Zoe down here to open it.'

'He's not likely to confide in her.'

'Look, she's a woman. They always poke their noses in places where they shouldn't…or maybe we got it wrong.'

At that moment the thing came alive. The mechanism was quiet, smooth, simultaneously disengaging various parts from the main body, the head from its shoulders, and the wings from its torso, an inner chamber was revealed.

Excitedly, they emptied the contents into their pockets. Cash, diamonds, and confidential papers, truly they had Edward and his three stooges by the balls.

'Okay, have your day, my man.'

With a delicious grin, Ruben dropped half a kilo of narcotics inside. But the difficulty of closing the statue met with the same difficulty of opening it.

'We have to go, my man.'

'If Zoe sees this, she'll flush it down the toilet.'

'Well stash it in his desk.'

Ruben clipped him round the ear. 'Where are your brains? The police will be wondering why it's not stashed in here. Now what did you do to make it open?'

'Me? What did you do?'

Then, suddenly it performed its magic again. The wings closed in on the body like a fallen angel, the head met with the neck, the whole thing locking seamlessly.

'How the hell did that happen?' Dingle asked.

Ruben shone his torch on the culprit. Against all reason and in this hour, it was the cat, not the owner or the soldier, who was master.

CHAPTER 29

Pinched of life, Ruben squinted to the morning light bouncing off a brilliant white ceiling and for a second confusion reigned. He propped himself up by the elbows and looked about a bare room smelling of wood and paint. No curtains, carpet, clothes, or cat, and no sound of friend or foe. Nothing but the bed he lay on and the blankets that covered him.

Sensing the shortages of everything that made life easier at this point in time, he endeavoured to stand on two feet. One foot in front of the other, he coiled to the floor like a heavy weight daisy.

At least it brought Charlie to the door. 'Wat do yew think you're doing?'

'What does it look like I'm doing?'

'Yew can't go traipsing about with nothing on.'

'Then where are my clothes?' At a hand gesture Ruben viewed the far end of the bed. Between layers of fresh underwear, clean blue sweater and jeans was Comeback, her wide eyes returning his look. 'How did you do that?' he asked her.

But it was Charlie who answered. 'I put them in Betty's washing machine and sewed up your jeans.'

'I should be with Ding.'

'He's alroit so stop fretting. He went back to keep an eye on the mansion, just like yew planned.'

Being much the better, both in mind and body for his one day confinement, with Charlie's assistance Ruben dressed and tottered around the room to wake up his leg. Thirsty, hungry and inquisitive to see the extent of a new build he limped in the steps of a strong old man who steered into a jaw-dropping kitchen made of white oak and marble. It was the culmination of Charlie's love for his grandson.

'Take it or leave it, lad. This place is now yours.'

'Mine?'

'No good to me. My home is with Betty, just like I said when yew left to sort yerself out.'

'I am lost for words.'

'Here, hev a cup of tea while yew find them.'

Poking his nose in cupboards and drawers which closed on a whisper, Ruben considered that without Charlie working the lathe there might not be a shop with a magical window display. And then there was Grey, her world so starkly different from his. He stared at the handset hung on the wall. Without her, the blueprint of his plan would be incomplete.

'Grey,' he said when she picked up, 'it's me.'

'Hi, me, how did it go?'

'It went good. The police arrested him.'

'Definition of a drug addict,' she said cynically, 'a holiday in Tenerife with a social worker.'

'No, Grey, he had a gun, recently fired.'

'You got shot?'

'Nothing serious, I can still walk…sort of. Anyway, it is now over to you to do what you do best with Smite and Frost. I shall deal with Plaid.'

'Have you incriminating evidence?'

'The tapes are with Ding. He's keeping an ear to the ground on Edward's place.'

'Well then, I shall kill two birds with one Stone.'

Her laughter echoed all the way to his heart, which rather made it difficult to ask, 'Grey, be truthful and tell me if you collected your half from God?'

There was a brief pause on the line. 'You know who killed Fuller?'

'That doesn't answer my question.'

'No, I never collected. It was sheer happenstance that Tag spilled his worries to God dining at the same club. So, I asked for a half a million in cash and Tag agreed.'

'I guessed as much.'

'Sam did it to protect you, Ruben.'

'Keep the money, Grey. And thanks. Speak to you later.' He replaced the receiver and glanced at Charlie beating out time with the frying pan, breathing a little heavily than before.

'Get that down yew, lad, then I'll show yew the workshop.'

'It's no workshop without you.'

'Is that the words yew found?'

'Maybe the only words ringing true. Everyone knows you've been my sheet anchor…do I really want to go it alone and make flatpacks by the dozen.'

'Yew hev Grey.'

Not quite, Ruben mused and filled his mouth with food, watched as his grandfather drew his chair closer to the table and picked up his knife and fork. 'When did you figure out it was Ding?'

'There are two kinds of people in this world, Ruby. Them that think of number one and them that climb down a drainpipe. It doesn't come any simpler than that. Now tell me about yew and Grey.'

Ruben leaned to his side and fed Comeback a piece of bacon. 'She feels it her duty to live among the ghosts of her ancestral past. That said, her brother, who guards her foolish exploits wishes me to step in his shoes.'

'Ruby, if I had another chance, knowing wat I know now I would hev married Betty. Love rarely comes knocking twice. Fer some, it never comes knocking their entire life. Yew lived twice and only found one woman yew really loved so wat's wrong in driving a taxi?'

'I wish to make a private deal with Tag. I step into Plaid's shoes in exchange for keeping the formula quiet.'

'Then yew sold your soul to the devil.'

'Charlie, the Government will never let it come to the table, not even if the law gets passed. Edward knew it. He guessed Tag would mothball my formula. At least I get to supervise the formula on animals. Let them grow intelligence. The world might be a better place with them in charge.'

Charlie cocked his head at Comeback. 'See wat yew done? Yew made him as daft as yew.' Then blinked twice when he thought he saw a hideous grin form on the cat.

Despite the difficulties which ought to have been present between them, Ruben observed her bushy white tail lash the air. 'There is only one language between us. Where I go, she comes too. And so it should be for Grey.'

With each passing second, the silence between them grew thicker. Ruben was so stuck on his thoughts that Charlie turned his attention to Comeback. She leapt effortlessly on to the work surface, sauntered to the sink, and lapped the water stagnating in the bowl.

'This ancestral home,' the old man said with his thinking cap on, 'has it got a garden?'

'Too big for a lawn mower,' Ruben admitted.

'Jack, yew remember him, had no shoes, liked to green his feet on grass. Not till the snow came did he slip on some boots without any laces.'

'It was economy and freedom.'

'There's no economy here if yew run this shop and much less freedom for your cat.'

Ruben smiled, shaking his head. 'And I could grow roses, get lost in a shed but it would not be my home, Charlie. It would be a staging post.'

While the old man dug out his pipe and struck up a match, remaining in the shadow of his thoughts, Ruben went to the handset on the wall and dialled his trusted friend.

'Hey, my man, how do you feel?'

'Good, very good, leg's a bit stiff. Why am I here?'

'Oh man, you went into a fever, had no choice but to get you a bed with Charlie. But hey, I got back in time for when the police arrived.'

'When was that?'

'Yesterday, 0800, sniffer dogs, the lot, you name it, Zoe went berserk and telephoned Plaid. She asked him to get Edward a solicitor.'

'Has he got bail?'

'Nah, he's going down, well and truly down. They got him on dangerous driving under the influence of drugs, illegal possession of a firearm, half a kilo of heroin, and that's just for starters. They're a bit confused about the body because it was reported stolen from the morgue, but what the hell, he gets done for dealing.'

'How does it stand with Plaid?'

'He's shitting himself. Zoe asked him to come and see her but he's keeping well out of it. I tell you, it's been great. Even Comeback had a laugh.'

'Excuse me?'

'She's okay. She preferred to stay with me.'

'That is not Comeback.'

'Course it is.'

'I'm looking at her now.'

'You're looking at her now?'

'Gee, is there an echo on the line or what. You picked up a stray.'

'Persian, white hair, green eyes, does that sound like a stray? Hey, perhaps there are two of them. I got the clever one, you got the idiot.'

Ruben clutched at his throat, silent, staring at the ceiling like a tourist in the Sistine Chapel. Was it possible two existed? Or was it possible Edward had a similar cat?

'Are you still there, my man?'

'It has to be Edward's or Zoe's.'

'Yeah, okay, what's the position with Grey?'

'She's coming to you. Give her what she needs, then come and pick me up. And keep hold of the cat, just in case.'

The kitchen, now filled with the heavy scent of pipe tobacco, had become the hub of Ruben's thoughts. Though clear thinking was not entirely possible, he was able to do some quick sums; two cats in the van and only one seen equals conspiracy. The more he told himself the idea was too far-fetched, the more convinced he became that Comeback had a twin. He looked her over without saying a thing, scanning her like luggage in an airport.

'Wat are yew doing?' Charlie asked.

'Ding claims the cat in his van is Comeback, better still there are two of the same and I cannot disagree, which begs the question which is which.'

'Thass Comeback.'

'Why so certain?'

'Ding blew her up so she wouldn't stay with him.'

'Charlie,' he said, picking her up, 'I cannot for the life of me argue with that.' Nuzzling his face into her full bodied fur, Ruben spoke in soft tones. 'Let's see what Granddad has done for a workshop.'

Cheerily they went downstairs where a shaggy animal was slapping on paint. 'Watcha, Ruby, how's it going?'

'Good, Bill, things are going good.'

'And who's this?'

'I call her Comeback.'

'Here!' Charlie had a thought. 'You can call the other Going.'

They burst into laughter, except Bill never really understood what he was supposed to be laughing about and carried on painting the walls yellow while Charlie showed off his pride and joy. The workshop, still sitting as a bedfellow to the main building, had all the elements that once drew them together on cold nights and secret days, though gone was the undisclosed chamber. In its place was an area for storing wood, slitting open boxes of screws and stacking rolls of coloured paper. Even now, nine, ten months later, it made Ruben smile to remember the rituals that went on in this space, the mixing of chemicals, the stolen hours on his computer and the way Grey sat on a pile of gold falling asleep in his arms. This space, the smell of it, the feel of it, pieces of things that happened when he was younger now no longer existed.

He sighed. 'I used to think there was no other life than the life I had here. Beyond that, it was too scary to face an alternative. Now I want to face an alternative and I'm lost, Charlie.'

The old man regarded him with a doubting look, which almost subsided into a smile. 'Ruby,' he said, knocking his pipe against the chimney-piece, 'yew came into this world with a timeworn past and liked wat yew saw. Here, roit here, not out there where the world's gone mad. Without Grey, yew would never hev faced your demons and faced them yew did. This is your home, always wus, always will be. Yew keep hold of it, lease out the bottom half, leave the top half fer yer bed in case yew make the wrong choice.'

'You really have given up the lathe.'

'It's not the same without yew, lad, and I don't say that to keep yew here. We had a good run. My place is with Betty and dare I say we shan't be coming back.'

'Why, Charlie?'

'I don't want to work in plastic.'

Established in one of the provincial towns of our favoured island, where society described as a happy mixture of agricultural and clerical, Charlie's ashes, at a future period, will probably be found mingled in a cemetery attached to a pile of iPods.

It was shortly after three when Sam Dingle arrived in his non-combatant vehicle outside the shop tooting his horn. Ruben bid farewell to Charlie, picked up Comeback and lamely shuffled into the passenger seat.

The soldier drove off. 'Grey said you were dealing with Plaid.'

'I am.'

'Mind telling me why?'

'I want his resignation.'

'She can deal with that.'

'Edward needed someone capable to work on the formula that's why he hitched up to Plaid. I need to know if he cracked it.'

'Is he likely to tell you if he had?'

'That's why you're taking me to Newmarket so I can give him the truth serum.'

Dingle shot on the brakes and steered on to the hard shoulder, the vehicle behind beeping its horn. 'Look, my man,' he said turning in his seat. 'You gave Jones the truth serum and look what happened to her.'

'I have to know, Ding.'

'Okay, so he tells you he has, then what? Kill him anyway, is that what you want, bring the police to your door? We had a plan. We stuck to the plan. It worked out good. Don't mess things up. You're home free.'

'Not while Plaid keeps his position on the board.'

'So, you want Plaid out and you in.' Dingle shook his head in dismay and continued with the journey. 'Oh, man, what sort of life is that, a bigger extension to your shed but you don't get to share it with anyone except a bunch of cats.'

Ruben craned his head to look in the back and at that point Comeback slipped from his lap and joined her confederate. 'Do you know its gender?'

'Do I want my face scratched?' Gone was the customary lightness and easy laughter. 'Okay, you want Plaid's resignation, that we can deal with but anything else, you can count me out.'

'Then what do you propose? If he's worked out my formula, he'll go underground and finish what Edward started.'

'You're not thinking straight, my man. Edward told you he kept the formula to his chest, yeah? He's too bloody crafty to give it to Plaid before he had control of the company.'

Ruben felt suitably stupid. 'It never occurred.'

'Like it never occurred Comeback has a twin…I tell you, Ruby, the more I think about this formula lark, the more I'm convinced there's going to be serious repercussions. One man alone can't handle it so how the hell do you expect the toss-pots in Government to handle it. They can't even handle the British economy let alone the warts on their noses. And don't think for a second Tag is jumping for joy. He knows he's got to tread a sticky path.'

'He will mothball it.'

'The trouble is, Ruby, if not him, someone else will come across the same dilemma but it might not be a good man or even in this country. It could be in a country where tyrants rule, which just about covers half this world. Imagine the Edwards getting hold of your formula, the consequences for the twenty-first century and beyond would be so profound that the ordinary bloke would be squashed like a pea.'

That scenario was cutting so hard into Ruben's brain that he was incapable of uttering a word. What had it all been for? He could discuss the moral and intellectual aspects of the formula for all the good it would do but the pictures emerging spelt disaster, whichever way he viewed it. There had to be another way to finish what he started.

When Dingle rolled on to the driveway and parked beside the Aston, he turned to look at Ruben. 'You sure you want to tackle Plaid?'

'Change of plan.' He dug into his friend's pocket and pulled out his mobile, dialling Grey's number. When she picked up, he said, 'Can you handle Plaid?'

'What's the matter, Ruben?'

'If I see him, I'm likely to dig myself deeper into a hole I should have climbed out long ago.'

'Are you thinking of doing something stupid?'

'Pretty stupid but hey, I'm entitled to be stupid. It's not often you meet a witch who turns your world upside down. Remember when we met, at the pub, you lost your glove. You ran off pretty sudden. Why?'

'My knickers were falling down.'

'Get away, were they really?'

'Yes, really, the elastic snapped when I got to my feet. In fact, when we danced my knickers were in my bag. What made you think of that now?'

'I'm just taking a short trip to the moon.'

'You will come back, won't you?'

And she said it so softly that he smiled while cutting the connection, returning the mobile to his friend. 'I need a drink.'

They piled out of the van, went into the house and grabbed a couple of lagers. The place was in a terrible mess, Edward's savagery touching all parts of the living room. Ruben never stopped to survey the scene, just carried on outside, limping to his shed with an entourage of two cats and a best friend. He had measured the risk in aiding Tag, the predicted backlash coming from Edward and the paradoxical dilemmas which had troubled him so. Only by releasing his formula for public scrutiny could he really finish what he started.

CHAPTER 30

An overcast as dark as an iron poker hid the sun. The day was wet and windy and Grey felt she was in the middle of lunacy. Out of pride in her undeniable intelligence to resolve all problems, and for the sake of Ruben, she was about to go against his wishes and blackmail Tag.

Sat in a ticking taxi outside his home, she closed her laptop in relative silence and looked at William's worried expression in the rear view mirror. 'You think I am making a mistake.'

'No,' he said turning in his seat. 'I just think you should speak to Ruben.'

'I will, afterwards. Give me half an hour then go round to his place. We can all have a nice cup of tea and you can tell him how much you enjoy defending me.'

Having responded to his dumb blinking, she raced up the drive in the pouring rain, struck in the door to the side of Tag's garage, and then up the stairs into his private domain.

'Gosh,' she said, slipping off her coat, 'where on earth does this rain come from?'

'The clouds,' Tag said so simply. He sat down and opened a file on his lap, exhaling loudly, as if he was about to embark upon a distasteful and worthless chore. 'You were employed to get rid of Harcourt without due publicity to this company. What I have here consists of nothing less than a ticking time bomb.'

This was expected. 'The only implication to your company is the three who sit on your Board crossing their legs and fingers. You should get rid of them.'

'Empty threats, Grey. They know I can ill afford to expose them.'

'Well, there I can help.' Again, that marvellous smile as she helped herself to a glass of sherry. 'Have you by any chance recently logged on to Doctor Hope's website?'

'No.'

'Let me save you the trouble. Ruben's formula is now exposed on the site.' She never paused for his comments. 'When the media finally twig it's no hoax, and they will, they will go searching for its source and that source will lead to Edward Harcourt because you will release his father's journal to the press. If not, I shall release the tapes which convey their plotting against you.'

'Are you blackmailing me, Grey?'

'Blackmail is such an ugly word. I would rather call it friendly persuasion. When you consider Ruben saved your bacon, gave your company a recipe to make billions from distressed pet owners and has just provided the perfect excuse for you to mothball his formula, I think you owe him a little bit more than just a handshake.'

Tag cupped his jaw, an air of calculation upon his furrowed brow. Without doubt he owed Ruben more than just a handshake. 'Let me wrap this around my head. By me releasing the journal I am giving accreditation to the formula.'

'Your excuse will be that Edward recently boasted of his father's achievement and provided you with evidence. Being a man of principle and in light of recent events you felt it your duty to put it in the public domain.'

'And Doctor Hope is Edward.'

'You believed it was him when we met.'

'And with Edward exposed it condemns the other three in a press sensation of unimaginable proportions.'

'You see how nicely we all gain?'

'Yes, it makes sense.'

'So, you will release the journal?'

'I will release the journal.'

'Then our business is concluded.'

With that, Tag went to a cupboard and pulled out a suitcase, the same suitcase which had travelled from Victor's hand to Ruben's hand to Shilling's hand to Tag's hand and was now back in her hand again, mutely accepting it.

Feeling both relief and anxiety, she left in the wet of the storm, crossing the border that separated the plots between Tag and Ruben. She tried his shed. That was locked. Then she tried his house. That too was locked. But there was something else far more disturbing than getting soaked to the skin. There were no curtains up at the windows, no furniture inside and moving round to the front she noticed the *For Sale* board.

William emerged. 'He's gone.'

'Gone to run a shop most like.'

'Do you want to go there?'

'Yes.'

Blip, blip, the windscreen wipers blipped all the way to that market town called Wymondham, and what would she say when she got there. *Hi, Ruben, can I stay awhile with you?* So, he would ask why. *Well, I thought fate had to figure in the equation somewhere. It always does for those large and defining moments in life.* So, what kind of twisted fate had led her to this strange moment, this crossroad? Deep in thought, she sat, feet pulled close, arms wrapped around her shins, and her chin resting in the valley between her knees. Her hair was wet and all things considered she was ready to take an even bigger plunge in the waters of love. Next week or perhaps next month, she mused, I will fall into his protective shield and share a lifetime of happiness.

It was all short-lived when she struck into an empty shop occupied by the soldier. 'Where is Ruben?'

'Not here,' he replied like a mournful harbinger of impending doom, and set his box of tools on the counter. 'Fancy a cuppa?'

Pondering on that question for a long while, she eventually drew her eyes over yellow walls and beyond. It looked so different, bigger, much, much bigger but so, so, empty. 'Is Charlie here?'

'He went down for some screws.'

'Yes, I will have a cuppa,' and followed Dingle upstairs. 'Will the shop be ready for Christmas?'

'We hope so.'

'I expect Ruben is…oh my goodness, will you just look at this kitchen. It's gorgeous, simply out of this world.'

'Charlie made it.'

'He's such a gifted man. Ruben's kitchen was lovely but it lacked planning.' Opening doors and drawers while the kettle was on the boil, she then went into the living room recognizing the furniture from the house in Newmarket. A bra was hanging limp on a picture frame, and suspicion zoomed in on an industrial scale.

'Hello there, my woman.'

She recognized the timbre of Charlie's voice and turned to greet him. 'You made a truly gorgeous kitchen.'

The old man tapped her arm and they went into the kitchen. 'Here, wat do yew think to him putting his formula on the www watever.'

'Charlie, it was a brave and wonderful idea,' but could not help herself from asking, 'Who fits into the bra?'

'Amy,' the soldier answered. 'Do you take sugar?'

'One teaspoon, please…when will he be back?'

'He's not coming back.'

Not coming back?

'Hev a seat, my woman.'

She seated slowly and the bra never seemed that important. 'I don't understand, Charlie.'

'Well yew wouldn't seeing as his furniture is here. He emptied his house and put it up fer sale, leaving me with Power of Attorney. I'm to put the money into gold and add to the pot in Betty's garden. Ding is living here now. He's going to run the shop selling things fer the home. Just to keep my hand in, I get to work at the back fer a couple of days a week making dollhouses.'

'But the little people, he made wonderful little people. Where is he, Charlie?'

'He found himself a new life.'

Her eyes got a little bit bigger, then a little bit smaller, knowing what a new life meant. Her hands clasped tightly around a mug of tea, mentally ravaging the loss of Ruben Stone. If she drank too deeply of grief, she would find herself in the cups of despair. Then a cat brushed soft against her legs. 'He left behind the people he loved. He should have stayed here.'

'He couldn't do that,' Dingle said. 'He put his formula on the net. The media would make his life, our life a misery.'

'But they wouldn't, Sam. I coerced Tag to release the journal thus putting direct blame on Edward.'

'Is your brother here, my woman?'

She only nodded her head.

'I hear yew hev a big garden.'

Again, she only nodded her head.

'Go home, my woman and take his cat. He would want yew to hev her.'

A momentary silence and she picked up the cat, caressing soft upon her face. 'Bloody stupid Ruben,' she said in the anger of wretchedness and left for the waiting taxi down the road. 'Bloody stupid Ruben,' she repeated over and over again, until she jumped in and told William to take them home.

'What's happened?'

'He took the easy way out,' she said hardening her resolve. 'We shall not cry over spilt milk, shall we, Comeback.'

In truth, she felt like wandering to the White Cliffs of Dover where many a despondent soul leapt to their death. She had buoyed herself up all day with a distinct idea that she would spend her life with Ruben and even entertained the possibility of serving in the shop. The last thing she said to him, just before the call ended, quietly, almost as though it was her secret, was 'you will come back, won't you?' But he was gone, actually gone. Misfortunes never come singly. Troubles were exceedingly gregarious in their nature, and, in the case of Ruben Stone, were apt to perch capriciously on a knife edge.

The rain had no excuse for stopping. The sky was dismally dark and the country lane leading to the daunting mass of her country seat was waterlogged and shedding no pleasure with its pot-holes. And then there was the wind. It came on sudden and strong, the trees bending to one another, like giants whispering secrets. It was as much as William could do to shut the front door by putting his whole weight against it.

And the home seemed extraordinarily quiet, no sounds, no smells, no Doodle the poodle, the boards creaking beneath their treads as if unaccustomed to the intrusion. In spite of this, greater wisdom appeared abruptly to the portal of the lounge.

'That's Going,' Martha said.

'She's staying,' Grey returned. Draped comfortably over her arm, the cat might have been a stole or a muffler. 'Her name is Comeback.'

'No,' a familiar voice echoed. 'His name is Going.'

It happened so unexpectedly, coming into the lounge where a fire burned its bottle blue light and so many tears Ruben went unnoticed, sitting there with Doodle on his lap as if they belonged forever. She neither spoke nor moved but gazed upon him as Going leapt from her arms and joined Comeback by the hearth.

'So… John Harcourt lays claim to my discovery.'

Wiping dry her eyes, she took a seat beside him, moulding herself against his ticking chest. 'You knew I would make Tag release the journal.'

'Perhaps.' His heart now beat a gentle rhythm, years of quiet isolation dissolving inside him. 'Perhaps a man never sees so much as when he is in a situation of extremity...and you, my Esmeralda Grey, what do you now see?'

Fixing her eyes upon two identical cats preening themselves by the fireside, linked mysteriously with the man she loved, the more able she was to give an adequate answer. 'You went sad and came back confused, carrying a formula believed to hold the key to mankind's future. But there is no future for your formula. That's rather disturbing, isn't it? Having said that, is it possible some are meant to come back for a reason?'

Ruben pondered. 'Yes,' he amused, 'I came back for you.'

ALSO BY LEVITY BROWN

GALLOWS HUMOUR

IT'S A MATTER OF LIFE & DEATH

Solomon Monday is ready to jump off the media rungs and accept his bizarre legacy, a converted mid 18th century courthouse tucked in the folds of Norfolk...and so begins an extraordinary mystery which has its roots in the eccentric staff, six poor souls innocently hung at the gallows. It takes the appearance of Izabo Tuesday to force Monday to confront his demons and find their ancestor's book, Week's Work, the element to clar Gallows Humour of its hauntings.

In a place where love and membership comes at a very high price, Gallows Humour is simply irrsistible.

PHANTOM JIGSAW

WAITING FOR REVISION

Strident Cutter, owned by third generation Tony Black, is on the brink of bankruptcy. His twin, Jason, an eminent chemist arrives from America to help with the sale, unwittingly walking into a nightmare. What first appears to be a blank jigsaw puzzle found in the store room, the phantom riddles catapult the twins into the realms of the paranormal.

This mystery is of a soul who needs Jason's expertise to

alter the course of history. There is rivalry, revenge and

forbidden love; an unforgettable impact of human relationships.

BOOK OF HORTUS

A TIME FOR HEROES

Sat naked in a puddle of mud, all that he knows of himself is his name - Quercus Coccinea. Befriended by Nina, a librarian, this legendary hero will never yield - one hundred years does not make a man forgive or forget. In a world of breathtaking beauty, Quercus gathers his thousand strong army to defeat an unbeatable enemy, gain immortality and find the lost halves to the Book of Hortus.

Suspenseful and endlessly exciting,

this mystery is sure to thrill anyone who enjoys action,

mysticism and nature on an epic scale.

GIDDY MIDNIGHT

THE GRAND EXIT

Warrior Queen Boudicca called upon the Goddess Andate for victory in battle against the Roman army. But what transpired gave rise to a curse inflicted upon two opposing bloodlines.

Lukas Giddy, disadvantaged by the curse, is determined to lift it.

Marcus Metellus, advantaged by the curse, is determined to stop him.

**For one woman caught between the two,
her love for Giddy and his furry companion is an act of courage.**